CALLIE CHENIER—Born to a fine old New Orleans family, she is a creature of the city's dark side, a child of voodoo and mystery, driven by forbidden desires. . . .

PERRY JAY DUBOISE—Cruel and ruthless, the Cosmetics King of the South created a shrine to feminine beauty—but could never possess the one woman he desired above all others. . . .

HONEY WINSLOW—The most dazzling superstar model in the world, she's every man's fantasy and one man's obsession—but her loveliness hides a horrifying secret. . . .

ELLIOT FITZGERALD—Forced to desert his family many years ago and believed long dead, his sudden resurrection would only bring heartbreak and tragedy to his surviving child. . . .

TESSA FITZGERALD—Driven to discover the secrets behind the celebrities she interviews, her own mysterious heritage could turn out to be the most devastating truth of all. . . .

LUC CHENIER—Impossibly beautiful, desired by men and women alike, he would stop at nothing to uncover the haunting secrets behind his heritage. . . .

NEXT OF KIN

Carly McIntyre

BANTAM BOOKS
NEW YORK · TORONTO · LONDON · SYDNEY · AUCKLAND

NEXT OF KIN

A Bantam Book / August 1990

ISBN 0-553-28595-5

Published simultaneously in the United States and Canada

Bantam Books are published by Bantam Books, a division of Bantam Doubleday
Dell Publishing Group, Inc. Its trademark, consisting of the words "Bantam
Books" and the portrayal of a rooster, is Registered in U.S. Patent and Trademark
Office and in other countries. Marca Registrada. Bantam Books, 666 Fifth Avenue,
New York, New York 10103.

PRINTED IN THE UNITED STATES OF AMERICA

RAD   0 9 8 7 6 5 4 3 2 1

For Kate Parkin and Susannah
Elizabeth Rose who was born without
knowing anything about this book.

And in memory of my father who
died without knowing anything about
this book.

My thanks go to Annabel Davis-Goff,
Elodie Constant, Suzanne Baboneau,
Babette Monteil, P.J-S,
A.S.M. and A.L.S.

PART I

CALLIE
1906–59

CHAPTER I

Callie Chenier was crazy. Queenie knew it for a fact. It made no difference that she was one of the St. Charles Avenue Cheniers, one of the oldest New Orleans families. She had been crazy from the day she was born.

Queenie had known the birth was going to be a difficult one because she had found a *gris-gris* underneath Madame Chenier's pillow only hours before she went into labor.

Everyone in New Orleans knew about *gris-gris*. Queenie herself used it from time to time. She would puff her way through the French Quarter to Basin Street, to the St. Louis Cemetery and make straight for the grave of the Queen of Voodoo, Marie Laveau. Marie Laveau had in fact died in 1881, twenty-two years before Queenie herself had been born, but she had grown up listening to her mother and her grandmother who had made frequent visits to the Queen of Voodoo and were firm believers in the power of her *gris-gris*. When she was alive, Marie Laveau had handed out her *gris-gris* (in return for a fee, naturally)— which could be anything from a ball of intertwined cockfeathers to a doll stuck with pins—to her clients who would then leave it under the pillow or on the doorstep of someone they wanted to influence or harm and wait for the results. Now that she was dead, believers knew all they had to do was to leave their own *gris-gris* on her grave overnight, then place it on the relevant doorstep or under a pillow.

Queenie always had one ready. The younger generation found it utterly ridiculous that *gris-gris* could still exist so far into the twentieth century, but when her granddaughter had a falling out with her beau, the unfortunate young man woke one morning to a foul smell. Under his pillow he found an old bone with a strange piece of string tied round it: Queenie's *gris-gris.* Within a week the couple were together again.

But the *gris-gris* she found under Callie's mother's pillow was truly an evil one, a tiny straw doll like a baby stuck with pins. Someone wanted the baby born dead and Queenie knew why.

Louis Chenier, the master of the house, was not the father of the child. His wife, Cécile, had been conducting an affair for the last two years with his brother, Jules. It would have been quite feasible for the baby to be passed off as Louis's but clearly Jules didn't trust Cécile to keep quiet. Queenie had told the young Master Jules everything she knew about *gris-gris* because of all the Cheniers he was her favorite. He had clearly put the information to good use.

Cécile was in labor for more than twenty-four hours. The Cheniers believed they had a healthy baby daughter, but the doctor who attended the long and difficult birth was secretly disturbed by the fact that the baby might somehow have been damaged by his extensive, although entirely necessary, use of forceps—her head, her brain even . . . Queenie didn't know this, of course. She believed as she watched the child grow up unstable and with a violent streak, that the *gris-gris* had done its work.

Queenie's domain was the kitchen because she was the cook. Callie took to visiting her every day and each time she came through the door Queenie would say: "Now if you just sit down there and act peaceable, child, you can stay here as long as you like."

The words were totally superfluous since Callie never opened her mouth. She just sat herself down every day on a cane-bottomed chair and went into a kind of trance, while Queenie fussed around her with blue crabs and filé powder, okra and red beans, pecan pralines and wild ducks, turtle soup and crayfish. Sometimes Queenie would take a slice of watermelon from the icebox and offer it to the child, but Callie would never take it. Occasionally, very occasionally, she would rise and stroll out into the courtyard to pick herself a fig from the tree.

She appeared to use the kitchen as a kind of haven from the bustling sound of activity going on in the rest of the house. Her parents entertained frequently on a lavish scale, but Callie rarely participated. She was not exactly the kind of child one presented to be fussed over by admiring guests. Once, during a momentary lull in conversation at a family lunch, she had looked up from her plate and announced in clear tones: "I want to be a whore when I grow up." There was a shocked silence, and Callie's parents exchanged horrified glances, but Uncle Jules slapped his knee and let out a huge guffaw. "It's all those oysters!" he declared. Uncle Jules had recently acquired the habit of taking Callie as his companion to the oyster bars in the French Quarter of New Orleans. She was too small to reach the bar so he handed down to her the freshly shucked oysters, one by one. "Folks always did say the damn things were supposed to be aphrodisiacs. Guess Callie's proved them right, ain't you, sugar?" He fondled her hair and everyone laughed and began to talk about other things.

It soon became clear that she was not going to grow into a Southern Belle. At an early age, she was a long, dark string bean of a girl with sallow olive skin which, in a certain light, had a dusky, almost negroid, tint to it. Her parents were disappointed in her and they showed it. No one ever came to kiss her good night, no one wanted to dandle her on their knee, no one made the slightest effort to entertain her. Mam'selle was exasperated by her sullen behavior in the schoolroom. Other children were never invited to play with her at the big old mansion on St. Charles Avenue and, for most of her childhood, she took to roaming around the house like a ghost, haunting the landings and scaring the servants when they came upon her unexpectedly, lurking in the shadows.

By staying in the kitchen it was as if Callie could pretend she was not part of the household. She was just biding her time there, waiting for something to happen, plotting, scheming. Day after day she came down to sit on her cane-bottomed chair and stared into space for hours, her only movement the imperceptible drumming of her fingertips on the armrest.

"Something's ticking over in that mind of hers," Queenie would say to the servants. "She's all pent up ready to explode and it ain't as if she don't know how to get herself something if she wants it bad. Child's mighty persuasive when she wants to be, so why is she waitin'? Beats me."

Queenie was right. Callie could turn on an intense charm and her victim would be caught in her web like a fly. And she needed it for as she grew up she became more and more ugly. Her body, instead of blossoming into soft, pubescent curves, remained straight as a board and repellently bony.

Yet she had a secret pastime which enabled her to escape into a fantasy world. Every so often, when Cécile Chenier went out, her daughter would creep into her room and play with the rows of little pots and paints on her mother's dressing table. Gradually she taught herself how to use them so that when one day Queenie came bustling in unexpectedly, she stopped dead when she saw Callie, shaking her head in amazement: "My, my, child, you is *pretty*! How you do that?" But Callie just smiled mysteriously and ignored her.

"She just don't know how to enjoy bein' a child," Queenie muttered. "She's waiting to grow up then ever'thing's goin' to be just fine for her."

Queenie was halfway there. Callie was just waiting for sex.

When Callie was ten the house next door to the Cheniers' on St. Charles Avenue came up for sale and was bought by a family newly arrived from France, the de la Salles. Callie's mother, who considered herself to be a warm and neighborly person, made a point of calling on Madame de la Salle at the earliest opportunity and was instantly transported straight to heaven when she discovered she could now hear first hand about the latest Paris fashions and exchange her old Louisiana recipes for haute cuisine ones.

Like the Cheniers, the de la Salles had one child, a daughter. Anita de la Salle's personality was as far removed from Callie's as it could possibly be. She was small, but already showing signs of being curvaceous at eleven years old. Her skin was purest white, scattered with a sprinkling of tiny freckles across her neck, chest and arms and she positively bubbled over with vitality.

Unlike Callie, Anita needed people. She hated being alone and having left all her friends behind in Paris she was desperately lonely shut up in the big old New Orleans mansion. What made it even more frustrating was that she knew there was a child her own age living right next door, but while Maman repeatedly urged Madame Chenier to bring her daughter when she visited, the girl never appeared. Indeed there was clearly some kind of mystery surrounding her. It would seem she was "difficult," "unsuitable," even, perish the thought, "a problem child." This much Anita's mother had gleaned from the other neighbors who called on her.

Then one day Anita saw her from her bedroom window. She watched, fascinated, as the tall, dark girl came out of the house next door and strolled across the courtyard to pluck a fig from the tree. Anita stared as the girl opened up the fig and devoured it hungrily, scooping up the flesh with her long tongue. Then she must have sensed that someone was watching her for she looked up abruptly, glared at Anita and rushed back into the house. Weeks went by before Anita saw her again and her frustration mounted until she thought she would explode with boredom. In the end the plan she devised to encounter Callie almost brought about her own undoing.

In Paris, amongst her friends, Anita had always been regarded as a madcap, a daredevil, who would stop at nothing providing she was egged on by a crowd of encouraging children. Now, as she hoisted herself up on to the six-foot stone wall that separated the de la Salles' garden from the Cheniers', she missed the row of anxious upturned faces to which she had become accustomed. She had reached the wall by climbing a tree and the bark had grazed the skin of her calves. She was in pain and she was also beginning to anticipate the fuss that would be made about the irreparable state of her dress. But speed had been of the essence. From her window she had seen Callie come out of the house next door and then Anita had raced downstairs and out into the garden. It was vital that she invade the Cheniers' garden to waylay Callie before she returned indoors. Even at eleven, Anita was subconsciously confident that her charm could work on someone once she had them face to face.

Only she slipped on the wet moss on top of the wall and crashed to the ground, landing at Callie's feet.

Anita waited for Callie to swoop down and fuss over her. Nothing happened. Rather late in the day Anita let out a howl of pain.

"You hurt?" Callie asked suspiciously in French.

"HURT? I think I might be dying! Help me up, please."

Callie didn't move.

"Oh, please, otherwise I'll scream the place down, see if I don't." Too late Anita realized she would do no such thing. The last thing she wanted to do was to attract attention to herself. Maman would be furious that she'd ruined yet another new dress, let alone trespassed in the Cheniers' garden.

"Scream all you want if it makes you feel better," Callie told her and began to walk away. Tentatively Anita pulled herself up against the wall, but when she put her weight on her left foot her scream of agony was quite genuine. Callie turned.

"You really are hurt, aren't you?" Her expression changed to a look of gentle concern never before witnessed by Queenie or Callie's parents. "Come," she held out her hand to Anita, "you're only a little thing. I imagine I can carry you. I'm strong," she said proudly. And she was right. She was able to lift Anita bodily and carry her in her arms.

For once Anita was so flabbergasted she didn't utter a word, too shaken even to notice that she was in fact being carried away from the house. Callie took her down to one of the buildings at the end of the garden which had once been part of the old slaves' quarters. She deposited Anita on a bed of straw on the ground and then turned her attention elsewhere. Anita quickly realized that the low-ceilinged hovel was some kind of hospital ward, a veterinary hospital to be more accurate. She was lying among four wounded beasts—a dog with one of its hind legs strapped to a crude makeshift splint, a cat with a bandaged paw and what appeared to be two unconscious birds. Callie was checking one of the birds and when she looked up her eyes were filled with tears.

"Oh, no, what's the matter?" asked Anita anxiously, forgetting her own pain for an instant. "Is it dead?"

"Yes," said Callie, adding fiercely, "I'm not crying, understand? You never saw me cry."

"No, of course not," Anita assured her, watching the tears now flowing freely down Callie's cheeks.

"So I suppose now I'd better have a look at you." Callie took Anita's foot in her hands and Anita flinched. Yet Callie's touch though firm was surprisingly gentle. After a while she looked up at Anita. "Nothing's broken so far as I can make out. You should rest though, keep this foot up off the ground for a while. It's probably a bad sprain. I know what we'll do, we'll wait till my mother goes out and then I'll carry you into the house. I'll say I invited you to play and you fell down the stairs. Queenie'll stand by our story."

"Queenie?"

"Our cook. You have a cook, don't you? Maman's always bringing back those disgusting recipes from your mother. They're your cook's, right?"

"No, my maman does our cooking all by herself," boasted Anita, unaware that it was something of a social gaffe to admit this on St. Charles Avenue, but Callie didn't seem to notice.

"So, what's your name?" she asked.

"Anita de la Salle, what's yours?"

"Callie Chenier and I'm a Creole."

"A what?"

"A Creole, silly. 'A Creole in the United States is a white person descended from the French or Spanish settlers of Louisiana and the Gulf States and preserves their characteristic speech and culture,'" Callie spouted parrot fashion as if reading from the dictionary. "Well, I don't know about the culture, whatever that is, but we speak French at home, quite a lot actually."

"Well, we are French and we speak it all the time." Anita's tone implied that she thought she'd won that round. "So, what's all this?"

"My babies, my pets. Whenever I find a wounded animal I bring it in here and look after it till it's better."

"But you're going to take me to your house?" Anita asked nervously, wondering if she was going to be left in this smelly place for days on end.

"I have to. You're a human. They'd come looking for you and I don't want anyone to discover my hideaway. I brought you here without thinking. I should have taken you straight to the house."

"Oh, no, I'm very pleased to be here," said Anita hastily. She didn't want to upset her new friend. "Oh look, you've got books and everything out here. Do you come here a lot?"

"Sometimes. It's my *cachette*, my hiding-place. So, don't go telling anyone, you hear?"

"I promise I won't, but can we meet here again when my foot's better, every day at a special time?"

"I suppose so." Callie didn't sound too sure, but Anita's enthusiasm was infectious. And, more important, she seemed quite happy to accept Callie exactly as she found her. Later, as she carried Anita up the garden, across the courtyard and into Queenie's kitchen, she acknowledged within herself the desperate hope that this French girl might turn out to be her first real friend.

If Queenie was surprised at the tenderness and solicitude Callie showed the child from next door she kept quiet about it. She had no idea Callie could be so kind, that she even had it in her to look after another person so well. Watching her Queenie thought she seemed almost maternal . . . At that Queenie shook herself. Callie Chenier a potential mother? No, sir, that was stretching the imagination too far.

But the two girls did become friends, meeting every day at five o'clock in the afternoon when they'd finished their nap. As Anita told Queenie excitedly, "We're best friends. We tell each other every little thing . . ."

That might have been true of Anita but there were some things Callie continued to keep very much to herself. Like Storyville . . .

Callie's body had always held a strange fascination for her. When she was sent up to her room to rest during the long hot summer afternoons, she would lie on her old French box bed with the huge pile of lace-edged pillows plumped up against the giant headboard and allow her hand to wander over her naked body. She loved the way the blinds made the sun cast shadows across her skin in a striped effect giving it the tawny look of a tiger. She would stretch out like a cat and twist and turn until she could feel on her skin the cool air of the overhead fan whirring above.

It seemed natural to touch herself. Unconsciously she sought relief: from the oppression of the steamy weather, from the claustrophobic atmosphere of the dark, gloomy house, from the pent-up frustration of her own tension. It felt right when she stroked her skin, it soothed her and when she accidentally brushed her hand against the little mound between her legs and an extraordinary sensation swept over her, she kept her hand there, allowed her fingers to probe and rub until suddenly she was beginning to shake. It was as if her body were a mass of liquid and she was swimming in it, swimming in her own skin, wallowing in it, warm, drifting, releasing her . . .

Yet she knew it was wrong long before Queenie walked in and caught her and cried, "Child! That's dirty. You stop that now," and slapped her hand away. But she didn't stop. Knowing it was forbidden somehow made it all the more enjoyable.

She knew about Storyville, the notorious red light district of New Orleans, but she had no idea that was where her Uncle Jules went every afternoon while she was taking her nap. One day, as she pulled down the blinds she saw him leaving the house and decided to follow him, more out of boredom than anything else. It was a blisteringly hot afternoon and she hurried after Uncle Jules as he made his way purposefully along the sordid streets.

Callie was only eleven but she was tall, and because it was so hot she slipped out of her dress. This was outrageous behavior for a young lady of good family from St. Charles Avenue, but in Storyville hardly anyone gave her a second glance. She did not look out of place for a perfectly good reason: Callie numbered among her ancestors several Creoles with more black blood than white, who had slipped in somewhere down the line on both sides. Callie's parents appeared completely white and when, in 1894, a law was passed in Louisiana which stated that any person who had black blood, Creole included, would henceforth be considered black, their family past was conveniently forgotten. But the black Creole blood lurking in their veins surfaced in Callie and as she sauntered down the scorched Storyville sidewalk after Uncle Jules, dressed only in her delicate lace-edged petticoat, she looked quite unwittingly every inch the sultry quadroon child prostitute.

Callie followed Uncle Jules into the hall of a rather grand parlor house filled with ornate Victorian furniture and ormolu-framed mirrors. She hid behind a potted fern on a pedestal and watched as he consulted with a skinny negro in a striped vest

and then disappeared up the staircase with a girl. Callie noted
that the girl did not appear to be much older than she was
although her skin was considerably darker, contrasting vividly
with the white silk of her petticoat. By the time he had reached
the top of the staircase, Uncle Jules had already divested himself of his jacket and was flicking his suspenders over his shoulders.

Callie sauntered across the hall waiting for someone to stop
her, but nobody did. Whatever they were doing behind the
rows of closed doors was far too pressing for them to be aware
of a stray child roaming the building. She climbed the stairs,
stroking the polished mahogany banister as she did so and
moving her skinny bottom from side to side as she had seen the
girl with Uncle Jules do.

Peeking through the banisters as she neared the top of the
stairs Callie saw Uncle Jules follow the girl into a room. By this
time he was pulling down his trousers and grabbing at her. The
next thing Callie knew the door was slamming behind them.

It was six weeks before she was able to find a way of getting
into the room before Uncle Jules. Now, instead of going
straight up to take her nap after lunch, she would hang around
to see if he showed any signs of going out. Sometimes she was
able to beat him out of the door. As she ran along the streets to
Storyville she unplaited her long dark hair and pulled off her
dress, aware that this slight alteration of her appearance allowed her a certain anonymity. She knew he always went to the
same house, into the same room, more often than not with the
same girl, but she did not know what he did once he was inside.

Finally the day arrived when she was able to arrive before
him, run up the stairs and rush into the room he always used
without anyone seeing her. The man on the desk never even
glanced up, she was so fast. In the room there was not much
furniture, no dressing table like Maman's, just a huge bed with
a brass bedstead and a walk-in closet. Callie slipped into it and
left the door open just a tiny crack. Through this she had a
clear view of the bed.

Uncle Jules came in about ten minutes later. He was carrying
the girl in his arms and dumped her unceremoniously in the
middle of the bed. Callie had time to see that the girl was half-
naked before her eyes became fixed on something thick and
pink and glistening poking out of Uncle Jules's breeches. She

watched, mesmerized, as Uncle Jules appeared to leap on the girl and begin to eat her, his head buried between her legs. The girl was shrieking with laughter and shaking her head from side to side. After a moment it dawned on Callie that Uncle Jules was licking the very part of the girl's body which always gave her, Callie, so much pleasure. As she watched, her hand moved to touch herself *there*.

Then the girl struggled to sit up and threw her arms round Uncle Jules's hips, pulling down his breeches. Where was the *thing*? Callie couldn't see it anymore. Then she realized why. The girl had taken it into her mouth. She was sucking it. Uncle Jules was naked now, his chest covered in black hairs like a bear. He threw himself on the girl and once more his thing disappeared, this time lower down the girl. She must have a hole down there, thought Callie and, feeling between her own legs, discovered she did too. The girl was screaming now, pulling Uncle Jules down on top of her. Callie saw his bottom heave up and down on her and, as she watched, she felt the familiar, liquid sensation beginning to creep over her.

It happened. The same thing that happened when she touched herself in her own bedroom. And just at that same moment when the girl gave one long scream, Uncle Jules joined her in a strange guttural sound and then there was silence. Just the sound of their exhausted breathing.

Two weeks later Uncle Jules was murdered.

Callie found his body.

He hadn't been at home all morning and during lunch she had become restless. She had not been to Storyville since the afternoon she had watched him from the closet. What she had seen that day had provided her with a stream of fantasies to conjure up as she touched herself. But his non-appearance disturbed her and she knew that it was time to go back there.

At first she thought his room was empty and she moved hurriedly to her hiding-place in the closet and there she found him. He was lying on his back. He was not entirely naked. He still had his breeches on, tucked into his riding boots. His crop still lay on the floor near his head. His eyes were still open, staring up at her. Callie didn't scream. She didn't even start. She stared right back at him.

He'd been stabbed at least four times in his chest. The blade was long, over six inches. It looked like a kitchen knife, the kind Queenie used to fillet fish and cut off their heads between the gills.

There was dried blood on his body and on the floor and Callie tiptoed around it. This was death, something she had not encountered before and she found it fascinating. She had no idea she was looking at the butchered body of her own father.

Somewhere at the back of her mind she knew she was experiencing fear, but it was not fear of the violence and trauma before her. It was fear of being caught. They might think she had killed him. She was propelled into action. She slipped out of her shoes and, clutching them in one hand, she ran barefoot out of the room and down the stairs, through the hall and out into the street.

Slap into Queenie.

"Child, I *declare*!"

Callie tried to run right past her, but Queenie reached out and grabbed her firmly by the elbow. "Stop right there, missy. If you is lost then I found you and I ain't gone let you go."

"I'm not lost, Queenie," Callie told her impatiently. "What are you doing here? Did you follow me?"

"I surely did. I seen you leave de house and I think where dat child goin'? So why you come here to dis *ba-ad* place?"

"It's Uncle Jules . . ."

"If your Uncle Jules comes here, dat's his business. Not yours. Now you stay here, child, while I go find him, bring him home."

Queenie's wail of anguish when she saw Jules Chenier's body reverberated all round Storyville. Callie, waiting for her on the sidewalk below, took to her heels and ran all the way back to St. Charles Avenue. If she was going to have to answer questions, Queenie's or anybody's, she'd rather answer them on her own home ground.

"Callie, is it true what they're saying about your Uncle Jules?" Anita and Callie were having their usual daily meeting in Callie's *cachette*.

"What about him?"

"That he was murdered in Storyville and you found his body?"

"Is that what they're saying?"

"Yes, is it true? Come on, tell me . . ."

"Well, what do you think, Anita? Do you believe that story?"

Anita frowned in exasperation. She couldn't bear Callie when she was in this kind of mood. It was as if she were another person altogether, someone who was determined to be as difficult as she could be. Anita had heard her mother describe "the Chenier girl," as she always called her, as troubled and sometimes this word fitted Callie exactly. It was as if her whole body were troubled. Anita couldn't quite find the words to describe it in English, but the literal translation of the French expression, *"je ne suis pas bien dans ma peau"* ("I don't feel right in my skin"), seemed the best way to sum up Callie when she was like this.

"I don't know what to believe, that's why I'm asking you."

"So, supposing it is true . . ."

"STOP PLAYING GAMES WITH ME, CALLIE! How can you expect me to be your friend when you're like this? It must have been terrible for you, I keep thinking about it . . . there, see? I do believe what they've been saying and I won't be put off any longer, so start talking."

For several seconds Callie stared in silence at Anita until the little redhead looked as if she might explode with impatience. Then she smiled and motioned Anita to come and sit beside her.

"OK. I'll tell you what happened, but you're going to have to hear everything, understand?"

"Yes, that's what I keep telling you. How can we be friends unless you tell me everything?"

Half an hour later Anita was trembling with shock at Callie's story. She had known nothing of Callie's afternoon visits to Storyville. For a while she giggled when Callie described how her Uncle Jules had gobbled up his girl between her legs. She positively squeaked with excitement when she heard about the long pink thing he had between his legs, but suddenly she didn't like the expression on Callie's face when she started telling her how the girl took it in her mouth. It didn't sound altogether nice to Anita. She'd never liked Callie's Uncle Jules much anyway.

Anita was not quite sure what upset her the most: the fact that Callie appeared to have enjoyed watching Uncle Jules behaving so strangely or the feeling of betrayal that she hadn't included her friend in the afternoon expeditions. But it was when Callie began to describe with such glee the bloody, butchered body that she found Anita really began to panic.

"There, Anita. Now you know my dark and terrible secret," Callie taunted her, "now you know everything just like you wanted to. So, please, just tell me one thing—are you still going to be my friend?"

"Of course!" replied Anita with absolute conviction, for she was a creature of pure instinct and her instinct told her she still loved the Callie who looked after the injured animals all around them, who loved the same La Fontaine fables as she did, who shared Queenie's pecan pralines with her and who spirited her up to Madame Chenier's bedroom when she was out and showed her what wonderful games could be played with the little pots of make-up. But the demon who every now and then entered Callie's mind and made her say cruel and vicious things—that was someone Anita was becoming increasingly worried about having as her friend.

The scandal was wild. Jules Chenier. Of the *St. Charles Avenue* Cheniers. Murdered in a brothel. Stabbed. Butchered. *Gris-gris?* Could be.

There was an arrest. The skinny negro pimp. Nobody thought he'd have a chance. The prosecuting attorney was Teddy Lenoir and nobody ever got the better of Teddy.

Theodore Auguste Panama Lenoir could trace his ancestors back to the early eighteenth century when New Orleans had been founded by Sieur de Bienville as a settlement named for the then Regent of France, the Duc d'Orléans. The Lenoirs had been French aristocrats and proud of it. While many other French immigrants had mixed their blood and intermarried with the incoming Spanish settlers after Louis XV of France cheerfully gave away the whole of Louisiana and its inhabitants to his cousin, Charles III of Spain, the Lenoirs remained 100 per cent French, keeping a careful eye on the suitability of marriage partners chosen by their descendants. The law firm of Lenoir, Lenoir and Beauregard had been started by Teddy's grandfather and had quickly established a reputation as one of the finest law firms in the South, let alone New Orleans. If you wanted to win a case you wanted Teddy Lenoir on your side.

Teddy knew the pimp hadn't done it. He had frequented the

brothel himself from time to time, although he'd have to put an end to that now. No, it had probably been that girl Jules had always gone to. *Crime passionel.* It happened all the time. Jules had led her on a bit, had promised marriage or something stupid. He'd gone too far and the girl had taken a knife to him. It was a scandal for the Chenier family, but someone had to pay and the girl was far too pretty. It was far easier to let the pimp go down.

But try as he might in court, Teddy couldn't make it stick and New Orleans society delighted in the additional upheaval of Theodore Lenoir losing his first case. The Cheniers, however, were strangely pleased with the way he had handled everything. His name was added to their guest list for invitations to all their parties. Apart from this little upset, his career was running right on course. All he needed was to find himself a suitable wife in about five years' time and his life would be complete.

They never did find out who killed Jules Chenier. Callie remained vastly relieved that Queenie never said a word about finding her down in Storyville at the scene of the crime. Maybe she'd just forgotten.

Queenie hadn't forgotten. But it wasn't the picture of *Callie* coming out of the brothel which stayed in her mind. It was the man she had seen running out of the building several minutes before. The man Queenie knew had killed Jules Chenier.

CHAPTER 2

The Cheniers could not ignore the fact that the time was fast approaching when Callie would have to make her début and enter the competitive field in search of a husband.

Her chances were slim. Piercing black eyes were the only feature in her long sallow face which could remotely be called attractive. The nuns who had taught her at the Sacred Heart convent school were from wealthy Catholic families themselves and had thus been equipped to instil in their students as part of their overall training such feminine virtues as "tact, quiet courage and the willingness to subordinate one's will to another's gracefully and even gaily." They'd had a problem with Callie from the outset. They had tried to turn her into a young lady, but the Cheniers had to admit to themselves that even they found their daughter awkward and gauche. The only consolation was that her flat-chested skinny frame was perfectly suited to the dropped waist fashions that had swept America in the early Twenties. Callie studied the dresses worn by the models in the Edward Steichen photographs in her mother's *Vogue*, but found them somehow too demure. Nevertheless she was able to convey what she wanted to her mother's dressmaker who ran up several creations made to Callie's specifications. She was particularly fond of scalloped hems and beaded bodices but it worried her parents that the colors she chose were so flamboyant—scarlet, fuchsia or emerald green.

Yes, Callie was becoming a problem. It was time for her to be finished properly, to be groomed to become the perfect gentlewoman and, more important, the perfect wife. But each time Cécile Chenier looked at her daughter, she shook her head and told herself it would be a miracle if that miserable pinched expression and the skeletal figure attracted any suitors.

To make matters worse Anita was sent away. The de la Salles decided she ought to go to a finishing school in Paris and make her subsequent début into society there. Secretly Callie was devastated and only Queenie noticed how apprehensive she was as the date for Anita's departure drew nearer. As usual Callie hid her misery with sarcasm.

"So, tell me, missy, what do you think they'll succeed in teaching you in Paris that you've been too stupid to pick up right here in New Orleans? Think you're going to come back quite the little lady, don't you? If you deign to come back to us at all, that is. . . ."

Anita ignored Callie's mocking tone. She understood why she was upset. She had been aware for some time how wretchedly unhappy Callie was, how when they went to parties together Callie was unable to relax for a second. She knows what she's like, Anita thought to herself. Here am I having such fun with all my new dresses, a different *coiffure* every night and more beaux than I know what to do with, while Callie just stands there rigid like a piece of wood. If only she'd move just a fraction, bend a little, unwind, laugh, frown, show *some* kind of animation. If only her behavior could even begin to match the flamboyant color of her clothes. It's the incongruity of it all which puts people off. It's not as if she doesn't draw attention to herself wearing those bright colors. She gets people to look at her and then she stands there as if she were dead.

The fundamental problem was that Callie just hated society. She didn't fit in because she was determined not to. She wouldn't even resort to make-up to help her which was the biggest shame of all as Anita kept telling her.

"You of all people know what a difference it makes. What

was all that playing about with your maman's pots and paints for, if not for this. You can make yourself look sensational with just a bit of rouge and lipstick. You know how to paint your face better than anyone else in this town, yet you won't even bother. You'd have them falling over each other to get to you . . ."

"There's no one I want, frankly," replied Callie, "beats me why you want to throw yourself at everyone, Anita. No wonder they're sending you off to Paris, way you're behaving around here. Talk about making a fool of yourself."

You're jealous, that's all. At least I'm making some effort. Anita bit back the words just in time. It was hard to sympathize with Callie when she was in such an unpleasant mood. Furthermore she was not about to apologize for her own popularity when Callie didn't even try to make herself attractive. But she hated it when the men talked about her friend: "Wouldn't touch her with a barge pole," "What do you mean? She *is* a barge pole," "Don't go near her," "Why not?" "Don't, that's all, she's strange, like a witch," "They never found out who murdered her uncle, don't forget, and she found the body," "She's dangerous," "Her father's worth a fortune," "Makes no difference, she's jinxed, keep away."

Anita always felt she ought to speak up for Callie, but the sheer delight of discovering her own success with the opposite sex somehow managed to put her on her guard when Callie's name came up. She didn't want to betray her friend, nor did she quite want to draw attention to the fact that they were close, so she just kept quiet. If Callie didn't want to play the game then that was her problem. Meanwhile she, Anita, was not going to let anything or anyone spoil her fun.

Anita paid her dues, however, as she knew she would have to. When the day came for her to leave Callie clung to her, sobbing.

"You won't come back. You say you will, but I just know you won't come back. And I'm not crying because you're going— it's just so hot and claustrophobic and Mamma's been on at me again about what I'm going to wear to the Duvaliers' tonight and I keep telling her I'm not going, but she won't listen. How can I possibly face going to anything anymore if you're not going to be there? But I'm not crying about you, understand? I'm not even really crying. . . ."

" 'Course you're not," Anita whispered soothingly, "and I will come back and we'll have lots to tell each other. Remember La Fontaine? Remember the Tortoise and the Hare? Silly, silly me—I'm haring off to Paris like a mad thing and no doubt nothing will come of it. You'll stay here and keep moving along at your own pace like the tortoise and who knows, you'll probably beat me to the altar, see if you don't."

Anita didn't believe a word of what she said to Callie and all the way to Paris the memory of Callie's forlorn face haunted her. She knew the extent to which Callie could suffer and she felt guilty that she had not made more effort to ease that suffering. She held out little hope that there would be any late blossoming in Callie and that she would return to find her friend had managed to transform herself into the belle of New Orleans. If anything, things could only get worse . . .

But miracles do happen and the Cheniers' manifested itself in the form of Teddy Lenoir.

He wanted Callie, had done so since he first laid eyes on her when she was twelve years old, right after the Jules Chenier scandal. He knew she would never be a beauty, but then he, Teddy, would never attract the attention of beauties. His eyes were too close together, his hair too stringy. But Callie had the dark, shady quality of the mulatto girls he had once encountered at the Quadroon Balls and whose bodies he craved, but was too fastidious to take, yet she came from a good family. She was a Chenier, one of the St. Charles Avenue Cheniers and so Teddy came a-courting bearing armfuls of magnolias from the Garden District.

Callie quite liked him. He was nothing to look at, but he had his advantages: he had potential, one day he would be rich; he was malleable—if she married him it would not be too long before she could begin to slip out of the house on various pretexts and seek out what she really wanted; and her parents approved, she would be free of them if she accepted Teddy. So she encouraged him, not too much, just enough to allow his hand to hold hers a fraction longer each day. Until one afternoon sitting in the conservatory surrounded by the flowers he had brought her, Teddy ventured to place a hand on one of her tiny breasts and tentatively, his hand shaking all the while, pull the bodice aside till he could look down at her nipple.

"C'est noir! It's black, just like I have always imagined. Callie, *tu es bien nègre, non?* That's why I want you so much," and his tongue darted out to swish from side to side, wetting his black moustache in excitement.

"Non!" shrieked Callie, leaping to her feet. "I am *not* black, I am white, pure white."

For some years now Callie had been worried about the possibility that there might be some negro blood lurking in her veins. She had heard her parents arguing about it, Louis Chenier always returning to the fact that one of Cécile's great-grandparents had been black and Cécile retorting that Louis himself could hardly claim to be without taint. Although this was never discussed outside their bedroom, when they started screaming at each other everyone in the house could hear, including Callie. Did she have negro blood? The thought horrified her and now here was Teddy suggesting it might be true. Of course he apologized profusely, denied having any proof, promised never to say a word, but his hopes of marrying Callie were dashed. Callie was too shrewd to banish him forever—he was on the point of becoming the family lawyer after all—but she didn't want him for a husband. Teddy Lenoir never married anyone else and if anyone ever came close to loving Callie besides Anita it was he.

Shortly after the Teddy Lenoir fiasco Anita came home from France for a week and the conversations between her and Callie were suffocatingly intense.

"Did *you* know I was black, Anita?"

"You're not black, darling, you're a Creole, you told me so. What's more you're beautiful. Is it really all over with Teddy?"

"You don't know what he said to me, what he implied . . ."

"So what if he did? If he liked what he saw it's not the end of the world. In Paris there were hundreds of *nègres.* Really dark. Everyone knows the history of the Creoles, Callie, *chérie.* It's not a sin for you to have a dash of dark blood somewhere. I bet plenty of our friends do, too, except that in you it's especially *exotique,* that's all."

Callie was not convinced. "I know it's why he liked me—it's just it was the *only* reason he liked me, I swear. I was a fool at first, I thought he wanted me for who I am, I thought he liked me like you do, I thought he *accepted* me, moods and all, I thought he understood me and all the time he was just looking forward to sucking on my black titties . . ."

"Oh, Callie, *please* don't say things like that. You know it isn't true." Anita added under her breath, "And it's rather distasteful." She hesitated; Callie had never referred directly to her black moods before. "So, how are you? *Dans ta peau?* How is your depression?"

"Depression? You make it sound like an illness, like there's something wrong with me. Well, I'll tell you something, my depression, as you call it, is worse than ever."

"You need to see a doctor, Callie."

"I know," Callie whispered, "I did."

"You *did*?" Anita was stunned. This was real progress. Did her parents know? "What did he say?" But Callie's reply was disappointing.

"Oh, you know, it was old Doctor LeBlanc. Mamma forced me to go and see him and when I got there I just didn't know what to say to him. I mean, I didn't have a fever or a cold and he didn't understand why I'd come to see him. It was awful. I have never felt so helpless, I just couldn't *explain* to him how I felt, so I got upset and he told Mamma I was making a fuss over nothing and then she got upset. Oh, Anita, it was so terrible. I wish you had been there. I've needed you so badly this past year. There've been times when I thought I was going out of my mind."

You *are* going out of your mind, thought Anita. Doctor Le-Blanc, the good old family doctor, what was the point of sending you to him? And how am I going to be able to tell you my news? How am I going to be able to tell you about the best thing that's ever happened to me in my life while you're in this appalling state?

But she had to and when she began to talk to Callie about Thierry, the young law student in Paris who had swept her off her feet, Callie's face hardened in an expression of miserable disbelief.

"I've no idea what he sees in me . . . I'm so silly and he's so terribly, terribly clever but I do so adore him and we've found this perfect little apartment in the *sixième* . . ."

"You're going back to Paris," Callie said flatly.

"But, of course—oh, silly me, didn't I tell you? Thierry and I are going to be married. Next month. And you'll come to Paris for the wedding, won't you, Callie, *chérie*? You'll be my maid of honor?"

"No," said Callie simply, "I won't," and with that she closed herself to Anita and refused to open up again before Anita left. Her manner was formal and polite, she congratulated Anita, kissed her on both cheeks and never again referred to her own problems. An invisible barrier had been erected between the two women and Anita realized that once again she had let her own happiness come before her attempts to relieve Callie's despair.

When Anita went back to Paris to be married, Callie's parents gave up on her and, dubbed an old maid at the age of twenty, she returned to the life she had led as a child: reading in her room or brooding in the kitchen with Queenie. Only Queenie knew she went out late every night and returned in the early hours of the morning, slipping in through the old slaves' quarters at the back, taking care not to let the screen door into the kitchen bang shut.

Callie had a secret life.

Storyville was long gone, but Callie had never forgotten her visits there. Seven years later she had returned and found that the brothel was still there. No one recognized the child who had been there at the time of the murder.

"You want to *what*?" the pimp by the door spat at the gaunt, raven-haired creature before him.

"I want a room here. There's one on the first floor. I want to use that room."

"We don't use that room anymore. No one wants to go in there. Man was killed in there. You ever heard of the Jules Chenier scandal?"

Callie shrugged.

"Yeah, well, it happened here, right in this building." He sounded proud, maybe he made a buck on the side, sold tickets to the tourists to show them the scene of the crime.

"Well, *I'll* use it. I'll pay you for it."

"Damn right you will. I take 80 per cent of anything you make if you work for me."

"No, I'll pay you for the rent of the room."

"Who are you?"

"That's not important. Now, do we have a deal?"

"You just want to rent the room, don't want to turn any tricks?"

"I didn't say that . . ."

"So, it's 80 per cent on top. You bring 'em in here, they pay me on the door."

"Whatever."

"First I gotta see you know what you're doing."

"You mean . . . ?"

"Yeah, let's go upstairs."

She was a virgin. She still touched herself every day and made herself come. The pimp hurt her and she cried out in pain. He slapped her and accused her of conning him, but she reminded him that she was not one of his cheap whores, that she would be renting the room from him for her own purposes.

She went there every day and often recreated for herself the moment when she had found Uncle Jules's body. Time and again she wondered who could have killed him and why. But, in spite of the ugly memory, she found the same kind of solace in the room that she had found as a child in her *cachette* at the bottom of the garden on St. Charles Avenue. Here, in this room, she could mourn the loss of her friend, Anita. Here she was as far removed as she could possibly be from the smart New Orleans society in which she knew herself to be a misfit.

Inevitably she became part of the establishment and it was not long before sailors began to seek her out. She didn't resist. And after a while, as she lay on the bed with her skirts pulled up to her waist, or found herself pinned against the wall as sailor after sailor thrust his way into her, she realized that in her own bizarre way she was beginning to find some kind of respite from her loneliness.

The night Cécile Chenier ran away, Queenie anticipated something was going to happen. Callie was out, Queenie didn't know where, but she praised the Lord that the "child," as she still called her, didn't hear the bitter words her parents hurled at each other.

"So what did your daddy do? Dye his skin white overnight?"

Cécile was screaming at the top of her voice. As usual she was referring to old Jean-Baptiste Chenier, Louis's father. *His* father had been one of the original black Creoles whose culture was based on the old French Caribbean one, who were artisans

and small businessmen, but who went on to become wealthy.
Jean-Baptiste had been born pale on account of his French
mother and when in 1894 the glittering half-caste society crum-
bled and the black Creoles were disenfranchised and relegated
almost overnight to an inferior position among the black steve-
dores and cotton-mill workers they despised, he took a gamble
and pretended he was of pure white stock, callously disowning
his own father in the process and leaving the old man to fend
for himself. Jean-Baptiste went on to buy a sugar cane plantation upriver, but kept his family in a small town house in New
Orleans, while his father died a pauper's death down on the
docks, forbidden to enter his son's St. Charles Avenue mansion
or to see his grandson, Louis.

When Louis fell for the beautiful Cécile Fontaine, Jean-Baptiste encouraged the union, knowing full well that the Fontaines
had had their own fair share of problems back in 1894 and
Cécile could be counted on to keep quiet about Louis's grandfather.

What he did not know was that behind her beauty Cécile
harbored a cruel mind. She took endless pleasure in taunting
poor Louis, threatening him with exposure of his black blood
always when he was about to close an important deal or enter a
new stratum of New Orleans society.

But Louis had his own retaliation: "Couldn't keep away
from him, could you? Think I didn't know all about it?
Couldn't keep away from my brother. Didn't you ever stop to
think that he might be riddled with disease? Look where he
went! Look what he did there! Look how he died! Diseased!
That's what he was and it's eating its way through you too,
Cécile. Every day another little piece of you is being sucked
away . . ."

"STOP!"

When Cécile left later that night, she didn't even take a valise
with her.

"Your Mamma just ran out into the night," Queenie told
Callie when she returned in the small hours. "Go to your
daddy, child. He need you now."

"Pah!" spat Callie in disgust, but even she was shaken when
they pulled Cécile's body out of Lake Pontchartrain a few days
later.

Louis Chenier never recovered. He had loved Cécile and

while he knew he had lost her years before, he was not prepared for this. Always a heavy drinker, now he clung to the bottle in desperation, allowing it to taunt and threaten him as his wife had done before.

Inevitably it killed him and Teddy Lenoir handled the probate of his will. Teddy had known all about the sugar cane plantation upriver, but even he was astounded to learn how lucrative it was despite the fact that it had an absentee landlord. In accordance with the instructions in Louis's will he sold it and informed Callie she was now worth several million dollars. But Callie just looked bored and instructed him to invest the money for her as best he could. And then she dismissed him.

She might be rich and her eyes might be shining when she returned to St. Charles Avenue from one of her nighttime excursions, but deep down she was ashamed and confused. Her body ruled her and while she might have found a way of scratching her perpetual itch, it was under the strain of this dual existence that she began to lose control of her mind.

"Callie, chérie, que faites, ma'fant? Po'quoi vo' visage si triste?"

Estelle always spoke to Callie in Cajun patois. She was just a simple Storyville whore, but somehow she had established a rapport with this tall dark woman with the piercing look in her eye who came to the *maison* every night.

She was strange, this Callie. Five years ago she'd just appeared out of the blue, no one knew where she had come from. She wore a wig, that was for sure, although from her skin it would seem she was dark anyway. And where did she go to every day? She just rented *that* room. Estelle hadn't been able to bring herself to go inside. But this Callie didn't seem to care. Not that it seemed to make her happy, why was she always looking so sad?

"You want to come with me see them?" Estelle was so nervous as to what Callie's reaction would be she spoke in her broken English, "See them. In the jailhouse. *Ils ont faim.*" Estelle licked her lips. *"Faim.* All those men. They real hungry. They love see woman. Come with me."

Callie shrugged. It might be *amusant* to see all those men with their tongues hanging out at her.

She shrugged again, a constant gesture for her now, nodded OK, she would go with Estelle to the penitentiary.

It was the last place on earth she expected to find her future husband.

CHAPTER 3

In later years when Perry Jay Duboise, the Cosmetic King of the South, looked back on the beginning of Bayou Beauty ("If you buy Bayou," the advertisements ran, "you too could be a Southern Belle"), he would have to invent the way he started. He might pretend that he modeled his early career on that of the revolutionary Charles Revson, founder of Revlon, but unlike Revson, whose first experimental batch of nail enamel was heated over a bunsen burner in a loft on West 44th Street in Manhattan, Perry Jay first thought seriously about going into the business when he was serving time in the Louisiana State Penitentiary for armed robbery.

They told him one day that he had a visitor. At first he didn't believe them. He had no family. He'd been born in West Texas and his real name was Perry Jay Dubbs. His father died when he was fourteen and about a year later so did his mother. During a tornado the family shack collapsed and Perry Jay began hitching a ride East. Pretty soon he started stealing for food and inviting anyone who challenged him to a stand-up fight. In Baton Rouge he got caught taking an old lady's jewel box. They gave him ten years and he gave them a long line of backchat about being let out on parole which they laughed at hard. So when they told him he had a visitor, he was suspicious.

When he saw her, he was downright disgusted. She was hideous. Tall, scrawny, with a miserable pinched-up face. He stared at her through the mesh.

"A Creole is a white person," she said without preamble.

"Is that so?" Who *was* this crazy woman?

"Yeah, I'm not colored. No, sir! Webster's Dictionary says 'a Creole in the United States is a white person descended from the French or Spanish settlers of Louisiana and the Gulf States and preserves their characteristic speech and culture.' Other dictionaries say otherwise, but we'll say I'm white, won't we?"

Perry Jay nodded. He didn't quite know what else to do. He noticed that her skin *was* tinged with a faintly caramel hue, but in such a way that she just looked dirty. Her pale scrawny figure had none of the voluptuousness he normally associated with Creole women.

"Well, my name's Callie Chenier and I'll be back next week."

They told him about her. Apparently she was from an old Creole family and she had lived alone since the death of her parents in the family mansion in New Orleans.

By the time the week had passed he'd forgotten about her till they told him he had a visitor again.

He didn't recognize her. She looked sensational. Beautiful, almost. After a while he realized why. She had applied makeup to her face, hiding the circles under her eyes, and transforming the gaunt bony expression of the week before into a finely chiseled face of such perfect symmetry that it was astounding to think he had ever thought her remotely ugly.

"Makes a change, huh?" She flashed dark eyes at him. "I liked the look of you, but you surely weren't going to pay me any attention."

"You only stayed but a second," Perry Jay felt moved to point out. "I hardly had time to notice you."

"You noticed me. You noticed me fine. You cringed. You didn't want to look at me, so I went and put on my make-up and now look at you jumping. Here, take a look."

She placed a little hold-all on the counter in front of her. The wire mesh between them prevented Perry Jay from reaching out and touching it, so he contented himself with watching while she unzipped it. He half hoped she might have brought him a bottle of bourbon on the quiet. There *were* bottles all right, but they were little bottles of what looked like paint and which turned out to be cosmetics. Perry Jay didn't know the names for half the stuff she produced, but she told him anyway. She had perfumes and bath oils, sprays and eaux de toilette and she managed to release all their scents directly at him. He glanced sideways at the other inmates seated in a line to the right and left of him, but their attention was concentrated on their own visitors.

Later the guards baited him unmercifully about the way he smelled.

"But you'll do fine if you stick by Callie," they admitted. "She's a wealthy woman. The word is she's been looking for a man on these visits. She ain't had much luck up to now. Oh yes, sir, she's crazy, but she's loaded and the man who wins her confidence is going to get himself a mighty fine reward. Times are I wonder what she'd do if we unlocked all these here barriers and let you all loose on her. Reckon if we ever let just one of you loose, she'd scream the place down. Shame to let all that money go to waste . . ."

The following week Perry Jay was ready and waiting when she arrived. He noticed she wasn't wearing make-up, but he said nothing, silently marveling that anyone could be so plain, that such a face could be transformed. But she had something on her mind.

"You want to see how it's done, don't you? You can't believe I'm the same person. Well, you can just sit and watch while I put my new face on. Won't take that long. I've been practicing since I was twelve. Can you imagine the fun I had? My mamma never knew a thing about it. She would have nearly died if she had caught me."

She propped up a shaving mirror on the counter in front of her and swept her black hair back into a ponytail. Then she covered it completely with a toweling turban. This isn't happening, thought Perry Jay. I'm in a jail, not a woman's bedroom. Callie smiled sweetly at him and proceeded to smear a light cream all over her face.

"So's the foundation'll go on all smooth," she explained. "Now, see, here's the powder." She waved a feathery powder puff at him, scattering a light film on the wire mesh between them. Perry Jay coughed and blinked and was suddenly mesmerized. Once again, the beautiful flower was blooming before him. How many women did this? More to the point, how many women looked as ugly as Callie did without their make-up? She'd finished now, was looking at him.

"See, now I'm a Southern Belle!" And she was. She bent over her hand laid on the counter. "I can't do my nails. They took away my nail file. Wouldn't let me bring it in to show you."

He was almost sorry when it was time for her to go. He'd forgotten the plain shrew she'd been when she arrived. But he groaned inwardly when he saw that she slouched instead of holding herself proud and high. He watched her slip past the guard, clutching her bag, jumping nervously when she was handed back the nail file, aware that very soon now she would be forced to leave her fantasy world.

Week by week, he drew her out of herself, learned that the money originally came from sugar cane plantations, that this was now all handled by the trustees of her father's estate; that in the beginning they had consulted her, but that after a while they drifted away leaving her in the dark; that she lived in just one room of the house; that her one dream was to be mistress of a big plantation. Then she would press her fingertips to the wire mesh and look at him expectantly. Perry Jay would place the tips of his own fingers to hers and pat gently.

"Soon," he whispered, "soon, Callie."

It came sooner than he'd hoped. He'd been in jail for only five years. The atmosphere in the room was cold and hostile, but the words meant freedom was just around the corner.

"First parole request for Perry Jay Dubbs."

"Duboise," he hissed under his breath. *"I'm Perry Jay Duboise now."*

"Legal counsel present?"

"Yes, sir. I'm Theodore Lenoir representing Mr. Dubbs." *Theodore Lenoir? Who the hell was he?*

"Perry Jay Dubbs, ten year sentence for armed robbery. First offense in the State of Louisiana. Mr. Dubbs has served sixty-two months of his sentence, present record satisfactory, applied for parole on 25 September this year."

Theodore Lenoir was on his feet. "I would like to point out to the committee Mr. Dubbs's good behavior while in prison."

"Notice is taken. The Board met in closed chambers last

week. Have you reached a decision regarding Mr. Dubbs's request for parole?"

"Request for parole is granted."

He was out in time for Christmas. On Christmas Eve, he married Callie Chenier in a small civil ceremony in the French Quarter. Theodore Lenoir was their witness and he and Callie conversed in French. Perry Jay realized that Callie really was of genuine French extraction and that when she spoke French, gone was the shy, gawky creature who affected a terror of men. She was cackling away with Teddy Lenoir, even going so far as to dig him in the ribs every now and then.

That night she lay in his arms in her giant four-poster bed. Her make-up was subtle, her face was glowing and peach-colored in the candlelight. Perry Jay had not had a woman in five years, but he knew he had to treat this moment with the utmost caution. If he upset Callie and abused her trust in him, trust which he had carefully built up over eighteen months of weekly visits, he could kiss goodbye to millions of dollars.

Instead of leaping in beside her, he sat down on the edge of the bed and gently stroked her cheek and smoothed her hair away from her forehead, murmuring over and over again how happy he was, how beautiful she appeared to him, how she need never worry about another thing, she was his Callie now, he would take care of her forevermore. As he talked, he inched himself closer to her till he held her in his arms and could begin to ease the thin lacy shoulder straps of her night-gown down her arms. As his hand closed over her now exposed breast, he slipped into bed beside her.

Callie was out of bed and on her feet in a flash. As Perry Jay began to protest, apologize, deliver promises to keep his distance, she slipped across the room. Well, that's that, thought Perry Jay. First chance I get I scare the living daylights out of her. I can only hope she doesn't divorce me tomorrow.

But Callie was not the least bit scared. Perry Jay's touch had awakened her and now she raised her night-gown to her waist and called out in a plaintive wail.

"Perry Jay! Perry JAY! PLEASE!"

Perry Jay saw his bride of a few hours writhing and moaning against the wall. As he ran to help her, he saw that her hand was rubbing her clitoris up and down. When he reached her, she pulled him to her by the draw-string of his pyjamas and deftly untied it. His pyjama bottoms fell to the ground as Callie dropped to her knees and took him in her mouth. She kneaded his buttocks as she did so. She seemed to be building herself up into a frenzy of excitement and the harder he grew the harder she worked on him.

For a split second Perry Jay recalled that this woman sucking greedily on his penis was supposed to be a shrinking virginal violet. Then, as he was about to come in her mouth, she slithered up the wall again, bent her knees outward and clutched him to her.

"Come into me, press me against the wall. Harder! HARDER!" she yelled as he hammered against her, crushing her frail skinny frame as he exploded inside her.

Later, lying awake while she slept curled up beside him, he came to terms with the fact that somewhere along the line he'd been conned, but when it came to marrying into millions of dollars and finding you weren't the first, even a guy who *wasn't* on parole would have to be crazy to complain.

They started *Bayou Beauty* in mail order and within ten years they had cornered the market in the South. Callie could play the little girl lost act to the hilt when it suited her, but underneath she revealed a shrewd business sense. It was utterly natural. Her father had never consulted her about anything and, except for Teddy Lenoir, no one had explained to her what went on in the world outside the family house. Yet she knew that Southern women held a special place in the world, renowned for their beauty, their manners, for being the kind of lady a man secretly craved as his wife, his fantasy woman. Callie had no time for this talk of women's emancipation which was starting to spring up all over the place. At the same time, she knew that there were a great many women in the South who were born anything but beautiful. And those were the ones they would begin with.

She left it to Perry Jay to find a chemist who would come up with a line of products. Then she set about writing a little booklet to accompany them. In it she gently and diplomatically acknowledged that it was possible to be born plain, but that with *Bayou Beauty* products a girl could outshine anyone. She included a series of photographs in the Before and After tradition, proving what she said and giving detailed instructions how to apply the make-up. Once again she brought Perry Jay in to start the mail order business rolling. They did it from St. Charles Avenue for a year, but soon realized that their customers were beginning to go into drug stores and department stores and ask for *Bayou Beauty*. Perry Jay's parole was up, he was free to travel the country. Using Callie's money, he found what was to become the South's largest cosmetics manufacturing operation. He also still used Callie. It was she who continued to analyze what every Southern woman wanted; it was she who came up with the idea of having a special sales force consisting entirely of women, who would sell right into other women's homes, calling door to door, encouraging their friends to have "Bayou parties." These women were hand-picked by Callie herself, who made sure they were all beautiful, but that they could pretend that underneath their make-up they were the plainest little things you ever saw. No Southern housewife they visited would dream of being so ill-mannered as to ask them to remove their make-up. Encouraged by thoughts of becoming like the delectable creature in front of them, they bought and bought.

Perry Jay opened factories all over the South. He also bought a fine old plantation house in Mississippi and Callie played the Southern wife to the hilt, never setting foot in the Bayou empire outside her home. She left the entire running of the business to Perry Jay, who was now sporting a thin black moustache and a permanent tan. He had also acquired a brilliant press agent and through him was fast becoming recognized as a force to be reckoned with in the cosmetics industry.

Callie was never mentioned except in society columns: *Callie Duboise, wife of cosmetics king, Perry Jay Duboise.* The marriage was a disaster.

They had only been married for a few years when Perry Jay realized that not only was his wife highly experienced in sex, but she was also an uncontrollable nymphomaniac. She had given him an edited version of her past. What he didn't realize was that it was still going on. It was shortly after they moved to the plantation, which they renamed *Coinchenier* (meaning Chenier Corner) to please Callie, that he found her one afternoon down at the stables, flattened against the wall of one of the stalls with her skirt hiked up to her waist while a hired hand thrust his way into her. Perry Jay fired the man on the spot, but

he knew he was not the first, nor would he be the last, and
when he came upon her for the sixteenth time in four months
he gave up. Instead he took care to select only the most discreet
hired hands, allowing Callie to look them over first and indicate
which ones took her fancy. Sometimes Perry Jay knew these
were men who could not be relied upon to keep silent upon the
weird habits of their employer's wife and he hired others instead. And noticed that they too found their way to the stables.
Callie didn't care.

Perry Jay worried about disease and as the years went by he
barely touched her again, except for an annual reunion on their
wedding anniversary on Christmas Eve.

Callie had long since given up worrying about getting pregnant. She had laid herself wide open for years and when nothing had happened she had concluded that she must be barren.

Queenie, of course, put it down to the *gris-gris* she had hidden under Callie's mound of pillows every single night since the
beginning of her marriage, a *gris-gris* which was supposed to
prevent her from conceiving a child. Queenie was terrified that
a child born to someone as crazy as Callie could be highly
dangerous.

Early in the New Year of 1940, Callie made an announce-
ment to her husband and while it only sent a slight shiver of
irritation up Perry Jay's spine, when it reached Queenie's ears
she wrung her hands and rolled her eyes and shuddered to
think what would become of them.

"Perry Jay," said Callie, clasping his hand in her bony claw,
"Perry Jay, I believe I'm going to have a little one and although
you maybe won't believe this, I just know it's going to be
yours."

He *was* a little one—tiny, a shrimp. Callie adored him from the
day he was born. She taught him to speak French before he
could utter a word of English. She insisted on giving him a
French name: Philippe-Josephe. Perry Jay, despite the fact that
he had changed his name from Dubbs to the French Duboise,
hated anything French. He elected to refer to his son as PJ.

At school they called him "pyjamas" and teased him unmercifully. After all, for most of his schooling he was a head
shorter than anyone else in his class and his father, instead of
manufacturing tobacco or cotton, made lipstick and nail polish.

"There's that beauty pansy's kid. Ain't he a pretty boy? How d'ya do, Miss Bayou?" they taunted him.

"Papa, qu'est-ce que c'est un pansy?" PJ asked his father at dinner one night.

"Don't talk to me in French!" roared Perry Jay. *"Callie!"* he continued to shout as if his wife were in the next room instead of sitting opposite him at the other end of the table. "PJ wants to know what a pansy is."

"Well, if you can't tell him, nobody can."

"What the goddamn hell do you mean? What do I know about ass-licking little fairies?"

"Perry, *chéri, pas devant . . .*"

"NO FRENCH!"

It was no wonder PJ grew up in a state of constant apprehension about his father. He was aware that he was somewhat of a disappointment to him. He was at a loss to understand why his father was so against anything French. PJ thought his father *was* French. West Texas was never mentioned, nor was the name Dubbs. As far as PJ knew, his father had always been called Duboise and somehow the notion lodged itself in his head that his father's family had emigrated to America from France, arriving on a boat sometime in the Twenties. He had this image of his father standing in the rain clutching a suitcase and a stuffed dog, shouting, *"On est arrivé!"*

Perry Jay was not interested in children. He was no longer interested in Callie Chenier Duboise. What occupied his time more than anything else was the phenomenal success of *Bayou Beauty.* If his son wanted to take an interest in it too, then fine, he'd encourage him. Till then he ignored him.

Every now and then, of course, PJ floated onto his horizon. Once, trailing around after his father and a group of shoppers through the endless halls of cosmetic displays on the ground floor of a large department store, PJ asked his father in a high-pitched squeaky voice, "Papa, what did they sell on the ground floor of department stores before they had cosmetics?"

Perry Jay stopped dead in his tracks. The group parted obediently as he strode through them to look down at his small son quaking before him.

"Nothing!" he roared. "There was nothing. Before cosmetics, all women looked like this," and he grabbed hold of a plain, middle-aged woman whose face was hot, shiny and totally de-

void of make-up. Gasps echoed round the group. Here was the legendary Perry Jay in action. Black hair slicked back from his forehead. A thin black moustache snaked across his upper lip. His pearl tie-pin nestled in the middle of his silvery gray silk tie. His boutonniere always seemed to be the color of his latest lipstick. There was no trace of the man who had sweated on a Louisiana chain gang.

Perry Jay's tours were very popular. Once a month he took a group of shoppers round the *Bayou Beauty* territory in department stores all over the South. He flirted, teased, shocked and joked with the women, displaying a kind of oily charm.

"Bring me some of my latest lipstick," he demanded, flicking his fingers at a nearby salesgirl. When she put it into his hand, he flourished it around and around in circles till finally he brought it down to the lips of the shiny-faced woman in front of him.

"Your mouth is crying out for this," he told her and before applying the lipstick, he kissed her briefly on the lips. She swooned into his arms and the surrounding women pressed forward to get a better view. PJ, cowering beneath them, was overcome with claustrophobia. Something like this always happened when his father took him anywhere near anything to do with *Bayou Beauty*.

PJ was an angel. He had an astonishingly beautiful face: wide-apart, black eyes fringed with long, curling lashes, a small straight nose, high cheekbones, gleaming even teeth which could flash the most heart-melting grins. Callie made him grow his hair long, which was another reason for the teasing at school. Her woman friends swarmed round him, all wanting to pat the little dark head. Callie purred with pride.

"Tu es joli," she would tell him as she placed his head in her lap, stroking his hair while she read him bedtime stories. *"On pourrait te prendre pour une fille."*

"Pas toi," he whispered to himself, well aware that he didn't get his looks from his mother. Her face without its make-up grew duller every year. It could still be transformed in under a minute by her skilful application of make-up, but PJ knew that underneath it all his maman was no Southern Belle.

Yet Callie was now one of the most stylish women in Mississippi. Despite her plainness, her figure was a couturier's dream, personifying the long, angular elegance of 1950s high fashion.

She traveled to New York and even as far as Paris to maintain a wardrobe befitting the wife of the Cosmetics King of the South. Balmain, Givenchy, Christian Dior adorned her tall, bony figure—little jackets nipped in at the waist, flaring out again in a frill above a calf-length pencil skirt, hair scraped back in an elegant French roll under huge picture hats. At home she wandered round the house in a succession of clinging silk housecoats, her hair hidden in a turban, her face exquisitely made-up, chunky earrings jutting out either side of her jaw like guard dogs. One arm was permanently bent at the elbow pointing up, the hand flopping back at the wrist trailing a long cigarette holder between two fingers. Two Pekingese snuffled along behind her wherever she went. They were called Tennessee and Truman despite the fact that they both appeared to be bitches. When she entertained at home, Callie invariably changed into one of her long-flowing, full-skirted, tight-bodiced white organdie dresses with the billowing sleeves nipped in at the elbow. She'd had her dressmaker model them on something she'd seen Grace Kelly wear in a movie and when she wore one, she would usually let her hair hang loose, held off her face by a velvet ribbon. The overall effect was quite ridiculous. Mutton dressed as lamb. *"Gigot, gigot, gigot!"* they cried at school whenever Callie came to pick PJ up.

When PJ was fifteen, he got his first big shock in life. It came about as a result of a practical joke he and Callie played on his father.

PJ was beautiful. Callie adored him. It was inevitable that the day would come when she would amuse herself by making up his face. She first started when he was about twelve. She emphasized the poignant hollows in his cheeks, smoothed blusher lightly upward and outward over his fine cheekbones, fluffed a film of powder over the freckles on his nose, outlined his wide slanting eyes with a black eye pencil, tweaked his eyebrows into two high arches and thickened his already dense eyelashes with a heavy coating of mascara. Finally, instead of slashing his full, pouting mouth with a dramatic red lipstick, she chose a soft, blushing pink and the overall effect was a terrifying success. Terrifying because Callie had transformed her son, as she transformed herself, into a strikingly attractive *woman*.

It became a game for them. Callie made up PJ every so often

in the privacy of her bathroom. Perry Jay was denied entry. It was her sanctuary. PJ enjoyed himself. He found he liked pretending, generally better than reality. At school, he pretended to be Elvis Presley. He swiveled his hips and brushed his hair forward so it flopped over his eyes.

"Since my baby left me," he would belt out suddenly in the locker room, *"I've found a new place to dwell, it's down at the end of lonely street at—"* and the other kids would all join in with *"HEARTBREAK HOTEL."*

"You sound just like him," said Honeychile Winslow, a blonde girl with breasts. Girls in school were automatically divided into those who had breasts and those who didn't. Honeychile, aged fourteen, had two little firm round balls which seemed to grow a fraction of an inch every day. Since Honeychile worshipped Elvis and had twice run away from home trying to get to Memphis, this was praise indeed. He tried "Don't Be Cruel" and "Love Me Tender" and she moved a little closer to him.

"Pyjam . . . I mean, PJ . . ." she began, hesitating and biting her lip in a way she knew to be irresistible. "PJ, d'ya suppose ya daddy would give me some Bayou Beauty, seein' as how we're friends?"

"NO! No!" PJ was on his feet, furious with her. He'd been about to fall in love with her, but this was outrageous. Honey was taking advantage, bringing his father into it *again.*

He went home in a temper and mooched into the kitchen. Queenie eyed him warily.

"Keep away from my shrimp gumbo, ya hear. Miz Callie bin askin' where you is. Company comin' tonight. Lucille's run off and there's no one to wait at table. Miz Callie, she frantic."

Callie had brought Queenie with her from New Orleans. Her *jambalaya* was without equal. PJ scared her. He didn't know why, but she was always watching him like a hawk. Now she glanced at him nervously as he took a stick of corn bread and wandered out.

He found his mother upstairs in her bathroom.

"Philippe! *Tu vas m'aider.* You've got to help me."

As she told him her plan, his mouth spread slowly into the lazy grin she loved so much.

"Perfect!" was all he said as she started to apply the moisturizer to his face.

His parents' guests had all arrived when he came in with a tray
of margaritas. He moved silently around the room, careful not
to catch anyone's eye as he offered them each a drink. Once his
high heels almost skidded on the parquet floor, but he caught
himself just in time. He'd only had half an hour to practice in
Callie's bathroom. The maid's dress fitted him like a dream.
The two tennis balls rubbing against his nipples unnerved him a
little, but when he looked down at the white frilly bib of his
apron jutting out provocatively, he was reassured. Queenie, of
course, had been horrified.

"Callie, she's new," he heard a woman say to his mother,
eyeing him appreciatively.

"Ye-es, just came today." His mother looked to see if anyone
was watching and winked at him.

"Mighty pretty, mighty pretty," muttered an old fool as he
maneuvered his tongue along the rim of his margarita glass.
"Like this drink, like it a lot, what's it called?" He looked
directly at PJ, who opened his mouth to answer and then shut
it just in time before his adolescent male voice gave him away.
Callie came to his rescue.

"It's a margarita, Eustace. We discovered them when we
were in Mexico recently."

"Oh, yes, how was that trip?" And the conversation veered
smoothly away from PJ. They hadn't thought of that, what he
should do if he had to speak. Lucille had never uttered a word,
just fetched and carried and handed food and drink to the
guests.

When they went in to dinner, he managed to serve them their
crayfish and their shrimp gumbo without a hitch. There was
one narrow escape when the old fool, Eustace Hooper, who had
achieved a certain amount of notoriety earlier in the year by
having a heart attack the same day as Eisenhower, choked on a
piece of crayfish and everyone thought he was having another
attack. Without thinking what he was doing, PJ dealt him a
hefty blow on the back. It happened so fast that no one saw him
do it except for Eustace who turned round and stared at him in
utter amazement. What was this ravishingly beautiful maid doing thumping him on the back? Boy, did she have some
strength to her! He was about to start drawing everyone's attention to PJ when he discovered several of the female guests were

plying him with water and perfume and cool lace handkerchiefs and he recalled he was supposed to be at death's door. He clasped as many hands as he could find and pressed them to his forehead.

The men ignored him and went on with their own conversation, discussing whether or not to buy Ford Motor Company stock which had gone on sale to the public for the first time, whether Ike would run again, whether they'd known anyone who had perished in the tragedy of the *Andrea Doria*, whether anybody knew anyone in that far-off place called Hungary and if Ike did run again, how much chance did Adlai have, and did Perry Jay have an answer to Suzy Parker as a model for Bayou ads?

"Well, if you don't *regarde pas plus loin* . . ." Teddy Lenoir motioned with his eyes toward PJ who was serving some coffee. "There might be something right here in your own backyard."

"NO FRE . . ." began Perry Jay before he remembered he was hosting a dinner party. Teddy always did it to annoy him, anyway. Best to ignore it. For the first time he took a good look at the new maid. The girl's profile looked vaguely familiar, short straight nose and long fluttering lashes as she concentrated on pouring the coffee. Her hair was swept back off her forehead into a little white cap which sat cheekily on the back of her head. Ears were rather large, mused Perry Jay to himself, otherwise she wouldn't make a bad model at all. As she went round the table, he glanced down at her legs and shook his head sadly when he saw they were rather muscular. Still, she could always wear pants or just do head and shoulder shots, worth investigating further, see if she'd cooperate in the initial stages . . . Oh yes, her cooperation looked like it would be most enjoyable.

PJ couldn't wait to get back to the kitchen. His father appeared to be taking an inordinate amount of interest in him. Had he guessed? Recognized him? But as he went out the door, he heard his father ask: "Callie, where's PJ? Thought he was going to join us tonight. I do want the boy to sit down to dinner with civilized folks just once in a while. Lord knows who he mixes with in school."

"He went to a movie. *The Girl Can't Help It,* I think." *Civilized folks indeed!* What would his guests say if she told them she'd met him dirt poor and in jail?

Queenie went to bed early in a huff. It occurred to PJ that he had no idea who cleared away after his parents gave a dinner party or who did the dishes. They had a butler, but he was away on vacation and anyway he would never sink so low as to do the dishes. After a while, it dawned on him that it must be Lucille who got to do all the worst jobs, which in this case meant him.

He was halfway through the knives and forks when he felt two heavy arms circle his waist from behind.

"I sure am mighty pleased you're helping out tonight," his father's voice purred in his left ear. PJ froze.

"I have some nice new lipsticks and eye shadows for you. We'll take them up to your room and see how they suit you. Hmmmm?" To PJ's horror, he began to unbutton the back of his dress.

"Must be hot in this uniform, let's take it off your shoulder a bit . . ."

PJ leapt away. Whatever he did, he mustn't open his mouth and let his voice give him away. On the other hand, he had to get away from his father who, undeterred, had started stroking his bottom again.

"All you have to do is cooperate, just a little, and you could find yourself becoming a model, earn yourself a pile of money, your face known to millions all over the South." He had moved in close again and was nuzzling PJ's neck.

"Perry, *chéri*! Are you in the library? I'm just going to have a nightcap, can I bring you something?" Callie's voice could be heard advancing upon the kitchen. PJ seized the opportunity and dug his elbow hard into his father's ribs. Perry Jay yelled and backed away.

"You need some of my perfume," he hissed. "You are one hell of a pretty woman, but you sure don't smell like one."

Fortunately, he had gone by the time Callie came in. She embraced PJ.

"You were wonderful, darling. Have you seen your father anywhere and what in the world are you *doing*? Leave all that and come sit with me."

"Mama, don't you think I ought to change first?"

CHAPTER 4

Perry Jay did in fact find a new model in his own backyard, although he didn't realize it at the time. Fourteen-year-old Honey Winslow knew it all right. The minute she learned that PJ's father was the legendary Bayou Beauty king, she latched on to him.

PJ took her to the house often. He had a huge crush on this precocious, gray-eyed, freckle-faced All-American blonde. Honey seemed years older than fourteen. Her father was dead and she lived with her mother, Louella, in a large rambling bungalow on the outskirts of town, a whole world away from the Duboise plantation. Her mother watched TV all the time and never noticed that her daughter had begun to use make-up, let alone that she was using hers. She barely noticed when Honey ran away to look for Elvis. When the sheriff brought Honey back and explained what had happened, Louella just looked at her daughter and asked: "Did you find him? What's he like?"

Every now and then, Louella would look up from the television to ask Honey: "Are you still a virgin?"

" 'Course I am, Mamma," Honey always answered and

frowned because she found the question insulting. Any girl who lost her virginity was dumb. She knew that was what kept boys sniffing round *her*, the fact that she always said no, but always implied that you never knew what might happen the next time she saw them. She dated boys older than herself. PJ was almost sixteen and he was the youngest. He was curiously shy when it came to necking, acting almost as if he didn't know what to do.

The only time he came close to uncontrollable passion was the night they saw *From Here to Eternity* and were discussing the beach scene afterward. "Let's pretend we're them," he suggested, meaning Burt Lancaster and Deborah Kerr, knowing that if he pretended to be someone else, he could let himself go. It wouldn't be him, PJ, kissing her, it would be Burt Lancaster. Honey nearly did lose her virginity that night, mainly because it was the first time she really wanted to.

"Why, PJ, I never realized you could be so exciting!" she squealed, pushing him away from her at the last minute. Burt Lancaster faded into the distance and PJ began apologizing profusely, winding up by inviting her to Callie's birthday party the following Saturday night.

When Honey walked into her home on the night of her fiftieth birthday in 1956, Callie Chenier Duboise was furious. She hated this trumped-up bit of white trash PJ had unearthed. She had to admit the girl was good-looking. She was tall for her age with her long beige-blonde hair pulled back in a ponytail. She had huge gray eyes with feathery lashes. Her nose was quite large, but it gave her face a strength which it might have lacked without it. Her mouth was big and wide and full and sensuous. At fourteen, she was still long, leggy, flat-chested and coltish, but it was clear that she was already very much what Callie called *séduisante*. She was wearing a little black dress. At her age it should have looked all wrong . . . but it didn't. It made her look at once sophisticated and little-girl appealing, so simple was the cut. Callie wondered where she'd got it. That slob, Louella Winslow, had never owned anything like this.

But the thing which infuriated her more than anything was the fact that Honey had a beauty spot on her left cheek. Callie had always wanted a beauty spot, but would never dream of painting a false one on her face. As she looked closer, she realized that Honey's was real, just a shade darker than usual with the help of an eyebrow pencil. What made it so striking was the fact that Honey was so fair. Her beauty spot stood out on her creamy complexion, competing with a few freckles on the bridge of her nose, but winning through as if to demand that everyone acknowledge Honey's loveliness.

Callie had forsaken her white organdie to wear, just once, a scarlet chiffon dress which was draped around her ever-bony frame in an attempt at a Grecian style. One shoulder was bare, the other had a long flowing extension of the dress tossed over it. A huge diamond clasp held it in place. Diamond-drop earrings hung from her ears. Her black hair was swept up into an elaborate chignon on the very top of her head.

We're opposites, she thought as she watched Honey. She's fair and creamy and I'm dark and dramatic. Even as she thought this, Callie wondered why she was comparing herself with Honey, almost as if they were in competition. But for whom?

She looked around for PJ. Where *was* he? If he didn't appear soon, she'd have to receive Honey herself. She was about to go over when she saw PJ arrive at the girl's side. She noted that he appeared unusually attentive, hanging on her every word. Poor Philippe, she thought, how boring for him to have to listen to what could only be a stream of inanities. What a darling well-mannered boy he was. But as she watched him stay close to Honey for the next two hours, she was aware of an unfamiliar *frisson* of something which she was surprised to finally recognize as jealousy.

PJ was hers. Her baby. He belonged to her, not to that little tramp. The girl was far too young to be allowed out to grown-up parties, but with a mother like Louella Winslow, was it any wonder . . .

They were calling her to come and blow out all her candles on her birthday cake and after that the dancing began. A dance floor had been laid outside underneath the oak trees and couples were getting up from the tables scattered across the lawn to move toward it.

Honey found herself separated from PJ and was rather relieved. She didn't want to be seen hanging round with him all evening. That might discourage any other potential action. Suddenly she noticed that Perry Jay was standing alone at the bar.

Perry Jay never knew what hit him. He felt a smooth little hand creep into one of his and he looked down. Honey's face at its most angelic gazed up at him.

"Excuse me, but I so want to dance and no one's asked me."

"Outrageous!" declared Perry Jay, gallantly ignoring the fact that since the dancing had only just begun, no one had had much time to ask her.

He led her out onto the dance floor and pressed her up against him. He immediately found he had the biggest erection he'd had in years. He looked about him; no one seemed to have noticed. He looked down at Honey and knew at once that she had. She reached up and whispered in his ear: "The only thing to do is to keep close together, that way they won't be able to see. It'll be our secret." And she pushed herself a little closer to him.

Perry Jay almost came on the spot. He positively ached. Who was this delectable little creature?

"What's your name, honey?" he asked her.

She giggled.

"You said it already. Honey. Short for Honeychile."

The words from an Andy Williams song, "Butterfly," popped into his head: *The honey that drips, from your sweet lips, can send me right out of my mind.*

"How old are you, Honey?"

"Eighteen," she lied. "How old do I have to be to be a model?"

"Whenever you're ready. Do you feel ready?"

"Yes," she breathed. "I'm ready now."

"Then we'd better go and start your career," Perry Jay told her and began to lead her off the dance floor toward the house. He couldn't believe it. Not one of his models had ever been this cooperative.

PJ saw them leave and cursed. What was Honey doing with his father? Callie Chenier Duboise watched her husband lead Honey across the lawn and into the house. "Damn, damn, damn," she almost swore out loud. She'd been aware of Perry Jay's "recruiting sessions" for new models for quite some time, but she had never imagined that little Honey Winslow might be a candidate.

Then she saw PJ moving toward the house after them and

she began to realize that perhaps there was a way to get Honey out of her son's life forever.

Perry Jay took Honey up to an attic storeroom. There was an old-fashioned double bed in a corner. He had long since dragged up a mattress for it. But there were no sheets or blankets or pillows and Honey wrinkled her nose.

"There's make-up in those boxes over there," he lied. "We'll look at it afterwards. Now, take your clothes off."

"What, *here*?" Honey pretended to look shocked. Perry Jay wasn't in the mood for teasers. He moved toward her and she hurriedly unzipped her little black dress and stepped out of it. This was just as well since when he reached her, he ripped her petticoat off her from the bodice down, grabbed her arm and flung her roughly across the bed.

At the back of her mind Honey dimly registered that she was still a virgin and this wasn't the best way to encounter the so-called act of love. PJ's father seemed to be in some kind of rage. He was yelling at her, calling her all kinds of horrible names, words she'd never heard before. He took off his jacket, but kept his shirt and tie on. He unzipped his trousers and pulled down his underpants. Honey screamed as loud as she could. She'd never actually *seen* one before, but she knew instinctively that this was one of the biggest ever.

Perry Jay raped her. While he was doing so, he told her over and over again that that was what was happening. He'd never done it before at his "recruiting sessions," not actually raped someone anyway. The girls up to now had been willing. This was a whole lot more fun. Why wasn't she screaming anymore? He looked down and saw she was almost relaxed.

"Scream!" he yelled at her and hit her across the face, "go on, scream!"

It had hurt Honey to begin with, yet at no point had she been as scared as she made out. It surprised her how much she began to enjoy it, even when he hit her. She screamed louder than ever.

PJ was coming up the stairs. Callie, who had just come up the main staircase, followed him, climbing slowly to the top of the house, unhurried, knowing perfectly well what she would find when she got there.

PJ flung open the door of the storeroom and stared at his

father's bare buttocks humping up and down. Honey caught sight of him out of the corner of her eye and in a split second changed her tune. She began beating and scratching Perry Jay's back.

"YES!" roared Perry Jay. "That's *right*!"

Then she scratched at his eyes and he pulled back. PJ saw the blood on the mattress between Honey's legs. Perry Jay saw it too and stared at her. He'd been so caught up in his brutality, he hadn't noticed that she was a virgin. He turned and saw his son standing in the doorway, watching them, felt him leap across the room and try to drag Honey out from under him.

"What in hell are you doing, boy?"

"She's in the class below me at school, Papa."

"She can't be. She's eighteen."

"I'm fourteen," said Honey.

Perry Jay shot off her. Grabbing his trousers, he pulled them on and ran through the door and down the stairs, never seeing Callie standing in the shadows on the landing outside.

It was the worst birthday Callie had ever had. She had wanted PJ to see that tramp thrashing about underneath his father, convinced that after that PJ would never want anything to do with her again. But now she could see him cradling Honey in his arms on the bed. As Callie watched them, Honey, her face partly buried in his shoulder, looked up and stared directly at Callie. She winked, but to Callie it was not quite clear whether it was her eye that moved—or her beauty spot.

It took Callie only two weeks to persuade Louella Winslow to send Honey away.

She invited Louella to come over for a cup of coffee. Louella arrived looking at once flabbergasted and suspicious. It was the first time she'd ever been to *Coinchenier*. Somewhere at the back of her mind she had vaguely registered that Honey was seeing the Duboise boy. His mother asking her here like this could only mean one thing: trouble!

"Honey's such a dah-ling child. We're so fond of her, Mr. Duboise and I. We've been so worried about her."

"She must be pregnant," Louella said flatly, not even bothering to make it a question.

"Why, surely not!" returned Callie sweetly. "By whom?" Silently she wondered that the possibility had not occurred to her

before. It could even be true, in which case there was even more
reason for getting the girl as far away as possible.

"No, no, no, she can't possibly be. She's just a child." Callie
prattled on gaily. "No, it's just that she doesn't have a father
and that makes such a difference in the life of a girl her age.
Mr. Duboise realizes this. He'd like to help. Things must be
very hard . . . financially, I mean."

"Very," muttered Louella, thinking how nice it would be to
have a TV set in her bedroom as well as in the living room.

"Well, as I was saying, Louella, we'd like to help. Do you by
any chance have any relatives living in any other part of the
country?"

"New York," said Louella. "My sister lives there. Honey
always did want to go to see her, but we never had the money
for the trip. Imagine that! Sissie's never even seen Honey since
she was a little bitty baby."

"Mr. Duboise and I would like to treat Honey to a trip to
New York City. We'll buy her a ticket and we're willing to
provide for her education there for the next two years, in the
very best of schools, of course. Mr. Duboise and I want to be
very particular about that."

Mr. Duboise couldn't have cared less. He had absolutely no
idea what Callie was up to. It was beginning to nag at him that
some of those other cooperative little girls might have been
younger than they said they were. He began to keep a very low
profile and finally decided to spend most of his time in his New
York apartment. Now that *Bayou Beauty* was expanding at
such a rate, the New York office seemed to be the hub of all the
activity in any case. Callie didn't give a damn. As far as she was
concerned, her husband could do what he liked. Their marriage
existed in name only. Besides, she had PJ and she didn't need
anyone else.

When, a month after PJ's graduation (which, for "business reasons," his father did not attend), Perry Jay sent for PJ to join
him in New York for a weekend, Callie became hysterical.

"Philippe, *chéri*, don't leave me. What could you possibly
want to do in New York at this time of year, all hot and
sticky . . . ?"

"It's not exactly frigid down here, Mamma," PJ pointed out.
He was keen to get away from *Coinchenier* for a while. Ever

since he'd graduated, the place had begun to get on his nerves and with Callie fussing over him all the time it was positively claustrophobic. Callie didn't seem to realize that he no longer wanted to spend time in her room, allowing her to make up his face. She hated it when he went out and became edgy if he invited friends over. Honey Winslow had disappeared right after his mother's birthday party well over a year ago, almost overnight in fact. It was all very strange. He had paid Louella a courtesy call and discovered that Honey had moved to New York. Of course, Louella kept quiet about the amount of money Callie had given her—enough to keep her in TV sets till the day she died. She didn't even mention that she'd seen PJ's mother and, as instructed, she refused to give him Honey's address. Rather belatedly, she began to wonder what her daughter had done to warrant such an elaborate and expensive operation.

"Well, please ask her to write to me, Miz Winslow," said PJ.

"Sure." Louella was aware that it was time to watch Perry Como and she wished PJ would leave.

But PJ never heard from Honey and as his plane landed at La Guardia he wondered if he'd run into her in New York. A ridiculous fantasy, of course. It wasn't as if New York was some little backwater in Mississippi . . .

That night at dinner his father came straight to the point.

"Well, son," he began and PJ cringed. He wished his father wouldn't call him *son* or *boy*. "What are you going to do now?"

"I don't know, Papa," said PJ innocently. "I don't know anyone in New York. Do you know of any place I might go, learn the new dances?"

"I meant work, you idiot. Are you going to come in with me? You could, you know. Start right here in New York where the action is." Perry Jay winked lewdly and PJ looked away quickly. He didn't think he would be able to stand it if his father was going to get all pally.

"What do you say, son?" To PJ's horror, his father reached across the table and covered his hand with his own. "Shall we make a go of it, just the two of us, try and cut the old lady out?"

So that was it. Perry Jay wanted to be rid of Callie and he thought he could use a cheap trick like getting PJ on his side to acquire what he wanted.

"I don't want to join *Bayou Beauty*, Papa. You know that."

"Suppose you got fancy ideas about going to college?"

"I hadn't even thought about it."

"There you are!" said Perry Jay triumphantly. "Haven't thought about a thing, have you? Callie's been filling your head with nonsense all these years and look where it's got you. Empty-headed and with no ambition in life. Anyway, I knew you wouldn't say yes right away. You need time to consider. Tell you what I'm going to do. I'm going to send you to Europe for a year, give you time to think about it and get some experience along the way." He winked again.

For a second PJ felt sorry for him. He was pitiful, really. He might run a giant beauty empire, but if Callie chose to shoo him away like a fly then that would be the end of him. PJ wondered how he had always known this, that his mother had the upper hand. Was it because of her money? Queenie had told him about his Chenier ancestors, and he was proud of the fact that he came from good stock. It was clear his father was nowhere near top drawer, in fact the old man had always been pretty cagey about *his* folks.

As for *Coinchenier*, what a charade. How the hell had he survived? Gradually the romantic illusion that he had harbored about the place throughout his childhood had trembled, shuddered and finally shattered altogether. Christ, what a place! If he were honest with himself, he had wanted to get away for years now and although he hadn't realized it, he had succeeded the only way he knew how—via his disguises.

No, if his father wanted to send him to Europe it was fine with him. The farther away he could get the better.

". . . Alphonse Lenoir—" His father's voice interrupted his thoughts. "You know Alphonse, don't you? Teddy Lenoir's ward. His sister's boy, the one who was orphaned about ten years ago. Philippe, are you listening to me, boy?"

PJ nodded. Everyone knew about Alphonse Lenoir, although very few people had met him. The way PJ had always heard it, Alphonse should have been sent straight to a nut house rather than an orphanage.

"Teddy wants to send Alphonse to Europe for a year, but he's still very young, so Teddy feels he needs a companion to watch out for him over there." Terrific, thought PJ, why can't they enlist him in the Louisiana National Guard instead?

Callie was devastated, of course. She saw it as a plot hatched by Perry Jay to steal PJ from her. She appealed to Teddy Lenoir, who still featured in her life as her lawyer even though he was getting on for retirement age. But Teddy wanted Alphonse out of his hair for a while and Perry Jay had come up with the perfect solution.

The first time PJ clapped eyes on Alphonse, he was instantly reminded of Callie. They both had that sallow, string bean look about them, although Alphonse was even longer at six foot four inches.

He was quiet and withdrawn and there was an air of perpetual misery about him. He cowered—inasmuch as anyone of his immense height was able—when people approached him as if he expected them to kick him away like a puppy not yet housetrained.

PJ almost felt sorry for him and made an effort to draw him out without much success.

"Uncle Teddy hates me," declared Alphonse in a lifeless monotone. "I'm such a disappointment to him. He'd like me to study law, but how can I when I'm an artist?"

"An artist? What kind of artist?" PJ was mildly intrigued, but Alphonse clammed up again and resumed his endless staring into space. Great, thought PJ, I'm going to have a ball with this clown in Europe. Meanwhile he was obliged to drag him around town and plan their itinerary, so they could get to know each other—except that Alphonse always had that mysterious, closed expression on his face as though he were locked away in some far-off place where no one could reach him.

Until they bumped into Honey Winslow.

They were sitting in Sam's drug store having a Coke, when Louella's little Nash convertible drew up and Honey stepped out. PJ gasped. She was utterly beautiful, a couple of inches taller than he remembered her. Her blonde hair had grown and hung around her face like a halo, held up and away by two turquoise barrettes. She wore a black sweater which plunged in a V at the front and back, revealing the tops of her milk-white breasts. A huge circular red felt skirt swirled around her hips, a wide black patent belt emphasized her tiny waist. Her feet were bare and her toenails painted the same color as the skirt.

"Well, hell-O." She sauntered into Sam's and came over to them. "I heard you little boys were off to Europe." She sat

down on the banquette beside Alphonse and put her arm
around his shoulder. Alphonse slouched down in his seat, his
long bony frame awkwardly constricted as he tried to make it
easier for her to reach across him.

"How *are* you, Alphonse darlin'?" she smiled sweetly up into
the string bean's face and to PJ's amazement, a slow grin
spread across Alphonse's face. PJ hadn't even been aware they
knew each other.

"I'm fine," Alphonse answered awkwardly, fully alert for
once, "I'm just fine and I sure am delighted to see you, Honey."

"So how are *you*, sugar?" She turned to PJ. "Bet you missed
me some while I been gone," she challenged him.

PJ shrugged. "How you doing in New York, Honey? No
one's heard from you."

"I'm doin' fine. I'm going to be a model. I want to make it
big and I will. Maybe your daddy can help. I've waited two
whole years, I'm through with school now and I'm ready for
him to help me. He owes me. Don't pretend you don't know
what I mean, PJ. And don't pretend you can help me either. I
don't need *your* help. You're just a kid. I want a man."

"Where you living in New York, Honey?" PJ asked her, ignoring her insult and trying to create a diversion. "I was up
there recently visiting my daddy. We could have got together."

"Oh, don't talk dumb, PJ. I wouldn't spend time with you.
Like I said, you're a kid. I live with my Aunt Sissie for now, but
that meal ticket's almost up. My Aunt Sissie gave up her job as
a receptionist just to stay home and take care of me. Ain't that
heartwarmin'? Well, the money's going to come to an end one
of these days. I can't imagine your mother's going to keep sending those checks forever . . . and when they stop one of us is
going to have to go out to work. And I'll lay good money it
won't be my Aunt Sissie. She's got used to sitting on her ass all
day courtesy your mamma, PJ."

"My mamma paid for you to go to New York? She paid you
off . . . ?" In his astonishment at learning this information, PJ
forgot to be angry with her for calling him a kid—after all, she
was two years younger than he was.

"Why, sure. I thought you knew that. She wanted to get me
away from you and away from your daddy. Your mamma offered and I accepted. Rather my mother did and I surely had
no objections. Got me away from Mississippi and jerks like

you, PJ. And him . . ." She dug her finger into Alphonse's ribs.

"I'm nnnn . . . ot a jerk," stammered Alphonse, his head shaking.

"Yeah, you. You're a dumb coot and you know what I think? I think you oughta be locked up. They shouldn't let people like you loose on the streets."

PJ was appalled. This was a little bitch talking. Alphonse stared at her in dumb disbelief.

"You're so pretty . . ." he reached out to grasp a strand of her hair and she jerked her head away.

"Sure, I'm a dream, Alphonse, but I'm not for the likes of you. Now, do you want to know why?"

He nodded, shook his head, nodded again, thoroughly confused. She let him have it anyway. "Because you're ugly, Alphonse, you're downright disgustin'. You're all long and lanky. I want me a man with grace. Grace and sophistication and you're a *dis*grace, Alphonse. Look at you, sniveling away."

It was true. To PJ's horror Alphonse had begun to cry. But Honey hadn't finished yet. "You're full of diddlyshit, Alphonse, and as for all those crackpot poems you been leavin' round at my mamma's for me—here," she pulled out a sheaf of papers from her pocket, "you can have 'em all back. Crazy load a shit!" She looked at him triumphantly.

"But I wrote them for you, Honey . . ." Alphonse whispered. "They are odes to your beauty, your *heavenly* beauty . . ."

"*Odes.* What in hell are odes?" shrieked Honey. "You mean odious more like, why, I never seen such—"

Suddenly Alphonse flipped.

He reared up to his full height, pushed over the table and slammed Honey down on her back on the banquette. He slapped her hard around the face and PJ reached out to restrain him. He didn't blame Alphonse one bit. Honey had been downright provoking but he could not stand by and see her hurt. It was only when he looked down and saw her face that he stopped and walked away. She was grinning up at Alphonse towering above her. She was loving every minute of it, taunting him, goading him and PJ knew that, in her own way, she was as sick as Alphonse.

He didn't see her again before they left and all the time he

kept hoping Alphonse's blows raining down on her hadn't in
any way marred her beautiful face. He didn't care if they'd hurt
her—she was a bitch and she deserved everything she had coming to her—but her face was the most beautiful he had ever
seen and he wanted to remember her that way.

Callie sat staring at a blank sheet of paper. She was trying to
compose a letter to Anita, but what she wanted to say would
have to be put across with a delicate touch which was something Callie simply did not have.

Their last meeting several years ago had been a disaster. Callie had appointed Anita PJ's godmother when he was born, but
omitted to tell her until twelve years later when she invited her
to stay at *Coinchenier—sans* Thierry, whom she had never been
able to forgive for spiriting away her only friend—to inspect
her godson.

After the war Anita had settled down to life as a somewhat
bourgeois Parisienne, a gossiping *bonne femme* of the first order, but her kind and generous nature had prevailed and she
had been overjoyed to learn of Callie's marriage and the growing success of Bayou Beauty. She had accepted Callie's invitation with alacrity and arrived at *Coinchenier* one summer in the
early Fifties in a state of characteristic overexcitement.

"Callie, *ma puce, ma belle, je suis ravie de te voir encore—
quelle éternité—allez, vite, montre-moi ton bébé . . .*"

PJ regarded with caution this apparition floating about in
pink chiffon at three o'clock in the afternoon wafting *L'Heure
Bleu* all over the place. She had called his mother her "flea"
and he was not to know this was a common term of endear-
ment in France. Worse, she had referred to *him* as a baby. He
watched nervously as she pranced about on backless high-
heeled peep-toe sandals and the pink chiffon pranced right
along with her.

"*Il est là.*" Callie gestured toward PJ.

"*Mais il est énorme,*" exclaimed Anita, "*il est déjà un jeune
homme.*"

"*Il est* twelve years old if you really want to know," drawled
Callie.

"Do I hear French?" Perry Jay had slipped into the room
and was looking threateningly at Anita.

"*Mais bien sûr,*" Anita flashed her sharp little white teeth at him in an equally threatening smile, *"vous êtes Perry Jay? Enchanté."*

"Callie, tell her to speak English or start packing."

"But, Papa, she hasn't even begun to *un*pack yet," ventured PJ unwisely, but Perry Jay had already left. "Maman," he turned to Callie, "Tante Anita can come and watch us in your bathroom, when I go to bed."

And so Anita had trailed upstairs after them assuming it would be some kind of twelve-year-old version of the bedtime story ritual. But even in her jet-lagged state she had been quite horrified by the make-up session she witnessed. Later she attempted to remonstrate in vain with Callie.

"Does Perry Jay know?"

"Do you think I'm mad? Of course he doesn't and you'd better not breathe a word."

"It's not right, Callie. No good will come of it, not for Philippe-Josephe anyway. He's almost a teenager. Supposing he goes on doing it? People will think he's perverted."

"So what?" Callie was barely listening. Suddenly Anita realized that as far as Callie was concerned there was no bad connotation attached to the word perverted. Here at *Coinchenier* it was the norm and the longer she stayed the more uncomfortable Anita felt. The boy was an angel—exquisite to look at, delightful manners—but he was in grave danger of being smothered by Callie's overpowering obsession with him.

"But I love him. He's mine. He's all I have to take care of now," she protested. "Remember my *cachette,* our *cachette,* Anita? You remember how I looked after my sick animals?"

"Philippe-Josephe isn't sick," Anita pointed out gently, adding silently to herself, *but you are.*

As for Perry Jay, Anita could hardly bear to be in the same room with him. She had known from the start that he was a beast. She could not imagine where Callie had found him and Callie was suspiciously secretive on the subject. He was so *vulgaire, un cochon* in expensive clothes. And he sweated profusely which was more than Anita could stand. A sweaty pig. Poor Callie.

During the flight back to Paris Anita kept repeating to herself those two words: poor Callie. It had not worked out for her after all.

Callie had not understood the reason why Anita's visit had

not been a success, but she had sensed her friend's distaste and
on her subsequent trips to the Paris fashion houses she found
herself too embarrassed to make contact with Anita.

But now she needed her. And somehow she had to convey
that need in her letter. She picked up her pen and began: *"Ma
chère . . ."*

Callie wouldn't say goodbye to him. For two days preceding his
departure she locked herself in her room and wouldn't come
out.

"She looks bad," Queenie announced. Queenie was the only
one allowed in to bring Callie trays of food which were always
returned untouched. "I gone make her a *gris-gris* to ward off
the evil spirits."

PJ rolled his eyes at her and patted her on her ample rump.
"You do that, Queenie chère, but just ask yourself one question
first. Are you 100 per cent sure you want her to come out of her
room? Mamma sure has been acting strange lately."

It was true. He had come upon Callie wailing in anguish,
backed up against the wall in the long dark corridors in the
upper regions of the house. Later the same day she would go
out and return home ecstatic, her mood lifted. She would fall
on PJ, clasping him to her, begging him not to leave her.

And Queenie would shake her head and mutter something
about "a curse on her daddy, a curse on Master Louis, it be his
fault, it be his fault all de time." But PJ knew better than to
listen to anything mad old Queenie said. It was a wonder she
hadn't let her *gris-gris* poison her cooking years ago.

When he left she handed him a small bunch of cockfeathers
encrusted with what looked suspiciously like dried blood and
entreated him to keep them somewhere about his person at all
times when he was away in Europe. "Otherwise something bad
gone happen to yo' mamma while you're away. You goin' to
come back a new man, anyways." He tossed the foul-smelling
feathers out of the car window on the way to the airport, but he
could not forget Queenie's words.

In one way she was absolutely right. PJ spent his year in Europe learning all about sex or, to put it more accurately, learning how to be a lover. He found that European women
gravitated to him in a never-ending stream. He acted like a

magnet. The fact that he was only of average height, perhaps, about five foot ten, didn't appear to put them off at all. He spent most of his time staying with friends of Teddy Lenoir's in France and his parents in other parts of Europe and in their villas, châteaux and palaces all over the Continent. At first it would be the daughter of the house, who would not be coy about showing him to his room after dinner and stepping in to make sure the maid had left soap and towels, and then lingering for a night of passion. Then the mothers would take over and it was invariably from them that he began to learn his craft.

First they went into ecstatics about his strong muscular build, his thick, glossy, black hair, his endless eyelashes, but he had heard all about this from Callie over the years and he was keen to move on and discover what effect it had on them.

He learned to eschew the quick fuck, that the twenty second in 'n out was of no interest. He learned that the greater the pleasure he was able to give his partner, the more enjoyment he too could obtain.

He learned that something as simple as scratching a woman's back could start it off and that tracing the palm of her hand round and round lightly with the tip of his finger could take things a stage further. A light touch with the tip of his forefinger was an essential part of it all and to this end he grew that nail on each hand a fraction longer than the others. Gently scratching inside an ear prior to a flick of his tongue in the same place, or trailing the nail up and down the inside of her thigh could bring a woman almost to the edge and have her moaning for more.

He learned the importance of skin, that a woman's should be soft and creamy, but so also should his. He learned about nipples and how to suck them slowly with his lips, encircle them with his tongue and then quickly nip them with his teeth.

He learned to lick. *Everywhere.* Her whole body, from the toes and the soles of the feet, all the way up the legs, the insides of the thighs and right inside the wetness between her legs. He learned to stroke the clitoris for hours, making her come over and over again, to stroke it not only with his finger, but also with the moist tip of his penis and, as she was about to come, to insert another finger quickly into her anus to heighten the pleasure.

They all taught him: daughters, mothers, aunts, cousins,

other guests. In between he dashed out to museums and scribbled notes on the paintings so that he would have something to report to Callie when he got home, but his mind was filled with endless erotic images.

As for Alphonse, he need not have worried. He never saw him, except for the odd meeting in a café when Alphonse would sit and sigh for hours over what, in his oddly formal way, he called "heavenly bodies" passing by. To PJ they seemed to be perfectly normal down-to-earth sexy girls, without exception blondes, who wiggled as they passed, tossing come hither looks over their shoulders. If Alphonse ever followed up with any cavorting of his own, PJ was never aware of it. PJ suspected that probably the most Alphonse did was to write one of his blasted poems.

Other than that the two went their separate ways and later PJ was to realize that while he had spent a year with this young man, he still barely knew him at all.

". . . And so, Anita, there *is* one big favor I want to ask you over and above having Philippe-Josephe to stay when he's in Paris. And if you don't even want to see him, please don't hesitate to tell me. We are neither of us young anymore, Anita, but there are moments when I feel I'm still a child and I want to run next door to you on St. Charles Avenue and ask for your help. I can trust you. I know you'll tell me if you don't want to see my Philippe and I won't mind. I realized I should have listened to you when you talked to me about him on your visit. I feel like a child now, Anita, and I need your help. I can feel my boy drifting away from me, drifting towards his father. All I want is for him to come back to me at *Coinchenier* where I can look after him. Make him understand that for me, Anita, when you see him, *if* you see him. *Please* see him. Tell him who I really am. Tell him how much I need him. Make him see how much I need him, make him see how much he needs me, that we are two of a kind . . ."

God forbid, thought Anita as she reread Callie's letter. Incoherent, crazed ramblings, but she could feel Callie's pain and it saddened her to think that there was no way she could do as her friend asked. PJ was on his way up to see her and she was curious to see what kind of a young man the angelic child had become.

He was a shock. A pleasant shock, but something quite unexpected all the same. He never took his eyes off her from the moment he was shown into the room by the maid and as he strolled towards her, he grinned at her lazily, irresistibly. By God, she thought, he's *sexy*. Before she could stop him—not that she wanted to—he had bent down and kissed her on both cheeks. But it was not the quick, embarrassed peck her friends' sons usually gave her. She was aware of an exquisite little puff of air being blown into her ear at the same time which made her skin tingle.

"Bonjour, Tante Anita," he whispered.

"Philippe-Josephe, look at you, mercy me—how you've grown." Anita was all a-fluster.

"How I've *grown*?" His grin was blatantly mocking. "Where exactly, Tante Anita?"

Well, it *was* a stupid thing to say. "Oh, you know, all over." She gestured vaguely toward him.

"Really?" He laughed. *"All* over?" Too late she followed his gaze—downward. No, really, this was too much. Surely he couldn't know about her little *aventures*? It wasn't her fault that Thierry had become so tiresome lately. He was always so busy, always so exhausted, it seemed as if he had forgotten the little pleasures of life. They never went out to dinner *à deux* anymore and as for anything happening *after* dinner, that was an event of the past. Yet Anita was not yet fifty and she barely looked forty. It was only fair that when young men began to make suggestions she should take them up. She was discreet, they only came in the afternoons. Like today. No wonder the maid had looked so amused when she showed him in. But it was unthinkable. Callie's son. Out of the question. Wasn't it?

He was clever as well as sexy. It was his brazen approach that did the trick and he knew it perfectly well. What a relief not to have to go through all the coy innuendo first. To just have someone look at you, want you, show it—and take you. Which is exactly what PJ did within an hour of his arrival.

Anita was in raptures. "Phil*eeee*ep," she squeaked over and over again as he brought her to climax.

"Freckles," he murmured, "beautiful white skin," knowing each woman liked to have her individual physical characteristics noticed and appreciated. Anita purred with pleasure. She was just like a satisfied ginger cat, but PJ resisted the temptation to point *this* out to her.

But the rapture didn't last. PJ had encountered guilt in his lovers before, but Anita's was different. She had vamped her friend's son. Actually it was the other way round, but she still felt guilty. She felt compelled to say something, knowing as she did so that it would ruin the glorious intimacy between them.

"How is your *maman*?" But he surprised her with his answer.

"You know her really well, don't you, Anita?" She was relieved he had dropped the *"Tante."*

"Well, yes, I used to, when we were children . . . until I left for Paris."

"What was she like?" He had propped himself up on one elbow and was looking at her intently. His black hair was tousled, but the expression on his face was deadly serious. And he was so *beautiful.* She couldn't resist reaching out and running her red nails through the dark hairs across his chest. He slapped her hand away.

"Ça suffit," he snapped. "Enough. I want to know. What was she really like?"

Anita shrugged to herself. Wasn't this what Callie had asked her to do? *Tell him who I really am.*

"You must understand one thing, Philippe. I loved your mother. Instinctively. She was one of those people it is not easy to love—or even to like. She distrusted the world and even as a child I knew I had to help her see that she could trust me. You see, she didn't like herself and if you don't like yourself—not just a tiny bit—you're lost. I don't know what happened in her early childhood, I didn't meet her till she was twelve, but I'll tell you one thing. There was no love in that house on St. Charles Avenue. Your mother had to keep seeking it elsewhere. She had this place at the bottom of the garden where she looked after wounded animals. Sounds corny, but it was true. We met there every day. She probably had other places she escaped to. But it was as if she was born lonely and no one in that house did anything about it."

"What about Queenie?"

"Oh, Queenie looked out for her. Queenie knew what was happening to your mother but she, Queenie, didn't *like* her. I could tell. She spooked Queenie. I was lucky. I managed to get through to the real Callie underneath, the person she never showed anyone else. Deep down she's kind and she's generous and aching to love someone. Your papa was not the right person to whom she could give that love and she realized that pretty early on, I suspect. But when you came along, Philippe, she found she had someone to love. Better yet, it was as close as she had come to loving herself. You were a part of her and you were beautiful—still are. Go back to her, Philippe. Let her love you. You don't have to give her love in return if you can't, but let her give it to you."

She waited, tense, to see what he would say. She had virtually done everything Callie had asked of her.

"I can't, Anita, and you know why. Oh, I'll go back and visit, but I won't stay."

"No?"

"No. And for the same reason my mother couldn't stay at St. Charles Avenue. There's no love at *Coinchenier*, no warmth. The only person who cares for me there is my mother, but it's the *wrong kind of love*. It smothers me. It suffocates me. There's something very strange about her, you sort of forgot to mention that. And it's true, *I'm* part of her and it's made *me* strange. That's why I have to get away."

"Mon pauvre," said Anita, pulling him to her. "Strange? Strange how?"

"Sex," he said without missing a beat.

"Sex isn't strange."

"I like it . . ."

"Of course you do. And that's why you're different from your maman. Callie didn't like sex."

"But I've had the feeling . . . Anita, it's weird, I've come across her in the corridors, *rubbing* herself, you know . . . ?" He was no longer the confident lover, but an embarrassed boy.

"She needed sex, Philippe, but not in the way you or I need it . . . or enjoy it. She's never had sex with love."

"Nor have I . . ."

"You will. Be patient. But you've had it with affection . . . even just now with me. And you must have had it like that before to be able to give it to me so wonderfully. You've been well taught, *mon chou* . . ."

"Teach me some more, *ma puce*," he added teasingly.

He stayed for four days—in the guest bedroom—while she

tossed and turned beside Thierry all night long. PJ never saw the sights of Paris, but he knew every detail of her freckled body. When Alphonse, who had stayed in Rome for a few extra days, caught up with him, PJ knew it was time to move on.

Anita knew it too. She was in danger of falling in love with him. She was sad, but if he left now it would still be all right. She had told him about Callie and even while she had not exactly followed Callie's instructions to the letter, she felt her words had made some kind of impression on PJ. She hoped desperately that he would find someone to love him as she might have been able to do, but somehow she knew that it would be a long time before he would be able to settle down.

And she knew she would never see him again.

Anita would have been hurt to know that PJ put her out of his mind. He had to. She had come perilously close to exposing him. The more she talked about his mother needing love, the more he realized that that was what he was searching for—albeit subconsciously. That was what made him such a good lover. Each time he *made* love to a woman he tried to give her his love. The only problem was that no one had yet given him any in return. And would he recognize it when they did?

On their return home he and Alphonse immediately lost touch and PJ was never to know that a year or two later, when the war really began to escalate, Alphonse's luck ran out when his number came up in the Vietnam lottery. He was a few years younger than PJ, who by then was too old for the general conscription, and no amount of string pulling on Teddy Lenoir's part could save him from being drafted.

PJ was resigned to a repeat performance of the dinner with his father a year earlier. What he wasn't prepared for was Perry Jay's first question: "Going to see a bit of Honey Winslow now you're back, boy?"

"Who?"

"Come on, son, you must remember Honey."

"Yeah, I remember, what about her?"

"Well, Philippe, you can't deny she was a pretty little thing. I mean you found her for me, didn't you? Took my hat off to you that night. Boy's got great taste, I said to myself. What ya get up to over in Europe, anyway, huh? You got an eye, boy, you surely got an eye. When you get back home to Mississippi, you let me know where the action is and I might just pay a visit, hmmmm?"

PJ would never know how he managed to avoid hitting him. Did his father really imagine they would go running round together as a pair, a kind of depraved double act, *droit du seigneur, père et fils*?

"But what about Maman?"

"Nothing to do with her. Long as she don't know. Don't ever discuss it with her, PJ. Man's business. Keep Callie out of this." Lord, was the boy going to have a cosy chat with his mother?

"But she knows, Papa. She was there!"

"She was where?"

"There. That night. Right outside the door. She saw everything—you, Honey. I went right past her when I rushed in."

"She *saw*?"

"I thought you knew."

"She ever say anything to you?"

"No. Never." This had worried PJ for weeks afterward. He could barely look his mother in the face, but she never mentioned it and he could not summon up the courage to broach the subject.

"Well, I declare," murmured Perry Jay to himself. So Callie had known all along. He felt distinctly uneasy. He was his own man. He was Perry Jay Duboise, Cosmetics King of the South, he ran Bayou Beauty. But Callie still retained a heavy percentage of the voting stock. She had power over him in that area. It didn't do to let her have anything else she could hold over him. He wondered what else she knew about his life. Knowing Callie, she'd keep it all to herself and use it when she needed to. Only thing was to make sure she never had the need. Meanwhile, it was the time to crush the Perfect Mother image in the eyes of her son.

"Your mamma's no Snow White herself."

PJ got up to leave.

"No, sir! Your mamma's got the itch. Always has had. Don't think I don't know all about it 'cause I do. She may be over fifty years old, but there's still no stopping her. Oh, she quietened down once right around when you were born. Fact is I thought she'd stopped altogether, but by the time you got to be about ten years old she'd started up again. She can't help it. She's seen doctors. I made her. And she's discreet, thank God. We struck a deal some time back. She sticks to the plantation. Anyone we hire to work for us down there has to swear they won't breathe a word. And we pay them good to keep quiet."

"It's not true." But PJ knew it was. He'd long been aware of his mother's strange behavior around certain men. She was fine with the dinner guests and business associates she and his father entertained. But her eyes had a hungry look when they followed the hired hands around the grounds.

"If you can't find Callie in the house after ten o'clock at night, try the stables . . . Haven't you ever wondered why we never keep a horse in the end stall on the right?"

Suddenly PJ felt incredibly weary. Once again he pitied his father, but was filled with contempt for him. Let him run down Callie, let him letch after Honey Winslow, he, PJ, didn't need either one of them. He knew who he was and what he wanted to do. He would need his father to help him and he knew that, like his mother, he would learn to have the upper hand over Perry Jay. He would pick his moment to ask for what he wanted, but for the time being he would steer clear of him.

Not saying another word, he pushed his plate to one side, got to his feet and left the room.

He didn't see Perry Jay before he left. The next day while his father was out, the telephone rang and when he answered it, PJ slipped naturally back into one of his old disguises.

"Duboise Residence," he said, pretending to be the butler.

"May I speak to him, please?" PJ instantly recognized Honey's voice.

"To whom, ma'am?"

"To him, to Mr. Duboise."

PJ was tempted to tell her she was talking to Mr. Duboise and almost as if she anticipated him she added: "Mr. Perry Jay Duboise."

"Mr. Duboise is out for the day. May I tell him who called?"

"Yeah, sure. Just tell him it's Honey and I wanted him to have my new address." She dictated an address down in the Village and PJ scribbled it down on a piece of paper which he slipped into his jacket pocket.

He never gave his father the message.

PJ's plane to Biloxi, Mississippi, the next day was not until the late evening. There was no one to meet him at the airport and he realized he'd completely forgotten to let Callie know that he was coming home. He'd wired her from Paris that he was going via New York and would be staying with his father, that he would call her and tell her which flight he'd be arriving on, but in the trauma of the last few hours it had slipped his mind to do so.

He took a cab from the airport to the plantation. The house was almost in darkness. The kitchen was deserted. Queenie and the returned Lucille were nowhere to be seen, probably fast asleep. Callie had written that she had fired the butler now that Perry Jay was never at home and she had long since ceased to entertain.

He went upstairs and put his bags in his room. As he bent down a slip of paper fell out of his pocket. He rescued it and tossed it onto his bedside table. Then he wandered round the house turning lamps on as he did so, smiling to see the familiar objects in the beautiful old house, the paintings, the huge bowls of magnolia, the old mahogany furniture.

He wandered out through the front door and sat on the stoop in a rocking-chair. The moon was almost full. A slight scratching noise made him look down. A scrawny-looking cat was trying to sneak past him. She had a kitten in her mouth. She saw PJ watching and darted off in the direction of the stables. He looked round and saw two more kittens nestling together, their eyes not yet open. The mother was back again, struggling to take yet another one in her mouth.

"Here, let me help you." PJ reached down and picked up the remaining kitten in the palm of his hand. The cat looked at him and then set off on her journey once more. He followed her and found she had made a warm nest for her babies in the straw bales outside the stables. Gently he lowered the last kitten to rest in a ball with its brothers and sisters. He was about to return to the house when he heard a sound from inside the stables. He glanced inside. There were dim light bulbs all along the roof. He glanced in the stalls one by one, but the horses were all settled. Besides, he could have sworn it was a human sound he had heard.

He remembered Perry Jay's mocking words too late. He had arrived at the last stall on the right. Callie was wearing one of her white organdie dresses, but the full skirt was pushed up above her waist. She was pressed against the wall and the man banging himself hard against her was naked to the waist.

He recognized the man immediately. It was Johnny the Cajun, a swarthy, heavy man who worked as a hired hand at *Coinchenier* at odd times during the year. He seemed to come and go whenever it suited him and PJ had commented on this to his mother, but Callie brushed it aside, saying the man worked hard and was welcome whenever he chose to come back to them.

Now PJ saw why. Instinctively, he had never trusted the man, but if he was shocked at seeing him servicing his mother, he was shattered by the man's words as he became aware of PJ's presence.

"Almost done," he grunted. "Y'all can have her in a minute." PJ was disgusted. This was the kind of sex he hated; no sensuality to it whatsoever, no point.

PJ grabbed hold of Johnny the Cajun by the back of his collar and tried to haul him off his mother, but the man was too strong.

"Hey, wait a second there. I told you I'm not done yet." And he dug his elbow into PJ's ribs, throwing him off balance. But Callie had seen him now and had slumped to the ground in horror.

"Hey!" cried Johnny, turning from one to the other. "Who's goin' ta finish me off?"

"Get outta here," muttered PJ. "Get outta here and finish yourself off. GO ON, GIT!"

Johnny the Cajun shuffled out, grumbling to himself. "Don't know why you're in such a hurry, she ain't that hot," was his parting shot.

PJ stared down at Callie, who had crawled into the far corner of the stall, her legs partly covered in straw, her arms folded across her shriveled breasts.

"Putain!" he hissed down at her, knowing the French would hurt her more than anything. "You're sick! I've got a sick, depraved whore for a mother. My father was right, *ma mère*, you've got the itch and it's disgusting. You *disgust* me, understand?"

"You saw your father?" was all Callie could get out.

"Yes, I saw my father and I'm going to be seeing a lot more

of him. Maybe I've been wrong about him all along. Maybe I ought to talk to him about having you locked up some place. I mean, how long has this been going on, Maman? Maybe you really are sick, maybe we ought to put you some place where you can get well . . ."

"NO!" shrieked Callie. "Don't take me away from *Coinchenier*. Don't leave me, Philippe, *please*, you're all I've got, you know you are."

"I know hell!" snapped PJ. He didn't want to see Callie put away somewhere, but he did want to hurt her right there and then as much as he could. Part of him knew he would regret it later on. He loved his *maman*, he always had, but stumbling on this side of her was too much for him. However much he might want to in the future, he knew he would never be able to bring himself to forgive her.

"I'm leaving now and I won't be coming back. You'll never see me again, Maman, *never!*"

Callie started to cry and on her hands and knees she crawled, weeping, along the stable floor ignoring the horses who peered over the stalls to stare down at her.

She reached the entrance in time to see PJ hitching a ride in a truck as it set off under the oak trees down the long drive.

Slumped against the barn door, she felt helpless to do anything to stop him. She made her way blindly back to the main house and stumbled up the staircase to PJ's old room, desperate to seek solace amongst his boyhood things. That night, clutching a bottle of sleeping pills, she crept into his bed and buried her face in his pillow. Her hand reached out to rest on the bedside table and touched a piece of paper. When she read the name and address scrawled on it in her son's hand she reached instinctively for the pills.

Perry Jay was fast asleep in the huge bed with the gray satin sheets while the Park Avenue traffic purred along outside his window twenty-five floors below.

He felt himself being shaken awake and came to. He looked straight into the ashen face of his press agent.

"What the goddamn hell are you doing in my bedroom? I said I was not to be disturbed this morning."

"They've been trying to get through to you since six o'clock this morning. It's Callie. PJ went down there last night, must have been there only an hour or so. Then he left. She's taken an overdose, Perry Jay. They say she may not make it. That's gonna be bad publicity for Bayou, Perry Jay. The worst. You better get down there right away. And who in God's name is *Honey*?"

"WHAA-AAT?"

"They found Callie in PJ's room. In her hand she had this piece of paper. It just said: 'Honey' and some address in New York. Who d'ya think it is, Perry Jay?"

"No idea," said Perry Jay. "Absolutely no idea."

PART 2

TESSA
1963–77

CHAPTER 5

Tessa didn't think about him often for the simple reason that she didn't really know much about him, but every now and then his distorted image would slip into her mind and she would begin to wonder.

She wondered what her life would have been like had he lived; whether his existence would have ensured that hers was a normal family (which God knows it wasn't); whether he would have given her confidence, encouragement, a sense of pride in herself. She knew she was beginning to feel capable of supplying herself with all of these, but it had taken a long time to realize this and she could have used a little help along the way.

She was a worrier by nature anyway and, inevitably once she began to wonder, the wondering soon turned to worrying and the worry festered inside her, culminating in the all too frequent explosion: "WHY WON'T ANYONE TELL ME ANYTHING ABOUT MY FATHER?"

Her grandfather winced. It appeared they were in for another of *those* conversations. How old was Tessa now anyway? Fifteen? No, confound it, it was 1963, she must be sixteen. Did she intend to continue these histrionic performances *ad infini-*

tum? "Grandpa, *please*, you haven't answered my question. Why won't anybody tell me anything about my father?"

The old man made a great show of putting down his book, removing his spectacles and knocking out his pipe. He adjusted his expression to one of everlasting patience and even managed a faint smile when he asked her: "Well, what is it you want to know about him, m'dear?"

"*Every*thing! I just don't understand why no one in my family, not you, not my mother, not even Granny Betty, is prepared to sit down and talk about him. You knew him, all of you, and yet whenever I mention him you all clam up, change the subject . . ."

"We told you how he died, as much as we were told anyway . . ."

"Yes, all right, he's dead, but what was he like when he was *alive*? What kind of person was my father? Am I like him?"

"NO!" The reaction was as explosive as Tessa's question had been a few moments before. "You're nothing like him, Tessa, nothing at all."

"Well, at least I know what he *wasn't* like. I suppose you mean his personality? Granny Betty told me I looked like him, my red hair I think. Did he have red hair?"

"No, he did not, he had blond hair. Granny's memory isn't what it was, surely you must have realized that?"

"Blond hair? He was fair? Really? Was he dashing? Was he wildly good-looking? There's a photograph of him on Mummy's dressing table in his uniform, but he's got his cap on and you can't see what color his hair is. Anyway it's a black and white photograph. But he was fair, was he?"

"Fair, dark, what on earth does it matter now?" snapped her grandfather. "Man's gone. It's unhealthy for you to keep raking him up like a dog with an old bone. You've survived sixteen years without him, haven't you? Start thinking about surviving another sixty-six. I won't have these maudlin questions, d'you hear?"

"But he looks so brave. Was he brave, Grandpa? Surely you can tell me that? Oh, if only I knew . . ."

"Well, you won't, my dear, not from me. Now, please leave and close the door behind you. I'm an old man and I want some peace. Run along now, there's a good girl."

·   ·   ·

Lady Heron-Sweeney sat in the summerhouse. *It is a terrible thing not to like your own daughter* were the words with which she tormented herself whenever she looked at Amy. It was just that she had always wanted a daughter; a *real* daughter, a laughing little girl she could dress up in pretty muslin dresses with velvet ribbons in summer and muffs and bonnets in winter; a little girl who would play with dolls and ride in the pony cart and sit demurely by her side on the footstool when she entertained people to tea.

It was quite clear from the outset that Amy was not going to turn out a *real daughter*. She grew into a slow, plodding lump, crowned with an incongruous mop of pale golden curls which might have been her saving grace. But they didn't save her from Betty Heron-Sweeney's bitter disappointment. It was plain to her that Amy would rather be the pony pulling the cart than the child riding in it and the only dress which ever remotely suited her was her night-dress.

To make matters worse, after Amy Betty produced only sons. Monty, Ferdy and Lucien: three beautiful little boys with the same mop of golden curls whose perfect manners and angelic looks made them endlessly in demand as page boys at weddings. It was they who inherited Betty's fine bone structure and perfect straight nose, while Amy missed out altogether and presented her father's enormous hooter and clear blue moonlike eyes to the world.

Inevitably the question of Amy's début had arisen. Deep down Betty had known she'd be doing society a big favor if she could refrain from launching Amy into it. What was the point of sending her to London? She wasn't going to find a husband anywhere. Let her stay in the country and continue her extended love affair with her blasted horse.

But where Betty Heron-Sweeney had failed, the horse succeeded. Amy entered him for the Ladies Race at the local hunt point-to-point and fell off at the first fence. She was helped to her feet by no less than a Coldstream Guards officer who was also riding that afternoon. Elliott Fitzgerald was young and dashing; he'd been a potential catch for the last three seasons, but somehow he had succeeded in eluding even the most determined débutante.

Perhaps it was Amy's pale golden curls, perhaps it was the fact that they shared a love of riding; Betty never could work it out, but when Amy brought this young man home to tea she knew immediately that all was not lost.

It was one of the happiest days of Betty's life when Amy and Elliott were married just before the war broke out, in the Norman church at Bellcloud, the rambling Elizabethan home of the Heron-Sweeneys for generations. But she had paid for it.

Now, nearly forty years later, Amy was still there.

Betty Heron-Sweeney had eventually got what she had always wanted, only it was not a daughter, but a *grand*daughter. Tessa grew into the tall, beautiful girl Betty had always dreamed Amy would be. Her face displayed her grandmother's delicate bone structure to perfection, even surpassing her in the height of her cheekbones. The nose was a little longer, true, but equally straight and the slightly wider flare of the nostrils only accentuated its character. The eyes were Betty's too, wide apart and gray-green in color with a direct, intelligent look. The mouth was large, full and sensual and broke frequently into a wide smile. But the hair, the long, dark auburn hair, was a mystery. No one in Betty's family had ever had red hair, nor could it be traced to a Heron-Sweeney. It must be Fitzgerald hair from those Irish ancestors on her father's side.

She looked up and saw Tessa walking toward her.

"Granny," Tessa called out as she crossed the lawn. "Granny, may I join you?"

The summer-house was another taboo. Her grandfather expressly forbade her to go near it, said it was unsafe. As usual there was no further explanation and for this reason Tessa always associated the eighteenth-century classical temple (moved to the garden from a nearby park and always referred to as the summer-house) with her father. She was more or less forbidden to talk about her father; she was forbidden to sit in the summer-house. Naturally the two must be connected. And she loved the summer-house with its triangular roof resting on two stone pillars. To reach it one had to cross the lawn, open a pair of carved wrought-iron gates and pass either to the left or right through the herb garden with the sundial in the middle.

Sir Hugh Heron-Sweeney watched her from his study window and reached into the left-hand pocket of his battered old tweed jacket with the leather patches on the elbows. As if the object he found there were contaminated, he withdrew it gingerly and dropped it on to the window seat in front of him.

It was an envelope. An envelope addressed to him with its top right-hand corner covered in foreign stamps.

The old man stared down at it for almost twenty minutes. Then he stooped, trying to bend at the knees as he did so—his back giving him considerable pain as always—and retrieved it. He hadn't opened it. He knew who it was from. The same person who over the last few years had sent all the other letters he kept in a locked drawer in his desk. He knew he should destroy them, wanted to, but each time a new one arrived it joined the others in their hiding-place.

He gave the typewritten words on the envelope one last glance before throwing it into the drawer.

Damn the man! Brave, indeed! Fellow didn't even have the courage to use his own handwriting. Why couldn't he leave an old man in peace?

CHAPTER 6

Tessa Fitzgerald was born and brought up at Bellcloud as her mother had been before her. She knew Amy was the eldest child of her grandfather, Sir Hugh Heron-Sweeney, better known in the academic world as Dr. Heron-Sweeney, professor of classics at Christ Church, Oxford. His children and grandchildren used to amuse themselves trying to repeat his full name and titles over and over again very fast. Those who cheated left off the "Sir" or the "Professor," but even so it was virtually impossible to say Hugh Heron-Sweeney distinctly more than about fifteen times.

Tessa knew that when her mother was in her twenties she had married her father, Elliott Fitzgerald, a young Guards officer who survived the war, but went into a deep depression when he returned home which not even the birth of an exceptionally beautiful baby daughter could alleviate. From then on the information became hazy. She was told that he disappeared two years after she had been born and that his body had been found washed up on a beach on the Gower Peninsula in Wales, but it was never explained to Tessa whether his death had been accidental or suicide. Shortly afterward, her mother had married again. Tessa's stepfather was called John Simpson, but to Tessa he was always "Uncle Johnny."

Tessa became very fond of Uncle Johnny. He would remain one of the most good-natured people in her life. According to his father-in-law, Johnny Simpson *was* idle—one of his favorite words. Nobody liked to point out that Johnny Simpson was rather stuck for cash and fearfully embarrassed because no one would give him a job. He blinked a lot and smiled and tried hard to be amusing, but no one took him seriously. Every now and then Tessa tried her luck with him on the subject of her father, but he was as much in the dark as she was.

"Jolly decent chap so I understand. I never met him myself, wasn't around these parts at the time. I met your mother in church. I was staying with some awfully nice people for the weekend and they insisted on dragging me to Matins. Amy was right behind us. All through the hymns she bellowed in my left ear till I turned round to see if I could get her to tone it down a bit. No such luck, but blow me if she wasn't a beauty. Bright blue eyes and pale gold hair—you don't have it, Tessa, but not to worry. They told me about poor Fitzgerald and frankly I'd've expected her to mourn the chap a bit longer. Not a bit of it. Whisked me off to help her organize the village fête the first time I asked her out to dinner."

Tessa was aware of her mother's inexhaustible efforts to persuade him to take Holy Orders since she rather fancied herself in the role of vicar's wife. Tessa often wondered if this was what ultimately drove Uncle Johnny straight into the arms of his fluffly little blonde secretary when finally somebody did give him a job. To Tessa's everlasting fury, he ran off with her while she was away at boarding school and she missed all the hulla-baloo. She came home at the end of the term to find that her mother, completely unaffected by the fact that her husband had deserted her, had thrown herself wholeheartedly into yet another of her "causes."

Amy's "causes" were the bane of her family's life and it was through their constant invasion of Betty Heron-Sweeney's privacy that Tessa came to sense that relations between her mother and her grandmother were somewhat strained.

Soon after Elliott's death, Amy had taken up charity work. Betty saw nothing wrong in it at the time. Indeed, the fact that it took Amy out and about was a huge relief even though it didn't *look* awfully good for a young widow to be seen charging about the county so soon after her husband's death. Betty had been genuinely horrified when they had learned that Elliott's body had been found washed up on a Welsh beach. When he had left Bellcloud and disappeared without a word, her immediate reaction had been that he must have had enough of Amy. And then, ridden with guilt at having such a thought, she had forced herself to admit that she had never been aware of any friction between the couple. She'd have known about it if there had been. They lived in the west wing at Bellcloud and she saw them every day.

Amy, as Betty had anticipated, did not take naturally to motherhood so when Tessa was born Betty invariably found herself having to step in and look after her. She had been only nineteen herself when she had had Amy which made her an exceptionally young grandmother. Her maternal instinct was still strong while Amy's didn't appear to exist at all. Yet marriage brought out a domineering side of Amy Betty couldn't recall noticing before. Amy bossed Elliott about all over the place: *do this, do that, fetch me this, fetch me that.* No wonder he'd left her, Betty reflected, but then again she had to concede that the young man had accepted his passive role quite cheerfully, as if he were really quite content for Amy to charge about laying down the law as if she were the husband and he the wife. He'd even resigned his commission and left his Regiment, which was something Betty always did find most odd, but she knew better than to interfere.

Betty marveled at her daughter's newly discovered ability to organize everything and everyone around her. Although of course she'd always been able to wind her father round her little finger. Hugh had allowed her to do exactly what she wanted, that was the trouble. He saw nothing unusual in the fact that his daughter appeared to be showing no signs of grief over her husband's death, but then he had been the one who had driven her to Wales to identify Elliott's body. Maybe Amy had poured out all her misery there. Betty had never heard a word about what went on despite the endless questions she had asked. All she knew was that ever since that time Amy had immersed herself in her causes, as they came to be known at Bellcloud, saving this or that, Meals on Wheels, The Rare Breeds Survival Trust, the Church of England Children's Society, Dr. Barnardo's, the St. John's Ambulance, lifeboats, the deaf, the blind, the list was endless, nothing escaped Amy, she rushed about helping them all. She even managed to replace Elliott with a second husband although Betty always reckoned that an idiotic lame duck like Johnny Simpson was just another of Amy's causes.

Betty put her foot down when the Morning Room came to be occupied three or four times a week by a constant stream of earnest would-be do-gooders. Betty remonstrated in vain with Amy until one dreadful day when Tessa heard the cruel words echoing after her mother down the stone-flagged passage to the Morning Room.

"How on earth could I have produced such a fat, ugly bore? Why can't you do something about *yourself*, Amy? You're the one who needs saving, for Christ's sake. All we ever hear from you is jumble sales, jumble sales and more jumble sales. Nothing but bloody committees, never you. Who are *you*, Amy? Answer me that. Is there a woman actually in there somewhere? Do you ever feel anything? Love? Hate? Anger? Do these words mean anything to you? Does it ever occur to you that you're involved with so many charities you can't possibly begin to care about the plight of the actual people or animals you're perpetually raising your pathetic funds for? You're a fraud, Amy. Your causes are nothing but a bloody substitute behind which you hide from life itself."

Betty had been driven too far. She had never come out and verbally expressed her contempt for Amy before. Now she held her breath, aware that she must have hurt her daughter beyond belief. Tessa, coming in from the kitchen garden, had heard everything. She froze in the doorway and together they waited for Amy to collapse.

Nothing happened. Absolutely nothing. Amy ignored the outburst and acted as if Betty had never said a word. This, of course, was what exasperated Betty more than anything; the fact that Amy never reacted, never retaliated, remained impervious to other people's emotions, hiding safe in her own insular cocoon. Tessa sympathized with her grandmother. She had the same problem with Amy. Her mother never appeared to listen to a thing Tessa said and as a result of this she invariably found herself going direct to her grandmother for advice, comfort or even just a chin-wag and a good laugh. But neither of them ever discussed their mutual problem: Amy.

So Tessa grew up feeling rather incomplete. No father, and no details of his death—or life for that matter. The idea of her bulldozing, white-haired mother ever having been married to the ethereal, poetic-looking young man in the wedding photograph on Amy's bureau was hard to accept. In another picture, under the glass on Amy's dressing table, he looked dashing, brave and powerful. Which had he been in real life?

"Tell me about him, Mummy."

But Amy as usual evaded the issue. "Now, I rather thought we might repair to the kitchen garden for the afternoon, plant a few potatoes, what do you think? I feel like a spot of digging. Come and join me, Tessa, do you good."

Get some fresh air and clear my head of all these awkward questions, you mean, Tessa thought to herself as she followed Amy down to the cloakroom. She watched her mother exchange her sensible brown lace-ups for a pair of gumboots, then she followed her along the dark stone-flagged passage which ran the length of the house from the hall to the back door. Amy marched through the door and on down the garden path to the kitchen garden.

"Come along," she boomed over her shoulder, "don't dawdle!"

Amy always sang hymns at the top of her voice while she was gardening.

"Fight the Good Fight," she bellowed, plunging her spade into the earth, *"with all thy Might,"* bringing her heel down heavily on top of the blade and making an opening in the soil.

"Spuds are over there in that brown bag. Now, Tessa, what I want you to do, are you listening to me? Jolly well get a grip on yourself, will you? I need you to help me out. Grab a potato and pop it into the hole I make with the spade. Try and get the thingy pointing upwards into the air, but even if you get it wrong, never mind, they'll squiggle their way towards the sun somehow. Ready? Off we go."

"WHERE'S HIS GRAVE?" Tessa shouted above her mother's hymn-singing. "Someone must have dug a grave for him just like you're digging holes for these potatoes. Can't you even tell me where he's buried? Why haven't you ever taken me to visit his grave?"

Amy wouldn't look at her. She leaned on her spade, head down.

"Your grandfather would not approve and you know better than to ask me to go against his wishes. We must be eternally grateful to him. He has taken us in and given us a home and we should be thankful for small mercies. It is unfortunate that your father is not with us, but we must be brave and not complain if the Lord has chosen to take him from us. We must pray that his soul may rest in peace wherever it may be and we must keep our grief and sorrow to ourselves and—"

"Fight the Good Fight," Tessa couldn't help finishing and shook her head in disbelief as she dropped the potatoes into the earth. When in doubt, hide behind religion was Amy's most frequent weapon. She kept everything tightly bottled up inside her, taking refuge in her prayer book or her hymn book if anyone made the slightest attempt to ease the lid off her emotions. Later, from her bedroom window Tessa watched her mother battling on. Her short gray curls and most of her face were now hidden by an extremely unflattering old sou'wester pulled down over her nose, her only protection against the faint drizzle which had begun to fall.

Tessa would have been amazed to learn that underneath the battered old hat, the tears were running down Amy's face almost as fast as the rain.

Sitting up in bed later that night Amy Heron-Sweeney opened her diary. She had kept a diary since she was a young girl. It was a secret diary. She had never divulged its contents, or indeed its existence, to anyone as far as she could remember, certainly not to either of her two husbands. The entries resembled a long letter she might be writing to a very close friend. They were chatty and, at the same time, often revealed her most intimate thoughts and opinions.

She generally jotted down her thoughts for the day just before she got into bed. Her diaries were not the fancy leather-bound kind with a key. Nor did she care for those five-year specimens. What was five years to someone like Amy who had lived more than forty-five? Amy found she could best express herself in large, lined exercise books which she covered year after year in her equally large, flowery handwriting.

She lay propped up against her vast linen pillow edged with lace, kicking absentmindedly under the bedclothes at a disgruntled golden retriever, who was stretched out across the end of her bed. She sipped the last of her Ovaltine and reached for a pen. But she couldn't find one and finally had to get out of bed altogether to look for it. Amy slept in a four-poster bed, adorned with heavy rugs even in high summer. A long tapestried ottoman stood at its foot. Two Victorian bedside tables tottered on either side.

Now she was up and out of bed, she didn't feel like going back to it. Instead she opened the trunk in which she kept all her old diaries. She picked out the one marked 1947. She turned to a well-thumbed page and read again the entry which had haunted her for almost thirty years.

Today I travelled to a small village near Swansea in Wales. They rang to say they had found Elliott, dead, on a beach near somewhere called Worm's Head, and they wanted me to identify the body. Papa travelled with me and I left baby Tessa with Mama. Throughout the long car journey Papa urged me to reconcile myself with the fact that Elliott was dead, so that by the time we arrived, I wanted to get the identification over as soon as possible and return home to mourn my husband.

They took me into a cold, tiled room which smelled horribly of some kind of strong disinfectant which could not quite obliterate the pervading air of death. My stomach heaved and I tried to run round and leave, but Papa had his hand in the small of my back and seemed to be propelling me forward, except he asked: "Can't I do it for her?," but they refused and even went so far as to ask him to wait outside.

They pulled out from the wall a kind of steel locker and there lay a ghostly white corpse with a label round its big toe. They had warned me that it would not be a pleasant sight. The cause of death was drowning, they said, the body had been in the water for some considerable time and the face was bloated and discoloured. I took a quick look and nearly fainted. It might have

*been Elliott, but I couldn't say for sure. I looked at an
address book, but it was full of indecipherable scrawls,
names and addresses long since washed away by the
sea water, and I looked at the silk spotted bandanna
handkerchief with the initial "E" embroidered in red
on one corner. I had given Elliott several such handkerchiefs for Christmas one year and, although I
rather thought they had had "E.F." on them, I had not
done the embroidering myself and it was not easy to
remember.*

*I answered their questions as best I could under the
distressing circumstances. Yes, Elliott had been missing
for quite some time; yes, he had been severely depressed
ever since he returned home from the war; no, he
didn't take sleeping tablets as far as I knew. Apparently sleeping tablets had been the cause of his death,
although I failed to understand how he could have
taken such an overdose and then been found washed
up from the sea. They did not seem interested in dwell-
ing on such a minor point and pressed me to identify
the body as that of my husband. By this time I was
exhausted, confused, anxious to leave this awful place
and return home. I confirmed that it was Elliott lying
there on the cold slab and Papa drove me away.*

*But I couldn't be sure it was him. Now I shall never
know unless Elliott comes back to me.*

Amy looked up as she came to the end of the page and felt the
familiar tears forming in her eyes. He had never come back but,
oh, if he ever did—if the corpse in that steel locker was some
other poor unfortunate—then perhaps he might one day return
and be reunited with her and his daughter. Elliott Fitzgerald
was always such a gentle, caring man . . . had he lived he
would have been the perfect father for Tessa.

If only her own father were not so uncompromising on the
subject of Elliott. Very soon now she knew she would have to
defy him and speak her husband's name at Bellcloud. Tessa had
a right to know about her father and she, Amy, would tell her.
But even then she knew she would be unable to tell her daughter the whole story. There was a reason why Sir Hugh would

allow no mention of Elliott Fitzgerald and only he knew what it was. Amy knelt down to pray to God to give her strength to tackle the old man about it before he took the secret to his grave.

CHAPTER 7

Apart from the fact that she grew up without a father and no one would tell her anything about him, Tessa had a perfectly happy childhood.

Initially she was sent to a school in the village where she soon became "best friends" with Nicola Woodhouse, the daughter of the local vet.

Tessa and Nicola were inseparable until Tessa was sent away to boarding school at the age of twelve. After that Nicola only saw her in the holidays. This was something of a mixed blessing since Nicola was not quite the true and loyal friend she made herself out to be. She was envious of Tessa: envious of her looks, her brains and, above all, of her background. Nicola would have given the world to live at Bellcloud and wangled every opportunity to be asked over there. But once Tessa was sent away to school, the invitations became less and less frequent and indeed were only forthcoming when the two girls happened to bump into each other in the village.

Nicola was amazed to find that Tessa, home for the holidays shortly after her sixteenth birthday, appeared to have no intention of continuing her education. She hadn't got any A-levels but that didn't seem to worry her. She implied that she wasn't getting on with her mother and was desperate to leave home and go to London.

"But you're so young, Tessa," Nicola told her.

"So what? I don't see what age has to do with it."

"But aren't you going to try for university?" Nicola was banking on going to a university herself, just what she needed to get on in the world.

"Well, I doubt I'd get in with just a few O-levels," said Tessa. "I thought I'd go to parties instead. Speaking of which, why don't you come to Mummy's boring do at Bellcloud next week? If you come you can have dinner there first. I'm going to wear a new green taffeta dress and I'm going to dance with my divine cousin Harry all night."

I wouldn't count on it, thought Nicola competitively and made up her mind to go.

Amy had finally persuaded her mother to let her use Bellcloud for a charity ball which filled Lady Heron-Sweeney with dread. Now Amy expected her to invite people to a dance at Bellcloud and make them pay for it. It was too frightful. She was hugely relieved that everybody was far too polite to quiz her about it. She just put it about that they were having a dance for one of Amy's causes and everybody bought tickets at five pounds a head. She was quite amazed. At any rate, Amy was organizing it all, hiring the caterers and the marquee and the band. She didn't have to do a thing except give this wretched dinner party for sixteen people beforehand.

She went into the dining room to check the table. Her black moiré silk dress rustled around her and her diamond choker dug into her wrinkled neck. She felt perfectly frightful dolled up like this, but what did it matter? It would be enjoyable to watch the young having fun. She did so hope that the girls would wear long. It was so tiresome the way nobody made any effort to dress anymore. The invitations said "Black Tie," but she wouldn't be surprised if some of the young men turned up in jeans.

"Of course they won't, Granny." Harry came into the room, magnificent in his evening dress. "You were talking out loud again, you know? You'd better not do too much of that tonight. Come and have a glass of champagne before our dinner guests arrive."

They went into the drawing room and were greeted with the sight of Sir Hugh in a dinner jacket and a pair of cricket whites.

"That won't do, Hugh," said Betty firmly.

"Won't do at all, Grandpa. Upstairs with you."

"But I *can't* find the trousers. I swear they went into the children's dressing-up box years ago and that's the last I saw of them. I never thought I'd need them again. Now Amy has to go and throw a *grand bal*, behaving like some silly débutante, well, she'll just have to take me as she finds me."

"It's too late anyway. People seem to be arriving." Hugh was peering out of the window. "Oh, it's only Tessa and her party. Why are they coming round the outside from the west wing when they could slip through the pantry door like always?"

"Shh, Hugh, they want to do things properly. Quite right too! How nice you look, Tessa darling." Betty held out her arms to her granddaughter. She really did look splendid. Her auburn hair was swept up into a little chignon on the top of her head and her gray-green eyes were beautifully offset by the swirling green taffeta dress. It was strapless, leaving Tessa's shoulders totally exposed, a little seed pearl necklace resting lightly on her collar bone. It wasn't quite enough. The child needed some real jewelery, Betty thought to herself, and made a mental note to see if she had any suitable pieces. Good God, what on earth did Amy think she looked like? Betty stared at her daughter coming in after Tessa. She resembled a tank in red velvet. Betty hastily brushed her aside and winced again. Who was *this*? Nicola Woodhouse? Oh yes, Tessa's odd little friend. Why wasn't she wearing long, Betty wondered. Hadn't Tessa explained? This child looked too frightful for words. A sort of white Grecian affair held together with bits of gilt, revealing almost all of her breasts and ending at least six inches above the knee. How extraordinarily nice of Harry to go over immediately and offer her a glass of champagne, make her feel at home. Really, the boy had such charm.

Several of Cousin Harry's friends from Oxford were invited to dinner and they too seemed fascinated by Nicola. Oh Lord, I'm going to be a wallflower, thought Tessa, but Harry was waiting for her at the bottom of the stairs when she came down after dinner.

"Where have you been? I've been looking for you. I want to

have the first dance with you. And several others throughout the evening if you'll let me."

"I've been powdering my nose. Or rather washing my hands since I don't wear powder yet. And of course you can have all the dances you want."

Tessa was looking forward to dancing with him. He had an appalling reputation, but she had a huge crush on him and it would give her a chance to be in his arms without running into danger. He could hardly feel her up in front of everyone on the dance floor. Or could he? She needn't have worried. As they shuffled round the dance floor, Harry whispered in her ear: "I've decided to respect you. I won't try anything funny. You can relax."

But strangely she couldn't and felt quite irritated. It made matters worse when the band started playing the current dance craze, the Twist, and they had to move apart. Finally she urged him to come and explore the discothèque which had been set up in the cellar.

It was almost pitch black and even though it was only about ten o'clock the cellar was packed with couples, locked in each other's arms, oblivious to the music and anyone else. Harry and Tessa joined them and Harry began to let his hands roam freely over her body. She brushed him away. He started again and once more she evaded him. Irritated, he grabbed her by the elbow and just then the lights came up. Tessa gasped. Right beside them Nicola was gripped in the arms of one of Harry's friends. One of his hands was placed firmly over one of Nicola's breasts and she was guzzling his neck quite happily. To Tessa's further amazement, Harry suddenly left her and pulled Nicola from the man's grasp.

"Do you want to?" he yelled at Nicola. "Do you want to? If so, follow me."

Do you want to? Do you want to *what*? Tessa wondered as she watched Nicola follow Harry out of the discothèque. She had a feeling she ought to find out.

Tessa watched them slip out of the marquee through an opening on the far side. She followed and saw them moving through the herb garden. She knew where they were going.

The summer-house.

It was the brazen way they went about it which shocked Tessa rather than what they actually did. If you were in the summer-house nothing you did was hidden. You could be seen by anyone approaching the herb garden. True, they were in shadow, but as she watched the movements of their silhouettes, Tessa unconsciously moved closer to get a better view.

She could make out the gleaming white of Harry's dress shirt in the moonlight. And below she caught a glimpse of his bare legs. He had pushed his trousers down to his ankles.

Nicola's white dress also stood out in the moonlight. Tessa could see that she was kneeling in front of Harry, kneeling between his legs, her head bent forward, jerking up and down in an odd fashion. Tessa watched, mesmerized. For some reason, all she could think of was that it must be awfully cold for Nicola, kneeling on the cold, stone slabs of the summer-house.

She was by the sundial now, recklessly indifferent as to whether or not they could see her. One of Nicola's breasts had slipped out of her dress and Harry was pulling at it, bruising it.

Tessa screamed when a hand grasped her shoulder and swung her round.

"I've warned you," said her grandfather, standing ghost-like by the sundial, *"never* to go near the summer-house." His hand had released her shoulder, but his arm remained raised above her as if he were about to strike her.

Tessa shot a quick glance at the summer-house and ascertained that all movement in it had ceased. Clearly Harry and Nicola had heard her cry out and had shrunk back into the shadows out of sight. She faced her grandfather, her instinct telling her to keep silent.

"It's a filthy place. It's for the scum of the world." Tessa was aware he was drunk. Whisky fumes attacked her as she leaned closer.

"Scum of the world," he repeated in a whisper. He must have seen them, thought Tessa and sprang to their defense.

"Grandpa, it's perfectly all right. They're probably just having a quiet talk. It's terribly noisy in the marquee."

"Not *them*," he hissed, "your *father*. Your father was *the scum of the earth*!"

"Oh, Grandpa, no, stop it. You can't mean that!"

"And you're his daughter," the old man leered. "All these years I've let you stay in my house and you know why?"

"Why?" she whispered, crying now.

"Because you're Amy's daughter too. I love *my* daughter in a way your precious father wouldn't begin to know about."

"But what did he *do*?" Tessa was nearly hysterical.

"If you ever find out what he did it won't be from me. You're Amy's daughter and while you're under my roof I'll protect you from such filth."

Tessa cracked. "Well, you can just keep your bloody roof, Grandpa. If I'm the daughter of such scum you can't possibly want me to stay. I'll leave. I'll leave and I'll never come back."

CHAPTER 8

For the rest of her life Tessa would look back on those first few months she spent in London as among the most miserable she ever experienced. Her impetuous decision to leave Bellcloud after the row with her grandfather had been an impulsive and reckless one and now she was paying for it.

Finding somewhere to live was the first hurdle and she could hardly believe her luck when Grania Henderson said she had a room in her flat. Tessa had called Grania on arrival at Paddington Station and woken her up early on a Sunday morning. Yes, there was a room and she could have it. Tessa breathed a huge sigh of relief. Now she had somewhere to live everything else would be perfect.

But it wasn't. It was quite awful. Tessa had always rather liked Grania Henderson when they'd lived at opposite ends of the county in the country, but sharing a cramped Kensington flat with her and Vanessa someone was stifling. Grania had gone so far as to give up her own room to share with Vanessa so Tessa could have a room to herself, but even so they always seemed to be on top of one another.

For the first time Tessa realized how spoilt she'd been at

Bellcloud. Granny Betty still had a live-in staff: a couple, Ben the gardener and Mrs. Ben, as she was known, the cook, plus Fanny who "did." It was Fanny Tessa missed the most. How on earth was she supposed to look after her clothes without Fanny? She dropped her things hopefully in the laundry basket in the bathroom to begin with, but a week later they were still there, going mouldy.

"What do we do about the laundry?" she asked Grania.

"Launderette," Grania told her, "go out into High Street Ken, walk along for about five minutes and then cross over the road. There's one about a hundred yards up on the left. Can't miss it."

"Launderette," repeated Tessa, nervously wondering what it was. "And the ironing?"

"In the cupboard under the stairs. Must dash."

Tessa succeeded in ruining most of her clothes in less than a fortnight. She either shrunk them, dyed them or scorched them.

Then there was the question of the flat itself. It was the bathroom which depressed her the most. She had never encountered such squalor. She never managed to take a bath without a pair of wet tights dangling in her face from the makeshift washing-line strung from wall to wall. There was a constant grimy line at various levels round the tub. The kitchen was equally daunting. Grease covered the stove and strange fungi inhabited the fridge. If she ever bought anything fresh and put it in the fridge it was immediately appropriated by one of Grania's or Vanessa's never-ending stream of chinless escorts. They arrived in droves every evening around seven to whisk Tessa's flatmates off to dine and dance the night away, only to return them in the small hours of the following morning and make a bee-line for the refrigerator to demolish anything they could find. The noise was unbearable. Once, unable to sleep, Tessa had got up to go and ask Grania and Jeremy or Simon or Nicholas or Jocelyn or whoever it was to *please* be a bit quieter, only to come upon them half-naked, grappling with each other on the living room floor. The sound of their smothered giggles as she hastily retreated haunted her for days afterward.

For Tessa had no one with whom to spend her evenings, let alone grapple. She was desperately lonely. And bored and homesick. And all this turned into a kind of lethargic depression when every morning Grania and Vanessa clattered out to their secretarial courses leaving her sitting with her elbows on the kitchen table waiting for the inevitable inertia to set in for the day. For several weeks she sat around and forced herself to come to terms with the truth: she had led a very sheltered life at Bellcloud which had prepared her for absolutely nothing in later life. On top of that, her upbringing had had a decidedly odd flavor to it when placed alongside other people's. She had not been raised by her parents. If anything, she had been raised by her grandparents. That would have been perfectly acceptable if her parents had not been alive and indeed her father *was* dead. But that left Amy. How did one explain Amy? "Well, she's as mad as a hatter. Spends her whole life organizing jumble sales."

No, she couldn't really talk about her parents. She dreaded to think what Grania might have told everyone about her. "Turned up on my doorstep. What *could* I do?" As a result Tessa was painfully shy whenever she encountered any of the chinless escorts in passing in the flat. She felt awkward and stupid as she bumped into them in her dressing-gown on the way to the bathroom and then had to stand aside and shiver while they went ahead of her to use the loo. "Won't be a tick, can't hold it back another second," as they dashed past her, and "Bit early to have a bath, isn't it? Going to bed already?" Or when they went into the kitchen and found her preparing her solitary supper. "No din-dins out tonight? Poor old Tessa. Come on, Grania, or they won't hold our table."

One evening Vanessa had a cocktail party at the flat and Tessa had no escape. She was obliged to rummage about in the back of her wardrobe till she found something which would serve as a cocktail dress. She spent the afternoon before Grania and Vanessa returned washing and setting her long auburn hair and was dressed and ready when they walked in the door.

"Crumbs!" shrieked Grania, "you look super, Tessa, doesn't she, 'Nessa?"

"Crikey! It's unbelievable, I mean, I just don't believe it's really you, Tessa. I'd better keep an eye on Jocelyn tonight. Once he sees you looking like that . . ."

Jocelyn made a bee-line for her as did virtually every other young man the minute he entered the room. The attention caught Tessa off her guard. She had read somewhere that girls who had been raised without a father unconsciously searched for father figures and invariably found them in older men with whom they became involved when they grew up. Yet here she was faced with an array of hungry youths all begging to be allowed to take her out to dinner. They wore their hair long, some to the collars of their pin-striped suits over pink shirts with white collars, others allowing it to flop casually across the shoulders of their velvet jackets which they wore over white shirts with frills down the front and flowing silk scarves knotted loosely round their necks.

Somewhere beyond the outer circle of these bee-like creatures swarming round her, Tessa was aware of the petulant murmurings of an army of abandoned females demanding explanations from Grania and Vanessa.

"Who *is* she?"

"What do you mean, she lives *here*?"

"I thought you said she was plain, never went out, hadn't an earthly . . ."

"Do you think she has any idea how stunning she is?"

"Well, so would you be if you had all day to tart yourself up like that, that's right, isn't it, 'Nessa, she's not doing a course and she doesn't have a job. Lady of bloody leisure."

"But Simon told me she was *awful*, said she hung around this place like a miserable ghost all the time. She's obviously one of those dark ones who comes out of their shell when it suits them and grabs whatever takes their fancy . . . lucky to be able to look so good with just a little bit of effort . . ."

Tessa caught snatches of their remarks and longed to tell them they'd got it all wrong. She was out of her depth. Nobody appeared to have noticed, but she hadn't actually opened her mouth to say something more than half a dozen times the entire evening. She didn't care for these languid young men with their drawling voices and their affected airs. Not one of them had attempted any serious conversation, nor had she found anything they said remotely funny. They, on the other hand, were amazed at their own wit, clapping each other on the back and filling the room with their braying laughter.

One man stood apart from all the others, a solitary figure

leaning up against the wall with his arms folded across his chest. He looked thoroughly bored by the proceedings and was on the point of leaving when a momentary gap in the throng of braying chinless wonders gave him a fleeting glimpse of Tessa.

He caught Tessa's eye and winked at her. Relief at finding what she hoped was a conspirator caused her to burst out laughing. He placed his index finger in front of his nose and beckoned to her in the manner of a master summoning a naughty puppy.

Without saying a word, he took her by the hand and led her from the room.

"Who's *that*?" she heard one of the abandoned lovelies whisper as she grabbed her coat.

"Francis Cottesmore," somebody informed her. "*Lord* Francis Cottesmore, fashion photographer. Our little friend has only gone out to dinner with the richest man in the room. By at least a quarter of a million, I should say. She's in for some good chow tonight!"

Tessa, not having been exposed to the status symbols of Sixties London, was not impressed by His Lordship's souped-up Mini. She made a complete fool of herself getting into it while he stood by holding the door for her. There was no room for her long legs and her knees kept getting in the way of his hands as he tried to change gears.

"*Alvaro's* okay?" he murmured as they swung into the King's Road.

"Fine," she stumbled, having no idea what it was.

Tessa had never been to a restaurant in London before. She'd hardly ever been to a restaurant in her life; the Heron-Sweeneys did not go in for family outings. Sir Hugh had been known to visit his club in London from time to time, but apart from that it was felt that the dining room at Bellcloud offered no incentive to rush out and eat elsewhere.

Now she sat in Alvaro's and studied the menu which appeared to be in a strange language, possibly Italian. She had no idea what to order and knew that she would be asked first when the waiter arrived.

"What are you going to have?" she asked Francis tentatively.

"Linguine, I expect."

"Wonderful, I'll have the same."

"Copy-cat," he laughed at her. "What will you have to drink?"

Another hurdle. Tessa had been forbidden alcohol at Bell-cloud. She was not used to alcohol. Would a glass of sherry sound ridiculous? Francis came to her rescue.

"How about a Campari and soda?"

"Mmmmm." She tried to smile appreciatively.

Francis was pale and wan with dark circles under his eyes. He always wore gray because he knew it contrasted violently with the lurid psychedelic colors of the Sixties and thus enabled him to stand out. He was rather on the thin side, but his brown eyes were large and expressive and he wore his dark hair shorter than most men of the time, but with a shaggy forelock hanging over his right eye which he perpetually pushed back with his fingers. He aimed to present a rather vulnerable, poetic image and he more or less hit the mark.

He was also a good listener, or he appeared to be. Sometimes he was miles away, merely pretending to be paying attention. But tonight he listened to Tessa's every word. He didn't have much choice. Two Camparis and soda and three glasses of Valpolicella and Tessa was pouring out the story of her life.

"When exactly did you leave school?" asked Francis, ordering her a zabaglione.

"Oh, just a few weeks ago, actually."

That explains it, thought Francis, *she's just a kid.*

"Are you going to be a model?" They usually were and they'd usually dropped huge hints about photographic tests by this stage of the evening.

"Me? Oh, don't be silly!"

By God, she means it. She has no idea about her looks.

"I'm not being remotely silly. I'm a photographer, didn't you know? If anyone can spot a model, I can. Give me a bell one day and we'll take some pictures in the Studios."

He gave her a card and watched her stuff it casually into her handbag.

"Oh, this is delicious." She demolished her zabaglione in an instant.

"Would you like another?"

"Yes, *please.*"

It took fifteen minutes to arrive and while she was waiting she had another glass of Valpolicella and Francis ordered cappuccino and Sambuca. As he watched her futile attempts to locate the tiny blue flame on the Sambuca and blow it out, he knew she was well and truly drunk.

He half carried her to his Mini and deposited her a few minutes later on the sofa in the living room of his town house in Lincoln Street. He reached up under her dress to roll down her tights and discovered to his delight that she was wearing stockings. He hadn't seen stockings in five years.

She came to as he was unbuckling her garters.

"Whash you doing?" she mumbled, making no effort to stop him. "I was going to take you on to the Ad Lib," he told her, "but I don't think you're up to it. You're all right," he added gently, "you're in my house and I'm taking care of you. Like this . . ." He bent his head and began flicking her clitoris with his tongue. Tessa reached out to stroke his hair and pushed his forelock back so she could see his face. Her body had never felt so relaxed and each time his fingertips touched her as he eased her stockings and then her panties down to the floor she felt a quiver between her legs and another rush of liquid pour out of her onto his . . .

"Oh my God!" She sat up. "Your sofa."

"Don't worry about that." He stood before her, unzipping his gray flannel trousers and holding his erect penis out to her between his hands. "Do you want to?"

Do you want to? At last she knew what that meant. And what her answer would be.

Lord Francis eyed the bloodstains on the cushion covers of his sofa the next morning. Did the girl have her period? Or could she . . . Surely not. Surely she hadn't been a virgin. Well, she wasn't now of course. He'd seen to that. Five times in one night, quite a marathon even for him. Poor kid must be feeling a bit sore, better take her up an ice-pack to hold between her legs.

But Francis Cottesmore had unleashed something called passion in Tessa Fitzgerald and he was going to have to pay for it. What did she want with a horrid block of ice inside her when she could have him?

Grania and Vanessa dubbed him St. Francis. He was all they heard about morning, noon and night. Not that they were there at noon, but as they struggled with touch typing at their secretarial college they could have sworn they could still hear Tessa going into raptures over him. She had gone through piles of back numbers of *Tatler* and *Harpers* and *Queen* and cut out all the pictures she could find of him (and then cut out of those pictures all the girls he was with). These she arranged in a collage which she hung above her bed. Then she realized she was looking at it upside down when she was in bed so she transferred it to the wall beside her.

Grania had a date for lunch with Suki Attwood and got a call from Suki asking her to come to an address in Lincoln Street off the King's Road. There was Suki still damp from the shower at a quarter to one.

"This is Francis Cottesmore's place," she told Grania by way of explanation. "I mean we only just got out of bed half an hour ago . . . it's OK, he's gone out."

"I didn't know you and he . . ." Grania looked at Suki who blushed.

"Oh, for God's sake, you know Francis. There's one bedded every minute."

Tessa got bedded by St. Francis every other night for about two weeks. Grania and Vanessa never said a word, except to tell her how to go about getting the Pill. They knew it was only a matter of time, but now that Tessa was beginning to mutter about the Norman church at Bellcloud being perfect for weddings and they *must* be bridesmaids, mustn't they? It seemed they might just have to intervene. They wouldn't enjoy it. She was a nice girl. A bit aloof, perhaps, to begin with and she still didn't seem to fit in with anyone else who came to the flat, but if one was prepared to talk about St. Francis she was really quite charming.

Tessa decided she wouldn't actually take Francis down to Bellcloud till after he proposed. She knew Amy wouldn't notice a thing, but she felt quite sure Granny Betty would detect the sexual electricity between them. She might be an old lady, but she didn't miss a trick. And of course she had been very firm on the subject of not giving in to a man until one was married. Well, she would be married soon. Maybe Francis would even propose today to celebrate the success of her photographic session. Silly, really. She didn't want to be a model. She was only doing it to please him. And he was such a wonderful photographer he was bound to make her look stunning.

On the way to Vogue House in Hanover Square she stopped off at Liberty's to browse amongst the fabrics. If they were to get married soon she would probably find herself living at Lincoln Street and quite frankly at the moment it looked just too much like a bachelor pad. It needed a feminine touch even if she only managed to get as far as changing the curtains in the bedroom.

Going down in the lift she noticed a small card by the panel of buttons: *Operator wanted. Apply Personnel.* What a dreadful job! thought Tessa and told herself for the umpteenth time that day that she was really very lucky to have found someone like Francis so soon after coming to London.

She arrived at Vogue House and told the Commissionaire that Francis Cottesmore was expecting her in the Studios. He told her to take the lift to the fifth floor.

She pushed open the door marked STUDIO and gasped as she entered. The area was cavernous. She couldn't see any corners. Everywhere she looked, dark spaces seemed to disappear into nowhere. Then she saw the backdrop and the lighting equipment. Francis's tripod stood poised for action. On the colorama in the foreground lay a pair of tights and a strappy high-heeled sandal. Where were the dressing rooms? They must be round the back.

Tessa stepped gingerly behind the backdrop and made out a shaft of light in the distance. Moving toward it she saw a wall of mirrors surrounded by spotlights. As she walked in, they lay at her feet stretched out on the floor.

Francis was on top pumping his way into the skinny, leggy blonde underneath him. His buttocks moved up and down, faster and faster below her as Tessa stood staring down at them. She was transfixed, could not tear herself away. The girl opened her eyes and saw her.

"We got company," she whispered in Francis's ear. He half turned his head, saw Tessa out of the corner of his eye and waved.

"I can't stop. I'm going to come any second. Get your clothes off, Tessa, and join in."

Tessa stumbled out, crashing into the backdrop, almost bringing it down on top of her. She made her way to the lift and managed to get inside before the tears began to cascade down her face. Within seconds she was uncontrollable, shaking, heaving, banging her fists on the walls of the lift.

Up and down she rode, hitting the button as soon as the car came to a stop at a floor. Once she had calmed down sufficiently to step into the foyer, she walked straight into the arms of the Commissionaire who escorted her into a taxi.

Grania and Vanessa found her huddled in bed, sniffling into Kleenexes. The collage of St. Francis was torn into shreds.

"He's a rotter," they agreed, "but you're well rid of him" (now one of them might have a shot at him), "and there is something else we really do have to discuss with you, Tessa. It's about the rent. You're way overdue. If you don't cough up soon we're afraid you'll have to go. Otherwise you're just going to have to get a job."

The next day, wearing Vanessa's owl-like sunglasses to hide her swollen eyes, Tessa took the Underground to Oxford Circus, marched down Regent Street and landed her very first job . . . as a lift operator at Liberty's.

For the next couple of weeks Tessa's life seemed to fall into two sets of monologues, the daytime one and the night-time one. By day she chanted out loud as she worked the lift:

"Going Up. First Floor: Fashions. Men's Shop. Children's and Toys.

"Second Floor: Dress Fabrics. Knitting Yarns. Needlecraft. Paper Patterns. Suitings.

"What's that, madam? No, you'll find China and Glass in the Basement along with the Crockery Shop and Wedding Lists.

"Third Floor: Bed and Table Linen, Carpets, Wallpapers, Furnishing Fabrics and what else? Oh yes, Ladies Room. Men's on the Fourth Floor, sir, along with Furniture and Lighting and the Restaurant . . .

"Watch your step, madam. Mind the doors now."

By night she hissed to herself in the privacy of her room: *"I hate him. I despise him! How could I have allowed myself to go anywhere near such a creep? What did I ever see in him? Just because he seemed a bit different to all the chinless wonders. But no, he turned out just the same, just as stupid. Maybe they're all like that? Maybe I should never trust a man again? One thing's certain: I'll never let a man make such a fool of me again. Ever!"*

Yet the pain remained and it exhausted her for everything she told herself went against the grain. She derived no pleasure from her nightly vitriolic seethings. She wanted someone to dream about, someone to put on a pedestal and love and admire. Inevitably the day arrived when she was so tired she launched unconsciously into her night-time vehemence going up in the lift first thing in the morning.

"Going up. Fourth floor only. I *hate* him. I'll never let him near me again, hateful bastard!"

"Of course you will." Fortunately she only had one passenger. Candida McCarthy was on her way up to the Press Office to discuss a promotion for the October issue of a new magazine of which she was the Features Editor. She tripped out of the lift leaving Tessa reeling in a cloud of Guy Laroche's *Fidji*. Tessa couldn't help remembering her grandmother's view, frequently expressed, that one simply didn't wear scent during the day. At least it had taken her mind off St. Francis for twenty seconds.

When he called two days later she was in the middle of revving herself up to hate him, so when his voice said softly in her ear: "Hello, sweets, sorry I haven't been in touch for so long. Been away on an assignment, you know how it is. How are you?" she was struck dumb. "What's the matter? You there? It was you, wasn't it? Or is it Grania? Grania, is Tessa there? I just . . ."

"No, no, I'm he . . . eeere," Tessa stammered. "It's mmmmme."

"Why did you rush off like that? You can't seriously imagine it was anything serious with that model? Happens all the time. Only way I can get them to relax before the session sometimes. They don't *mean* anything to me. Now, how are you fixed for dinner tonight?"

"Fine. I mean, nothing. I'd love to." And she believed everything he told her, because quite simply she wanted to. She wanted it all to be all right. She wanted to believe he cared for her, that she meant something to him and if he went so far as to tell her it was so, it seemed pointless not to trust him. It was part of his job screwing those girls, that was all. Part of his job. She'd just have to get used to it.

In the small hours of the morning, lying in bed at Lincoln Street, Francis remembered to ask her to forgive him and found her fingers placed against his lips and her soft, low voice suggesting there was nothing to forgive. Christ! Francis thought to himself, Tessa the Romantic strikes again. Too bad she's such a knockout in the sack, otherwise I'd give her the elbow once and for all. This girl's going to get her heart broken from here to eternity.

CHAPTER 9

He was absolutely right. He broke it himself a few months later when he ran off to the Bahamas with a blonde French actress who never worked again. And Tessa came down to earth with a bump.

She felt foolish and more than a little trapped. She couldn't go crawling home to Bellcloud with her tail between her legs so soon after the scene with her grandfather. It would be a downright admission of failure. She hadn't heard a word from Amy, of course, but her grandmother had written faithfully every week, long, reassuring letters demanding details of parties and London life. Tessa had mentioned Francis in her replies from time to time, but mercifully her grandmother had not demanded further information about him.

She could not go home, nor could she stand much more of being cooped up with Grania and Vanessa. They were pleasant and good-natured girls, but something told Tessa that all they were waiting for was a husband. The secretarial course and the search for work was only a pretense until the real thing came along. The vision of wedding plans at the Norman church at Bellcloud had disintegrated altogether by now and to Tessa's surprise she realized that it really wasn't what she wanted. Not yet anyway.

What she needed was a job. A real job, not shunting people up and down in the lift at Liberty's. She had no qualifications whatsoever, but listening to Grania and her friends chattering aimlessly on the telephone, Tessa realized she was not exactly the most stupid person in the world. It was 1963, she was ready, willing and able and despite the fact that she was not yet eighteen and had no experience, she was determined to go out there and make something of herself. Somewhere along the line Amy's "Fight the Good Fight" attitude had also instilled itself in her daughter.

She answered an advertisement for an assistant to work on a new magazine and was duly summoned for an interview. She deliberated for hours on what to wear. Should she appear what Granny Betty called presentable in her best coat and skirt and hat to match, or should she go in what she herself felt most comfortable: her new Mary Quant *Bazaar* dress, black with white zigzags just above the hem, a hem which barely covered her thighs? She opted for the latter. After all, it was ostensibly a fashion magazine as far as she knew and they'd probably appreciate a bit of up-to-the-minute rags.

Her interview was with the Features Editor and the minute she walked in Tessa knew she had made a mistake. The woman who rose to greet her was impeccably groomed in a pink Chanel suit with ropes of pearls hung round her neck. She was petite with tiny feet in exquisite lizard skin court shoes and Tessa felt huge and gangling and awkward.

A familiar smell hung in the air but Tessa couldn't quite place it. Her CV was being studied, a work of highly creative fiction concocted by her and Grania the week before at the kitchen table.

"Tessa Fitzgerald. Twenty-two. A-level French, German, Latin, English Literature. You don't say anything about university, but that's not essential."

Tessa breathed a sigh of relief. It was bad enough that she had lied about the non-existent A-levels.

"And you've spent some time at *Vogue*. That's enormously useful. What exactly did you do there?"

Well, as a matter of fact I popped over there to have Francis

Cottesmore, my erstwhile lover, take some photos of me, but when I got there he was otherwise engaged . . .

"I, uh, did some photo captions . . ."

"Did you? Well done you. Then you had a stint at Liberty's. Wonderful store. What department were you in, the Press Office?"

"Yes," lied Tessa. "I absolutely loved it. It seemed a natural step from there to look for work on a magazine again."

"But of course. Tell me, did you work for Lady Arabella while you were there?"

"Ah no, I didn't really know her. Her office was at the other end of my floor."

"And how long did you work in the lift before you moved upstairs to the Press Office?"

Tessa choked. The smell. Guy Laroche's *Fidji*. Never wear scent during the day. She'd smelled it before in the lift at Liberty's.

"There's no one called Lady Arabella working in the Press Office at Liberty's," Candida McCarthy told her gently. "How much truth was there in the *Vogue* job?"

"Not much," admitted Tessa, "but I do want to work here. I'll do anything you want if it means I can learn what goes on. I'm sorry I lied about my past experience, but I was just terrified that my lack of it would stop me from even getting my foot in the door. I'll come clean with you. I can't type, but I can learn. Any fool can answer a phone and take messages. I'm sorry I'm looking a bit casual, but it's the way I feel most comfortable."

"You look fine," Candida told her and it was true. The girl had an extraordinarily vibrant quality to her. Young and energetic. This was just what Candida needed after the string of apathetic, spoiled debs she'd had to put up with.

"Let's give it a three months' trial," she told Tessa and was rewarded when the girl's face came alight with a positively heartwarming smile.

Candida McCarthy was rarely wrong in her instinct about people. This girl had potential written all over her. She could have been a model, but clearly that thought had never entered her head or if it had it had long since been dismissed. Candy watched her for some time. Her organizational skills were first rate, she followed through on everything she was asked to do and proved to be a first-rate assistant, but within a few years she had completely outgrown the job. What Candy could not have predicted was that Tessa would develop such a natural talent for journalism. She started with short pieces—book reviews, gossip items, beauty tips—and progressed to features on the Pill, the Problems of Sharing an Apartment, low budget fashion and How to Kiss Your Lover Goodbye. But it was when she was sent to interview a visiting American film director that her real talent came through: *profiles.*

Sam Montefiore was an American director of Italian extraction whose films were currently all the rage. Yet he was notoriously difficult to interview. Some claimed his hot Latin temperament got the better of him, others found him withdrawn and morose.

His films were good copy, but thus far he was not. His claims to be a very private person were anathema to the Press who liked flamboyant, extrovert people who would feed them lots of anecdotes about their lives into the tape recorder so all they had to do was get someone to transcribe their tapes. But Sam Montefiore wouldn't go away. He was an enigma, he was good-looking and his films were big successes. When he came to town every journalist worth his or her salt had to go through the motions of trying to get a good interview out of him.

Tessa did her homework thoroughly. She was now twenty-seven years old and it was time to move up a notch or two. She should really have moved to another magazine in order to get a promotion, but Candy McCarthy had taken a gamble on her and she was more than prepared to repay her by sticking around. Besides, there was no better magazine around to tempt her away.

In amongst the backdated paraphernalia on Sam Montefiore in the cuttings library she came across a small item which mentioned his autistic child. *"Sam Montefiore and his family, including Eric, his autistic son, left today for their annual summer vacation in Montauk,"* the caption ran under a blurred wire photo of the director and a group of children about to board a plane.

"Why can't you people understand I just don't like talking about my pictures? I like the public to see them and decide for themselves. I have nothing to say," he told her in his suite at the Connaught.

"I don't want to talk about them either," she told him. "Tell me about Eric. As the father of an autistic child, what can you tell me about this illness, do you feel it is a form of childhood schizophrenia? Do you believe there is a chance Eric will ever recover?"

"He's been in Bellevue's children's ward for a year," muttered Montefiore, "why don't you ask them?" But his attitude toward her had changed. He was alert, waiting to see how she would go on.

"It's just I've heard that the prognosis is pretty bleak for most kids," she hurried on. She was way in deep now, too late to turn back. He would either turn on her or stick with it. Her only hope was to be blatantly provocative. "Is it true what I've read that sometimes the parents, especially the mothers, can have a smothering effect on the very young child which exacerbates the illness? Is this why Eric's in Bellevue? Do you plan to institutionalize him for the rest of his life . . . ?"

"NO!" It was a cry from the heart and over the next few hours Tessa discovered that this man had a very big heart indeed. He and his wife had suffered agonies throughout the first three years of Eric's life, agonies the public never heard about as Montefiore was too busy filming all over the world, making his name, often leaving his wife alone for months at a time. He was wracked with guilt since at first he had not believed his wife when she said something was wrong with Eric, that he had a communication problem, that he would scream for hours on end with no reason. He had even gone so far as to suggest it might be something his wife was doing wrong which brought on these attacks. His child was not ill. A Montefiore would never be in any way retarded.

Then finally he had to face up to the truth. Eric was autistic and there was very little that could be done. At the moment he was all right, but a remission at puberty was always possible. He and his wife had elected to keep him home with them, although more than two-thirds of the parents of autistic children in America surrendered their children to the special care and supervision of institutions. But he and his wife could not bear to part with Eric. They loved him every bit as much as their other children.

The interview was a sensation. Montefiore talked about his work with the National Society for Autistic Children in America. He exhorted parents of autistic children in England to be brave, they were not alone. Every other magazine and newspaper in England ran the same old Montefiore interview, so when Tessa's appeared it read as if it were about a different man. And in a way it was. Tessa had found the real Sam Montefiore where nobody else had ever bothered to look and she had made people care about him. A year later she would interview Eric himself when Montefiore brought him on a trip to London. And finally, Maria, the wife.

Tessa's career was made. She loved people and remained endlessly fascinated by them. She had the ability to get her subjects to confide in her, she clearly respected them and showed it and in turn they trusted her. She began to put her own mark on her interviews. The public wrote in saying they looked for her byline, suggested people they would like to see her write about. And as the demand for her grew, Candida McCarthy knew she was going to have to let her go.

Tessa's life changed. She went freelance. She rented her own flat, found herself to be a sitting tenant paying a ridiculously low fixed rent with her landlords unable to get her out and eventually she was able to buy the place from them for less than half the market value. Even so, her mortgage nearly crippled her but the *Tessa Fitzgerald Interview* was still a big pull and barely a week went by when she didn't work.

Betty Heron-Sweeney lay in her four-poster bed at Bellcloud reading a letter from Tessa which informed her that her granddaughter was doing well in her new job on a magazine. Poor girl, thought Betty, still no talk of any young man. What have we ever done to help her on her way? Poor girl. Pushed out into the world with only her beauty to support her. Would that I were a little younger, I'd take her under my wing. Too late now. She's on her way. Will I last another decade to see her happy and settled? Please God, spare me that long. Forgive me for not loving my own daughter and recognize my love for my granddaughter. Protect and guide her for she is still but a child . . .

Downstairs in his study her husband did something he had wanted to do for a long time. He unlocked a drawer in his bureau and withdrew a small bundle of airmail letters which he threw onto the fire. As he watched them burn he poured himself a large brandy from the decanter and raised his glass. "Here's to you, Elliott. To the end of you—forever." A short while after that the new letters began to arrive.

Men came and went over the years. Tessa had long since got over her crush on Francis Cottesmore. In fact she bumped into him quite often now and found herself able laughingly to dismiss his attempts to start something up between them again. She enjoyed sex and in the permissive Swinging Sixties and early Seventies she found plenty of it. She made a point of never sleeping with anyone she didn't actually like, but she never allowed a relationship to develop into anything more than a relatively casual affair. It was as if she had cut herself off from them, could not allow them beyond a certain point and if they got near it, she sent out certain signals and they retreated. She was always the interviewer, never the interviewee, and she was an expert at turning the attention away from herself when things got too close for comfort.

Until she slipped up and fell for Jeremy.

Jeremy was an accountant, about as far removed from her immediate circle of friends as could possibly be. She'd gone to him because she needed an accountant. Her affairs were in total disarray. She was self-employed, but as far as she could remember, she hadn't paid tax in several years. She needed help and Jeremy gave it. He asked the questions. He had to, it was part of his job, he had a right to. She felt relaxed with him, trusted him. The pressure was off. He was behaving in an official capacity. They weren't at a party. She was not expected to go out to dinner with him afterward or wonder whether she should let him go to bed with her.

But she did. It happened almost without her noticing, but she could not have been more delighted. This soft-spoken, tall young man with his prematurely graying hair and laugh wrinkles around his eyes gave her a new kind of reassurance.

It was a shame he did not tell her he was married. Yet perhaps even that was not a problem. Things had not been right with Shirley for quite some time. They barely saw each other and she had probably guessed he had someone else. She usually did. With luck he would be able to devote more and more of his time to this beautiful redhead. Maybe he could even pick up some new clients through her, she seemed to know so many prominent people.

When he asked if he could meet some of her friends, Tessa was a little wary. Did she want people to see them as a couple? Wasn't it a bit too soon for that? He wouldn't really fit in with her crowd, but maybe she was being too cautious. She had thought of very little else ever since she'd met him and that had to mean something. OK, she'd arrange a dinner party as soon as possible. She'd call Nicola Woodhouse, her childhood friend who had recently moved to London, to come round and help. She'd been meaning to invite Nicola over for ages. It would be really interesting to see what Nicola made of Jeremy.

Nicola let her tongue wander round the inside of Jeremy's mouth one last time before he firmly pulled his head away and withdrew her hand from between his thighs. They were sitting in his car outside her flat and they were due at Tessa's for dinner in half an hour.

"You're . . ." he began and struck his fist against the steering wheel without finishing the sentence.

"Insatiable?"

"Insatiable, yes. But actually what I was going to say was you're a bitch."

"What do you mean?"

"You know exactly what I mean, Nicola. You're supposed to be one of her best friends. Over the past fortnight I must have screwed you twice as many times as I have her and she doesn't even know we've met."

This was true. They'd met on Tessa's doorstep late one night. Nicola had spent the evening with Tessa and left around eleven. On her way out she'd almost bumped flat into a tall, thin man craning his neck up at the second-floor windows and knew instantly that this was Jeremy. Tessa had talked of nothing else all evening. Nicola couldn't resist it.

"Jeremy?" she asked softly. He jumped and looked down at her suspiciously.

"Who are you?"

"Nicola." Still softly.

"Tessa's friend?"

"The very same. She's asleep. I just left her."

This was a lie. Nicola had left Tessa wide awake in front of the television, quite convinced that Jeremy would be dropping by for a "nightcap."

"Fast asleep," continued Nicola. "In fact she was coming down with a rotten cold, so I made her a hot lemon drink and laced it with brandy. She's dead to the world. I doubt if you'll get much out of her tonight. My flat's just around the corner. Come in for a quick one."

Which was how it had started. Jeremy had had several quick ones both in and out of Nicola's bed. And from then on he'd found her waiting for him at Reception every night when he left the office. They'd have a "quick one" at her flat every evening before he walked around the corner to meet Tessa.

"Aren't you coming up?" Nicola was half out of the car, aware that he was still sitting hunched over the wheel.

"I thought you were going over to help her get the meal ready."

"I am, but we've got time . . ."

"No, we haven't, Nicola. Cut it out. Hasn't it occurred to you she's going to see us together tonight for the first time? In the same *room.* Hasn't it occurred to you that she's a very bright woman who's going to put two and two together in a flash unless we're really careful? Haven't you even given the poor girl one thought at all? You're a bitch, Nicola. Can't you even admit that?"

"Sure, if you want me to. And I have thought about tonight and I can tell you over and over again till I'm blue in the face that she won't suspect a thing. She thinks it's love. She always does. She's quite convinced you're absolutely dotty about her and no one else. If she knew you were married she'd probably imagine you'd leave your wife. And, as you've already pointed out, she's no idea we've even met. Personally I think it's going to be fun 'meeting' for the first time all over again. So let me ask you something. Hasn't it occurred to *you* that we ought to work out how we're going to play it? Don't you think we ought to go up to my place and rehearse a little? Besides, where are you going to go while I pop round the corner to help? You don't want to go all the way home to Chiswick for a quick cup of coffee with the little lady and be here in an hour, surely? Come up and have a bath with me, then I'll go on ahead and you can follow later. It makes sense. You've got to admit that."

"Are you going to clean your teeth?" Jeremy asked her softly as he lay soaking in her bathtub fifteen minutes later.

"I expect so." Nicola grinned. She knew what was coming. She wondered if he ever asked Tessa to "clean her teeth."

She searched for her special toothbrush. The ritual was always the same. He lay in the tub and watched as she slowly squeezed the toothpaste along the bristles. Then she gave her teeth a cursory token brush and flashed them at him.

"How's that?"

"Fine. Now, don't forget to rinse the brush."

This was where the fun began. She rinsed off the toothpaste and turned toward him. In what appeared to be almost an absent-minded accident she allowed the toothbrush to wander slowly down to her nipples. She began to stroke them very gently, occasionally letting the bristles flick them up. Once they were hard, she began to "brush" her way over her ribcage, across her stomach and on down to the triangle below.

"Brush your hair," grunted Jeremy, his hand circling his erection rising up below the bathwater.

"Of course I will and then I'll brush yours," replied Nicola, reaching down to pull out the bath plug. The water trickled out leaving his engorged penis exposed. Nicola gave his pubic hair a perfunctory scratch and moved on to let the bristles of the toothbrush rotate almost imperceptibly over his balls, sometimes slipping down to slide softly in the crease around his anus.

"Time for the electric one . . ." he muttered and Nicola dutifully reached for the electric toothbrush.

"Wait a second," she told him and streaked into the kitchen to run the toothbrush hard over the ice tray in the refrigerator. She returned to inch the still chilled bristles up and down his penis before suddenly switching on the electric motor and flicking them over the glistening tip again and again. By now she was leaning right over the side of the bath, her head directly above him. Anyone coming into the bathroom would have thought she was brushing her teeth until, at the last minute, she threw the toothbrush over her shoulder and took him in her mouth.

Later she bathed alone after they'd made love twice in the bedroom. He was still lying across the bed as she applied the finishing touches to her make-up. No further mention had been made of the way they were going to "play" their meeting later on.

"We're going to have to tell her sooner or later," she heard him murmur as she went out of the door.

"Aren't you going to change at all?" Nicola was perched on a stool in Tessa's kitchen. She said she had come round to help, but she was really rather enjoying watching Tessa getting redder and redder in the face.

"How the bloody hell can I? They're due in about half an hour and I've only just got home." She opened four cans of plum tomatoes in rapid succession and flung the contents into a pan. "Anyway, nobody will give a damn."

No, they won't, thought Nicola. Tessa can get away with anything. If it were me, I'd have started planning the whole thing about a week in advance. I'd have been to the hairdressers today at lunchtime. By now the table would be laid, the cushions plumped, the candles burning. I'd have redone my make-up three times and be wafting scent everywhere. How on earth does she do it? She looked around the kitchen. Chaos as usual. She picked up some cans of flaked tuna fish and opened a cupboard. Better make some kind of gesture to clear the place up.

"No, don't do that." Tessa grabbed the tins and then promptly handed them back to her. "On second thought, why don't you make yourself useful and open them for me, or do you just want to sit there all evening?"

Nicola glanced up. Tessa sounded a bit waspish. She couldn't know, surely?

"Nervous?" she asked as innocently as she could.

"Yes, if you really want to know."

"Why, for heaven's sake? Your evenings are always wild successes. You know that."

Tessa took the opened cans from her and emptied the tuna into the pan with the tomatoes.

"Damn, I forgot to put the oil in first. Oh well, might as well shove it in now. Where did I put the basil?"

"Here." Nicola handed it to her. "So what are you nervous about?"

"Jeremy."

Here it comes, thought Nicola. How the hell could she have known? "Jeremy?"

"They'll hate him. No, maybe that's too strong. But you know, Nicola, he's not like anything I've had before. They'll be expecting another Bob or a Jonathan or some visiting producer or something."

"Not some dreary little accountant, you mean?" Relief made Nicola tactless. Tessa stiffened.

"No, not some dreary little accountant, as you so sweetly put it. And that's not what they'll get either. Is that really how I've made him sound? He may be an accountant, but he's not dreary, not at all. You wait till you see him, Nic. With luck he'll come early and you can have a sneak preview. Oh, Jesus, now I've gone and put too much black pepper in. I'm going to ruin this if I don't look out."

Jeremy never showed up.

There was a very simple explanation for his non-appearance: he had decided he couldn't cope with the situation any longer. His wife was beginning to notice how exhausted he was every night and he knew he couldn't go on much longer. He didn't love Tessa. He only wanted an entrée into her circle of friends. It was a pity that things had got so complicated. The truth was that he really rather liked Tessa and felt he owed her an explanation, so he called her in the morning and told her he was unable to go on seeing her. When she asked why, he told her, perfectly calmly, that he had been fucking Nicola for the past fortnight and he assumed that Tessa, knowing that, would have no wish to go on seeing him.

He was right. Tessa had had enough. She wanted out. Away. As far away from London as possible.

Once again Candida McCarthy came to her rescue.

"Ever heard of Honey Winslow?" she asked Tessa over lunch at Crank's, the health food restaurant near Carnaby Street. Candida was only five foot two and while she could sometimes get away with being described as *petite*, tottering about on her size three high heels, there were days when she "blossomed" as she put it, and with her geometric Leonard hair cut framing her round face with its turned-up nose she resembled a Pekingese in a pink Chanel suit. Those were the days she headed for Crank's and their salads.

Tessa picked at her tofu burger. "Honey Winslow? Rings a bell."

"She was as big as Shrimpton in her day," Candida told her, "but that was way back in the mid-Sixties. You'd know her face if you saw it. She didn't do that much over here, but she was huge in America. Didn't you ever buy *Honey* perfume?"

"No."

"Ah, well, anyway, I've got this piece lined up on models *then* compared with models *now*. I've got three or four of the current ones who've agreed to say their bit, Marie Helvin and Jerry, and then Jean and Celia Hammond have agreed to be interviewed about what it was like in Swinging London. Twiggy too, maybe, but I really do want the American angle. Honey Winslow's agreed to do it and I had someone fixed to talk to her in New York, but they've gone and let me down at the last minute. I *could* find someone else over there, but I was wondering if you might be interested. Of course it would mean leaving London for a while . . ."

"Candy, *please* let me do it . . ."

"You'd have to find your own accommodation. I could help with the air fare somehow, but I'd only budgeted for someone in New York to do it on the spot. I don't have anything down for a hotel . . ."

"Doesn't matter. I'll find a place. I've got a friend over there who could put me up. What's she like, this Honey Winslow?"

"Honey*chile* Winslow. That's her full name, I understand. Never clapped eyes on her—in the flesh, I mean. She photographs like a dream, or did at any rate. Probably still does. Bones like that don't crumble that soon. Which reminds me, we'll have to get a photographer lined up over there, we'll need pictures of her to go with the pieces. She's a gorgeous honey blonde. Sun-kissed, I believe the expression is. And Southern. From the Deep South somewhere, a real Southern Belle, what more could you want? In fact, the more I think about it the more I like it, the idea of putting you two together. It might well turn out to be a big profile we could run on its own. But watch out, I hear she's quite an outspoken lady, sassy, flirty, wild about the opposite sex, not too keen on her own. But see if you can get her to take you out and about a bit, show you the wild spots of Manhattan. Do you good. You could leave next week, as soon as you've found somewhere to stay. Why don't you take a few days off to prepare yourself? Go down and see your family for the weekend, tell them all about your exciting new assignment. Bet they'll be proud of you . . ."

The sad look of irony which flashed across Tessa's face did not escape Candy and she instinctively reached across to take the other woman's hand and give it a squeeze. "You never talk about your family—" she began. But Tessa cut her short. "No, I never do," and then switched abruptly to, "So what are they wearing in New York these days?"

Two days later, as she rode out to Heathrow in a taxi, she made a promise to herself: New York, here I come and I'm going to have a great time.

She arrived in New York and went straight from Kennedy Airport to an address on the Upper West Side where she was to rent a room in the apartment of a friend of a friend.

His name was Larry Parker and he had thick glasses through which he peered at her as she stood in his hall wondering which room was hers.

"What about tonight?" he asked, looking her up and down in a way she was not at all sure she felt comfortable with, although he looked harmless enough. "You got dinner all sorted out? My friend Hank's coming over. We're going to have a few beers and watch TV and maybe send out for Chinese. You're welcome to join us." He looked hopeful.

"I said I'd go over to my friend Nancy's. We've got a lot to catch up on."

He wasn't much good at hiding his disappointment, but he tried.

"So, you wanna take a shower, freshen up a little before you go? It's right down the hall before you get to my room. Know how to get to Nancy's from here?"

She nodded.

"Well, you take care now. We got a guy on the loose in this town. He's runnin' around killin' women—"

"—with beauty spots?" Tessa interrupted.

"Yeah, matter of fact that's exactly it. They heard 'bout him over in England already?"

"No, no, my cab driver said something about it on the way in from the airport."

"Yeah, well, I guess it's on their minds. Happening all the

time. They drop a girl off, drive off into the night, next thing they read it in the *Daily News* she's been found with her throat cut. Only connection is they all got beauty spots."

"So I'm all right then?"

He gave her a tentative grin.

"Yeah, but like I said, you take care even so. See you later. If you change your mind about dinner, we'll be here."

He went out whistling. Whistling rather well, in fact. Not a song she recognized, but whatever it was, she knew it was in tune and ten minutes later, as she stood under the shower, she could still hear him.

She spent the following morning setting up her offices at Larry's apartment and then put in a call to Honey Winslow only to find that she was out of town and wouldn't be back for a few days.

In order not to waste any more time she called the photographer who would be taking the pictures of Honey to accompany the profile. Maybe he'd be able to fill her in on her elusive subject.

She called him at PIA—Photo International Agency, a huge photojournalists' cooperative like Magnum or Sygma—of which he was a member and, in a brief conversation, arranged to meet with him the following evening at his apartment on Riverside Drive on the Upper West Side. He apologized for not being able to talk longer—there'd been another murder, a model this time, someone he knew he'd taken pictures of in the past. He wanted to dig them out. The police were keeping the details close to their chest.

"Does Honey Winslow have a beauty spot?" Tessa asked him on impulse.

For a beat there was silence, then he whistled softly down the line.

"Well, I'm damned! It just so happens that she has . . . See you tomorrow, Tessa, looking forward to it."

She hung up, smiling. She liked the sound of Jack Fern. Maybe she really was going to have a good time.

CHAPTER 10

When Jack Fern decided it was crazy to keep on laying out four hundred dollars a month for an apartment he never used more than a few days in every month, he knew his decision was a throw-back to his mother's paranoia about their holiday home when he was a kid. To call it a holiday home was being generous. It was a boat-house, really, by a lake on the land of some old millionaire, who charged his father a small fortune to lease it. The idea was that they would spend the summers there, basking in the sun, swimming in the lake, going for long hikes and picnicking in the forests, enjoying boat trips up and down the lake. The shack was sheltered from the sun by high pines which loomed over it casting oppressing shadows. The lake was covered in green slime; nobody in their right mind would want to take a dip in it. Anyone who ventured a walk in the forest was set upon by the millionaire's dogs. The Ferns did not own a speedboat. And on top of everything, the lake was only about seven miles from their home in the small town in upstate New York. It wasn't even as if they were going anywhere. But no matter how much Sarah Fern nagged her husband to give up the lease and put the money that they spent on it to better use, he refused. Five years went by and still Jim Fern wouldn't change his mind.

Jack hardly knew his father. This was because he never saw him. Jim Fern was a night security guard for the millionaire who rented him the shack. He started patrolling the grounds around ten-thirty every night and returned home just before daybreak when he fell into bed to sleep till noon. By the time Jack came home from school, he was gone again. The grounds he patrolled were not extensive and indeed nobody knew why the old man bothered to hire a security guard at all. Jim Fern clearly knew, but he wasn't telling anyone.

His mother, a sad, quiet little woman, who wept when she listened to music on the radio in the evening, gave piano lessons in the front sitting room. She was an extraordinarily gifted player whose talent went unappreciated until one day she was heard practicing by the millionaire, who had come to look for her husband. He made her play for him for the best part of two hours and then asked if she would entertain his house guests that evening after dinner. So while Jim Fern wandered about the grounds outside in the rain, in a rage (for some reason he had been dead against his wife going to the big house), Sarah Fern, dressed in a soft lilac wool dress two sizes too small, hastily borrowed from a neighbor, spent one of the happiest nights of her life. Every piece she played was received with requests for more. The fourteen-year-old Jack went with her and sat quietly upstairs in a gallery from which he could look down on the room where his mother was playing. He watched her and saw her relaxed and happy for the first time. She was alive and glowing, and she played on and on as if she were caught up in some kind of whirlwind which would not let her fingers rest. And then something happened which Jack would remember for days to come. He heard the slam of the front door at the bottom of the sweeping marble staircase somewhere behind him. Then Sarah Fern's music was interrupted by a tall redhead in a fur coat who rushed into the room. Jack saw the man who had invited his mother to play rise to greet the redhead, extending his arms toward her only to find them filled with the coat. Then Jack noticed a change in his mother. Her hands were frozen above the keys and she was staring at the woman. A look of terror flashed across her face and, like her glowing expression only a few seconds before, this was something he had never associated with his mother. The look was fleeting and the next moment she had composed herself enough to rise and smile at the redhead. But the redhead didn't smile back. Sarah Fern was out of the house in fifteen minutes, edging her car gingerly down the long, dark unfamiliar drive to the highway with Jack hunched up on the passenger seat beside her. Sarah was never asked to play at the big house again.

A few weeks after the incident, the parents of one of her piano pupils called to tell her they couldn't pay their bill, so would she take something in lieu of money? She told them not to be so stupid, they could pay later when they had the money, but they insisted and turned up at the Fern house clutching a battered little Kodak camera and a home-made chocolate cake. Sarah took one look at the couple and knew there was no way she could go on saying it didn't matter. They were proud people, they wouldn't take charity, but they wanted their daughter to continue her piano lessons. When Jack came home from school, she showed him the camera. "Learn how to take pictures with this," she told him, "and you'll be able to capture anything you want and look at it forever." And Jack knew that what he wanted to capture was the glowing look on her face when she played the piano at the big house. And also the look of terror which followed when the redhead appeared.

A classmate in high school taught Jack to develop and print photographs in his parents' kitchen. He discovered pretty early on that his real interest was in taking pictures of people, trying to capture what they were thinking, what they were really like, their emotional side, their feelings underneath the surface. He reckoned to himself that being a photographer posed much more of a challenge than painting a picture. An artist painting a portrait could determine the expression and feeling he wanted portrayed in his subject's face in advance. If he were a good painter, he merely had to transfer that picture from his mind's eye onto the canvas. A photographer had to wait until the expression he wanted appeared on a person's face and then catch it. But still he had to know what he wanted, what he was looking for, every bit as much as the painter did. And he had to be a whole lot quicker off the mark.

Jack started hanging round the offices of the local paper hoping for tips from the photographers working there. One of them told him about the three Cs—the Composition, the Communi-

cation and the Clicking of the shutter. Jack found himself con-
centrating on the most abstract of the three: communication.
His photos had to communicate to the viewer the anguish, the
pain, the joy, the anticipation he himself was witnessing whenever he clicked the shutter. Anyone looking at his photos must
see what he had seen and, more important, feel what he had
felt, understand the situation which had moved him to take the
picture. His photographs would therefore always only be as
interesting as his own perception.

It was one of these quick changes of expression which se-
cured for him his first newspaper photograph. One Saturday
the picture editor sent all his photographers over to a blazing
warehouse which was threatening to spread and destroy a local
mill and consequently had no one to cover the local beauty
contest. Jack was watching the fire when he heard one of the
photographers mention this. He raced home, grabbed his camera and hid it under his sweater as he entered the dance hall
where the girls were lining up. He never knew what made him
decide to concentrate on one particular girl throughout the
contest. There was nothing about her which indicated that she
might turn out to be the winner, except that *she* clearly thought
it was a cinch. Jack thought he had never seen such a con-
ceited, smug, superior expression. He snapped away, caring less
and less as time went by whether anyone would challenge his
right to take pictures. The girl soon became aware of him and
flashed her gushing smiles his way. He never left her alone and
suddenly realized what he was doing. He was banking on the
fact that she would lose. He was right. The judge announced
the winners from the third runner-up. It wasn't her; she continued to smirk confidently. But her name was read out next. She
hadn't won. She was second. This was the moment Jack was
waiting for. He clicked furiously. A faintly bewildered expression filtered onto her face followed by a slow dawning of real-
ization, then the face began to crumple as she almost gave in to
tears until rage took over and she turned to glare at the girl
who had won. For a split second Jack thought she was going to
spit, but she composed herself and the little rosebud mouth
stretched itself into a smile again. But the eyes continued to
glint and Jack continued to catch them. He turned in a series of
eight photographs of the girl to the picture editor who ran the
whole story. The text was harmless, an attempt to point out the

agony encountered by the contestants, but Jack's pictures said it all. He had managed to include some of the other girls in the background and it was clear they had none of the mean-spiritedness of his main subject.

Jack was on his way, although he didn't really know it. Sarah and Jim Fern insisted that he finished High School and that meant another year before he could attempt to take pictures for a living. He contented himself with practicing, shooting as wide a variety of material as he could find: sports photography and athletics, where he learned to pit his talents against those of speeding athletes to record their split-second moments of glory; parties, still-lifes, parades, buildings, church suppers, weddings, funerals. His pictures were praised all over town and printed frequently in the paper. But Jack was bored, and the more he tried to pretend to himself he didn't know the reason why, the more frustrated he became. The one thing his pictures lacked was violence. The only deaths Jack had ever photographed was when he sneaked into the morgue to shoot a few stiffs. He knew he was becoming tired of his gentle hometown material; he wanted to take pictures of scandal, action, brutality, drama, material which would get the adrenaline going, material with an edge—real anguish and poverty rather than the synthetic, sentimental, cosy country life which surrounded him. Not since he'd captured the over-confident beauty queen eighteen months earlier had Jack encountered real shock. And, much as he despised himself for it, he wanted to, even if it was just in the eyes of someone caught in a road smash.

It never occurred to him that it would be he who was in for a shock and that in its aftermath he would leave his hometown forever.

It struck him one weekend that he had not spent enough time photographing the rather spectacular landscape surrounding his home. He decided to hitch a ride out to the estate his father patrolled at night and wander around taking in the scenery, photographing the wildlife on the lake. His father had never told him he was welcome to go there, but then he'd never forbidden him either. Jack arrived at the grounds at about three o'clock in the afternoon and started to wander down the drive. He avoided the house and veered off down a footpath toward the lake. Suddenly he saw a figure emerge from the wood on the far side of the lake. He was convinced it was his father, which was strange because Jack knew he didn't come on duty till about six-thirty. Then he saw the man making for their shack by the lake and realized it must be his father. He'd join him there.

It took Jack a good forty-five minutes to walk the whole way round the lake to the shack and as he approached it he noticed smoke coming from the little brick chimney. He therefore anticipated the blazing fire which greeted him as he quietly pushed the door, but he was totally unprepared for the scene in front of it. His father was lying on his back on the rug, totally naked. Crouched over him, also naked, was the redhead who had interrupted Sarah Fern's piano playing. She knelt astride him, her bottom hovering over his face, her breasts brushing his stomach as she moved her mouth up and down his erect penis. For a second she lifted her head to laugh and Jack took her picture. He knew exactly what would follow. She heard the click and her expression turned to shocked horror as she stared at him, her chin resting on Jim Fern's penis. The support collapsed the moment Jim saw his son. He pushed the redhead aside and lunged toward Jack, who continued to shoot the ridiculous naked figures. His father was on his feet and coming at him, his now limp penis long and swinging between his legs. Jack, panicked into mechanically shooting film, stupidly marveled at his father's equipment at the same time. Suddenly the redhead began to laugh. She rolled over and over on the rug in front of the fire, clapping her hands in the air, bringing them down to squeeze her breasts as if she thought that might arrest her uncontrollable laughter. Jim Fern stopped, confused, not knowing whether to grab his son or the redhead. But the redhead stumbled to her feet and came toward Jack. "Take my picture," she demanded and started to run her hands up and down her body, tweaking her nipples at the camera. Mesmerized, Jack released the camera to let it hang by its strap around his neck. The redhead moved forward and began to rub her naked body against him, grabbing his hair and plunging her tongue into one of his ears. The next thing he knew he was being flung out of the shack and as he started to run off along the side of the lake, he heard his father's voice yelling, "That's my son, Goddamnit. My son, don't you understand? That's Sarah's boy."

Jack was too shaken up to think about hitching a ride back

home so he walked. It took him three hours and gave him time
to calm down. OK, so he'd been shocked, but once he had had
time to think about it, he found he was beginning to admire his
father. Who'd have thought the old son of a gun . . . all those
years. No wonder they never used the holiday home. His father
had been having his holiday up there every day probably. He
knew he ought to feel badly on his mother's account, but that
redhead just seemed to make sense. She sure was a whole lot
more appetizing than his mother, better even than the pictures
in the girlie magazines stashed beneath his bed. He rushed to
develop the pictures as soon as he got home, sneaking into the
little larder off the kitchen which he used as a darkroom. He
heard his mother come in halfway through the evening and
called out to her not to disturb him, he'd get his own dinner.
He hung the prints up to dry and dragged himself up to bed,
carelessly forgetting to lock the door. When he awoke the next
morning, the euphoria of the night before had gone. The
thought of facing his father filled him with dread. He heard his
mother downstairs in the kitchen, heard her footsteps going
towards the larder . . .

He raced downstairs, past his parents' bedroom, barely taking in the open door through which he could see the empty bed
—his father had not returned. He found his mother in the larder staring up at the pictures. To his horror, Jack's first instinct
was to rush upstairs and get his camera to take a picture of her
shattered face. He half thought she might try to comfort him
about the shock of his own discovery or even question him as to
why he had taken the pictures. But she said nothing. Very
slowly she unclipped the photographs and gently laid them out
on the shelf. Then she pushed past him and he heard her going
upstairs. She returned with something in her hand which she
placed beside one of the pictures. Jack moved to see what it was
and found it was another photograph, a snapshot of two beautiful girls of about seventeen or eighteen. One was his mother
and the other was the redhead. There was a vague resemblance.
"Would you believe I was as pretty as she is—once?" was all his
mother said before she left the kitchen. A few moments later he
heard her begin to play the piano.

For the next few weeks all Jack seemed to hear was his father's raised voice, his mother's weeping and the sound of that
piano. His father never mentioned the day at the shack and

when Jack tried to raise the issue, he threatened to confiscate his camera. When summer came, his mother told him they were sending him away to stay with his aunt, his father's sister, in Westchester County. Soon after he arrived, she wrote him a long letter, the only one he ever received from her in his life, telling him the redhead had once been her closest childhood friend who had run away from home when she was seventeen. She, Sarah, had been engaged to his father at the time and she had caught them together then, all those years ago. Till that night when the redhead had walked in on her piano playing at the big house, Jack's mother had never known that her friend had even returned to the neighborhood, let alone as the millionaire's girlfriend. Jack's mother went on to tell him that his father had tried to get Joan, that was her name, to run away with him, that somehow the millionaire had found out and fired his father, who had now disappeared. The only good news was that the millionaire had hired her to play for his guests on a regular basis. She was earning good money. She would send for Jack soon.

But Jack never went back. Aged only sixteen, he got a job as a photographer on the local paper in his aunt's town. From there he moved to New York where he hustled relentlessly till he was taken on by one of the big wire agencies. He was sent to Vietnam for two years where it scared him that he became so obsessed with taking pictures of death. He concentrated on the expressions of the dying, the final expression followed by the face of death itself.

His pictures won prizes and when he returned to New York, he was taken on by a big photographic cooperative with offices all over the world. He traveled extensively wherever his work as a freelance photojournalist took him—Europe, Africa, back to Southeast Asia, Australia, twice even to Russia. Eventually he requested to be given assignments only in America, but the sheer size of his home country still required him to be away from home three weeks out of every month. And he had a home now, had had one for nearly a year, an apartment way up on the Upper West Side of Manhattan, overlooking Riverside Drive with a stunning view of the Hudson. It wasn't that expensive, but it wasn't cheap either and since he knew there wasn't likely to be any let-up in his traveling, he might as well let it for the rest of the year. He wasn't supposed to sub-let, but what the hell, everyone did. He hadn't the first clue how to go about it, but he knew where to start.

He called Doodle.

She picked up on the first ring.

"Hi, Fern. Haven't heard from you in a while. You need something, right?"

He could picture her, a younger version of Miss Moneypenny in the James Bond films, telephone crooked between her shoulder and ear, both hands doodling away in front of her. Ambidextrous Doodle. Her real name was something like Beatrice, but everyone called her Doodle because she did, all day, all of the time. No one could ever make head or tail of them. Telephone messages were handed over half-obliterated by squiggles, but everyone forgave her because Doodle was a gem. She would do anything for anybody and was quite the most sought-after person in the New York cooperative which sold Jack's pictures. No one ever let her near the pictures themselves because no one wanted to see their prints covered in doodles, but everything else was her responsibility.

"You want to rent your apartment? Is it clean? Do you have enough plates, pots and pans? Is there a doorman? Do you have plants? Will they need looking after? I'd better come over and sort it out." Which is exactly what Jack hoped she would say.

She breezed in twenty minutes later with details of a new assignment.

"Where is it this time? Alaska?"

"Tulsa, Oklahoma. You'll be back in no time. Sure you want to go ahead with the rental?"

Jack was sure and Doodle went into action.

"Sort out the stuff you want to take and start packing," she ordered him. "Everything you don't need we'll put in this closet," and she produced from her purse a large padlock, which she proceeded to start fixing onto the closet door.

"You have to move out today, Jack, otherwise you never will. Tomorrow I'll have someone come over and clean the place and I'll go shopping to buy the things you don't have. Looks like you only got one saucepan in the entire kitchen. I'll call a rental agency first thing in the morning, have them come over and take a look, see what they figure you'll get for it. How long do you want to rent it for? Six months? Why don't we just advertise? Forget the agency, cut them out. Start getting your camera bags together. What's this locked door?"

"My darkroom."

"Well, you can't take it with you. You use the one at the office anyway. Can we store the stuff in here? Get on the telephone and book yourself a hotel room. For three nights. You leave for Tulsa tomorrow. When you return for the odd night, we'll get you fixed up with a room in a nice little hotel I know in this neighborhood. You like this neighborhood or would you rather move downtown?"

She prattled on and on and Jack grinned to himself as he collected his stuff together. Doodle came on as a raving eccentric, but when it came to getting people organized she was Little Miss Efficiency. By seven o'clock that night he was checking into a hotel room having handed the keys to his apartment to her, knowing full well she wouldn't allow him near the place till he moved back into it again.

"I'll pick up the mail. I'll take the plants to my place and look after them there. Seems like they need a vacation anyways. You don't need to worry about a thing. When you get back from Tulsa I'll have someone handing you a fistful of dollars a month for that place. Now let me make a note to send you a copy of the inventory . . ."

Tessa left Larry mooching around the apartment the night of her appointment with Jack Fern. He'd made his pitch, "You got dinner all sorted out?," and she'd refused as politely as she knew how. At least this time she had a genuine excuse. Nothing could be more legitimate than a meeting with the photojournalist with whom she would be working over the next few weeks. It was pure business, surely Larry would understand that. She waved goodbye at the elevator and wondered if he would still be standing at the front door when she arrived at Jack Fern's apartment building.

When he opened the door, Tessa knew without a shadow of a doubt that she would go to bed with him. Men like this one didn't come along every day.

She was almost certain it would be that night. What she didn't bargain for was the fact that it would be within the hour. Almost immediately, it became clear the man had nothing else on his mind.

He didn't exactly look like an uncontrollable rapist. For a start he wasn't tall, but he had a pair of sensational shoulders. His chest was quite broad, his legs slender, his sweater and jeans looked custom made for his body. His sneakers were filthy. His hair was thick, black and glossy. His eyes were almost black too and glistened beneath curling lashes. It was the eyes and the way his mouth curled which told her what was on his mind.

"Looking for Jack Fern?" he asked her.

"Yes, I am, is he . . . ?"

"You got him."

"Oh, hello, I'm Tessa Fitzgerald, we spoke on the telephone, we said we'd meet tonight to talk about the Honey Winslow job, perhaps you've forgotten, I could always come back another . . ." Why was she babbling in such an idiotic way?

He had his arm under her elbow. She felt herself being propelled across a bleak, empty hall into a vast room. Two huge windows faced her, no curtains. Polished wooden boards on the floor. To the left a fireplace broke the harsh expanse of white wall, to the right bookshelves reached from floor to ceiling. There were very few books. Instead huge blow-up photographs were propped up on alternating shelves. Tessa started to move across to look at them, but he steered her toward a sofa in front of one of the windows, its back to the door.

It must be a full moon, thought Tessa. It was uncommonly bright even though he hadn't turned on a light and it was almost eight o'clock at night. He released her gently into the depths of the sofa and bent to pick up her feet and rest them on the low coffee table in front of the window.

"What'll you drink?"

"Do you have any wine? White wine?"

He came back with a bottle of ice-cold Chablis, already opened, a wine glass for her and a large Scotch and water for himself. He flopped down beside her and gestured toward the wine.

"Help yourself."

When she leaned back with the glass in her hand, she found his head in her lap, a lazy, teasing expression on his face.

"Now, listen . . ."

"I'm listening . . ."

"What is it? Are you tired or something?" The sarcasm

didn't come across as strong as she'd intended, but it was there all right.

"Sure, I'm tired. I'm tired and depressed and a little . . . well, never mind. I just liked the sound of your voice on the telephone. And you must have liked mine, otherwise you wouldn't have come over here in the first place."

She looked down and saw he was grinning up at her. His head was becoming heavy on her thighs. Warm, heavy and not entirely unpleasant. This was all wrong. They should be sitting at opposite ends of the sofa making animated conversation, talking about Honey Winslow, exchanging stories about their work. Yet somehow work was the last thing Tessa felt like discussing. She looked around her. The place felt empty. There was nothing in the room except a sofa, a coffee table and them.

"You're a photographer." What a stupid thing to say. She knew he was. That was why she was here, wasn't it?

"If you like."

What was *that* supposed to mean?

Silence.

"I'd like some more wine."

"Help yourself."

He wasn't about to move. She leaned forward, reaching for the bottle. Her breasts touched his face, he raised his head and nestled against them for an instant. To her surprise, she didn't stiffen, but withdrew her hand to stroke his hair. He didn't react, just slowly lowered his head to bury it against her stomach. She smoothed his hair, black and soft, away from his face and let her fingers wander around his ear. Slowly she eased his face away from her stomach and ran her index finger over his eyes, closing them, down his nose to run back and forth across his mouth until he opened his lips and started to suck it gently, running his tongue rapidly against the back of her long nail.

She drew his face up to hers and let his tongue into her mouth to meet hers. Their lips didn't meet for several seconds and then she felt him try to take her whole head into his mouth. The inside of her mouth filled with a warm wetness identical to the feeling between her legs. He was sprawled across her in such a way that she knew the sofa was getting the benefit of his hard on. She shifted slightly and felt it pressing against her left hip. To her amazement, he suddenly rolled over and lay across her on his back, flaked out, one arm dangling down, the other reaching up to stroke the back of her neck.

Tessa couldn't stop. Her hand went straight to his zip. She took out his penis and held it, expecting him to stop stroking her neck and press her head down. He didn't. She ran her hand up and down, pausing now and then to find the throbbing path along which to trail her nail, barely touching it. He shivered. She reached below, took his balls in her hand and squeezed gently. He gripped her hair at the back of her neck and held on hard. With his other hand, he reached for hers. Together they worked his penis furiously and she wondered somewhere at the back of her mind if it might not come off altogether.

He let go just before he came, but she let her hand stay there, bathing in it, smearing it all over her wrist, in his hair, on his thighs. He brought her hand up to his face and held it against his cheek.

"Like I said," he murmured, "help yourself." Then he slipped off her and lay on the floor. She knelt beside him and took off his shoes. She pulled his jeans and pants off him and left him there. She went to stand by the window and felt him come up behind her to grip her shoulders and bury his head in her neck. It began to pour with rain outside till the windows were just a sheet of water, almost obliterating the buildings across the street.

She felt his hands come around and cup her breasts. They moved down to press against her stomach, forcing her buttocks back against his nakedness. Slowly, he unzipped her jeans, pushing his hand under the elastic of her briefs, finding her mound and kneading it gently with the flat of his palm. She felt herself about to sink and he flung his other arm around her, holding her up from under her armpit. He reached lower and his finger swam into her. He withdrew it fast and plunged again. She shuddered and arched back against him as his finger inserted itself time and time again. She felt him look up and stare out of the window over her shoulder. They bucked back and forth together. Her jeans still covered her buttocks, but she could feel him kneading against her.

When she came, he pressed his whole hand against her and held her until she withdrew it to hold it against her cheek. When he released her, she fell to the ground.

She was aware after several minutes that he was no longer in the room. She turned her head. It was pitch black. He must have turned the light out in the hall. Mechanically she began to grope around for her clothes in the dark and then realized she had not even undressed. Suddenly she couldn't wait to get out. She edged her way across the room like a blind person, arms extended in front of her, feeling in the dark.

As she found the door to the apartment and opened it, she heard him laughing softly down the hall.

"Come again soon," he called as she stepped into the elevator.

Going down, she found she was shaking. It was all very well having adolescent fantasies of making love with a complete stranger, but in reality it was nerve-wracking dealing with the after-effects. Still, he wasn't a complete stranger, at least she knew his name.

Except that she didn't. The man posing as Jack Fern closed the door behind her and went back to the sofa to pour himself another Scotch.

"Tessa, you won't believe this but there's someone called Doodle for you on the telephone. *Doodle?* Is that a name or what?"

Tessa restrained herself from grabbing the receiver from him and reached out casually to take the call.

"Hello," she said cautiously, "this is Tessa Fitzgerald."

"Oh, Tessa, I'm calling from the PIA photographic agency. I just can't tell you how sorry I am. I plumb forgot to call you. He went off in such a rush and we had to let his apartment and all . . ."

"Who went off?"

"Jack. Jack Fern. He had to rush off to Oklahoma yesterday. I was supposed to call and cancel your meeting with him last night. I'm Doodle by the way. I guess you showed up and he wasn't there, I'm just so sorry, let's see if we can reschedule . . ."

"He was in Oklahoma last night? Jack Fern wasn't in his apartment last night?"

"No, that's what I'm trying to explain to you. He's away in Oklahoma for a week. I rented his apartment out. I called the guy around ten to explain you might show up. Crazy, of course, far too late. Your appointment with Jack was for seven or eight, wasn't it? Anyway, there was no answer."

No answer. So her mystery lover had gone out after she'd left.

"Hey, Tessa, you still there? You want to reschedule?"

"Yes, yes, of course. Maybe Honey Winslow will be back in town then too. Doodle, can I ask you something? Whom did you rent Jack's apartment to?"

"Why? You want it? You have a place to stay, don't you? You gave Jack the number."

"Yes, it's just I want to go over there and leave some material for him to look at on his return. It'd be nice if I knew the tenant's name, so I could give them to him to keep." Tessa was grabbing at any excuse to find out the identity of the man.

"Oh, Jeez, bring it here. I'll keep it for him. Jack probably ain't going back there for a while anyway."

"Oh, that's sweet of you, Doodle, it's just that Jack's apartment is just near here, only five minutes' walk away and I'm *so* busy right now, I really didn't want to have to come downtown . . ."

"Oh, OK, no problem . . . uh-oh, wait a second, I can't remember it. I'll have to call you back. I'll call you at the West End Avenue number, right, once I've looked it up?"

"Thank you *so* much, Doodle. You're so kind."

"Think nothin' of it. Hope we get to meet soon, Tessa. 'Bye now."

As soon as she put the telephone down, Tessa grabbed her coat, rushed down to the street. She needed some fresh air to help her sort out this new development.

When she got back Larry was watching the news on TV.

"Hi, Tessa. They just found another girl murdered. That's the second this week. But listen here, this one they found in our neighborhood, over on Riverside Drive. That's real close, you know. I told you you oughta take care. They found her last night . . . they gotta catch this guy and fast. Hey, Tessa, you got dinner all sorted out?"

Tessa slumped down on the sofa and stared at him.

"They found her last night?"

"Yeah, Riverside Park. Tessa, you OK? You gone all white. By the way, there was a call for you. Doodle again. Can you beat that? *Doodle!* Said to tell you the guy's name was . . . wait a second, I wrote it down . . . boy, another weird name: *Philippe-Josephe 'PJ' Duboise.*"

PART 3

PJ AND HONEY
1960–61

CHAPTER II

At the beginning of the Sixties, PJ began a period of drifting. He had no idea that his mother had attempted suicide. His immediate aim, following that horrendous night when he had caught Callie in the stables, was to put as much distance between himself and *Coinchenier* as possible. He toyed with the idea of going through a mourning period given that it was quite likely he would not see either of his parents for some considerable time but quickly tired of it.

Women weren't a problem. Of course he knew already from the success he'd had in Europe. But now, as he began to drift around the country, moving swiftly from place to place, he found that he drew them to him like a magnet. For whatever disguise he selected, however different he looked from day to day, his eyes never changed. He only had to turn to a woman and stare intently at her for a second or two through his long black lashes and she melted. Better, she often offered him a bed for the night.

His jobs were often menial, whatever he could pick up when he arrived in a town—delivery boy, gas station attendant, elevator operator, barman—and the women he met through them

were a far cry from the Southern Belles who'd come calling at
Coinchenier. But he'd never had much time for *them* in any
case. They'd bored him most of the time with their fey, affected
ways. None of them had been real. None of them except for
Honey Winslow. *White trash,* Callie had called her, but she'd
been something more than that even if it was only a tough
bitch. He'd catch up with her again when he was ready. Meantime he just had to keep on the move. He had long since realized this had nothing to do with keeping away from
Coinchenier. He was just so restless he found he couldn't sleep
nights if he stayed in the same place for longer than a week.

To his amazement, he discovered his monthly allowance had
not been stopped. Surreptitious calls to his bank in New York
revealed that his father's money continued to flood in. And PJ
used it to keep up his various disguises, to be able to travel from
place to place, checking in and out of motels, renting apartments here, studios there, even going so far as a villa in Capri
one summer to support the notion that he was the rich young
son of an Italian contessa.

PJ realized that his father must have learned of his visit to
Coinchenier and his estrangement from Callie. He didn't expect
Perry Jay to try and get in touch with him immediately after
that, but when month after month went by and it became clear
his father was making no effort to find him, PJ began to feel a
little uneasy. Had something happened to Callie? Had his father cut him off? But no, when he checked the bank, his allowance was still arriving on the first of every month. He tried to
reach Mr. Wade, the manager, but he never returned PJ's calls
personally which was odd, although he was always assured by
the staff that everything was in order. He called the various
offices of Bayou Beauty from time to time, disguising his voice
and asking to speak to Perry Jay. Somehow he could not summon up the courage to identify himself. He always said he was
"a friend of Mr. Duboise's son, Philippe, from High School,
trying to get in touch with him. Did they know where he could
be reached?" The minute he mentioned his own name he was
always referred to the Press Office who would inform him that
Mr. Duboise understood his son was "traveling right now, but
if he liked to leave his name and number, they'd have Philippe
get back to him just as soon as he returned."

Looking back on these calls—he always got the same response time after time—PJ had to laugh. *Traveling!* Well, in a way it was true and right now it looked as if he wasn't ever going to arrive anywhere.

But at the end of 1960 he found himself in Los Angeles working once again as a barman. One night a customer asked him for some boiling water and he watched as the man poured it over a shot of brandy and squeezed in some lemon juice.

"Coming down with a cold?" PJ asked conversationally.

"Real stinker," said the guy. "Got a big job tomorrow, don't know how I'm going to get rid of it in time."

"What line of work you in?" PJ asked.

"Make-up," replied the man and PJ only just managed to stop himself saying, "Oh, yes? So's my dad." Instead he asked: "How d'ya mean, make-up?"

"Movies, commercials, TV stuff. Make-up artist, you know? Make the faces up for the camera, see they look good under all them lights. Make 'em look ten, twenty, fifty years older if their part calls for it. 'Scuse me . . ." The man sneezed violently and ordered another brandy. When the bar closed for the night, PJ had to carry him home and found it wasn't too far from the motel where he was staying.

It was more of a weird hunch that his chance meeting with the make-up artist could lead to something, rather than concern for his welfare, which made PJ pay him a visit the next morning. He found the man, whose name was Frank Farmer, in no condition to get out of bed and as he lay there, PJ studied him. Then he asked abruptly: "Where d'you keep your clothes?"

"Over there," replied Frank, too astonished to retreat from such an odd question, "in the closet in the hall."

"And your make-up?"

"My make-up?"

"You know, the stuff you use for your work."

"Aw, that. They keep that at the studio or wherever the location is, but I keep a little stash of it in the bathroom. It's in a black box behind the john."

PJ disappeared. Half an hour later he walked back into the bedroom and Frank gasped. Fumbling with the sheets, he staggered out of bed and dragged himself over to look in a full-length mirror. PJ came to stand beside him.

"I'm outta my skull!" screamed Frank. "I'm seeing double. There's two a me."

But there was only him—and PJ who had been instantly struck by the fact that he and Frank were very similar in terms of size, height and facial bone structure. The only main difference was that Frank had dark reddish-brown hair, even though his eyes were dark and long-lashed like PJ's.

"Well, I dye it a little," Frank confessed, starting to simper. Pansy! thought PJ to himself, echoing his father's old war cry.

"And of course mine's a wig which I just happened to have on me," PJ admitted, pointing to his own newly reddened hair.

"But, it's the face! The face is a dream!" Frank purred, reaching up to stroke PJ's cheek. "Where d'ya learn to use make-up like that? You're a natural."

"At my mother's knee," replied PJ quite truthfully.

It was all so simple from there on. He put Frank back to bed, made him run through the details of the day's work, wrote down a quick resumé of his life—his mother's name, how many brothers and sisters he had, his star sign, favorite foods, his hobbies, the kind of casual conversation he usually made while he was working. Luckily Frank had a pretty good idea of what would be required for the day's work. He had already been primed by the director of the commercial as to what look was wanted for the three or four models who would be taking part. He was able to tell PJ just exactly what to do. Then he reached for a glass of water, swallowed a couple of Bufferin and settled back to spend a day in bed recovering, happy in the knowledge that in the evening PJ would return having done his work for him. He could still bill the agency and, as agreed with PJ, they would share the fee 50/50. It was a whole lot better than losing the job altogether.

What Frank never realized at first was that PJ really was a natural and he did the job twice as well as Frank himself would have done it. Frank recovered from his cold, but before too long he fell ill once again. Frank confessed to PJ that he picked up viruses all the time and each time he did so, PJ went to work for him. One thing led to another. PJ's work was so much better than Frank's that he started getting more and more bookings—people just assumed Frank was improving. PJ upped Frank's rate accordingly until finally Frank reckoned it was just getting too risky for him to work at all. The day would come when someone would figure them for two different people if only, as Frank was forced to confess to himself, because PJ's work was so noticeably superior to his own. Besides, now his rate was so high, getting only 50 per cent out of it when PJ worked for him was almost as much as the 100 per cent he'd been getting before he met PJ.

Inevitably Frank got more and more greedy. After only six weeks he told PJ: "You oughta go to New York, where all them big ad agencies is. Madison Avenue. That's where ya oughta be. Ya'd clean up. *We'd* clean up. Definitely! I ain't too crazy about the city myself, but it's where the action is."

"Is that a fact?" PJ was getting a little tired of Frank always going on about the *action*. It wasn't as if he was sweating his guts out for it himself, just taking a hefty piece of it.

"How d'ya like this guy?" Frank poked him in the arm. "Cash just waitin' to be made and the guy just sits there. Why dont'cha knock it off with the negative waves and take the Red Eye, go check it out. Ya don't score a bundle ya can always come back."

"Tell me about it . . ." PJ didn't even look up.

"Trouble with you is you can't stand the heat."

"I can't, huh?" PJ stood up. The truth of the matter was he couldn't stand Frank Farmer's *heat* anymore. "You got any connections in the East, Frank? Any contacts? Or do I have to hit the town cold?"

"I got plenty names. By the time you've packed your bags I'll have a list for ya. Whatcha say?"

PJ caught the Red Eye to New York that night. Frank Farmer's problem was that he never came back.

"You can lose yourself in Manhattan," the man sitting next to PJ in the Red Eye told him, "believe me, ya want it that way, no one knows you're there. Think about it, Monday to Friday close to four million people ride the subway, but they never see the guy in the booth sellin' 'em the tokens and the guy don't see them, just their hands. Nobody sees faces. You can be anonymous, I'm tellin' ya. It's no place to live. It's like a jungle."

Sounds perfect, thought PJ and, of course, for him it was. He'd been there before, but he'd been passing through. No, he had come back to stay and pretty soon he realized there was no better place for him to live his dual life.

He arrived with the dawning of a new era, the start of a brand new decade, the Sixties. Everyone was raving about the youthful Senator John F. Kennedy and his glamorous young wife, Jackie. PJ adored her.

"Youse a romantic," Barney told him, "youse all the time dreamin' with ya head in da clouds." Barney was PJ's local barman. His bar was right around the corner from the walk-up PJ had rented on 56th Street. P.J. Clarke's and Michael's Pub were also within walking distance, but PJ liked Barney's better. Barney was one of the few people with whom he could be himself.

"Why so nervous? All the time ya nervous. *Relax*, take it easy, have a drink, what ya here for?" But PJ would sit there twitching night after night his first week, tapping his foot impatiently against his barstool. "What's ya name?" Barney asked him. "Going to come in here every night, ya gotta have a name."

"PJ," PJ told him without hesitation.

"Jeez, ya oughta be round the corner. Don't tell me ya last name's Clarke."

"No, it's . . ." PJ stopped himself just in time.

"What's PJ stand for?"

"Phili . . ." Again he stopped himself. He didn't want to broadcast his identity to the whole world.

"Phil. Well, good to know ya, Phil. What'll ya have?"

Frank Farmer's contacts were good. PJ found work almost right away. He used the name Phil Joseph and, despite his youth, everyone was amazed they'd never come across him before, never even heard of him.

But there was one place he refused to work. *Bayou Beauty.* It wasn't too difficult to avoid it. It seemed every make-up artist and his mother were crazy to work on the sessions there. If "Phil Joseph" didn't want those jobs it meant less competition.

He found he was using his father's products all the time. He wondered if Perry Jay ever got to hear such things as the name of a bright new talent among make-up artists. Phil Joseph wouldn't fool him if he heard it . . . and yet? The money was still pouring into his account and one of the first things PJ did was to go to Louis Feder on Fifth Avenue and order a new supply of wigs and hairpieces. The blond wigs were made from German women's hair; the brunette from French and Italian.

American women had too many rinses and permanents, apparently, which made their hair too weak to be used. As PJ strolled around the streets of Manhattan, ideas for disguises flooded in every day. He stared for hours at the mannequins frozen in the windows of Saks, Lord and Taylor, Bergdorf's and found himself unconsciously adopting their poses while he stood there on the sidewalk, head tilted back, arm outstretched, toe pointed. Nobody noticed him. Beside him tramps and bag ladies carried on long conversations with the plastic women in the windows and no one even took any notice of *them*.

Inevitably PJ realized he was going to have to face his father for two reasons. First, he needed his father's financial support for the project he had decided to embark on and second, he wanted news of Callie. His feelings about his mother were confused. He knew it would be a long time before he could bring himself to see her again, if ever, but he had a strange intuition that all was not well. He decided to start off with a trip to the New York offices of *Bayou Beauty,* partially disguised, to see if he could find out any incidental information about his parents, other than the endless stream of meaningless guff which appeared in the Press about his father. He had noticed that his mother never seemed to be at his father's side anymore when Perry Jay was photographed at all the receptions and parties he went to. If he actually hung around the office a while, PJ felt he might just get somebody to spill a few beans.

The offices were on the eleventh floor of a huge building in the midtown section of the Avenue of the Americas. Security was tight. The bank of elevators leading directly to the *Bayou Beauty* floor was cordoned off by a red rope and all visitors had to sign in with the security man and be given a visitor's badge. PJ signed himself in as Willie Franks, posing as an assistant manager of a small department store in Alabama, who had done so well with *Bayou Beauty* products he had been invited to have a guided tour of the Manhattan office by the Press Office if he ever happened to be in the city. He did the "Aw shucks, I knew I shoulda called first" routine, but the guard wearily pinned a visitor's badge on his lapel and ushered him into the first elevator.

The elevator was already crowded and the doors were just about to close when a tall blonde vision in skin-tight black matador pants and a black turtleneck sweater streaked in calling out over her shoulder: "S'me, Mr. Montgomery, Honey Winslow. You know *me*. I don't need a badge. We're old friends now, ain't we?"

"Sure thing, Miss Winslow, but I still think I oughta . . ." Montgomery could be heard mumbling as the door shut in his face.

Honey turned round to beam at everyone else in the elevator.

"Hi, y'all," she announced, her smile even more brilliant than PJ remembered with the help of some newly capped front teeth. She looked straight at him, but if she saw through his disguise she didn't let on. She turned round again and quite deliberately began to wiggle her behind from side to side, tapping her foot impatiently on the floor as the elevator crept up to the eleventh floor. PJ watched as seven pairs of male eyes moved from right to left with each wiggle.

They continued to stare as Honey sailed through reception waving gaily at the girls behind the desk. They didn't notice PJ for a minute or two while they gossiped about Honey.

"Get her!"

"She's here for that new perfume publicity. They're gonna take her picture in the studios up on the fourteenth floor."

"She's real pretty."

"Tough as nails."

"Maybe so, but pretty with it. She'll go far."

"You bet! Word is the old man himself is taking an interest in her."

"You mean . . ."

"That's what I heard. Been screwing her for quite a while now."

"Can I help you, mister?"

PJ gulped.

"No, no, I guess not. I'm sorry," and he backed hurriedly into the elevator. Down in the lobby Montgomery gave him a quizzical look.

"Quick tour, Mr. Franks."

"Well, they seem real busy. Figured I'd take a rain check." PJ took a risk. "Who was that delectable creature who rode up in the elevator with me?"

"Oh, she's delectable all right. That's Honey Winslow, *Bayou Beauty*'s new discovery. Sure does brighten up my day when she comes by."

"How long before she'll be down?"

"Oh, you rascal you, aimin' to take another peek, ain't you now?" Montgomery was beginning to have some fun. "She'll be down in an hour or so, soon as she's had all her pretty pictures taken. You go on over to the coffee shop over there and sit by the window. You'll see her go by when she leaves. Iffen you ain't got better things to do . . ." And he chuckled away to himself as he approached a new batch of visitors.

A week later, PJ went back and this time he marched straight up to the gossips on the reception desk and asked for his father.

"Do you have an appointment, Mr. . . . ?" They didn't even bother to look up.

"No, but he'll see me."

"I'll ask his assistant to step out. May I have your name, please?"

"Duboise."

"No, *your* name, please, sir."

"I just told you. Philippe-Josephe Duboise. I'm Mr. Duboise's son."

All heads swiveled. Eyelashes fluttered. He was entreated to take a seat, was told Melissa would be right out.

In fact it was Perry Jay himself who hurried out to collect him.

"My, my," he cried cheerfully for the sake of the watching receptionists, "look who's here. Good to see you, son."

"Hi, Papa. Please don't call me son." PJ decided it was high time a few things were changed in his relationship with his father.

"Well, yes, OK, but you might want to think about calling me Father or Dad instead of that French shit . . ."

"Dad, *pas devant* . . ."

PJ rolled his eyes toward the receptionists who were sitting gaping, listening to the family reunion.

"NO FRENCH . . ." yelled Perry Jay, but he smiled too and they both laughed at the old family joke.

"I don't know, Philippe," said his father, throwing an arm around his son's shoulders and propelling him toward his office. "We don't hear from you in a year and now you turn up out of the blue just in time for your twenty-first birthday. We'll have to think about throwing you a really big bash."

"At *Coinchenier*?" PJ asked nervously, and was surprised at his father's emphatic reaction.

"No! Not at *Coinchenier*. Hick place. Much better to do it in New York, where all the action is."

The same old corny line. "But what about Maman?" PJ asked.

"Precisely. It'd upset her to have it at *Coinchenier*. Remember the last birthday party we had there?"

Callie's disastrous fiftieth. PJ shuddered. "So how is Maman?"

"Pretty good. Pretty good."

"Does she come to New York?"

"Never."

"So you go down there?"

"Not much."

"So you don't see her very often?" But Perry Jay wasn't going to let this go on any further. If PJ didn't know what had happened to his mother so much the better. He changed the subject.

"So here you are, son, sorry, Philippe. Does this mean you've decided to join me?"

"Absolutely not."

Perry Jay recoiled. The jovial manner was dropped in an instant. The guard between father and son was re-erected.

"And I don't want a twenty-first birthday party either."

"Well, that's just as well since you aren't going to get one, no, sir."

"But I do want a twenty-first birthday present."

"You've got a damn nerve . . ."

"Want it to get out Perry Jay Duboise is as mean as hell, won't even give his son a . . . ?"

"You blackmailing me, boy? 'Cause if you are you can cut it out right now. Waste of time. OK, you're entitled to a little present. How much d'you have in mind?" he asked wearily.

"A magazine."

"I'm sorry?"

"A magazine, Papa, sorry, Dad, I want you to buy me a magazine."

"Buy one yourself. I've been paying your allowance. I know you're not that broke."

"No, I mean a magazine to run. The whole kaboosh. Doesn't

need to be a big one, I want to edit a magazine, Dad. I've been thinking about it for some time. There must be a publication out there in bad shape, something you could pick up for a song and I can reshape."

"Damn pansy thing to want to do."

"Yeah, maybe, but it is what I want."

"Will you run Bayou Beauty ads for free?"

"DAD!"

"Well, will you?"

"Let me get started first and then I'll think about it."

"Gotta keep it in the family, son."

PJ ignored the "son." He wasn't home and dry yet.

"But there's one condition, Dad."

"Philippe, gimme a break here . . ."

"Once you've bought me a magazine you have to leave me alone to run it without any interference."

"Leave you alone? Be glad to. What do I want with some pansy magazine and the disappointment of a son who's running it? Give me some free space for Bayou and you're on your own."

"Don't you even want to know what kind of magazine I'm going to turn it into?"

"I couldn't care diddlyshit. Now get outta here and stop wasting my time. Leave your number with Melissa and I'll have her call you with the details when I've closed the deal. Oh, and by the way, *Philippe*," he gave his son's name a particularly sarcastic accent, "don't expect me to keep on paying your allowance. You want to be left alone, then you will be. And it could be I won't interfere, as you put it, when I come to draw up my will either. Now git . . ."

Perry Jay had his lawyer cast his eye around town and finally bought his son a small trade publication with sleazy offices around Union Square whose circulation had dwindled to below profitability.

PJ was ecstatic. It was perfect for his needs. He was the proprietor, now all he had to do was find an editor to run the thing. He had lied to his father. He didn't want to go near the place himself, he wanted to remould the whole thing from afar. That was going to be part of the fun, that way he could contribute material himself under a pseudonym. He wanted his identity kept away from it, he wanted to be able to continue his disguises. The staff might quit when they realized just how drastically he planned to change the content of the magazine, but that was too bad.

For what PJ had in mind was an erotic magazine. *The* magazine for lovers. But a class act, not just smut and beaver. High quality photographs and literate features and fiction with a sensual, erotic slant.

He met his editor at a party. Susan Walker was a tall butch brunette and currently editor of a highly successful literary magazine. The next day PJ had his father's lawyer call and offer her double her salary to be his editor. The details of the job would be waiting for her in an envelope at the bar at the Sherry-Netherland at six o'clock that evening. Without revealing his identity or even making his presence known to her, PJ watched from a corner of the bar as she opened the envelope and read the contents. When he saw that her eyebrows failed to rise even a fraction of an inch, he knew he had his editor. For she had been informed that while she would never meet her proprietor, she would be expected to obey his every whim. She would have to carry out his instructions to the letter from day one of her employment. And not until she started work on the magazine would she know the nature of its contents. She would be the editor in name only.

She was hired the next day and the old editor fired.

Now all PJ needed was a name for the magazine and a face and body for the cover of the first issue.

And it was the second problem he decided to tackle first.

It was easy to get Honey's address. When he took it down from Melissa, PJ thought it sounded familiar and realized it was the same one he had written down that time in his father's apartment just prior to the last time he had seen his mother.

PJ took a cab down to the Village and climbed the two flights of stairs in the walk-up till he got to her apartment. Even before she opened the door he could smell something sweet wafting at him from her tub. She must have just settled in to soak after a hard day's work when he rang her doorbell. He heard her say, "Aw, shit!," as she looked through the security peep-hole in the door to see who was there. She opened the door to him wearing nothing but a towel hastily wrapped around herself.

She retreated into the bathroom to dry herself and called out:

"Fix yourself a drink. Second cabinet on the left in the living room."

She reappeared, wafting into her tiny living room in a totally transparent violet-colored *peignoir* with matching violet ruffles and frills at the neck and sleeves. PJ winced inwardly at the sheer tackiness of the robe.

"So what's a little boy like you doing in the big bad city?" She poured herself a liberal amount of vodka and PJ noticed she drank it neat with just a couple of cubes of ice.

"Do you drink that much every night, Honey? You'll get old before your time. Don't you have to think about your looks, your face? Do you photograph well in the morning with a hangover?"

"Have I taken one sip? Have I even touched my first drink of the evening and already he's talking about a hangover. So happens I'm expecting company and I may drink a little, but it's none of your Goddamn business."

"Well, in fact it is," PJ told her. "I want you looking good tomorrow morning."

"You're adorable to be so concerned," she said sarcastically.

"You're going to have to look good for the pictures."

"I'm not working tomorrow as a matter of fact."

"Yes, you are. For me," he told her.

"PJ, what in hell you talking about? You're a little baby boy, you don't even have a job probably—" she hesitated. She hadn't seen him since that time back in Mississippi before he went to Europe. She stopped. "Do you?"

"I run a magazine and I want you for the cover."

"You do WHAT!"

"So, OK, it'll be the first issue, but it's going to be a huge success and the first issue will be a collector's item. Wouldn't you like your face and body to make history?"

"They already are. Any day now," she added hastily.

"This'll clinch it."

"What's the magazine?"

"It's a high class erotic magazine."

"I don't do pussy."

"Oh, no?" PJ eyed her transparent *peignoir*.

Honey hadn't even sat down yet. She turned to him.

"Look, PJ, it's sweet of you to drop by. I guess you've just arrived in the city and you're looking up old friends in the hope they'll introduce you to new ones. I know how it is—a boy can get lonely, but I'm afraid right now you're going to have to leave. This is New York. You can't behave like a Mississippi hick up here, knocking on people's doors and expecting them to throw them wide open, drop everything and entertain you. What you do is you call first and ask them for a date. Here, I'll give you my number . . . not that I'll have much time to see you. Boy, am I busy . . ."

She was standing close to him now and PJ reached out, almost lazily parted the *peignoir*, ducked his head down and buried it in her snatch.

Honey slapped it away. He caught her wrist as she did so and forced her down onto the couch. He bent his head again and bit her nipples through the violet nylon and before she could do anything else he covered her mouth with his own and nipped at her lips, bruising them, and plunged his tongue into the space between her teeth. He felt her tongue connect with his and for a while he kissed her passionately and slowly, true PJ style. But he knew the way to treat Honey was rough and as soon as he felt her relax he gave her a shove so she fell off the couch landing heavily on the wooden floorboards. While she struggled to get to her feet, he unzipped his pants and showed her his rock-hard erection.

She didn't realize she was coming toward him and when she was close enough he pulled her roughly to him and lifted her onto him, forcing her legs to wrap around his waist. He stood there, easing her onto his hardened penis, pulling her off, pulling her back on again. She was like a limp rag doll, no longer fighting him. She was going to come at any second, he could feel it, but before she could he hurled her away from him and she landed back on the floor in a heap. Now she was angry again, coming at him like a hissing cat. But he was on her, pinning her to the ground, forcing himself onto her, into her. He wasn't enjoying it, but he could feel her excitement and it spurred him on. He pulled himself out of her and rising up, plunged his penis into her mouth, but only for a second. He wouldn't put it past her to bite hard.

He got to his feet. "Get up," he ordered and when she didn't move, as he'd known she wouldn't, he took her hand and dragged her, half-stumbling, into her bedroom. Still holding her firmly to him, he threw open her clothes closet and rummaged around till he found a little black dress not unlike the one she had worn to Callie's birthday party when his father had raped her.

When she'd changed he selected several expensive pieces of jewelery from her dressing table, gifts no doubt from his father, and threw them at her to put on. She stood up, resplendent in her glory, a sleek model once again, smiling at him, playing for the camera.

For there was a camera now. PJ had brought one and he knew this was the time to bring it out. She dropped her eyes from time to time to his erection and her hand rose instinctively to her breasts. She stood there barefoot and stroked herself, hitching the dress up to give him a peek at her bush from time to time as he clicked the shutter.

But they were exactly the kind of pictures he didn't want for his cover. Coarse, blatant sexuality totally lacking in subtlety. Before she realized what was happening, he had ripped the dress off one of her shoulders and hurled her into a corner. The shock showed in her face, she was taken totally by surprise and slumped slowly down the wall, sinking into a trembling heap.

This was his cover. A rich, classy woman, breathtakingly beautiful, normally out of reach to the average man, reduced to a bruised and vulnerable state, dress torn, feet bare, knees drawn up in a protective position to ward off any further attack.

He took his pictures and left her crouched in the corner. As he walked out the door he ripped his silver identity bracelet from his wrist with the little charm in the shape of a dolphin hanging off it and threw it at her. It had been in his family for two generations, but he didn't want to wear it anymore. It reminded him of Callie. Honey and Callie: both of them liked it rough. "Something for you to remember me by," he shouted. With luck his father would recognize it and it would give the old man a bit of a jolt.

But Honey had the last word: "Come back, PJ. We haven't talked about my fee."

It was raining when he let himself out into the street and as he hurried away he saw a long black limousine draw up to the curb. He watched as his father stepped out, pulled up his collar to shield him from the rain and ran up the steps into Honey's building.

While PJ was watching his father, someone else was watching him. A wet, lank figure stood at the end of the street making a feeble attempt to shelter from the rain under an already soaked awning. Alphonse had seen everything. He had seen PJ go in and come out and now here was Mr. Duboise arriving to pay a visit. Well, soon Honey would have another visitor. As soon as she knew he, Alphonse, was downstairs, she'd send away the others and invite him upstairs.

"Nothing doing," said the doorman. "Miss Winslow won't see anyone. She has a visitor right now."

"Oh, she'll see me," Alphonse told him firmly but politely. "Call up to her, if you will, and tell her that a Mr. Alphonse Lenoir is here to pay her a call."

The doorman shrugged and did as he was asked, but leapt away from the telephone when Honey's raucous voice came screaming down: "I TOLD YOU NO VISITORS AND CERTAINLY NOT HIM!"

"You heard her," the doorman said apologetically. "I guess the entire Village heard her."

"But I'm going overseas. I'm going to Vietnam, she'll want to say goodbye! She may never see me again," implored Alphonse.

"Imagine that," said the doorman, propelling him firmly outside and slamming the door behind him.

Alphonse stood in the rain for a long time staring up at Honey's windows. "When I get back," he whispered, "if I get back, she'll see me then all right . . ."

Eros, as PJ ultimately decided to call his magazine, was not an overnight success, but the first issue established it firmly as an alternative publication with a cult following.

PJ culled the material for the first year's issues from a variety of sources. He maintained that erotica could be found in every walk of life and, continuing to use his disguises, he embarked on a constant search for it. He decided to take work wherever he could find it and look for the erotica as he went, then instruct Susan Walker to put a writer on whatever he found.

Countless occupations presented themselves the minute he started looking—at various times he was a dog-walker, a florist's delivery boy, a librarian, a sales assistant at Rizzoli's on

Fifth Avenue, a hand model (he didn't have particularly beautiful hands, but had no trouble keeping them steady which was a
big plus when the camera came in for the close-up). And he
was prepared to stoop low when the mood took him. He was a
supermarket checker and a night-watchman, a hospital aide
and for one week even a grave-digger. He joined unions and let
his membership lapse. And all the time he remained a loner,
keeping himself to himself, inviting no one back to his apartment.

For every job he had a new disguise and a new identity. For
six months he enrolled at a school for masseurs and for a further six months he was on nodding terms with scores of uni-
formed East Side doormen as he whisked in and out of
buildings, up and down elevators, in and out of the apartments
of rich female clients. They adored his rub-downs, the feel of
his firm hands on their bodies, easing away the aches and pains
in their muscles, but all too often they wanted to turn over and
gaze at his beautiful, dark-eyed face and eventually he had to
pack it in. Yet it made way for another way of life: that of the
lounge lizard. The name Philippe Duboise was sufficiently elegant to get him invited to the chic parties of real high society, a
far cry from the social climbing circles Perry Jay was known in,
if only because he was something of an unknown quantity. A
beautiful, elegant young man, with exquisite manners, a slight
Southern accent and clearly not short of cash (not yet anyway).
He positively *adorned* penthouses in his white tuxedo, but he
was slippery as an eel. Just when it was time to collect a gathering to go to dinner he was nowhere to be seen, slipped away
into the night.

He became a night owl. It suited him. Endless cigarettes,
walking the streets passing tired jazzmen on their way home.
Inevitably he discovered Clubland starting with the Peppermint
Lounge in 1962. Every night it was *"Meet me, baby, down at
45th Street, where the Peppermint Twisters meet."* His lithe
body was a natural for the Twist. Discothèques, as they became
known, were imported from France, tiny clubs where *disquaires*
spun records on the turntable. The Peppermint Lounge was one
of the first New York clubs to install stereo equipment and PJ
became one of the first New York club DJs. He moved on to
Arthur, Sybil Burton's club, The Scene, 12 West, Enchanted
Garden in Queens, 2001 Odyssey in Brooklyn, and a host of

others. He narrowly missed being profiled by Bob Colacello in *Interview* magazine as the handsomest DJ, although a couple of gossip columnists did pick up on him, but had to resign themselves to describing him as New York's mystery DJ. At four o'clock in the morning after the clubs closed, he walked the streets or took a shift as a night-watchman till seven-thirty, eight o'clock when it was time to go over to 42nd Street and go to the movies. The movie theaters between Times Square and Eighth Avenue opened at eight every morning and PJ often joined the derelicts and alcoholic bums in search of a soft seat in a smoky anonymous atmosphere for a couple of hours. He watched westerns, horror movies and a load of foreign films at the Apollo.

And each week he sent over a package to Susan Walker with the details of the stories he wanted to see in the magazine. The cover of the first issue with Honey crouched in a corner had caused a stir, because it fronted a photostory inside showing a florist's delivery boy arriving at an apartment and coming upon just such a poor, little, beat-up rich girl.

His job as a hand model made him think of another successful photo-story of hands in a variety of erotic poses, fingers probing, fists . . .

The grave-digging stint inspired him to commission *The Necrophiliac*, an award-winning short story about a man who stalked his beautiful female victims, murdered them and then made love to their corpses. He buried them lovingly in the middle of the night, digging their graves in romantic spots all over his land.

The masseur job threw up a series of erotic New Journalism which took *Eros* out of the cult category and moved it up into the society magazine market. The whole of the East Side was in an uproar while the series ran. Who was the person who had leaked the ladies' most intimate demands? Servants were fired. No one suspected the dark-eyed masseur who had brought them such pleasure several months earlier and then mysteriously disappeared.

He never heard from Honey as to what she made of the cover. He never heard from his father except that, true to his word, he cut off PJ's allowance. As *Eros*'s circulation grew, so did PJ's income. Susan Walker never once asked to meet him. Apart from the creative content, she had complete control and this seemed to suit her fine. Her only attempt at contact was to once send him a note via his father's lawyer (she didn't even know his name) asking if she could commission a lesbian piece. He had known when he had talked to her at the party when he first met her that she was a lesbian and he approved of her blunt approach in asking for the piece and said yes. He wondered if she had ever figured that her proprietor had to be the quiet, dark man she had talked to briefly at that party, yet her only clue could have been that the job offer had come the very next day. Of his mother there was no sign whatsoever and he decided to leave it this way.

The years went by fast. The permissive Sixties ended and it was not until they were mid-way through the Seventies that he began to wonder if he would ever settle down, get married, have children, lead a normal conventional life. He had women, but he never asked them back to his apartment. It always had to be their place. He talked to them endlessly on the telephone late at night before he went out to clubs, but he never gave them his number. He wanted his apartment to be his escape hatch, his hideaway, his retreat. Yet once he had taken a particularly persistent blonde to the building where he had been working as a freight elevator operator. He had enjoyed the job in that it gave him plenty of time to think, to dream, except when a truck driver with a heavy load and a tight schedule would sit on his horn down in the loading bay. He showed the blonde the freight elevator, kidded her, told her he worked there, *lived* there, in that cage. She'd wanted to see his home, well, there it was, right before her eyes. She'd known he was only kidding, but she played along never realizing that this charming young man who had just taken her to dinner at the Four Seasons actually did work there. He had pretended to pour her a drink in a corner of the cage and then he had stripped her and made love to her on the floor as they rode up and down the twelve floors of the deserted warehouse. She never heard from him again.

He solved his problem by renting other people's apartments for short spells and taking women back there. There was an additional attraction. While he lived in these apartments he "adopted" the identity of the real owners as best he could. He had a brilliant ear and when he met them briefly to take possession of the apartment he listened intently to their voice so that he could impersonate them on the telephone.

Except this latest rental had given him a problem. He hadn't had a chance to meet the guy who normally lived there. He'd had to take the keys from someone who worked for him, a woman with the crazy name of Doodle. All he knew was the guy was a photographer, a photojournalist away on assignment in Oklahoma. But the place was good, big and spacious. Except it was empty of personal possessions, hard to get a fix on the guy's personality. Just these big bare walls with his photographs pinned up here and there. Then that Englishwoman had showed up with some story about a meeting with the photographer, what was his name? Jack Fern. Had that girl been onto him? He knew he should never have rented the apartment in his real name.

"Damn!" He should have picked up on that one. He'd let her slip away too quickly, probably never find her again. Well, wasn't that how he liked it? Strangely enough, he found he wanted more of this Englishwoman. She'd been different; he'd had the impression that he could have talked to her. Maybe he was kidding himself. Anyway, it was too late now. He'd let her get away. "Damn," he swore out loud again.

"What's the problem?" Barney was wiping the bar, his eye on the Met game on the TV set above him. PJ still made it back to Barney's to drink wherever he rented the other apartments.

"OK, so you don't wanna answer. Women! Has to be. Guy doesn't answer it's always some'n to do with a dame. Am I right? Who are ya tonight, anyways?"

PJ looked up.

"What do you mean?"

"I mean, who *are* you? Don't be a wise guy. I know you're always changin' appearances. Think I hadn't noticed, all these years you been comin' here? Last week you was a perfect Puerto Rican, first few seconds even I was fooled. You had the accent, I mean you had the voice like that, just like a spic. Week before you was a society type, Boston accent, so who are you tonight? All I know is your name's Phil and you come in here dressed different all the time. Ya could be murderin' people all over the shop and lookin' different each time. See what I mean? All I asked was who was you tonight?"

"It's me. Phil."

"Right. So that's the real you. Now I know. Hey," his attention switched to the TV, "the game finished and I never got to see who won. Let's catch it on the news anyway."

He changed channels and a man's face flashed across the screen. PJ dropped his drink.

"That's Perry Jay Duboise, the Cosmetics King. Guy who runs that Beauty operation, what's it called?" Barney asked.

"Bayou Beauty," muttered PJ.

"Sure, sure."

PJ's eyes were riveted to the TV set. *Coinchenier* filled the screen. As the camera pulled out and back a long black limousine could be seen coming down the oak-lined drive.

"The cosmetics tycoon, Mr. Perry Jay Duboise, today put paid to rumors that his wife has disappeared. 'If you go down the Mississippi you'll see her coming and going,' he told our reporter, 'she just prefers to live in the country and why not?' Family friends have long been concerned at Mrs. Callie Chenier Duboise's long absence from public life and her failure to come to the telephone, but her husband's claims that she has expressed a desire to lead a quiet life in the country were borne out today by the appearance of Mrs. Duboise leaving the family home *Coinchenier* and refusing to talk to reporters."

PJ watched as the limo swung out onto the highway. In the backseat could be seen a woman in dark glasses and a black turban, waving a black-gloved hand. He hadn't seen Callie in sixteen years. The woman in the back of the car could have been anyone.

He sunk his head into his hands. What the hell was he doing? What had happened to Callie? What kind of son was he that he hadn't been to see her?

Barney refilled his glass. He was obviously looking to hand out some advice.

"Ya ever think about settlin' down? Ain't you ever wanted kids, Phil?"

PJ nodded. But no one could be further away from settling down to married life. What chance did he have of ever having a kid?

He would have been astounded to know that in the months following their last encounter back in 1961, Honey Winslow discovered she was pregnant.

CHAPTER 12

It was ironic that Honey Winslow had made her mark as a model via her fresh-faced All-American-honesty look when, as her own mother, Louella Winslow, had once been heard to remark: "That little girl was *born* devious."

When the money from Callie Chenier Duboise ran out, Aunt Sissie, who had seen through her niece the minute she stepped through the door, gave Honey a week's notice. Honey wasn't unduly surprised. She was well aware that she had never lifted a finger to help her aunt while she'd been her guest; that she'd been fed and waited on for two years and there was only so long you could get away with something. She had been attending an elite private school in the East Eighties, courtesy of Callie, but her classmates had been a spoilt, indolent, decadent, ill-mannered crowd and she had brought them home to interrupt poor Aunt Sissie's sleep night after night. The only plus in the whole operation as far as Aunt Sissie was concerned was the fact that Callie's funding of it meant that there was always a bit left over to enable Sissie to visit the best beauty parlors, to buy herself a nice new closetful of clothes from Bloomie's, to take a quick trip to the Virgin Islands one winter. Now that the

money was coming to an end there was no way she was going
to tolerate Honey without the perks which went with her. She
and Honey were basically two of a kind—they didn't give anything for nothing, so when on the day Honey left, Sissie went to
her pocketbook and found her niece had relieved her of over
two hundred dollars, it was her turn not to be unduly surprised.

Honey used the money to rent herself a loft in the Village.
Her initial notes to Perry Jay Duboise had elicited no response
whatsoever. Honey decided it was time to take matters into her
own hands. She flitted up and down Seventh Avenue every day
for a week watching carefully the wheeled racks of garments
being pushed to and fro across the street by the manufacturers'
and designers' porters. By Thursday she had taken stock of
what was available and which of the garments she'd seen that
would suit her. On Friday she "acquired" them. She did this by
chatting up the porter, promising untold delights later that day
if he let her try on such and such and then, once decked out in
a lynx coat or whatever, she hailed a cab and leapt into it.
There were very few people who would take the word of a
garment porter against that of a woman in a lynx coat.

Honey's next scam was brazen in the extreme. Decked out in
her newly acquired finery, but retaining her Southern accent,
she marched into a series of modeling agencies and declared she
was a personal friend of the Duboise family and Mr. Perry Jay
Duboise himself was sponsoring her entry into the modeling
world. The bitches who ran the agencies weren't born yesterday, but Perry Jay was away in Paris that week, probably
wouldn't be back for three or four. The New York office didn't
actually know a Miss Honey Winslow, but Mr. Duboise did
have a great many friends back home in Mississippi and who
knew what he had said. Then there was the question of this
girl's clothes. Clearly she was no ordinary little hick. They all
knew they ought to try to track down Perry Jay or wait until he
came back to see if she was on the level, but at the same time
they each knew that her basic looks were too good to turn
down there and then in case one of their rivals snapped her up.

Honey had her choice of agencies, but she didn't pick up the
most famous. Very shrewdly for her young age, Honey reckoned that here at the dawning of a new decade, the Sixties,
things were bound to change and she didn't want her career to
be tagged onto the end of a whole lot of others. She wanted

somebody who would help launch her as something New with
a capital N. She knew she wasn't right for the sleek, sophisticated, *mature* look of someone like Suzy Parker or Barbara
Goalen. She was *young* and she wanted to exploit her youth as
her deadliest weapon. She wanted to make everyone look
younger and fresher and more outdoorsy. She wanted to make
everyone come out of the night-clubs and into the fields. And so
she acquired an agent, a bubbling little button of a woman from
Kentucky, whose own ideas these were. Honey quite simply
stole them and promoted them all round town in all the photographers' studios when she went for her go-sees and as she
spieled, simpered and charmed them and exuded sheer healthy
sexual wholesomeness, it wasn't too long before a number of
them began to get the message. When later she had her first
spread in *Vogue* modeling chiffon evening gowns as she planted
potatoes, she knew Perry Jay Duboise would see these pictures
and that was the time to go and see him.

Perry Jay came back from lunch slightly intoxicated. This was
unusual for him; he rarely drank during the day, but he felt he
was justified in indulging in a few well-earned martinis as a way
of celebrating the news that the laboratories had finally succeeded in pinning down the right formula for *Bayou Beauty*'s
first perfume.

Now he had to get the Creative Department thinking about
the campaign to launch it. They could start by coming up with
a sensationally original name.

He walked past his secretary, Melissa, who appeared to be
trying to tell him something. But he ignored it.

Sam was his Creative Director. Quickly Perry Jay outlined to
him again the details of the new fragrance.

"It's new, it's fresh, it's above all *young*. It reminds you of a
warm summer's afternoon. It's outdoors. It's like nothing we've
ever done before," he concluded, "and the first thing we have to
do is think of a name for it."

It was at that precise moment that he was aware that he had
a huge erection. Very occasionally this did happen when he
became worked up while he was talking passionately about
something connected with *Bayou Beauty*, something connected
with the sales potential of millions of dollars. But right now he
was excited by the fact that his balls were being teased by what

felt like long feminine fingers. And now those fingers appeared to be reaching for the zipper to his fly and pulling it down gently, gently . . .

Perry Jay had had his desk built specially to his own design. The full semi-circular curve ran around over seven feet. Dead in the middle was an opening measuring three feet wide by two and a half feet high and running back as far as three and a half feet. This enabled him to sprawl comfortably in his chair while sitting at his desk and spread his long legs out wide underneath it. He was sitting like that now and when he glanced down to see what the hell was going on with his private parts, he saw that there was enough space for Honey Winslow to be kneeling stark naked between his legs. She almost seemed to be praying to him with her hands up in front of her running up and down his engorged penis, her pointed little breasts crushed between her elbows.

"Honeeeeeee!" he breathed.

"Honey? Honey! That's it, Perry Jay. That's perfect. That's what we'll call it." Sam's head was nodding enthusiastically.

"It says it all—warm summer afternoons, bees buzzing lazily around, smooth creamy smell, milk and honey complexions wafting the scent of *Honey* everywhere thanks to our new fragrance . . ."

"Shit!" shouted Perry Jay, as he felt Honey take him in her mouth and her teeth graze his foreskin for a split second. "Get out of here!" as he came into Honey's mouth. "Get the hell out of here and start working on the campaign. I want to see layouts and specs first thing in the morning. Now git!"

Sam got, staring at him all the while until Perry Jay began to wonder if perhaps he had special powers to see through the wood of his desk, that he was experiencing a voyeur's dream watching Honey's naked little behind bouncing gently up and down as she worked furiously on him. He reached down and his hand met a hard little nipple straightaway.

"For the last time, OUT!" he roared.

"We're going to have to find the right girl for the campaign," said Sam as he slipped out of the office. "Wonder what the hell's got into the old fart," he said to Melissa on the way out. "I've never seen him so excited. This fragrance must be real important to him."

"He's right, you know," Honey told Perry Jay as she

stretched along his now naked form as he lay on his back, "you're going to have to find the right girl . . ."

Honey had several more "interviews" in Perry Jay's office, most of them on the putting green. Her idea of providing a new hole as she lay spread-eagled on the green felt in front of his desk brought a whole new dimension to his putting practice. Every now and then he struck the ball that extra bit harder to see if she complained, but she never did. Perry Jay had never forgotten the force with which she had allowed him to violate her that first time during Callie's birthday party. Would she let him attack her like that again? It would be risky to try it. She'd been under the age of consent then and would always have that over him. But, just as long as he gave her what she wanted, he was pretty sure she would keep quiet. And he was pretty sure he knew what she wanted now.

He told her she could be the *Honey* girl, but he let his "Creative" team supply a whole stream of beautiful girls for him to "interview" in his own inimitable way. Then, when it looked like they were beginning to scrape the barrel, he introduced Honey to everyone at the New York office of *Bayou Beauty*. Right away they congratulated him on his choice. They'd seen her in *Vogue*. She was just perfect and the fact that her real name was Honey added an extra promotional gimmick to the campaign. And he thanked his lucky stars that the Press Officer he had had at the time when Callie had taken her overdose, the one who had told him about the piece of paper in her hand with the name "Honey" on it, had long since had the misfortune to succumb to a rare blood disease and was no longer around.

Before long Perry Jay began to visit Honey in her little apartment in the Village on a regular basis.

Honey was far too busy taking care of business—in other words herself—to ever have any twinges of regret or sadness about other people. But PJ's visits to her when he got his pictures for the first issue of *Eros* coincided with the beginning of the shooting of the *Honey* campaign. For weeks Honey scoured the magazine stalls to see if she could find it. She was terrified it would destroy the image she was building up of herself as the *Honey* girl. Time and time again as his father rammed himself into her, Honey had to bite back the question: "Say, Dubee" (she'd developed a nickname for him since she had found herself calling him Mr. Duboise all the time and couldn't bring herself to say 'Perry Jay'), "d'ya happen to know where PJ is these days?" But she never said it aloud.

Soon she was so taken up with the *Honey* campaign she barely had a moment to herself. Her face was everywhere: on double page spreads in all the magazines, on billboards, on showcards in department stores. Within two months her face was known to Americans coast to coast and they took her to their hearts. All over the States her wide wholesome smile was torn out of magazines and pinned up on walls in offices, teenage bedrooms, on truck drivers' dashboards and locker room closets. She smiled at the people who looked at her picture and they went on their way smiling with her. Men bought *Honey*—for their wives, their mistresses, their daughters, and the women bought it for themselves. "Hiya, Honey!" was the catchphrase which caught on and every time someone caught a whiff of the vital, euphoric fragrance they smiled at the wearer and called, "Hiya, Honey!" And Perry Jay sat back and watched the profits roar in.

Honey had reached the peak of her modeling career much faster than she had anticipated and she intended to stay there, but a month later when she arrived at a photographers' studio to pose for a swimwear session she was in for a shock. She had a considerable struggle to squeeze herself into the electric blue Lycra one-piece swimsuit she was to wear for the pictures. There was something wrong here. It was her size, maybe even a shade too big if anything given her miniscule measurements, but when she pulled it up over her breasts and turned to look in the full-length mirror of the dressing room, she was aware that it fit much too tightly over her hips and stomach. And it was her stomach which was wrong. It was no longer flat. There was a distinct bulge, a little round protuberance which had never been there before.

The next week the sickness started. Every morning when she woke up she found herself rushing to vomit into the toilet bowl. Honey's periods had never been regular. Listening to other models gossiping here and there, she had overheard talk of how if you were extra specially thin it messed up your regularity. She'd been assured by *Bayou Beauty*'s own doctor that there was nothing to worry about, she should just note down when she did have a period, the force of the flow and how long it went on.

When she went back to him with her little chart he saw that she had not recorded any sign of menstruation for four months. Two days later, he told her she was pregnant and while it was hard, given her unusual record, to pinpoint how far advanced she was, he said he would estimate that the fetus was already as much as twenty-two weeks old. Honey absentmindedly consulted a calendar hanging on his wall and realized that she had very probably conceived the week of PJ's visit to her apartment.

The doctor was babbling away. "You're too far gone. Why didn't you come to me sooner? There's nothing I can do. You're young, with the right exercise afterwards your figure will be back in no time." Suddenly he stopped, realizing what he was saying. Usually they asked him straight out. "When? How much?" The word itself was never mentioned. Perry Jay knew what having a baby could do to a woman's figure. He had an arrangement with a clinic. Sometimes the girls barely even knew what they were in there for; all that mattered was that they were out quickly and back to work. But Honey would have to go through with it. He wondered who the father was.

So did Honey. It was either PJ or his father.

She couldn't hide the bulge from Perry Jay for much longer. She had to tell him and to her utmost amazement he was pleased. So pleased that she let him believe he was the father beyond a shadow of a doubt. But she was bewildered as to why he should want her to have it.

"What about your wife?" she asked him. It had worried her that there had been no sign and no mention of Callie since she'd been working for *Bayou Beauty*. In the old days Callie had been part and parcel of the organization even if she did spend most of her time at *Coinchenier*. Honey had never dared ask Perry Jay before. Now she had to.

"Callie was institutionalized a few years ago. PJ, well, he ran away, told her he never wanted to see her again. It was too much for Callie. PJ was her whole life. She took an overdose. They found her just in time, pumped her stomach, saved her life, but then she had to return to *Coinchenier* knowing PJ would never come home again. She wasn't ready. They told me it would take months before she could come to terms with the fact that she would never see her son again, that he was never coming back."

"Why did he run away?"

"Hate to say so, missy, but that's none of your business. He discovered somethin' about Callie that he just couldn't accept."

"But surely you know where he is? Couldn't you get him to come home?"

"Sure I know, but I don't want him upsettin' his mamma, goin' to visit her. Won't do her no damn good at all. Matter of fact, I'm goin' down to see her tomorrow."

"How much longer will she be there?" Honey asked.

"Oh, a while, quite a while. Long as it suits me to keep her there."

"You mean you had her *committed*?" Honey was quite shaken by this revelation.

"You could say that. She ain't exactly insane, but she's got bad blood in her. Haven't I ever told you about . . . ?"

What Perry Jay then told Honey about Callie startled Honey more than anything she'd heard in some time. It also started her brain ticking over at double its normal rate. Knowledge was power and boy, did she have knowledge now. But she feigned only moderate interest and instead asked innocently: "And my baby?"

"You go ahead and have it. I'll take care of all the financial details. You know that. It is mine, after all. Maybe it'll be a little girl who'll grow up to be as pretty as her mother."

But Honey wasn't listening. Perry Jay was still in touch with Callie. Callie wanted PJ. Callie had skeletons rattling around in her closet waiting to be exposed. As Perry Jay fondled her already swollen breasts, Honey began to hatch out in her mind the best little scam she'd had in years, a way to get her hands on the Duboise fortune.

And that was her first mistake.

CHAPTER 13

The following day she hung about *Bayou Beauty* until she heard that Perry Jay was back from his day's outing. In the corridor she contrived to crash headlong into Marcus, Perry Jay's chauffeur, as he was coming out of the Men's Room.

"Marcus! How clumsy of me. I'm so sorry. Here, let me get you a cup of coffee in the canteen."

Marcus was thrilled to bits. The drive down to the institution had been deadly dull. The place had to be the most boring town in the world and he'd had to kick his heels around in it all day waiting for Mr. Duboise to finish visiting his wife. A cup of coffee with the delectable Honey Winslow was just what he needed to restore him. And she seemed so interested in him, asking him how he was and how his day had been and seeming so concerned when he told her it had been a wash-out, asking why, where had he been . . . ? Well, where was that? And so he'd told her and afterward felt a whole lot better. Later, after he'd dropped Mr. Duboise off at his Park Avenue apartment he remembered that he wasn't supposed to tell *any*one where Miz Callie was in case the Press got hold of it. But that Honey Winslow, she wasn't *any*one now, was she?

"I had no idea you and Mrs. D. were so close," said Marcus for the umpteenth time as he swung Perry Jay's long black limousine through a pair of high wrought-iron gates which had swung open, electronically operated by a security guard, when the car approached them. The limousine purred smoothly up a long winding drive underneath a continuous archway of tall oak trees which seemed to bend toward each other, obliterating the blue sky above. Suddenly they emerged into a wide open space and Honey gasped and wound down her smoked glass window to peer through her sunglasses at the building in the distance. Even though it was almost half a mile away, it was instantly recognizable to her.

"Why, Marcus, I've been here before."

"No, you ain't, Miss Honey. You ain't crazy. You just think you have."

"No, that house, it's familiar."

They were closer now. The house was immense and ugly, a mansion built in the sixteenth-century Italian style with a red tiled roof and a profusion of arches and pillars. Ivy all but covered the west wing giving it a dark and sinister appearance.

"It's 'The Breakers'!" shrieked Honey. "It's just like that Vanderbilt place at Newport, Rhode Island."

" 'The Breakdowns' more likely," muttered Marcus darkly. "You want to take warnin', Miss Honey, place is full a crazies. I ain't never seen nobody look happy. Why, even Mr. Duboise hisself is shaken when he comes out. Never says a word that entire drive back to the city. Shakin' like a rabbit he is and he ain't scared a nobody."

Wanna bet? thought Honey to herself. Time will tell.

The limousine glided to a halt outside the flared sweep of marble steps up to the main entrance. Honey stepped out and wrapping her voluminous camel-hair car coat around her to hide her pregnant figure, she strode up the steps and into the cavernous entrance hall.

"Ah, Jeez, Marcus, it *stinks* in here!" It was true. There was a faintly sour smell of sweat and urine permeating the area. Honey reached into one of her coat pockets and brought out a small dispenser of *Honey*. She flung her arm high above her head, depressed the nozzle and sprayed liberally in huge circles. Marcus, who had removed his chauffeur's cap on entering, now pressed it over his face. The combination of what he called "crazy smell" and *Honey* guaranteed instant nausea.

" 'Scuse me . . ."

Honey turned to see a little woman of about fifty-five dressed in a neat little blue poplin blouse with a Peter Pan collar tucked over her ample bosom into a navy blue pleated skirt. A whistle hung around her neck on a chain along with a pair of spectacles and one of the largest penknives Honey had ever seen.

" 'Scuse me . . ." she said again.

"I'm Honey Winslow," said Honey, assuming that would explain everything as it usually did. "Here to see Mrs. Duboise."

"We have no Mrs. Duboise here."

"Well, she was here yesterday," Honey informed her brusquely. "Where d'ya think she could have gone since then. Marcus, tell this person who we are here to see and make her *understand*."

"This here's Miss Honey Winslow and she'd like to visit with Miss Callie Chenier," translated Marcus.

Chenier! Wasn't that Callie's maiden name? So, she wasn't registered as Mrs. Duboise. Interesting. Old Perry Jay clearly wanted it kept a secret that his old lady was shacked up in a mental institution, probably told them she was some old cousin he had to come and visit. Honey wondered how many of the staff recognized Callie as *Mrs.* Perry Jay Duboise, former socialite and wife of the Cosmetics King. The Press might like to know too, but there was plenty of time for that.

"Do you have an appointment? We like for our visitors to make appointments. That way the patients can get adjusted. Surprise visits can be so disturbing."

I'm here to be disturbing all right, thought Honey.

"Oh, I'm *so* sorry," she purred. "Didn't Mr. Duboise say anything about it? He was here yesterday, wasn't he? I'm an old family friend and when he told me poor Aunt Callie was here, why, I just *had* to rush down and see her. Didn't he say I was comin' today? Why, surely he did?"

" 'Scuse me?"

Honey pressed her fingers into the palms of her hands in frustration and decided to try a different approach. She took a step toward Mrs. Clift and loomed over her.

"Take me to Miss Chenier right now, do you hear? I've

driven all the way from New York City and Mr. Duboise told her I was coming. She'll be waiting for me. We would like complete privacy and I do mean complete. While we're talking, my chauffeur will have his lunch. You *can* lay on some refreshment, I take it?"

This worked. The little woman nearly jumped out of her skin. She leapt to attention and for one glorious moment Honey thought she was going to salute. Probably been a WAAC in the war, working out her petty little aggressions on the crazies. Well, she was going to be no match for Honeychile Winslow.

"Why, surely, right away. Just slipped my mind you were coming today. Miss Callie, she's in the OT Department—and I didn't mean just doing it. She's a teacher. You're going to see a big change in her, she's *expressing* herself so well nowadays, you'll see. We just pray she won't be going home too soon. 'Course, that's mighty selfish, we know, but we just love having her here. Come along now, Mr. Chauffeur," she beckoned to Marcus, who had resumed his hovering position behind Honey, "let's find you some refreshment. Why, *I know you*, you're Mr. Duboise's chauffeur. Well, now I know it's all right. You never asked for lunch before. All you gotta do is ask. Come now, I'll have someone show you the dining room."

"She gonna put me with the crazies? I don't want ta eat with the crazies . . ." But Honey grasped him firmly by the elbow and propelled him in front of her as they followed Mrs. Clift down a long pale green corridor.

Honey was beginning to wish she hadn't come. Mrs. Clift shepherded her into a sinister cage-like elevator which creaked its way to the fourth floor at a snail's pace. Mrs. Clift never stopped talking, but Honey couldn't bring herself to listen. It wasn't until she realized the little woman was trying to fill her in on Callie's history with them that she made the effort to take in what she was saying.

". . . 'course she wasn't always no trouble. My, when she first arrived was she a handful? Had these delusions of grandeur, ya know? A lot of them have them. Thought she was a fine lady, been living on a plantation or something and we all had to call her Miss Callie. Funny thing, though, it kinda stuck and most of us still do. Seems she does come from some old family in the South, but she's just a poor relation. That kind Mr. Duboise fixed it for her to come here. He's done everything for her, paid her way, she oughta be mighty grateful to him, but when he comes visiting they don't hardly speak to one another."

"Why is she in here exactly?"

"Why, don't you *know*? I thought you was family."

"Friend of the family," Honey corrected her. "Well, I know she had some sort of trouble with her son but . . ."

Mrs. Clift looked at her oddly.

"Her son who don't exist, you mean? It's *so* sad! She thinks she has this son who won't speak to her but, like Mr. Duboise told us, she's *Miss* Callie Chenier, she's not married, she has no son, she just pines for a son she never had."

Honey was shocked. So this was Perry Jay's game. For a split second she almost felt sorry for Callie. After all, she owed her a thing or two. If Callie hadn't bumped her out of Mississippi and paid for her to be educated in New York, who knew how long it would have taken her to get her foot in the door of high fashion modeling? She realized she hadn't seen Callie for about four or five years, not since that night of the older woman's birthday when she'd looked over PJ's shoulder and seen Callie watching them. The woman must also know she'd been raped by her husband, probably been watching that too. Now that she had to confront her, get the better of her, she was beginning to wonder if she could do it. Mrs. Clift was still prattling on. Some of what she was saying filtered through to Honey until suddenly one sentence made her stop in her tracks.

"Mind you, we all soon found out another reason for Miss Chenier needing treatment. She was a roaring nymphomaniac. Kept escaping from her room and pouncing on the orderlies, pushing them back up against the walls and trying to tear open their zippers." Mrs. Clift's tongue rippled across her lips in memory of the excitement. "See, she couldn't stand it when she found she had to be cooped up with the girls, kept screaming for a man, kept screaming for what she wanted, described it in every detail every day at the top of her voice. 'Course, Mr. Duboise, he wanted this kept real quiet. Paid us real handsomely to keep it that way and we have, but seein' as how you're such an old friend of the family . . ."

Well, well, well! thought Honey to herself. Randy old Callie had a problem, the old lady had an itch. Question was, did she still have it?

"Did she respond to treatment?" Honey asked Mrs. Clift, well aware by now that the little woman loved nothing better than to talk about the seedier side of her patients' illnesses.

"Well, we *think* so, but we can never be sure. See, we doped her up real good for the first two years and never let her see any man 'cept Mr. Duboise who, of course, is like a father to her."

"Of course," agreed Honey quickly.

"We don't allow no pictures of men, young men that is, anywhere near her and she can't watch television. She's only allowed books provided they don't have any pictures in them. Now, we don't believe for one moment that she's forgotten they exist, but it seems they don't bother her too much anymore. She hasn't asked for one in two years. Well, see now, *here* we are . . ."

She unlocked and swung open a door and Honey walked in to witness one of the most bizarre sights of her life.

Immediately she sensed that Callie might actually be insane, although ironically she was the only one in the room who looked perfectly normal. The scene before Honey had the appearance of a schoolroom with a lesson in progress. About a dozen women were seated at two long, wooden trestle-tables. Dotted along the tops of the tables stood a hotchpotch collection of mirrors: self-supporting circular shaving mirrors, wood-framed glass rectangles hinged between two wooden posts, the kind which could be tilted to the desired angle, triple-paneled dressing-table vanity mirrors whose wings could be adjusted to reflect the profile.

In front of the tables, on a raised podium, stood Callie, dressed in a navy turtleneck underneath a navy gingham artist's smock over tight navy ski pants. Despite the looseness of the smock (where *did* she get the clothes? Honey wondered, everyone else wore drab green overalls), Honey could see that her frame was as scrawny as ever. Her scrawny neck rose out of the turtleneck and the outer edges of her gaunt face were drawn tightly into a navy toweling turban giving her eyes a slanting, elongated, almost Oriental expression. But how those eyes gleamed between the two enormous gold hoops protruding from her ears. For Callie was in her element: *she was conducting a make-up class.*

Honey was mesmerized. The teacher was oblivious to all but one of her pupils. She was in the process of applying pancake to

the cheeks of a dark sallow-skinned woman who slumped de-
jectedly on a lone wooden chair on the podium. Tears streamed
down the woman's face and obliterated Callie's work as quickly
as she applied it. Undaunted, she slapped on more pancake,
more rouge, until the woman's face was covered in what looked
like a series of mudpies.

Honey looked round at the rest of the "pupils." Several of
them had their heads buried in their elbows on the table. Some
were valiantly trying to make up each other with grotesque
clown-like results. One woman, as soon as she saw Honey,
promptly removed all her clothing and began to suck sugges-
tively on a fully extended blood-red lipstick until Mrs. Clift
stepped forward and gently removed it. Another woman was
angrily hurling loose powder, liquid foundation and mascara at
a wall in an attempt to form some kind of abstract mural.

Mrs. Clift beamed contentedly. "Isn't it just wonderful," she
asked Honey, "the way she gets them to *express* themselves?
Mr. Duboise supplies us with all the materials absolutely free.
Isn't he the most generous-hearted man you ever knew?" With-
out waiting for an answer, she signaled frantically to attract
Callie's attention away from the sobbing woman.

"Miss Callie, look, here, you have a visitor."

Callie turned toward them and Honey's chest suddenly tight-
ened in apprehension. She'd come to fight a battle, or at the
very least make a deal, but now she was face to face with the
enemy, she realized she had managed to avoid thinking about
Callie as a flesh and blood adversary. Yet here she was: Perry
Jay's legal wife, still emanating an air of gaunt elegance despite
the unfortunate circumstances, clearly dangerously close to insanity yet due at any moment to be released back into the
world.

And that smile! It sneaked and flashed across her face revealing still a row of even, gleaming white teeth.

Fangs! thought Honey, all the better to sink into my tender
young flesh, and found that she was extending her hand to
Callie's outstretched one, feeling it held in a bony, jagged
ringed grip. Well, she's not going to get away with it. Well, I'll
be Goddamned, the bitch doesn't even recognize me.

It was true: there was absolutely no sign on Callie's face as,
still smiling, she drew Honey to the center of the podium.

"Look, everyone!" she appealed to her totally indifferent

class. "Today we have the *perfect* model. Maria, dear . . ."
Gently she prodded the sallow-skinned woman who promptly
flopped off the wooden chair and began to bang her fists on the
floor in despair.

Honey took her place on the wooden chair almost automatically.

It's hardly surprising she doesn't recognize me, she thought.
When she last saw me I was still at school and now I'm a top
model.

Callie took her chin between forefinger and thumb and tilted
her face upward.

"*Look*, everyone," she urged again, "look at the *exquisite*
bone structure on . . . oh, excuse me, dear, what *is* your
name? You're new here, aren't you?"

Mrs. Clift rushed forward to correct the error.

"No, Miss Callie, Miss Winslow's not an inmate. She's your
visitor. An old family friend of you and of Mr. Duboise. *You
remember* Miss Honey Winslow."

Callie let go of Honey's face so fast her nails scratched the
younger woman's lower cheek, drawing a thin trickle of blood
which ran down Honey's neck and inside the still upturned
collar of her camel-hair coat.

"Class dismissed!" she snapped, but no one else in the room
was listening to her except Mrs. Clift, who began to back nervously out of the room. "Well, I'll leave you to have a nice
reunion . . ." she murmured.

Honey got to her feet and backed away to the other side of
the podium. To an outsider she and Callie might have resembled a pair of actresses set to give their all in a powerful dramatic two-hander. The podium looked like a stark stage set
with the solitary wooden chair and the now silent, depressed
woman lying prostrate on the floor between them.

"So," Callie began, "it *is* you, isn't it? What the hell brings
you here?"

Honey decided on the sugary approach.

"Why, Miss Callie, when I heard I came straight here . . ."

"Bull!" retorted Callie. "I've been here for quite a while. You
need to wash your ears out if this is the first you've heard of it.
How *did* you hear, by the way?"

"Pillow talk, truth to tell," replied Honey sweetly. "Bin

screwing your husband." All of a sudden she remembered the line of attack she'd planned all along.

"Welcome to him." Callie feigned indifference.

"And your son."

Callie's head whipped up.

"Philippe?" she whispered.

"PJ," confirmed Honey, and very slowly she began to let her coat fall open to reveal her swollen stomach.

"WHERE IS MY SON?" roared Callie.

"Oh, Miss Callie, you *know* you don't have a son." Mrs. Clift came bustling through the door behind which she'd obviously been eavesdropping.

"Please leave us alone," demanded Callie.

"Oh yes, alone . . . you want to be alone. I'll leave, of course." She gave a rather bewildered glance at the other women in the room, but decided to leave them where they were. "Alone," she said again, shaking her head as she retreated once more through the door, closing it behind her.

"Now, listen," said Honey, turning to Callie to tell her a blatant lie. "I *know* where Philippe is. I came here because I knew you would want to see him when you got out of this place. Now, I don't know the exact reason you're here, but I do know your husband intends for you to stay here a while."

"He does? That's ridiculous. There's nothing wrong with me now." Callie was astounded. "How *is* my boy?"

I've got her exactly where I want her, thought Honey. She continued her assault.

"He's real fine. Now, if I guarantee to tell you where you can find your son, you're going to have to do something for me in return, ain't you, Miss Callie?"

"Hell I will!" It wasn't in Callie's nature to go down in the first round. "First of all, I must get out of here."

"Well, if you feel like that, I'll be on my way." Now Honey slipped right out of the coat and began to walk across the podium with an ugly, exaggerated gait, feet and knees turned out, a palm placed squarely in the small of her back, pressing forward her pregnant stomach. "Congratulations, any old how . . ."

"What for?" asked Callie, bewildered by this bizarre performance.

"This!" Honey pointed crudely to the bulge under her maternity smock. "You're going to be a granny, Callie."

With each sentence, Honey was becoming less respectful, more openly contemptuous of the older woman.

"That can't be Philippe's . . . How can you prove you've seen him?"

Then Honey stared as Callie's mouth dropped open in astonishment. Her eyes were fixed on the silver dolphin bracelet hanging from Honey's left wrist. Honey couldn't know it, but seeing this Callie knew her son must have given it to this girl, had to have seen her . . .

"Of *course* it's his baby. You *know* he was always *crazy* about me. Now, I know he told you he was never going to see you again, but I'm here to tell you I can change that. I'm having PJ's baby and I came down here to share that news with you." Moving in close, Honey switched tactics, bent down, held Callie's head to her stomach and whispered: "There now, can't you hear him? Your grandson. I just *know* it's going to be a boy. Philippe thinks so too . . ." she lied. "You're going to want to share him with Philippe too when we get you out of this place. I've been working on Philippe, I almost got him to come with me to visit you today."

"Well, why didn't you?" Callie looked at her suspiciously.

"He was frightened of running into his father. Your little boy simply had no idea you were in here till I told him. Isn't that a sin? But it's you he wants to see, not his father, so he's prepared to wait till you get out when it's safe. Then I'll put you in touch with him. But first—" Honey was almost crooning now. "First, you have to do just one little thing for our child."

"And it's for Philippe too, right?"

"Oh *yes*! Definitely! Philippe *wants* you to do this."

"Well, what do I have to do? *If* I decide to do it," Callie added quickly.

"It's so simple. When you next see Perry Jay, you tell him you know about the baby, but you give him to understand that you think the baby's *his*. His child, Perry Jay's. Now, you never mention PJ's . . . I mean, Philippe's name at all. Not once. You need to act shocked, just a little, about the fact that you know your husband's been fooling with me, don't overdo it, but you forgive him. He'll be curious as to why I came and told you, but I'll sort that out with him. He'll be mad at me at first, but he'll come round. I can always handle him. Have you got that so far?"

Callie nodded. The thought of the possibility of being re-united with PJ and the excitement of the intrigue caused her to focus all her attention on Honey.

"Now comes the important part," Honey continued, standing over Callie and looking down on her. Somehow the school-room atmosphere was back again with the roles reversed; this time Callie was the pupil. "You tell Perry Jay that he's got to consider his new child's welfare, his education, his future as a Duboise and his potential role at *Bayou Beauty*. What about his will? In the event of Perry Jay's death—God forbid, but you never know—in the event of his death, who currently stands to inherit?"

"I don't know anymore," Callie told her. "He cut Philippe out of it when he ran out on me. Lord knows how the poor boy survives. Do *you* know? I guess you must. How's he going to provide for your child?"

"Exactly!" Honey clapped her hands in glee as Callie fell right in with her plans. Clearly Callie knew nothing about PJ's budding career as a magazine publisher. Honey had been watching *Eros*'s progress from the sidelines. She'd found the first issue with her picture on the cover eventually. She had been amused to find that no one else appeared to know who was behind the new publication. Well, he clearly wanted it kept secret for a while and she'd keep it that way for him until it suited her to spill the beans. Meanwhile, if Callie thought he was broke, so much the better . . .

"I've been worrying about that too, Miss Callie. Now I'm a fashion model in case you don't know, but that's precarious work and it won't last forever. Now, poor old Philippe, bless him, isn't going to earn us a bean. I've come up to see you, Miss Callie, because I *need* your help . . ."

"How, missy? I can't persuade Perry Jay what to do with his will. That's not something a person can do. You know the man. I know the man." Callie was almost colluding with Honey now as a matter of course. "He just won't bear it. Now, why don't I give you the money to bring up my grandson, if that's what you need? Although, from the looks of you, you seem to have done all right for yourself. Always did say you'd turn out to be a pretty little thing," she added generously, if a little patronizingly. "I've got plenty of money of my own. Between us we wouldn't need Perry Jay."

"Do you own *Bayou Beauty*?"

"I've got stock."

"Voting stock?"

"Yes."

"How much?"

"50 per cent."

"How much?"

"You heard. I'm entitled to it. We started the business together, Perry Jay and I, when you were still in diapers. Without me he'd have had *nothing*!"

"Callie, *Miz* Callie," whispered Honey patiently, as if talking to a child. "You're in an institution. How do you know Perry Jay won't find two doctors and have you declared insane, forever, have your 50 per cent made over to him on the grounds that you aren't fit to vote by reason of insanity? He must have power of attorney for voting your share at the moment whenever there's a board meeting. Time's running out. You have to do something now. You have to get him to give back your stock and persuade him to leave his 50 per cent to his child."

"You mean *your* child . . . and Philippe's."

"I'm talking about your grandchild. Maybe the only one you'll ever have. What about *Coinchenier*?"

"Perry Jay bought it for me and it's in my name. That's mine. We could raise PJ's baby there and PJ could come home again . . ."

"I want my child to have 50 per cent of *Bayou Beauty* and everything that goes with it," said Honey firmly. "And I mean everything. I'm assuming you'll leave *Coinchenier* and your 50 per cent to PJ. That's OK. But I want something for my child. Will you speak to your husband?"

Callie stared. She'd had private investigators searching for PJ ever since she had been inside the home. They'd drawn a blank everywhere, or so they told Callie. (The simple truth was that Perry Jay had found out and paid them double to come up with nothing.) If Honey was telling the truth, that she genuinely did know where to reach PJ, if she really was carrying his child, it was an opportunity too tempting for Callie to pass up. No amount of pleading to Perry Jay would get *him* to tell her where their son was. It would be tough getting him to agree to change his will, but whom else did he have to leave his share to? It could be done, and Honey was right to make her start thinking of ways to get out of here, but it would mean she would have to play her trump card, the one she'd been saving for an emergency like this ever since her marriage to Perry Jay had gone sour. She had been tempted to play it several times before, but at the back of her mind she'd always known the time would come when it would prove invaluable. Now was the time. Especially if the rat planned to leave her in this place indefinitely.

"I'll do it," she told Honey quietly, the emotion she had shown earlier evaporating, replaced by her usual hard exterior.

"How?" Honey asked her.

"That's my business."

"OK." Honey shrugged. "Tell him when he next visits and get him to write it down on a piece of paper, sign his name to it."

"Then you'll tell me where I can find Philippe?"

"I'll do better than that. I'll persuade Perry Jay to get the doctors to release you from here. He can do it. You recall what he did on your fiftieth birthday? I was under age then and he knows it. I know he figures I won't do anything about that after all this time, but he's wrong. I'll use it if I have to. I'll use it to get you out of here if you guarantee to get him to leave his share of Bayou Beauty to my child."

"Sounds like you ought to persuade him to do that too," Callie told her.

"No, no, we need a two-sided attack to bring him down. Between the two of us we can do it . . ."

"Where *is* Philippe?" Callie persisted.

"Oh, no. I'm not going to tell you that till the baby's born. That wouldn't be fair now, would it? When the baby's born I'll get word to you and you can come see me in the hospital, come see your grandchild. First you've got to get out of this place, get yourself adjusted to the outside world, get yourself in good shape to see your son again. No, you're just going to have to trust me, Callie. You can do that, can't you?"

Callie just stared at her.

"Get out of here. I'll do what you want, but if you don't come through with your side of the bargain, God help you, 'cause nobody else will, I'll see to it."

"I'm leaving now, Callie dear. Next time we meet I'll be showing you your grandchild. Just you stop and think about that and all the things you're going to tell Philippe when you get to see him again."

She sashayed out and, ignoring Mrs. Clift, who was hovering outside the door, she made her own way down in the creaky elevator, collected Marcus and told him to get her back to New York as quickly as he could.

She had no intention of talking to Perry Jay about Callie. If he brought it up she'd tell him he was the one who was crazy if he made any attempt to bring Callie back to the outside world. But if Callie would get her old man to leave only a fraction of his share to Honey's child, then she, Honey, would be ahead of the game. She'd slip down and see Callie again and once she knew he'd given Callie that piece of paper confirming that he would change his will she'd go to him and make damn sure that he did. A piece of paper wouldn't stand up in a court of law, but it was a start in the right direction. It would mean Callie had managed to make Perry Jay see sense. And then it would be up to her, Honeychile Winslow, to cement what had been started. She knew she could charm Perry Jay into letting her hire the most expensive nursemaid she could find to take care of the baby. And then she'd use the child, play them off against each other, let Callie go on thinking it was PJ's, let Perry Jay go on thinking it was his, till they coughed up enough cash to satisfy her and if she could get a piece of Bayou Beauty thrown in for good measure, all well and good.

It was going to be a question of juggling from here on in. She had something on Perry Jay. She had something on Callie which Perry Jay had told her (and which even Callie herself didn't know about), she had Callie thinking she could lead her to PJ (which she would never do even if she did know where he was), and in a little while she would have the baby. Right now she had everybody exactly where she wanted them.

It never entered her head for a second that Callie would double-cross *her.*

CHAPTER 14

The next time Perry Jay Duboise paid a visit to his wife h
wasn't entirely prepared for her opening line: "I hear you'v
been fornicating with Honey Winslow."

"What's that, sugar?"

"Don't you *sugar* me, not for one second. I *know* about yo
and Honey Winslow. I *know* about the baby. *Your* baby. Bu
what about *our* child? Our son? Tell me honestly, Perry Jay, d
you know where PJ is?"

"I have not the slightest inclination to know where he is
Damned little pansy . . ."

"Find him for me and send him to see his mamma. *Please*
Perry Jay."

"No can do. Boy's gotta come home of his own accord."

"Boy? He's not a boy anymore. Even I can recognize tha
Perry Jay. It's been years since I saw him."

"No, honey, you're absolutely right. He ain't a boy no more
All the more reason for him to make up his own mind. But I'r
tellin' you, Callie, and you better understand this, whether he'
a boy or a man, he won't come. *He won't come.*"

"Then I want the baby."

"What are you sayin'?"

"I want your child. Honey Winslow's child. I want to come home and raise it at *Coinchenier* as my own to take the place of my baby."

"Callie, you are seriously crazy. You're in an institution. How could anyone possibly let you take care of a little baby? 'Sides, you're way too old. You're no spring chicken no more. You're old enough to be a grandmother, you ain't gettin' that baby. Not now, Callie, sugar, not *ever.*"

"SHUT UP!" Callie was rigid with fury. "Shut up and listen to me. I want us to take a nostalgic trip back in time. Tell me, Perry Jay, can you remember the day we met?"

Perry Jay felt his mouth go dry. He couldn't speak. That subject was off limits. *Taboo.* She knew that, damn it. They'd agreed never to talk about the fact that he'd been in jail. Well, it was true she had that over him, but she wouldn't use it, would she? Sure she would which was why he'd already had a private little talk with his lawyer to make sure the right people in Baton Rouge and at the Louisiana State Penitentiary had been sufficiently bribed to keep their mouths shut. Let her try to dig up the dirt; she wouldn't get very far.

"Why, sure I remember. We met at the Louisiana State Penitentiary. I was a poor boy from West Texas and I'd stolen some food from a lady's house in Baton Rouge and I got caught."

Callie mimed playing a violin. "Stop! Perry Jay, you'll make my heart bleed. My, my, my, I never knew you were so creative. It wasn't food you were stealing, Perry Jay, it was jewels. An old lady's jewels. An old lady who subsequently died."

"What did you say?"

"She died, Perry Jay, from those terrible blows you inflicted on her body when she wouldn't tell you where she kept her jewels. Or maybe you were just hitting her because you enjoyed it, we'll never know because that old woman died from what they call 'grievous bodily harm'."

"My partner . . . it was him . . . I never touched her . . . he struck her, I remember now, he struck her over and over again. They never caught him, I took the rap . . . all those years in jail . . ."

"What was his name?"

"His name?"

"Yes, your partner, what was his name?"

"Ah, Christ, Callie, gimme a break. It was over thirty years ago, I can't remember . . ."

"You can't remember because there was no partner. We found a witness, Perry Jay, that's how you got caught in the first place. There was only one man who came out of that house and it was you. The old lady was still alive by the time you went to jail, but she died not long after. But you got lucky. See, by that time I had come along. When that old lady died they could have slapped a manslaughter charge on you instead of armed robbery, but my family had a lot of power in the state of Louisiana and our lawyer, old Teddy Lenoir, did some skilful negotiation to get you off the hook. Of course you served your time for armed robbery and there's no way you could be retried for manslaughter, but if Teddy Lenoir started spreading the word . . . He's real tight with someone on the *Times-Picayune* and if they ran a story about a little chapter in your past, I just couldn't bear to think how quickly it would be picked up elsewhere."

"All right! Enough!" Perry Jay could already see himself trying to impress upon reporters that he had never known the old lady had died, falling into their traps, saying too much, hanging himself, ruining himself . . .

"So," Callie strung out the word in an attempt to soften him while she switched tacks. "Let's talk about when I'm getting out of here, let's talk about my 50 per cent of the voting stock of *Bayou Beauty* and, most important, let's talk about my return to *Coinchenier*."

Callie might be in an institution, but in her head she was right back at the helm and Perry Jay didn't have a prayer.

It irked him considerably to have to pay the same two doctors who'd had Callie committed a similar bribe for her release, but when the day finally came he settled his wife into the passenger seat of his Mercedes which he used on the rare occasions when he drove himself, wrapped a rug around her, thanked Mrs Clift, discreetly handing her a check as he did so, and within moments he was swinging the car off down the drive with Callie at his side. He felt strangely at peace with the world. Somehow he'd always known he'd never be able to get the better of Callie. Now she was coming home and once again the two of them would be able to present themselves to the world as a couple. Appearances counted, hell, yes! He'd had to do some fancy talking over the past few years, to stop the Press finding out where Callie was. Oh, they knew she didn't like New York, preferred to live in the South in the very heart of *Bayou Beauty* country as he kept trying to explain to them. But they wouldn't be fooled for long. Maybe he'd give a big party at *Coinchenier* again, throw the house open, invite everyone, fly people in from New York, London, Paris, show them a real good time. Show them the home of a real Southern Belle, put Bayou Beauty back on the map and pretend that this is what Callie had been building up to all this time—the party of the decade . . .

Beside him Callie sat in silence wondering if that little tramp Honey Winslow would keep her word and tell her where Philippe was.

All she could do was wait for the baby.

The baby was late.

In the final month Honey had begun to wonder what the hell she thought she was doing having a baby. To begin with, it had been a kind of game to her, unreal, something which happened to other people, but which was not something she would ever experience herself. One day someone would turn around and say, *OK, lady, time's up, there's no baby inside there, you can stop pretending.* But her stomach continued to grow and when she went for her check-ups she was pronounced one of the healthiest mothers-to-be anybody had ever seen. There wasn't going to be any problem. Oh, no siree, this was going to be one easy birth, she had nothing to worry about.

As she lumbered around her apartment, taking warm baths to ease her discomfort, she wondered whether she ought to let Louella know. She knew she ought to feel guilty about Louella, but she didn't. She'd spoken to her mother precisely eight times in the last four years and had never once been back home for a visit. Since her face had become famous from coast to coast, her mother had tried to get her to return; not directly, she was far too frightened to call Honey herself, but via calls to Aunt Sissie. Aunt Sissie too appeared to have had a change of heart and had begun calling *Bayou Beauty* all the time, saying she was Honey's beloved aunt. Honey assumed she was looking for a handout, or two, or three, but Aunt Sissie was the last person who was going to benefit from her success.

Yet Honey had always felt she ought to do something about her mother. She was kin after all. So was Aunt Sissie, she supposed, but there was kin and then there was real close kin. And then she would remember that Louella had had no problem about accepting money from Callie Chenier Duboise to get her daughter sent away and once again she would feel her heart hardening toward her mother. She tried to remember if Louella had ever said anything much unless it related to television. And if Honey called her to tell her she was about to have a baby, surely the first thing Louella would ask (assuming she was listening and not watching the set at the same time) would be, "Who's the father?" And that was the big question. Who *was* the father? If you made love with a man and then again with his father later the same day, it was rather hard to tell.

Honey had been miserable ever since the day she had looked down and realized she couldn't see her own feet anymore. This was no way to live! She went out and bought a pound of her favourite soft-center chocolates and a stack of magazines. She arranged the chocolates in a delicate porcelain bowl and put it on the table beside the couch. Then she lay down and put her feet up on the arm where she could see them. She flicked idly through the magazines until she came to an article entitled "Are You Ready For Your Baby?" No, she thought, not at all!

The first pains started while she was in the middle of painting her fingernails. Vicious stabs like the worst kind of period pains. Honey surveyed her smudged fingers in disgust. She was aware that she was shaking from head to toe. This was it. There was no going back now.

She telephoned the clinic and screamed down the receiver: "I'm having my baby. *Quick!* Come quickly! *Now!*"

They asked her if the water had broken and she didn't know what they were talking about. She hadn't listened to a word of anything the doctor had told her during her pregnancy. She hadn't a clue what to expect. Suddenly she was little Honey Winslow, poor white trash from Mississippi, again. She was in *their* hands; she had no control. She didn't even have her beauty anymore. Her wrists were swollen and her nail polish was all over the place. Her ankles were huge—she knew that even though she couldn't see them. And now they were trying to stick something up her.

"What the hell are you doing?" Honey was terrified.

"It's just the forceps to pierce the membrane and break the water."

Over the next eleven hours Honey was aware of floating, disjointed words and sentences—"Shall we give her a drip?," "Measure the cervix," "No problem" and then, more urgent, "Push! PUSH! NOW! GO ON! YOU'RE DOING FINE! PUSH! NOW!," "Here's the head," "It's a boy, a little boy," "Take him, Honey, he's all yours."

And as Honey held him in her arms and looked down at the little wrinkled face, she was sure she saw PJ's eyelashes starting to grow.

"We've got to take him now, Honey. We got to take him now and wash him. We'll bring him back soon. You just rest."

But she couldn't sleep till they returned and laid the baby in a cot beside her bed. Honey stared at him.

"He *is* mine, isn't he?" she asked the nurse in a disbelieving whisper.

"No question. You just gave birth to him. More natural birth than I've seen in a long time. You're going to be a good strong healthy mother. Everything was just fine. There's no problem with him, and no problem with you except you need some rest. That's all."

The next day Honey was sitting up in bed painting her nails when a surprise visitor walked in and gave her the shock of her life.

"Where is he?" Callie Chenier Duboise asked. "Where's Philippe?" She didn't bother asking after Honey's baby. She had her own priorities well mapped out.

Honey could only stare at her and mouth: "How did you get out?"

Callie grinned triumphantly. "I'm so grateful to you, Honey, for reminding me it was time to get out. Now, where is he? Where's my son?"

"Search me." Honey held up her palms.

Suddenly she felt her shoulders being gripped by Callie's bony hands and she was being flung backward and forward as Callie shook her, her face peering into Honey's like a myopic vulture. "We made a deal. You've had your baby. Now, I get to know where *my* baby is."

"Not from me, you don't," Honey taunted her in a sing-song

tone, her voice rising on the "me" and coming down again on the "don't." "I ain't got a clue . . ."

"You never knew, did you?" Callie was holding her at arm's length now. "You were lying all the time."

"I haven't seen PJ in nine months," replied Honey sweetly.

"But you know where to reach him if you want to?" Callie asked her hopefully.

"No idea."

Callie slapped her hard across the face.

"You little bitch. You cheap double-crossing piece of white trash. I was crazy to trust you for more than a second."

"You're crazy period!" snapped Honey, holding her smarting cheek. "NURSE!" she bawled, "I'm being attacked here. Come take this woman away right now."

But nobody came and Callie leaned in closer, grabbing the sheet and pulling it away from her head. Honey summoned up her last resources of energy and spat in the older woman's face.

"Get out," she hissed, "get out and stay out. Don't you ever come near me again."

"Oh, I won't," returned Callie, smiling a hideous smile. "I surely won't, not for a *very* long time. Don't worry about that."

And she had risen and swept out of the room almost before Honey realized she had gone. Nor had she noticed Callie whisk her silver dolphin bracelet off the bedside table and into her pocket.

Callie found a telephone by the elevator and dialed Perry Jay's private line.

"Stay right where you are," she told her husband. "You and I have to *talk!*"

Back in her pale pink room Honey ranted and raved until they gave her a sedative to calm her down. Before long she fell into a deep sleep and dreamed she was holding her baby son in her arms. When she woke up she asked for him. Once. Twice. Endlessly.

But they never brought him back to her.

"Cheap double-crossing piece of white trash," was Callie's opening gambit as she stormed into Perry Jay's office.

Perry Jay groaned inwardly. He assumed she must be talking about Honey. He'd had a report from the clinic that Callie had made a fleeting visit to New York and visited her and he had known it would only be a matter of time before she brought up the subject of the baby.

He studied his wife for a second or two before answering, not that her remark really required an answer and he wasn't about to get into instant hot water by rushing to Honey's defense. The woman standing before him was wearing a lilac cashmere sweater and a matching accordion pleated skirt which sashayed smoothly around her legs as she moved back and forth across his office. She looked like an elegant, if rather gaunt, Latin woman although there would always be that rather smoky side to her coloring, sort of Lena Horne without the beauty. Callie could be beautiful, of course, when she applied her make-up, but somehow the twisted, crazed expression on her face invariably made her look ugly.

"Little bitch," Callie continued, getting into her stride. "You're going to be sorry you ever laid eyes on her, Perry Jay."

"Uh-huh," Perry Jay tried to sound noncommittal. "Why are you here, Callie? I don't have much time, I . . ."

"That baby Honey Winslow's just had. It's very simple, Perry Jay. I want him. I want that baby."

"Well, what am I supposed to do about it?"

"He's your baby too. Give him to me."

"Just like that? Callie, you're crazy!"

"So you keep reminding me," she told him drily. "I don't care how you do it—just get me that baby within twenty-four hours or I'll talk to Teddy Lenoir."

She told him she was going back to *Coinchenier* and would wait for him there. On the return flight to Biloxi she found herself wondering just how he would go about getting her the child. After what she'd told him about the death of that old lady in Baton Rouge, he'd do it. He'd do *anything*.

It all happened very fast.

"Kidnapped!" shrieked Honey Winslow when Perry Jay told her the news. "How could that possibly happen to my baby? I thought you owned this place, this clinic. Don't you have no security? How could someone walk in and snatch a kid in broad daylight?"

Perry Jay didn't actually own the clinic, but he exercised a lot of power there. He had put a lot of business their way over the years. All his models had their abortions there and now here was Honey Winslow having a baby there with Mr. *Bayou Beauty* picking up all the tabs. It had been all too easy for him to "arrange" for someone to walk in and "snatch the kid in broad daylight" as Honey herself put it. He hadn't bargained for the fact that Honey saw the "kidnapping" as a wonderful way to get herself some free publicity. Once she got home to her apartment she was on the telephone right away.

"HONEY'S BABY KIDNAPPED" screamed the *Daily News* headline. Perry Jay groaned. The baby was tucked up in a cot in one of the guest rooms in his Park Avenue apartment. A temporary nurse had been hired to look after it. She had been told the mother was a relative who was away for a couple of days, but would be back to take care of it soon.

"They want to know who the father is," Honey screamed at him down the telephone, "and how much ransom is being asked."

"Two million dollars," Perry Jay told her, "but don't breathe a word who the father is. Keep my name out of it."

"But can I say you'll be paying the ransom, that you see yourself as my guardian?"

"Christ, Honey! Don't overdo it. Say I'm your benefactor and that's it. Say you've asked me to help and I'm thinking about it." That would make him look good, a generous fatherly figure coming to her rescue in her hour of need. Mr. *Bayou Beauty* took care of his own. Come to think of it, there could be quite a bit of mileage to be got from this whole thing and in *Bayou Beauty*'s favor too.

"Well, think quick. I want my baby back. Soon!" Honey hung up. It occurred to Perry Jay that she didn't sound remotely perturbed. Knowing Honey, she was having a ball with all the Press dancing attendance on her.

Only there were two things which couldn't possibly happen and the sooner she realized it the better. She was never going to get her baby back. And he, Perry Jay Duboise, was not about to be parted with two million dollars.

"Dead?"

"It was a terrible place. Way uptown. Tenement block. Real fire hazard. My men had instructions to go to an apartment on the fourth floor. Place was empty. Door was open even. They found the baby in one of the rooms lying on the bare floorboards. He was dead." He could be pretty creative when he tried.

"I hope you got to keep your two million dollars," Honey told him bitterly.

"I'm sorry."

"Well, I know it's an old line," she spat at him, "but is that *all* you can say? You're *sorry*? *You're* sorry? What about me? I had to spend nine months of my life walking around like a bloated old slob, probably ruined my figure forever, and all for nothing. Where does this leave me, Perry Jay, tell me that. Where does this leave me?"

Honey brooded for days about her loss. *Her* loss, not the baby's. Without the baby her plans were utterly thwarted. Somehow Callie Chenier Duboise had got the better of her and it enraged her. She was forced to take stock of her life. That she was barely twenty years old and already a successful public figure whose face was known to millions of Americans was immaterial to her now. That it was inconceivable that a woman of Callie's age and experience should succumb to the wiles of someone like Honey, who was really little more than a precocious teenager, had never entered Honey's head. Callie had been a sick woman once and temporarily vulnerable to the ploys of others, but Honey's visit to her at the institution had come at a time when she was on the brink of full recovery. Honey would never know it, but her words had served as a tonic to Callie, prompting her scheming mind to return to action.

But Honey, for all her outward worldly sophistication, was still a child at heart. A child who wanted her own way and was not, it appeared, going to get it. Not for the time being at least. She wanted money and while she had above average earning power as a model, she also had enough sense to know it could not last forever. If she had chosen to reveal her thoughts to even the most amateur psychologist he could have told her that such a desperate desire for money and concern for her future at so young an age could only mean she was blessed with the kind of ambition which could only lead her in later years to serious financial success. But she did not. She was too concerned with the fact that she had failed with the Duboise family, would never get her hands on their money and Perry Jay would probably never speak to her again.

If she did but know it, her fears and worries would prove to be groundless.

The long black limousine sped through the night. Perry Jay sat in the back, the baby beside him in a covered basket. They'd been traveling most of the day already. New Jersey, Maryland, Virginia, Tennessee and on down to Mississippi. It took forever, but if Marcus found it strange that Mr. Duboise was not flying down to the South, he knew better than to comment on it.

It was rare for Perry Jay to feel any kind of guilt, but he did so now. Damn it, he felt ashamed of himself telling that beautiful young thing all those lies about her baby. *His* baby too, why did he keep forgetting that? Thing was he just didn't want to be bothered with raising another child, not at his age. No sir, Callie could have the baby, but she couldn't keep him at *Coinchenier*. Callie would have to go and the baby along with her. And once they were gone he would start thinking about little Honey Winslow.

There just had to be a way he could make it all up to her.

Alphonse had only been in Vietnam six months when he read about Honey Winslow's baby in an old edition of *The New York Times*.

Honey Winslow. His heavenly angel. All around him in Saigon, Oriental women propositioned him seeing him as a "round-eye," a meal ticket, little realizing that he would never be interested in them. He had only one thing to fight for: to get back home and save Honey from her tormentors.

And he fought. He had never been popular with other men in his unit, but with an M16 slung over his shoulder, Sergeant Lenoir achieved their wary admiration. Nevertheless he kept himself to himself, eschewing all offers of drugs, women and booze and the story went round camp that only one thing could get him through the night: killing.

PJ followed the story about the kidnapping of Honey's baby with dread. When he read that it had been found dead, he almost breathed a sigh of relief. He'd noted the fact that his father had been standing by to pay the ransom and assumed that the child was his. It never entered his head for a second that he might be the father.

Queenie opened the door at *Coinchenier* in her night-gown when Perry Jay arrived in the middle of the night. She bent forward to peer at the bundle in his arms.

"What's dat?" she asked and glared when he marched straight past her, ignoring her question.

"I'll put a *gris-gris* on you one of these days, Monsieur Duboise, you see if I don't," she muttered darkly as she heaved herself up three flights of stairs to her bed in the attic. But she had no chance of getting any more sleep that night.

The sound of the bickering two floors below between Callie and Perry Jay rose higher and higher as their argument became more and more heated. Bitter, ugly words were being hurled back and forth. Queenie tried to block out the noise by burying her head under the pillow. The rowing upset her. It was bad enough that Miz Callie had returned to *Coinchenier* in such a strange mood, but if this was the way things were going to continue she was not sure she was going to be able to stand it. Still the noise penetrated until she gave up and, wrapping herself in her robe, she sneaked downstairs to take a look at the bundle Perry Jay had brought in and laid in a basket in the hall. As she passed Callie's room the dispute had risen to fever pitch.

"I can't leave here, this is my home, damn you!" shrieked Callie.

"Whaddya mean?"

"What if PJ comes home?"

"He won't be coming home. Can't you get that through your head? You've got your baby, what more do you want? I want you out of here and I want you to take the brat with you."

"What about Honey Winslow? Will you still see her?"

"That's my business."

"I hate that bitch, I want her dead."

"Hush, Callie, you'll wake the baby."

"I don't care. She's trash and she deserves no more."

"Never mind her, you have to go. You can't stay here and raise a baby. What will people say?"

"If I go, what's in it for me, for this baby?"

"What do you mean?"

"I mean when you die . . . who gets *Bayou Beauty*?"

"Well, you know you've got 50 per cent yourself."

"Who are you going to leave your share to?"

"My business, Callie, my business."

"But I own *Coinchenier*. You gave it to me. It's mine. You can't get me out of here."

"You'll go, Callie. Maybe one day you'll return, but right now you'll go."

"Only place I'm going right now is back to my room to get some sleep. I'll take the baby in with me. You need never see him again. Go on back to New York, Perry Jay. We don't need you here. Go back before I take it into my head to tell folks things about you which will make you wish you had stayed in the penitentiary . . ."

"Queenie told me a few things about you while you was in the institution . . ."

Callie froze, but did not turn around, keeping her back ramrod straight as she waited to see what he would say next.

"Told me you got bad blood, Callie. You ain't a Southern Belle at all, you're a Negro lady. Oh yes, you got black blood but worse, you got *bad* blood."

Callie turned to face him, still not saying a word.

"Your Uncle Jules, the one who was murdered," Perry Jay continued, "they never did find out who did it, did they?"

Callie shook her head.

"Well, I know. Queenie told me. Queenie was there in Storyville the day it happened. She saw the murderer coming out of the brothel. She saw the blood on him. She knows who did it."

"Who was it?" whispered Callie.

"Why, it was your own father, Callie, sugar. He'd gone to that brothel to kill his brother Jules on account of Jules had been seducing your mother for Lord knows how long. *Crime passionel.* Same old story. But that makes you the daughter of a murderer, Callie. The half-white daughter of a murderer. You tell anyone about that little old lady in Baton Rouge and I'll tell them the other side of the story."

Callie knew it had to be true. She had been there herself and she knew Queenie must have been there too, must have seen the man, her father . . .

She went out onto the landing.

"QUEENIE!"

Queenie came rustling in. She'd been looking at the tiny baby boy sleeping downstairs in the hall.

"Come here, Queenie, come close," Callie said in a gentle soothing voice as if talking to a recalcitrant animal. "Mr. Perry Jay has been telling me things. He says you told him my father killed my Uncle Jules. Is that true?"

"Yes'm."

"Thank you, Queenie. That will be all." Outwardly Callie was all icy calm, but inside she was boiling with rage.

Later that same day in 1961 Callie Chenier Duboise boarded an Air France flight from Idlewild Airport to Paris carrying her tiny bundle in her arms.

As she settled herself and her baby in her First Class seat, she decided on a name for her grandson. She would call him Luc. Luc Chenier. And one day she would be back to claim what was hers.

PART 4

TESSA
1977

CHAPTER 15

"Tessa?"

Still blurry with sleep, Tessa reached for the telephone under her bed, cursing the day she'd let Larry put one in her room. He never answered the telephone first thing in the morning. It always woke her up and it was always for him. Whom did she know in New York who would dream of calling her so early? How many people did she know in New York who would call her anyway? Nancy never called period. Tessa had a strange feeling maybe she'd had a thing going with Larry in the past and was not entirely happy about Tessa living in his apartment, but then she'd been the one who had set it up. Anyway, the early morning calls were always for Larry and she had to get up, pad down the hall and go in and wake him up. But this time the voice was asking for her and she knew it was a voice she'd heard before.

"Tessa Fitzgerald, is that you? It's Jack. Jack Fern."

"Jack." Tessa repeated his name mechanically, still in a trance.

"That is you. Tessa, I'm so sorry. Doodle told me what happened. I should have called you myself to tell you I was going

away to Tulsa. It was one of those last minute things, you know
how it is. Anyway, I'm back now, thought I'd have to stay
there a week, but in the end it only took two days. I was calling
to find out when we could get together about this Honey Winslow job. What's your schedule like?"

"Honey Winslow," was all Tessa could get out. This was all
too much for her. It seemed like only yesterday that she'd been
making uninhibited passionate love with someone she thought
was Jack Fern only to learn that he was actually away in Oklahoma. She hadn't been able to address herself to the question of
who the mysterious "P. J. Duboise" might be. Whoever he was
he must have thought she was crazy. Yet she couldn't forget
him, couldn't get the forty-five minutes they'd shared together
out of her mind.

Now here was the real Jack Fern calling her. But did she
know it was the real one? Her heart was hammering. She
needed to hear him say a few more words . . .

"Is Honey Winslow back yet?" she asked him.

"I understand she is, but then I figured you'd know more
about that than I would. Have you contacted her yet?"

No, it wasn't the voice of the man she'd met at the apartment
the other night. The reason she recognized this voice was because she *had* heard it before, but only on the telephone, when
she'd called Jack Fern in the first place. And then she realized
what was different about the man she'd made love with: he'd
had a Southern accent.

"So, when can we meet?" Jack was asking. "Want to come
over to PIA, my agency, and then I'll take you out for some
lunch? How'd that be?"

"That'd be fine," Tessa told him, pulling herself together.
The man was really being very pleasant and after all they did
have a job to do. She glanced at her alarm clock. It was nine
o'clock, high time a working girl was up and about. "I'll come
to PIA, I'd love to see it. As for Honey Winslow, I left a
message for her to contact me once she got back and I haven't
heard a word so I thought . . ."

"Honey call you?" He sounded incredulous. "Ah, well, you
just don't know Honey. She doesn't exactly go out of her way
to make life easy for other people, just herself. But we can track
her down from here when you come. Come over around twelve,
OK?"

"OK."
"See you later, Tessa, 'bye."

She was shown into the PIA offices and was momentarily taken
aback by the glare of the lightboxes with a myriad of trans-
parencies laid out on them, being scrutinized by people with
microscopes. She knew a little about the agency, that it was a
repository, a base, an office for freelance photographers. It
seemed to her that they had all been called in on that particular
morning. The girl who had brought her back from reception
stopped and pointed.

"There's Jack, over there in the corner. See him? Hey, Jack,
someone from England to see you."

Tessa watched as a tall, sloping frame hunched over a
lightbox straightened up and turned in her direction. Immediately he raised an arm in welcome.

"Hi there! Come on over, I'm just looking at my stuff from
Tulsa. I was there to photograph a golf championship, would
you believe?"

His smile was wide and warm and, for the first time since she
had arrived in New York, Tessa got the feeling that someone
was genuinely pleased to see her. She found herself rushing
over to him, automatically extending her hand to be shaken by
his, a good, strong, firm grip.

"It's great to meet you. Truth is I've never worked with
anyone from England before but, hey, don't worry, I'm not
going to make you sit and talk about the country for hours on
end. There's nothing worse than the All-American Anglophile.
Let's go and eat, there's this place across the street that has just
about everything unless you'd like some Chinese or something . . ."

"Anything's OK with me. I'm delighted to meet you too,
Jack. Before we go, you said something about tracking down
Honey Winslow."

"I already did it. You get to go to her offices right after
lunch, just for a quick meeting. She said she had fifteen minutes
free. I thought it would make a lot of sense if we went over
there, you two met and we set up a series of interviews between
you and her. I can take the pictures separately or maybe I can
come along to one of your sessions with her, we'll see how it
goes. She's wild about the idea of the piece you're doing, any-

thing that'll put her back center stage. That's why she's willing
to give you lots of time. Believe me, Tessa, by the time you're
through you'll really know that lady . . ."

"You make it sound like you don't exactly envy me . . ."

"Well, I wouldn't say that, but then Honey Winslow, she's
some lady. Come on, I'll tell you about her over lunch."

Tessa followed him out of the elevator, noting that she had
quite a stride to keep up with him. That was rare. He was long-
legged and rangy, like a cowboy she thought, but realized that
probably had more to do with the fact that he was wearing a
plaid shirt, jeans and cowboy boots. Still, with her own long
legs, it wasn't often that she couldn't keep pace with a man.
This one had *Leader* written all over him, he clearly took it for
granted everyone would follow wherever he went. And there
was a wholesomeness to him, maybe he'd been a Boy Scout.
Did they have Boy Scouts in America? Well, whatever he was,
he was extremely good-looking and she felt quite proud of herself when she saw a number of women turn their heads to look
at him when he escorted her into the restaurant. Nor did she
miss the looks of envy they flashed at her a second later.

They were sitting in the glass-covered extension which jutted
right out onto the sidewalk of Columbus Avenue. Jack asked
her what she'd like to drink and then said: "I have a confession
to make. I've never seen any of your work."

"Well, actually I've never seen any of yours either," Tessa
laughed and stopped quickly. He was looking terribly offended.

"They've run my pictures in *Time* magazine," he told her.

"I'm quite sure they have. I suppose I must have missed
those particular issues, that's all. Does it matter? I mean, they
used my story on Sam Montefiore years ago, but you probably
never saw that either."

"Wait a second. I did read a story on Montefiore in *Time*,
about his autistic kid. That was you?"

She nodded. Instead of congratulating her, he looked suddenly uncomfortable. I see, thought Tessa, he's competitive and
probably more so with a woman, no doubt. How boring. Well,
she wouldn't let it bother her. She was confident in her writing,
enough to ask him: "Will you tell me about your work?"

And he did. For the entire lunch. Every now and then when
there was a break she would wait for him to ask her about
herself. But he didn't and whenever she volunteered some in-

formation he always contrived to bring the conversation back to himself saying something like, "Oh, yes, *I* had an experience like that once—it was about three years ago, I was in Los Angeles . . ." and off he would go again.

But he was cute. And funny and entertaining. She enjoyed listening to him or rather she found she was able to relax and enjoy the meal secure in the knowledge that she was not required to keep the conversation going. In fact every now and then she caught herself tuning out and thinking about other things—like what was happening in London for instance. To her amazement by the time coffee arrived she found herself comparing him with Jeremy—and favorably.

As he was getting the check he even managed to find someone else to talk about other than himself: "You know what? I *could* tell you about Honey Winslow's background."

"Oh, *please.* Where is she from?"

"The South."

"Oh yes, I remember hearing about that. In fact, I've done quite a bit of homework on her, about her rise to fame as the *Honey* perfume model."

"What's your angle exactly on this piece? Models then and now? Or is it more what Honey Winslow thinks of models then and now?"

"It could be either. To be perfectly honest, I want to leave it open, see what she's like to interview, see if there's any depth to her which might make it more than a profile of just another model, if you see what I mean . . ."

"Well, I'm not too sure about *depth.* Deep is not a word I'd use to describe Honey Winslow. It's all right out in the open with her. But you'll certainly find out she's more than just another model . . . *now.*"

"What do you mean *now?*"

"She recently became a successful businesswoman and I warn you that's what she'll want to talk about. Matter of fact, it's *all* she talks about these days, *Winslowear.*"

"What on earth is *Winslowear?*"

"It's this leisurewear line she's designed herself and has formed her own company to manufacture. In fact I brought along this piece someone did on it last week. Honey Winslow's just started talking to the Press about it. Here, you'd better read this, it's pretty banal stuff and it might give you an idea of what not to ask her when you start interviewing her . . ."

He dug a magazine out of his jacket pocket and passed it across to Tessa. She started to read where he indicated while he ordered coffee.

At the end of the article Tessa looked up.

"Says here she had a baby . . ."

"Really? I don't think I got that far. Is it the kidnapping story?"

"The what?"

"It was a big story in the Press about sixteen, seventeen years ago. She'd had this baby and it was kidnapped right from the clinic where it was born. Then it was found dead."

"But that's terrible! Who was the father?"

"She never said, and the Press moved on to other things after the baby's body was found. There was a lot of hoo-ha about the ransom demand and then when they went to pay it, they found the baby dead in some tenement block, so the story goes."

"Who put up the ransom money? Was she rich enough herself by then?"

"Could have been, I don't know. No, it was Perry Jay Duboise who helped her out."

The name was like an electric shock to both of them. *Duboise*. Tessa stiffened. Surely that was the name of the tenant in Jack's flat, the one she'd . . .

Jack slapped his head. "Of *course*! Why didn't I make the connection before? See, I've got someone of that name living in my apartment right now. I wonder if he's any relation. Never occurred to me before."

"Perry Jay Duboise is the Max Factor of the South, isn't he?" she asked, to cover her confusion.

"Yes, that's how Honey Winslow got started. He has this company, *Bayou Beauty* . . . Oh, you've heard of that? Well, he's Mr. *Bayou Beauty* and when he launched this new perfume called *Honey*, as you know, Honey Winslow was the model like Lauren Hutton and *Charlie*. She maybe knew the Duboise family from her childhood in the South, that'd be something you might want to ask her . . ."

"Or who the father of her baby was . . ."

"This doesn't sound to me like it's going to be an article about models then and now . . ."

"Hallelujah," said Tessa and laughed.

"I'll get the check and walk you over to *Winslowear*. It ought to be on Seventh Avenue seeing that it's part of the garment industry, but since it's run by Honey Winslow it's on Fifth Avenue."

Twenty minutes later they waited in the reception area of *Winslowear* while Honey Winslow was told they had arrived to see her. The whole of one wall was a bank of photographs of the lady herself, a montage which set out to tell the story of her life in pictures, starting with a baby picture in the top left hand corner and ending three rows down with Honey doing the split in one of her own velour *Winslowear* track suits in the bottom right hand corner.

Tessa's eye went straight to the end of the first row of pictures. There was Honey with a Fifties bouffant hairdo, a corsage pinned to the shoe-string shoulder strap of her dress. A typical Fifties High School picture. But it was the boy in the white sports coat with the carnation in his buttonhole on whom Tessa focused her attention. It was an old picture, grainy black and white, but she could still recognize the man who had made love to her earlier that week. P. J. Duboise.

As she looked at the picture of the smiling couple and waited for Honey Winslow to summon them, she knew she had the beginnings of her story.

Honey Winslow kept them waiting for forty-five minutes and each time they tried to leave the receptionist leapt up and stopped them.

"But she was only going to give us fifteen in any case," Jack protested.

"Yes, I know, but she'll be with you directly. She's been delayed and she's running a little late. She would hate for you to leave without seeing her. Please sit down," and she guided them back to the navy banquettes which ran along the wall opposite the bank of photographs. They sat down under a giant brass "W" (for *Winslowear*) which hung on the wall above them.

Finally Jack got to his feet again. "I've had it with hanging around this place. I've got work to do. I'll catch you later, Tessa," and before the receptionist could stop him he had gone.

"Thanks for lunch," Tessa called after him. Suddenly she

began to feel nervous. Her job depended on how she got on
with Honey Winslow. She'd been curious to meet the woman,
but not especially so. Up to now she had never really seemed a
reality, just a face in a magazine photograph. Any minute now
she would be a flesh and blood woman and by all accounts
someone to reckon with. And then there was the question of
P. J. Duboise . . .

Two models in *Winslowear* leotards came wandering through
the reception area.

"*Madame*'s jumpy as a cat in heat today," said one.

"Well, maybe she's got the rag on. She has to get it too just
like the rest of us." The other one laughed.

Terrific, thought Tessa, I'd better be on my way. But just as
she was about to leave, the doors burst open.

"Are you the limey journalist come to see me?" were the first
words Honey Winslow ever said to Tessa, who nodded. "Well,
listen now, we're going to have a reschedule. How about dinner, you free for dinner? Sure you are, get me Plaza 4-9494,"
she snapped at the receptionist and reached for the telephone to
be put through. "Hello? This is Honey Winslow, I want my
usual table for eight o'clock. Tonight? Of course I mean tonight. 'Bye."

She turned back to Tessa. "See you at the Four Seasons at
eight. Nice meeting you. Goodbye now."

And she was gone. Nice meeting me? I didn't say a word.
And she didn't even bother to find out if I was free tonight, just
took it for granted. Manners, Tessa concluded, were certainly
not Honey Winslow's strong suit.

What the hell was she going to do with herself for the rest of
the afternoon? Without realizing what she was doing, she left
the *Winslowear* building and caught an uptown bus for Broadway. She told herself she was going back to Larry's apartment
for a couple of hours, but before she could stop herself, she had
left the bus on 97th Street and was walking all the way down to
Riverside Drive.

She was going back to Jack Fern's apartment.

She rang the doorbell and when P. J. Duboise opened the
door and saw her standing there, he didn't seem at all surprised.

"Want some coffee? I'm just making some. Come on in."

He was naked to the waist and his feet were bare. She

watched his neat arse in his tight jeans as she followed him into the kitchen.

"I'm making coffee and I bought some donuts from that shop on the corner. Know the one I mean?" She nodded. "They've got jelly in them, raspberry jelly." He took them out of a paper bag on the counter.

"I know who you are," Tessa said.

"Shhh. Here." He plunged his index finger into a donut and quickly redirected it, covered in jelly, into Tessa's mouth. "Suck it," he told her, then lifted her bodily onto the counter. He was surprisingly strong.

"You're P. J. Duboise, aren't you?" She felt helpless, knew what was going to happen, wanted it to happen, knew that was the real reason she had come.

"So what?" he said, almost rudely, and began unbuttoning her shirt. He squeezed her breasts out of the black lacy cups of her bra until the nipples were exposed, then he bent his head and began to suck them. As she sat above him on the counter she could look down on the top of his black curly head as he moved his mouth from one breast to the other. She extended her legs and wrapped them around him. He pushed her back until she was lying flat across the counter, the small of her back lying in the powdered sugar spilling out of the donut bag.

PJ unzipped her skirt and pulled it off her. He took off her high-heeled shoes and stood them on the counter behind her head, next to a tall glass jar with spaghetti in it. He removed her panties, but left her stockings and garter belt. She was now lying half on, half off the kitchen counter and, gently, he lifted up her legs so that they lay flat, resting, reaching almost to the sink.

He bent his head again, but this time he moved to the area between her legs. As he tongued her and nipped at her, he reached for a donut and dangled it above her mouth. By the time she reached the jelly inside the donut, her own juices were flowing freely into his mouth. After she had come, he removed her bra and she lay, spent, along the counter reaching up idly to scratch the dark hairs on his chest as he stood over her.

"In England we have donuts with holes in them."

"So do we," he told her. His eyes narrowed and she looked up to see them glinting in excitement between his long black lashes. "Do you want one?"

"In a moment. Help me down." He did so and she pushed him back to stand against the counter. Now it was her turn to unzip him and his erection poked through his underpants as she lowered his jeans down his legs. She gave the tip of his penis a quick lick and he groaned.

She made him step out of his jeans while she pulled down his underpants.

She found a donut with a hole in the middle and hung it on his erection. She took an agonizing four minutes to nibble her way around it, imperceptibly grazing his penis with her tongue as she did so. As she took the last crumbs into her mouth he flung her down on the floor and thrust himself into her. He raised himself above her to the full extent of his arms, pulling his penis all the way out and then plunging back into her again. And again and again, harder and harder. She wrapped her legs around him and rocked herself from side to side, contracting her muscles as she did so, sucking him into her, moving him with her. She wanted him even more than she had the last time, more than she had ever wanted any other man in her life. Above all, she wanted him to come, to explode into her.

As he did so, she could have sworn he told her he loved her, something no man had ever said to her before.

They lay naked on the kitchen floor and drank coffee and finished the donuts. Every time Tessa opened her mouth to say something he filled it either with a donut or his tongue, devouring her mouth with his own, biting her lip until she could taste blood. Finally they relaxed, almost slept, their arms about each other.

The telephone on the kitchen wall suddenly began to ring, shattering their peace.

"I know who you are," Tessa reminded him although she didn't know why.

"The guy who lives here has an answering machine. He's a photographer. It'll pick up. Wait a second."

It was Jack himself calling. The machine recorded his message and then played it back into the kitchen. It was eerie lying naked on his kitchen floor listening to his voice echoing through the apartment.

"Hi! This is Jack Fern. I was just calling to say I'm back in town and was wondering if I could stop by tonight around six to pick up some of my stuff. If you're not there I have my own key. Hope to meet you. G'bye." There was a click.

Tessa got to her feet and dressed silently. PJ lay on the floor and watched her. She waited for him to speak, to ask her when he would see her again, but he just stared at her, not saying a word. Finally she blurted out: "I'm having dinner with Honey Winslow tonight." Surely that would provoke some reaction, but his face became if anything even more impassive.

"You know Honey Winslow, don't you? Weren't you at High School with her? Only I saw your picture at her office, on the wall. When you were kids, at a dance it looked like. I'm here to do an article on her, I'm a journalist, maybe you could tell me something about her? *Oh, why did you pretend to be Jack Fern the other night?*"

She knew she'd gone too far. She should have stopped when she saw how he shut himself off at the mention of Honey Winslow. The clock on the wall said it was getting on for five forty-five. Jack Fern would be arriving any second. She had to go. As she picked up her bag and turned to leave, he gave her a nonchalant little wave of the hand. But his face remained without expression, cold, withdrawn—a far cry from the passionate creature who had writhed above her a short while before.

As she let herself out of Jack Fern's apartment for the second time that week, she never noticed PJ's bags lined up in the hall, packed and ready for departure.

"Sex is everything!" pronounced Honey Winslow at the top of her voice. She was sitting opposite Tessa in the Grill Room at the Four Seasons and Tessa flushed. Did it show? Could Honey tell just by looking at her that she had had sex that afternoon?

After leaving PJ in Jack Fern's apartment she had rushed home to take a shower. While she was washing her hair she heard Larry come in and realized she hadn't closed the bathroom door. He'd have a clear view of her body through the shower curtain as he passed by on his way to his room. Well, to hell with it. She could handle Larry.

She had tied her toweling robe firmly around her and marched defiantly into the kitchen to pour herself a glass of wine. Larry had just fixed himself a Scotch and raised his glass to her. She knew what was coming before he even opened his mouth.

"Hey, Tessa, you got dinner all sorted out?"

"I have, as a matter of fact, I'm going to the Four Seasons."

Larry's jaw had dropped open. Literally. The Four *Seasons*? Who the hell was taking her to the Four Seasons? He looked crestfallen. "You musta lucked into a real rich guy if he's taking you to the Four Seasons for your first date . . ."

"It's work," she told him, "and it's a woman who's taking me."

He brightened considerably. "Don't forget to bring me a doggy bag."

Tessa selected basic black: a silk T-shirt and a silk jersey wraparound skirt. She hung a long string of pearls Granny Betty had given her around her neck and added her favorite pearl and lapis earrings to give some color. When she swung her long auburn hair over her shoulder the blue of the lapis could be glimpsed in her ears.

American women—or rather New York women—were extremely chic, Tessa had noticed. They were not chic in the way that Frenchwomen were. Their style was different, more executive chic, but it was a studied look, a contrived casual appearance. They were not as hard-looking as the French, but like the Frenchwoman, the rich American took her grooming seriously. The Frenchwoman's look said, *I am dressed to perfection,* naturellement, whereas the American woman declared, *I've spent a fortune and it'd damn well better show.* The British woman, thought Tessa, just says, *Well, here I am.* But she had to admit to herself that she'd been making more of an effort since she had been in New York.

When she walked into the Four Seasons she felt perfectly confident. In fact she was glowing and her eyes were shining. Sex always did that to her. It probably did it to everyone. But few people turned to look at her and, as she sat waiting for Honey Winslow, she acknowledged that it was because she did not look rich. She looked natural, attractive, warm. But she did not look like a million dollars, as the saying went.

When Honey Winslow arrived all heads turned. She too was in black, but the difference between hers and Tessa's was approximately fifteen hundred dollars. She was wearing a tight-fitting black suede jacket with a stand-up collar and plunging *décolleté*. Her hair was swept off her face and up into a chignon. A heavy gold choker gripped her long neck and huge gold egg-shaped earrings gleamed from her ears. The matching black suede pants were skin-tight in the matador style and ended just above her ankles. The heels on her black crocodile shoes added a good three inches to her height.

Tessa felt her confidence evaporating. Already the stark, cavernous ambience of the Four Seasons had begun to depress her. She found it so gloomy, so overpowering. She would have derived a certain amount of comfort had she realized that many of the diners would have felt equally overawed if they had found themselves about to sit down to a full-scale dinner in the oak-paneled dining hall at Bellcloud.

Honey Winslow didn't apologize for her lateness, merely snapped her fingers at a passing waiter and demanded a kir royale.

"You?" She looked at Tessa to whom she had not even said hello and Tessa realized she was being asked what she wanted to drink.

"A white wine and . . ."

"Bring her a spritzer," Honey told him. "So, what's it you want? What's the angle?"

"That all depends."

"On what?"

"On you." Suddenly Tessa decided she was going to give as good as she got.

"I can be happy, I can be blue, it all depends on you . . ." sang Honey. "What do you mean, it all depends on *me*? You're the one who's writing the damn thing, but let me tell you something up front, I'd sure appreciate a big mention for *Winslowear*. I'm coming over to England to launch it there. You do know about *Winslowear*, don't you?"

"I certainly do," Tessa said, "but that's not why I came across to interview you."

"Oh?"

"No, I'm doing this piece for a magazine and they're putting together this article on models then and now and . . ."

"Yeah, yeah, yeah, and I'm supposed to be part of the *then*, right? Thanks a lot."

"No, wait a minute, that's why I said it all depends on you, Honey. May I call you Honey?"

"Ah, Jesus, you Brits are so goddamned polite. It's my name, isn't it?"

"Thank you. Please call me Tessa."

"You were saying something about it all depends on me?"

"Exactly. What I'd like to do is just talk to you over a period of time, say the next two or three days, about anything *you* want to tell me . . . about your childhood, how you became a model, what it meant to you, what tips you might have for other girls starting out, how you became such a high-powered businesswoman . . ."

Honey reached across the table and patted Tessa's hand. A broad smile spread across her face. "High-powered businesswoman. *Now* you're talking! Where shall I begin?"

"P. J. Duboise," replied Tessa and hid behind her menu.

"What about him?"

"What about him?"

"Yeah. That's what I asked you. What about him?"

"Well, you knew him?"

"Of *course* I knew him. I knew the whole damn family. His father got me started. What's it to you anyway?"

"I saw the picture of the two of you on the wall at *Winslowear* and I thought maybe you were childhood sweethearts, perhaps he had introduced you to his father and that's how your career started. I thought maybe we could start there . . ." Tessa's voice trailed off. Honey was giving her a look filled with suspicion. Had she hit on the truth by accident?

"Now, why on God's earth would I want to spend time talking about a deadbeat Southern boy like him? Seems to me that you've been doing a bit too much thinking. Now, let's eat. No more talk about P. J. Duboise. What are you going to have?"

While they chose their food Tessa made a mental note to go back to the subject of P. J. Duboise at some point in the future.

Honey reached for her purse and pulled out an ornamental silver cigarette case and lighter. She offered one to Tessa who declined and lighted one for herself seconds before a passing waiter brandished a match under her nose almost setting fire to her eyelashes. She waved him away and beamed at Tessa.

"So, tell me about yourself. One of Britain's hotshot journalists, are you?"

"Oh, no, far from it, I'm just—"

"Oh, for heaven's sake! Why are you being so modest? That's so typical of you British women. You never want to stand up and tell the world how sensational you are."

"We don't have to. Everyone can see it a mile away."

"Hey, hey, *touché*! That's more like it, sweetheart. But I don't see nothing sensational about most of you Englishwomen. I'll admit you got your beautiful complexions and all, but you're born with those and the moisture in the air keeps them that way, but not forever. You British girls just don't know how to look after yourselves after you reach a certain age. Time you reach thirty-five all you got left is a shiny nose and ruddy cheeks with broken veins all over the place and it's downhill all the way after that. So what is it that's so special it shines out of you from every scrubbed little pore?"

"Our individuality, our class, our *savoir-faire*, our ability to laugh at ourselves, our subtlety, our good manners, our attractive melodious voices. Furthermore, underneath our basic reserve which, incidentally, some people find most refreshing, we are invariably more perceptive by nature and have been known to stop and think before opening our mouths. For example, I suspect that you, Honey Winslow, were not born to the wealth to which you are accustomed today and that is why you flaunt it and yourself all over the place." Tessa was aware that she was being unpardonably rude, but nothing would stop her now. Honey Winslow had asked for it.

"Look at it this way, you're world famous, just about everybody recognizes you, yet you persist in drawing attention to yourself as if you were frightened nobody would notice you. I suspect this comes from a perfectly natural feeling of insecurity within yourself, which is something we all experience, yet in the American woman it manifests itself in the most extraordinary ways. She will endure and deliver a never-ending stream of plastic platitudes. If she arrives to have an abortion she will no doubt be told to 'have a nice day.' She is, by and large, unable to admit to her insecurity with calm and composure; she dare not own up to the fact that she might be a smidgen less than 100 per cent Miss Success from top to toe. The only person to whom she will do this is to her analyst. British women do not have analysts, Honey. Not many of them anyway. They have friends instead. And they have themselves. Your British woman admits to *herself* that she has failings, that she is human, that things do go wrong in her life and, God help her, the only thing to do is pick herself up, dust herself down and start all over again."

Tessa paused for breath and Honey butted in.

"Well, same here . . . Believe me, I've had some knocks in my time and I've come through, but I like to think it's on account of my *American* spirit and don't you go quoting that 'look who won the war' crap, you weren't around during the blitz. Besides, you're talking about New York women. Have you been anywhere else in the States? No? OK, so I make a big noise, but if you're going to make it over here, Tessa Whatever Your Name Is, you have to do some shouting. You might get by on your cute little British accent for a while, but not for long. The time will come when you'll have to enter the rat race, especially in New York City, otherwise they're going to take you for a loser and walk all over you. Life's too short for refined little Minnie Mouses in Manhattan. And by the way, I just don't happen to believe there's anything wrong in striving for success, in trying to be a winner . . ."

"Ain't what you do, it's the way . . ."

". . . *that you do it.* Yeah, I heard that one too. So let me ask you something. I've done it my way. The American way. And you've done it the British way. Which one is the most successful?"

"Point taken."

"You have to be assertive. Make demands. You're not the little kid anymore. You gotta act like an adult . . . ah, hell, I'm going to get off my soap-box. What'll we talk about now? What about men? You like men?"

Tessa laughed. Honey Winslow was outrageous, but she was beginning to like her for some inexplicable reason. Or was it so inexplicable? She says exactly what she thinks and I like her for it. She may be infuriating but she's got guts. I'm going to enjoy doing these interviews, Tessa thought to herself.

Aloud she said: "Yes, Honey, I like men."

"Me too. Tell you what I think? *Sex is everything.*"

And now everyone turned to look at them, she had said it so loudly. Their food arrived and for the rest of the meal Tessa thoroughly enjoyed herself. She steered clear of potentially inflammatory subjects like P. J. Duboise, although she would have loved to learn more about him. A nagging voice which she pushed repeatedly to the back of her mind kept asking, would she ever hear from him again? Not that she'd heard from him

in the first place. On both occasions she had gone to him . . .
Would she have to do so again?

"Excuse me, Miss Winslow, there's a call for your guest." A
waiter hovered at their table with the telephone in his hand.

It was Larry. It had to be. He was the only person who knew
she was at the Four Seasons.

"Forgive me?" she turned to Honey, who shrugged her
shoulders and nodded go ahead.

"Tessa, is that you? There's been a call for you from England. They say it's urgent, wouldn't tell me what it was. You
gotta come home and call your mother."

Now it was Tessa's turn to shrug her shoulders at Honey.

"Afraid I have to go home and call my mother. Thank you
for a wonderful meal. I'm only sorry I can't stay for coffee."

"My pleasure. You call my office tomorrow and we'll fix up
some meetings for the interview. Check please!" she hailed the
waiter. "Who knows, I might even tell you all my secrets, you
never can tell . . ." and she wagged a finger playfully at Tessa.
"You just never can tell."

As Honey left the restaurant, Alphonse Lenoir stood silently in
the shadows on the steps leading up to Park Avenue. He recalled the moment when he had returned home from Vietnam
and seen her picture hanging high above Times Square. It was
then that he had known that what he had always predicted had
come to pass, that while he had been away she had become
truly a goddess. He wanted to approach her but he dared not
and knew he must be content to worship her from afar. For the
time being . . .

Jack Fern had been out to grab some Szechuan take-out on
Broadway and was returning to his apartment when he saw one
of the most shapely legs he had ever seen emerging from a cab
on 97th Street. The other followed and the owner's skirt was
pulled up her thigh as she leant back to pay the driver. Finally
she stepped out onto the sidewalk.

"Tessa!" called Jack and crossed the street. She looked
rushed and nervous.

"There's been a call from England. Something's happened. I
must ring them."

Jack put his arm around her shoulders.

"Hey, hey, hey. Take it easy. Come to my place. Make your call from there."

He guided her down to Riverside Drive and up to his apartment, helped her place the call.

To Tessa's surprise, it was her grandmother who answered the phone.

"Brace yourself, darling. It's your grandfather. He's dead. I'm sorry to have to tell you like this, but there's no other way. It was terribly sudden, Tessa dear, and they say he suffered no pain which is a mercy, but then they always do say that, don't they?"

Tessa had begun to cry. She couldn't help herself. The last time she had seen Sir Hugh they had had that terrible argument and now he was dead and she would never be able to make it up to him. She was aware of Jack taking the receiver from her, heard odd words, *funeral, Saturday, see she makes it, all that can wait, of course I will, my condolences* and then he was holding her in his arms, stroking her hair, telling her everything was going to be all right.

Tessa felt only his strength. She clung to him even when he lowered her gently down onto the sofa. After a long while her sobbing ceased and she lay against his chest. She felt dazed. "Where am I?" she whispered. "In my apartment." And looking up, she recognized it. "But your tenant . . . ?" Only that afternoon she had been . . . in the kitchen . . . "He's gone. Disappeared. Taken all his stuff. He paid until the end of the month, but he's gone. P. J. Duboise. Vanished into thin air."

Over the next twenty-four hours Tessa was reminded constantly of something Honey Winslow had said about Jack Fern during their dinner: "He's a take-charge kind of a guy." Jack organized everything for her and drove her to the airport himself.

As she was about to go through the gate to the Departure Lounge to board her flight for England and Sir Hugh Heron-Sweeney's funeral, she turned back to thank Jack for all he'd done.

And once again she found herself in his arms, moulding herself against his long, tall, comforting frame. Only this time when she looked up into his face he lowered his head and kissed her on the lips. It was a gentle, relaxed kiss, but he put a lot of feeling into it and right at the end he moved his mouth to blow in her ear and whisper: "I'll be thinking of you. Come back to me soon."

CHAPTER 16

Betty Heron-Sweeney noticed a distinct change in her grand-daughter when Tessa came home to Bellcloud for the funeral. For a start there was an air of self-confidence about her which the old lady had never seen before.

Tessa had made the odd visit to Bellcloud since she had left, but Betty couldn't help but notice that it was always when Hugh was away. What had happened to cause them to be so estranged? Hugh had been like a father to Tessa when she was growing up, taken the place of her own father. Well, at least she had taken the trouble to come back for the funeral. She'd never thought she'd live to see the day when one of her own family became a—what did they call them now?—jetsetter and now here was Tessa nipping across the Atlantic as if she were cross-ing the Thames.

Betty Heron-Sweeney watched her striding down the plat-form toward her. Those loose, baggy trousers reminded her of the ones Amy used to wear in the Forties, but unlike Amy, Tessa had gathered hers into her trim waist with an extremely stylish leather belt and Amy's had never had those flattering tucks over the stomach, nor would she have worn with them such a beautifully tailored shirt. Shapeless woolly sweaters had always been more Amy's line. Betty sighed. It was immensely gratifying to know that Tessa had inherited her own interest in clothes. Betty knew she shouldn't be thinking of such trivial things as fashion with poor Hugh hardly cold in his grave, but she couldn't help it. Anyway, he wasn't in his grave yet, wouldn't be for another two days. Now what had the darling child done with her hair? It looked different. Ah, that was it . . . as Tessa turned her head Betty was able to see the elegant plait hanging down her back. *Very* stylish. Pity Hugh wasn't there, he'd have been proud of his granddaughter. Betty held out her arms, wincing as she noticed how Tessa had to stoop to embrace her.

"Tessa, my angel. How sad that it should take something like this to bring you back to me. You look quite enchanting, my dear. Now, come on, darling, is that all the luggage you've brought? It doesn't look as if you are planning to stay with me very long. What a shame, but never mind, we mustn't waste a second. Ben's waiting in the station yard with the car."

"Ben? Didn't Mummy drive you to meet me?"

"No. I'm afraid Amy's been locked in her room since it happened . . . Now, darling, no more now because I don't want to discuss matters in front of Ben. Just give me one more hug and tell me you're glad to be home."

"Oh, Granny, of course I am. How awful that you should have to ask me to say it—now, let's get home for tea. I want to hear all about it."

"Wonderful to see you, Miss Tessa," Ben told her, pumping her hand up and down. Dear God, thought Tessa, he looks far too old to drive. But clearly Granny Betty felt safe with him and once they got going Tessa understood why. Ben drove at fifteen miles an hour for the entire journey. It seemed like an eternity before the huge wrought-iron gates which marked the beginning of the drive loomed before them.

And then she saw. Bellcloud. The sprawling Elizabethan house, its red brick basking in the rosy glow of the afternoon sun, looked as inviting as ever.

Ben deposited them at the front door and lifted out the luggage. Tessa walked into the vast hall with the sunlight streaming down through the oriel window. There was a strange sound

not unlike caterwauling echoing through the house and she
could not make out what it was.

"That's your mother," her grandmother offered by way of
explanation. "She's been singing hymns ever since poor Hugh
collapsed."

"Tell me what happened, Granny. Was it awful? I feel so
terrible not having been here."

"There would have been nothing you could have done. He
was here, in his study," she motioned Tessa into the room,
"pouring himself a brandy after dinner when I heard a crash,
glass shattering. I rushed in. He'd dropped the decanter and he
was lying there on that rug. It's funny, Tessa, I knew he was
dead. Of course, I did all the things one does, called the ambulance, Dr. Manners, begged Ben and Mrs. Ben to *do* something,
yet I knew from the moment I saw him that he was gone, there
was nothing we could do."

"Poor Granny. And Mummy? What did she do?"

"Nothing. Not a single thing. She was absolutely useless.
You know, it really is most odd. Last night after dinner I
dragged her in here and made her sit down and have a chat
with me. The thing is, if anyone must know what it's like to
lose a husband, it's Amy. I thought she might be able to help
me, it might be something we could share, discuss together.
Lord knows how I've tried to get close to my own daughter
over the years and if it takes an occasion as sad as this one for
us to have something in common, so be it. Not a bit of it. Do
you know what she had the audacity to say to me? She said I'd
never loved her father. I think she's going round the twist or
whatever you call it. You see, Tessa—and believe me, darling,
this is not meant as a criticism—you don't come here very often
so you haven't seen much of her lately, but she's been getting
steadily worse. I just have this terrible feeling that one day she's
going to explode and it's all going to come pouring out and I
won't be strong enough to deal with it."

"Do you think she should see someone?"

"You can't mean a *psychiatrist*? Tessa, darling, there are limits."

"Everyone in New York sees one. They call them analysts."

"Well, we can't send Amy to New York. Out of the question."

"No, Granny, they have them in England too."

"Oh, no, no, heavens no. It's unthinkable. Next thing they'll be locking her up."

"Granny, honestly, it's not like that now. Lots of people go to them. It's just a way of seeking help in solving your problems."

"Tessa, surely you're not saying, I mean you don't . . ."

"No, I don't, but that's because I don't need to, but if I did think I needed help I wouldn't be ashamed of going to one. It makes sense. In fact there have been moments when I've wondered if I ought not to see someone about my father."

"What on earth for? He's dead."

"I needed to find out more about him and no one would ever tell me anything. It's worried me for years, Granny."

"Has it really? You astonish me. I thought we'd told you everything we could and I'm afraid I'm no use about what happened when he died as they left me behind when they went to Wales. Besides, I really cannot see how a psychiatrist is going to be able to tell you about him, unless you think you could lay your hands on one who knew him."

"It doesn't work like that, Granny. You learn to discover yourself through talking about your parents and their effect on you. Or the fact that they weren't there and the effect *that* had on you."

"Oh, stuff and nonsense. I will have no more talk of these people and Amy is certainly not going near one. No, darling, what I thought might be best would be for you to have a little talk with her."

"Oh no, please, Granny," Tessa said, desperately.

"Well, darling, you know there is one really rather serious matter. Bellcloud."

Tessa sat down suddenly on the sofa. "Surely nothing's going to happen to Bellcloud now that Grandpa's dead?"

"Supposing he's left it to Amy? She'd turn it into a haven for all her causes."

"But surely he'd have left everything to you, Granny."

"Who knows what Hugh might have done? Changing his will was one of his favorite occupations. I had your Uncle Ferdy on the telephone this very morning. Of course he pretended he was calling to ask about the arrangements for the funeral, but he managed to slip in a quick question about the will. Monty and Lucien were marginally more restrained. They telephoned your grandfather's solicitor instead of me. But you know, Tessa, the old boy had a soft spot for Amy. She was his only daughter and he knew I never could abide her. No, don't shake your head like that. It's best I face up to the fact. I dislike my own daughter and I have no compunction about telling you that, Tessa, even if she is your mother. It's you I feel close to, always have, always will."

"I know, Granny. I feel the same way about you, but I feel so awful. She's my mother. All I ever wanted her to do was to show that she noticed that I was around. To her I'm just a person who could help her in the garden. She's never realized I'm a human being."

"Darling, don't upset yourself. There's nothing wrong with you. She's the one who's in trouble. So could you have a talk, Tessa, work at her, draw her out, please . . . before you go?"

"I'll do it tonight, Granny, after dinner," said Tessa. Inwardly she dreaded it.

"Bless you. Now, before you go upstairs to wash, tell me about New York. Are you happy there? Are you going to stay?"

"I don't know. I mean I don't know if I'm going to stay there, but in answer to your first question, yes, I think I am happy there."

"Forgive me if I'm prying, but did you leave London because you were unhappy there? Problems with a young man?"

"Granny, you're amazing, but I'm not going to tell you anything about that. I don't know if you would like New York. It's dirty and the pace is very fast. I feel enormously stimulated from just walking along the streets, but at the same time, I can feel utterly defeated a second later. There's a strong feeling of competition everywhere and it requires a lot of energy to feel on top. You expend much more energy somehow. There's a constant demand on it, no matter what you're doing, a strong pull, a force propelling you along whether you like it or not and if you don't feel up to it for some reason or another, then it can really get you down. But the thing that really interests me is that I'm learning a lot about people. They're tough over there, but they're genuine."

Betty sounded rather dubious.

"I have to confess the ones I've met were awfully loaded and brash."

"Well, that's probably because we make them feel uncomfortable. They overcompensate for the excruciating modesty of the British by showing off all the time. But they're warm, Granny. I'm only talking about New Yorkers, of course, and they say New York is not America, but there's a great community spirit in New York, everyone knows everyone on their block, rather like the village here."

"Well, I've read stories about people being mugged and murdered on the street and everyone turning a blind eye. Doesn't sound like community spirit to me." Betty Heron-Sweeney turned away. She *had* been nervous of Tessa going to New York, but had so far kept her feelings well hidden.

"Granny, there *are* a lot of crazy people in New York. I'm not saying there aren't. There's a murderer running around the city right now killing women, but if you suddenly saw a man with a sawed-off shotgun or a switch-blade going for the person on the other side of the street, would you actually run over and get involved? I don't think so somehow . . ."

"But you do have some *nice* friends?" Granny Betty asked uncertainly.

"I have some fantastic friends, but it's wonderful to be back here, Granny. I'm going to go and unpack now. Dinner at eight as usual?"

"Shall we make it seven-thirty if you're going to have that little talk with your mother afterwards? You'll hear the gong. And please don't be too critical about the food. Mrs. Ben isn't as young as she used to be, but I haven't the heart to replace her."

"Nonsense, Granny, you're all heart but I know what you mean. See you later."

How I love that girl, thought Betty Heron-Sweeney as Tessa left the room. How I wish she could stay here with me instead of my own daughter.

The dam burst during dinner when Mrs. Ben served the cold watercress soup. Tessa knew after one spoonful that she was going to have difficulty in finishing her bowl. There might be watercress in there somewhere, but she couldn't taste it. Yet she was not prepared for her mother's outrage.

"Watercress soup!" shrieked Amy. "We can't have watercress soup. Papa hates it."

Betty Heron-Sweeney and Tessa tried not to look at each other. Mrs. Ben stood beside Amy looking most uncomfortable, clutching the soup tureen to her chest.

"I suggest you take it away immediately, Mrs. Ben. If Papa sees it I wouldn't like to be in your shoes."

Mrs. Ben dropped the tureen and stumbled out of the dining room. Watercress soup trickled into the cracks between the floorboards. Nobody moved until Amy, as if emerging from a trance, said: "Of course, he's dead," and slowly she rose and walked out of the room.

"*Now*, Tessa," said Betty Heron-Sweeney firmly, "go to her now."

Tessa was unprepared for her mother's opening shot. It was almost as if Amy had been expecting some kind of confrontation with her daughter.

"You couldn't possibly know what it's like, Tessa. After all, you hardly knew your own father and you were much too young to understand or feel anything when he went."

Tessa said nothing. Her instinct told her to remain silent, to offer no provocation. She was right. Amy looked at her and it all came tumbling out.

"I was never a beauty, Tessa. Mama wanted a beauty, I've always known it. There was nothing I could do. But Papa understood. He never said anything, but I knew he understood how I felt. I felt comfortable with him. And your father, he was the same."

Tessa held her breath. This was the first time her mother had ever brought her father into the conversation of her own accord.

"Elliott did not require me to be beautiful. He only wanted me to be me. He never challenged me, never seemed to notice that I was plain, that I had no interest in parties and dancing and those silly dresses everyone was wearing. He understood my interest in things like the British Legion and the Church, far more than your Uncle Johnny did by the way. Your father was the closest thing to a saint I have ever come across. Of course," Amy swung away, and began fiddling with a hairbrush on her dressing table, "there were moments when he was . . . *persistent*, especially when he returned from the war, but I suppose otherwise we should not have been blessed with you."

This was the closest her mother had ever come to saying she

was pleased to have a daughter. Tessa wondered if the time had come to offer a reciprocal gesture, say something which might bring them together as mother and daughter for the first time. But Amy was not finished.

"Then I lost him. And at the same time I lost my father."

At the same time? Tessa was confused.

"Something happened. Papa turned against Elliott, would not speak to him. And then he died and he forbade me ever to mention his name again. From that day on my relationship with my father changed. We no longer talked or shared our feelings. Yes, Tessa, I have feelings too. Don't look so surprised. Oh, Papa tried to engage me in the kind of chats we used to have together, but I was always aware of Elliott standing there, invisible, between us. I no longer trusted Papa. I knew I had lost them both and there was only one person I could turn to."

Tessa was about to ask if she meant Uncle Johnny when she realized her mother meant God. She switched tacks abruptly.

"I'm sorry, Mummy," she said gently. "I'm sorry I plagued you with questions about my father. I never knew all this. But don't you see, I'm here and Grandpa's gone. You can talk about my father now, you can talk about him to me, you can tell me everything."

"No, I *can't*! You don't understand. Now Papa has gone it makes it worse. He is dead, but I must still respect his wishes. It would be terrible if I started to disobey him the minute he was gone. One day I shall be reunited with Elliott again and I must just be patient and wait until that time."

And until then she'll Fight the Good Fight, thought Tessa grimly. She's a psychiatrist's dream, there's so much inside there waiting to be unlocked. Poor Mummy. Instinctively she moved to put her arms around her mother as she sat on the edge of her bed, but Amy moved away. No, Tessa realized, she doesn't want me to penetrate her cocoon. I must remind her of my father, of what she lost. She will never be fully aware of who I am. She has not asked a single question about me, she has not even asked me how I am. It's not that she doesn't care, it's just as Granny said, she's not aware that she cares.

Moving very slowly so as not to disturb Amy as she sat in her trance, Tessa went to the dressing table and picked up one of the photographs of her father in its silver frame. Gently she placed it in her mother's hands and while Amy looked down to

gaze at the picture, Tessa quietly kissed the top of her head.
Amy never noticed, but Tessa didn't mind. She realized it was
something she had wanted to do for a long time and if she had
to do it when her mother was unaware of what was happening,
then she would. There would come a time when she would be
able to embrace her mother whenever she wanted. But that
time was a long way away. Meanwhile she must be patient and
as she closed the door to her mother's bedroom she heard the
echo of her grandfather's voice: *Patience is a virtue, virtue is a
grace, and Grace is a little girl who wouldn't wash her face.*

The question of the will was solved the next day. Sir Hugh's
solicitor called Betty Heron-Sweeney to fix a time for the reading and at the same time informed her that she was the main
beneficiary. Bellcloud was hers to do with what she wanted. He
suggested that she might want to keep her eye open for any new
will he might have made when she went through his things.
Just in case. Betty sighed. There was so much to be done. She
had stoically tackled the mass of papers deposited all over his
study, but when she had ventured up to the vast room which
ran almost the entire length of the house under the roof of the
kitchen wing and the servants' quarters, she had balked. Sir
Hugh had succeeded in filling eight trunks with files and correspondence and she had been only too happy to accept Tessa's
offer to help sort it out. But the real reason they were getting
together was to have a chance to decide what to do about Amy
and they both knew it.

But if Tessa thought it was just an excuse she was mistaken.
Granny Betty had kept her at it in the attic hall all morning
and it was only when they sat down to lunch that she raised the
issue.

"Tessa, dear, I've been thinking about Amy."

Ah, finally the old lady was getting round to it.

"Yes, you see, Tessa, there's the question of the family history your grandfather has been compiling for years. Heaven
knows why, because if anybody wants the basic details they
only have to look in Burke's *Landed Gentry*. There are pages
and pages of Heron-Sweeneys going back at least two or three
centuries."

"Really, Granny? Am I in it?"

"I expect so. Hugh was responsible for updating it whenever

hey sent him a copy for the revised editions." Tessa made a
nental note to go and dig it out of the library after lunch.

"But the thing is, he'd almost finished it and if you can be-
ieve this, he'd actually managed to interest some idiot pub-
isher in London. The whole thing is quite beyond me. I
ictually sat down and began to read a bit of it the other day
ind I tell you, my dear, I swear he's made most of it up. But
hat's neither here nor there. He may have kept quiet about it,
»ut it was the old boy's passion towards the end. I really feel I
»we it to him to see that it gets finished, so I thought Amy
could do it. She can turn it into one of her causes. How did
our talk with her go, by the way? She seemed a shade less
morose this morning."

Tessa paused before answering. It was possible that Amy
emembered nothing of what she had told Tessa the night be-
ore, but even if Tessa repeated the odd sentence, she knew that
she would feel disloyal to her mother. It would be a betrayal of
some kind. She couldn't do it. Yet it was her grandmother who
had supported and comforted her throughout her childhood,
not Amy. How could she hold out on her? She had to compro-
mise.

"I didn't get a chance to say much, Granny." Lord knows
hat was true.

"Didn't you? Ah, well, I suppose it was wishful thinking on
my part. But what do you think of my plan to put her onto the
amily history?"

"I think it's an excellent idea, Granny. But who's going to
»ut it to her? Rather you than me, she'll listen to you at least."

"Oh, I wouldn't be too sure about that. Hugh was the only
»ne who could get her attention. She adored him, you know,
Tessa. I'm ashamed to admit it, but she probably does miss him
more than I do. I shall have to tell her that it was Hugh who
isked that she complete it in the event of his death. The whitest
ie there ever was, but it's the only way."

After lunch, pleading the need for fresh air, Tessa walked out
nto the garden. She had to come to terms with the summer-
rouse. As she sat on the stone slab which served as a bench,
nemories of her grandfather came flooding back. What had it
»een about her father which had enraged him so? What had
rappened to cause him to forbid her to come here? She closed
ier eyes and could feel only the warmth of the hot afternoon

sun. It made her feel sensual, even slightly aroused, it made her think of Jack Fern. No, not him, the feeling was more intense, something she hadn't yet experienced with Jack. It was pure, unadulterated lust which swept over her now as she sat in this hitherto forbidden place, lust for that strange man with the Southern accent who had infiltrated her defenses and given her such unashamed pleasure. P. J. Duboise. Had he disappeared forever? And what about Jack Fern? Would he become part of her life when she returned to New York?

Her mind was not on Hugh Heron-Sweeney's papers at all in the attic that afternoon. Several times her grandmother had to give her arm a tug to bring her back to reality. It was only when she came to a square box of neatly typed letters that Tessa's attention managed to focus fully on the matter at hand.

They were typed on old-fashioned quarto paper, a format rarely seen nowadays, she reflected. The address at the top was a Post Office box number in France. They were all typewritten and began "Dear Professor Heron-Sweeney" and when she turned over the page Tessa saw that instead of a handwritten signature the sender's name was also typewritten: *Eric Christian.* Good heavens, the thriller writer. How wonderful to think that her grandfather had been carrying on a correspondence with such a famous author all these years.

"Granny, would you mind awfully if I kept these? They're some letters from Eric Christian, the crime writer, and there's really not very much known about him."

"Of course you can, my dear. I found a mass of those trashy paperbacks downstairs, but I'm afraid I threw them all away. Hugh used to devour them after dinner. I don't care what you do with the letters."

Tessa carefully folded them back into the box; there seemed to be a surprising number of incomplete words on the page. Looking closer, she found that the "O" key of Eric Christian's typewriter was clearly bent or broken.

The good weather broke the day of the funeral and the rain came pouring down. The service was held in the Norman church at Bellcloud and afterward they all trooped out to the open grave.

Tessa found herself surrounded by a rain-sodden crowd of Oxford academics and their ruddy-cheeked wives with straggling gray hairs wisping down underneath their dull green rainhats. The umbrellas poked her in the eye and when she stooped to place a bouquet of red roses on Sir Hugh's casket as it was being lowered into the ground and her skirt slid up to reveal her long and beautiful legs, they tsk-tsk'd away like a bunch of disapproving adders.

Betty Heron-Sweeney, who had already buried three brothers, hated the pomp of funerals and was anxious to get indoors and start dispensing cups of tea and the odd brandy. She was also becoming slightly embarrassed by Amy's highly audible sniffing. Her sons were all behaving perfectly well. Trust Amy to let the side down. Tessa was doing her best to steer her mother away from the graveside, but she insisted on staying, trumpeting into her handkerchief.

Johnny Simpson had come down from London bringing with him his little blonde wife.

"Don't see why he had to bring Fluffy with him," grumbled Amy between gulps.

"Her name's Doris, Mummy," said Tessa, by now exasperated. "Do try to remember. They're coming over."

But Amy turned away. The mist was clearing and so was the crowd of mourners. They were making their way across the south lawn to enter Bellcloud by the conservatory and start stuffing themselves with the tea laid out on trestle-tables amidst the tropical plants.

"Time for tea, Mummy," said Tessa firmly, but Amy wouldn't budge.

"I don't want tea. Please leave me be and let me stay here with the old man for a while. They don't want me in there. His stuffy Oxford friends never liked me anyway."

So Tessa left her and began to walk across the rain-sodden lawn toward the conservatory. As she was about to enter something made her pause and look back toward the churchyard. There were two figures left standing at the graveside, one at each end of the grave. Tessa could make out her mother in her black felt hat with the round crown and wide brim, still staring down. The other figure was a man of about Amy's age, tall, thin and a little stooped, supporting himself with a walking stick. Even at this distance she could see he was bareheaded with longish silver-streaked hair smoothed back over his rather narrow head, and he looked as if he might have a beard.

The man seemed to be staring at Amy, who was on her knees now, praying, her hands together. As she struggled to her feet he took a few steps backward, turned and started moving swiftly away into the mist. Amy began to run after him, but there was little hope of her catching up with him. By the time Tessa reached her, she had slipped and stumbled in the mud. As Tessa took her arm to help her up, she saw that her mother was weeping silently, tears pouring down her face. But she was no longer mourning her father. Amy was reaching out toward the rapidly disappearing man. Bending close, Tessa thought she heard her whisper, "Elliott!" and then again, louder, *"Elliott!"*

CHAPTER 17

Elliott Fitzgerald caught the train by the skin of his teeth. It was the *Capitole du Soir*, the express train from Paris to Toulouse which left the Gare d'Austerlitz every night at six o'clock. It didn't stop at Gourdon so he would have to go on to Cahors and drive his battered old Citroën the twenty-odd miles to Arriac.

The flight from London had been late arriving and he had only just made it to the Gare d'Austerlitz in time to dash in the direction of the *Grandes Lignes* and charge through the barrier, flicking his ticket at the official. Thankfully, Elliott sank back into his seat to reflect on the last few days. Perhaps it had been a mistake to go to the funeral especially since he had not really gone through with everything he intended to do. He had meant to make his presence known to his family, have a talk with Amy, explain everything.

But how did you explain your presence when you were supposed to have been dead for almost thirty years? When he had read of Sir Hugh's death in a two-day-old copy of *The Times*, he had thought that showing up at the funeral would be the simplest way. Yet one look at Amy's face when she'd recognized him at the graveside had been enough to tell him it would be an impossible task. Perhaps by slipping away quietly into the mist as he had, he might just have succeeded in leaving her with the impression that she had seen a ghost.

Poor old Amy. Of course he should never have married her in the first place, he realized that now, but when he first married Amy Heron-Sweeney there was much about himself he had not yet come to terms with.

He had met Christian de Saint-Cyr during the war on a weekend leave in Paris. It was at a small dinner party given by an ageing *comtesse*, who was a friend of Elliott's mother. Christian was roughly the same age as Elliott and arrived, like the young English officer, on his own. Christian gave him a lift back to his hotel and the following day showed him around Paris. He seemed to take it for granted that Elliott knew he was a homosexual and began to speak about it almost immediately. He spoke of his *petit ami* rather than his *petite amie* and Elliott's French was sufficiently advanced to make the distinction. Christian was not one to keep things to himself. He described to an astonished Elliott, who had never met a homosexual before, how his *petit ami* (whose name was Jean-François) could arouse him instantly by reaching out and rubbing his nipple in a circular movement. How it felt when Jean-François put his tongue in his ear, his hand on his penis and when he put his arm around Christian's chest from behind and inserted his penis into his slippery hole and blew tenderly on the back of his neck.

Not once did Christian touch Elliott, yet not once during the whole day did Elliott's erection show any sign of subsiding. Finally when Christian deposited him back at his hotel he reached up and gently stroked Elliott's cheek as the Englishman leapt out of the car. It was enough to trigger an explosive ejaculation which Elliott only just managed to keep in check until he reached his hotel room and lay heaving, face down, on the bed.

The trouble started when he returned to Bellcloud after the war. He found himself unable to make love to Amy. She didn't really complain; lovemaking was not a high priority for her. It was a luxury she'd done without during the war and she could perfectly well continue to do so. She was quite happy knitting in the evenings or they could listen to the wireless together and when they were tired they could go to bed—to sleep.

Yet Amy was not insensitive and she was aware there was something troubling Elliott. At first she had thought it was the problem of what he was going to do with himself now the war was over. For some reason he had resigned his commission and was now no longer in the Army. But he would not tell anybody why he had done it. Then she began to wonder if he had had some terrible experience which had left him in such a vulnerable state. But he wouldn't talk to anybody about that either.

Eventually she decided the only way to coax the truth out of him was to engage him in some warm and gentle sex. It was just as well that Amy liked a challenge. It was several weeks before Elliott managed to maintain an erection long enough to penetrate her. Amy would have happily settled for some cosy cuddling and intimacy focused on conversation rather than anything else, but Elliott seemed to be obsessed with the idea that he must satisfy her. Yet it was not until he gave in to the temptation to think about Christian that he was able to do so.

Tessa was born nine months later and Elliott began to feel that he could after all look forward to peace of mind. There was nothing wrong with him. He had a wife, a baby daughter and his father-in-law had given them a wing of Bellcloud to live in. He had a role in life: family man.

Then Christian de Saint-Cyr reappeared.

Elliott and Amy were invited to lunch with the Heron-Sweeneys. Betty met them in the hall in an unusually excitable state.

"We have a surprise guest for you, Elliott. Turned up about an hour ago. A *French*man! So exciting! His mother knows yours and now he's come to look you up. He's *so* charming, kissed my hand, don't you know? But that's the French for you, isn't it? Do hurry up, Amy. The poor man's been trapped by Hugh in the library and he's probably bored to death. Give Tessa to me and go on in."

Lunch was a nightmare.

Elliott could not stop thinking about the fact that their guest could be sent to prison for his sexual preferences, and that those preferences were obviously also his own. Not that Christian seemed the slightest bit out of place. Nor, mused Elliott, did he, otherwise Amy would never have married him. It was obviously a case of *it takes one to know one*. Christian must have spotted him right away at the dinner party in Paris despite the fact that he had not yet been awakened. Elliott wondered how many others had recognized him for what he was. If they had they'd done nothing about it. He speculated on whether or not he would ever have been aware of it had he not encountered Christian.

After lunch Betty insisted on showing Christian her herb garden. After all, the French did such wonderful things with herbs surely he would want to see it. After about twenty minutes she returned to the house alone.

"I've left him sitting in the summer-house, Elliott. High time you two had a chance to have a chat on your own. Off you go. Amy's taking a nap and I'll keep an eye on Tessa. Hugh's gone down to the orchard with a pile of papers . . ."

Of course, Elliott wasn't listening. The second his mother-in-law had mentioned that Christian was waiting for him alone in the summer-house he had felt himself begin to quake with excitement. He raced over to the herb garden and paused at the sundial in the middle of it. He walked around it several times, knowing it was madness to go any further.

Christian was sitting quietly in the summer-house smoking a cigarette. He was completely naked. Uncrossing his legs, he patted the bench beside him.

"Come. Sit." Elliott sat and waited to be told what to do next. But he did not have to do anything. Christian chucked his cigarette out through the arched doorway of the summer-house and knelt before Elliott. Slowly he began to undo Elliott's fly. Just as he was about to take Elliott's engorged penis into his open mouth, Sir Hugh Heron-Sweeney walked into the summer-house.

"Don't do that," he said, *"méchant!"* He pushed vaguely at Christian and looked at Elliott, who was sitting rigid with shock. "Put it away, there's a good fellow. Better come and see me in my study after dinner tonight, hmm?"

"But where did he *go*?" asked Betty for the umpteenth time. "Why did he have to rush off like that? He didn't even come to thank me for lunch and he seemed like such a nice young man. I simply *don't* understand it."

Dinner was drawing to a close. Amy had been at a loss to understand why they had to stay to dinner at all. They'd only been invited for lunch, now she'd have to go all the way back to the West Wing to fetch Tessa's feed. Elliott hadn't touched his watercress soup, cold roast lamb or his rhubarb fool and he knew Betty was on the point of asking what was the matter with him.

"Elliott's having coffee with me in my study," announced Sir Hugh. "Want to have a bit of a man-to-man with him."

"Oh, Lord," said Betty to her daughter, "I hope he doesn't go and say something upsetting to poor Elliott."

Sir Hugh poured Elliott a large brandy and pushed him onto a large chintz-covered sofa. He stood directly above his son-in-law, feet wide apart, bending down every now and then to poke the young man in the chest.

"It won't do, m'boy, won't do at all. The Siwans of North Africa, the Arunta of Australia, the Keraki of New Guinea, they all have a go at anal intercourse among men and boys, but I'm afraid we don't. I know I didn't witness any anal intercourse, but you'll have to toe the line. Now, what are we going to do? You've married Amy and there's nothing I can do about it now. If we start thinking of divorce Betty will have a fit. I think what you need is a holiday, pop off somewhere quiet, sort yourself out, come back right as rain. How does that sound?"

Elliott was so relieved that he didn't have to give a detailed account of himself that he agreed immediately that yes, he did need a holiday, that the war had really got him down, made him vulnerable to the stranger side of life, that it would never happen again, that he would return to be a wonderful husband to Amy and a loving father to little Tessa.

"Just so long as you understand one thing, Fitzgerald," Sir Hugh warned him. "It must never happen again."

Elliott dozed off and woke to find they were past Limoges and the countryside had begun to rise and fall on either side of the railway. Grubby little goats were bucking about in abundance on the hillside. After Brive-la-Galliarde the sun went down on the horizon selfishly hugging its crimson glow to the immediate area around it, leaving the train below out in the cold. The hills, now smothered with forests, loomed up to the right and left in smoky-rose silhouette gradually becoming darker and darker until all Elliott could make out was the occasional sharp black outline of a hilltop château against the moonlight.

Elliott shivered, remembering the train which had taken him

on his "holiday" following the showdown at Bellcloud. The boy had been sitting opposite him for most of the journey, a young lad of about sixteen or seventeen. He had stared at Elliott quite openly until Elliott's spine began to tingle. He was mesmerized by this bony little face with the large blue eyes fixed on him. He found he could not look away and finally had to ask: "Why are you looking at me?"

"You're the spittin' image of the actor, 'Enry Fonda. Sorry, but for a while I thought you was 'im. Didn't mean to stare."

"Oh, it's quite all right." Elliott was so relieved that the boy was not angling in another direction that he cheerfully slipped into conversation with him.

"Yes, several other people have said that, too. To tell you the truth, I'm not sure I'm familiar with the real Henry Fonda. Terrible, isn't it? I'm not one for the picture shows."

"Well, they say I'm a bit like 'im meself," the boy told him, obviously very proud of the fact.

"Well, I expect you are." Elliott smiled, amused by this chirpy youngster. "Where are you from?"

"London. Going down to Swansea for me 'oliday."

"Do you have family there? Friends?"

"No—I don't know anyone. Just 'eard it was peaceful."

"That's what they told me. I'm going to the Gower Peninsula. I hear the beaches are spectacular."

At Swansea, the boy stood up to retrieve his suitcase from the overhead rack and Elliott saw he was no child: he was nearly as tall as he was.

"Cheerio then," he said, "maybe we'll bump into each other."

They did. A few days later Elliott recognized the gangling figure coming along the beach. Once again they slipped easily into conversation, sitting on the beach throwing pebbles into the surf. He learned that the boy had no family and that he had decided to spend his last few pounds on traveling to Swansea to try and find a job there. He was fed up with London, he wanted to be as far away from there as possible. Idle conversation with a total stranger was just what Elliott needed. He relaxed and almost told the boy why he was there. Instead he invited him to have a drink in the pub.

"You are old enough?" The boy just looked at him and winked. By closing time they were pretty far gone and the talk had once again got around to Henry Fonda. They were jokingly competing against each other as to who looked the most like him and finally appealed to the landlord to settle the argument. The landlord took his time, but arrived eventually at a conclusion.

"Well, see, look you now. The lad here has the facial expression, but in those clothes he doesn't look at all like a film star. But you, sir," he turned toward Elliott, "you've got the cut of his cloth, I reckon."

"Tell you what," said Elliott to the boy, "let's swap clothes and see what he says then. I'm not going to admit defeat yet." Almost helpless with laughter they repaired to the outside Gents and tossed their clothes to each other over the dividing wall of the cubicles, but when they emerged from the Gents the pub was closed.

"Bloody poor show!" said Elliott, now very drunk indeed. "Might have waited for us. Come on, let's go and have a swim."

Arm in arm they lurched down to the beach and into the sea.

"I can't swim," the boy told him, "you'll have to hang onto me."

"Can't swim? Henry Fonda can't swim? Never heard such nonsense."

The boy giggled. "Well, I'll 'ave a go. But, mind you stay close."

The current swept him away almost immediately. In his drunken state Elliott was vaguely aware that the boy was calling for help, but when he looked round he couldn't see him.

Elliott started to sober up fast. He opened his mouth to call to the boy and realized he didn't even know his name. The boy had called him sir when he'd called him anything at all and he, Elliott, had not even gone to the trouble of finding out his name.

Elliott never knew what made him go and sit on the beach instead of going for help. He told himself afterward that he must have gone into a state of shock. Just before dawn he slipped into a cave in the cliff face and fell asleep, propped up against a boulder. He was awakened by the sound of holiday-makers arriving to spend the day on the beach. It took him a few seconds to realize where he was and then he looked down with horror at his unfamiliar clothes and remembered what had happened.

The grubby white shirt and baggy gray flannels the boy had been wearing fit him rather well though the tennis shoes were a bit of a tight fit. Elliott rolled up the gray flannels to his knees. They were shriveled and slightly damp from the dip in the sea the night before. Clutching the tennis shoes in one hand he padded barefoot out of the cave and along the beach, staring out to sea every now and then as if he expected the boy to suddenly bob up and wave to him.

They found the body a few days later, washed up on the beach. Elliott had not been able to bring himself to venture up to the village and had continued to spend his days and nights in the cave, living off ice-creams and the hot sausage rolls vendors sold on the beach. His beard had grown and in the by now filthy clothes of the boy he was virtually unrecognizable as the elegant young man who had arrived and checked into a boarding house as Captain Elliott Fitzgerald.

Crowds swarmed onto the beach and he hovered behind them as the boy's body was carried up to a waiting ambulance.

"His face is all bloated," called someone.

"Looks fit to burst any minute," called another.

The next day confirmed Elliott's worst fears. The "nice young captain" who'd drowned was the talk of the beach. They'd found his handkerchief, an address book and a watch and chain with an inscription on the back with his name on it. His wife was on her way to identify the body.

Elliott started. He was about to cry out that it wasn't, he was there, it was someone else they had thrown the blanket over, but he found he couldn't say a word.

He stayed in the cave. If necessary, he would starve to death rather than face those crowds of people who had already written him off as dead. Would Amy do the same? Apparently yes.

"The wife arrived, said it was him. Her father brought her."

Her father brought her! Sir Hugh was here. Elliott knew he had to get away fast.

He decided to make a dash for it at dawn, run along the beach and sprint through the village to the station where he could catch the first train to leave in the morning. The boy's pockets had revealed five soggy pound notes which Elliott had dried out on a rock. He'd only used a small amount so far on ices and sausage rolls and had plenty to get him to London. Once there he'd have to think again.

Having not been able to look in a mirror since the night of the drowning, he had no idea of the bizarre sight he presented as he loped along the beach very early the following morning. But Hugh Heron-Sweeney, roaming the cliffs above, recognized the bearded figure immediately and roared down to him, "Elliott! Stay right there, man." He came down to the beach as quickly as he could. "I've been looking for you. I saw through this nonsense about your being dead. All over the village they're saying you were wandering around with a young boy. It just won't do, Elliott. You were supposed to come here to sort yourself out. You said you weren't going to go in for that sort of thing anymore. What have you got to say for yourself?"

"The boy was just someone I met on the train coming down. There was nothing *like that* . . ."

"Expect me to believe that? D'you think I'm a blithering idiot? Get a grip on yourself, man. It's bloody lucky for you that they're so feeble-minded down here they don't seem to be conducting a proper inquest into the death, otherwise they'd soon find out that boy was a good deal younger than you are. He *was* wearing your clothes and he did have your things on him, so how do you explain that? I can't stand a man who doesn't stand by his word and I can't stand a man who doesn't own up to the truth. As I've said before, Fitzgerald, it just won't do. You'd best stay dead."

"What?"

"Dead, man. You'd better go on being dead. Everybody already thinks you are, including Amy. If you try and show up again at Bellcloud, I'll have you sent straight to prison, if not for one thing then for another. I take it that young boy's drowning *was* an accident . . . ?"

Sir Hugh had given him fifty pounds in cash and promised not to say a word providing Elliott didn't ever come near Amy and Tessa again. He bought some clothes in the town for Elliott and Elliott changed into them in the cave. Then Elliott caught the seven-thirty to London and from there he took the boat train from Victoria to Paris. He never knew why he wound up in the Lot, but deep down he suspected it might have had

something to do with the fact that Christian's family had originally come from there.

On the first train journey down to Cahors he had whiled away
the hours scribbling down an account of the horrendous events
of the past few weeks. To his amazement, he found that even
though the story was action-packed at the outset, he could not
resist the temptation to embellish it even further. On reading it
through at a country inn he discovered that he had written a
rattling good little thriller which was barely recognizable as his
own story.

He had sent it to a London publishing house so well known
that it reached them in spite of the fact that he only put their
name and London, *Angleterre*, on the envelope. They replied,
using the pseudonym under which he had sent the manuscript,
saying they didn't accept anything which wasn't typed, but
they had forwarded his work to a reputable literary agent
whose name and address they enclosed. Four weeks later one of
their rivals received the typed version of the book from the
agent and immediately offered for it. The literary agents wrote
to Elliott about the sale and advised him to buy a typewriter
with the proceeds. It was clear he was going to be needing one.
They had taken the liberty of having his original manuscript
typed up by one of their secretaries, but they regretted they
would be unable to continue with such a service in the future.
Would he please send a photograph of himself, some biographi-
cal details for the jacket copy and the name and address of a
bank where the advance payment could be deposited. After
they had claimed their 10 per cent, of course.

Eric Christian, as Elliott had elected to call himself, gave
them nothing but a Post Office box number in Cahors. Even
when the sales of his third book enabled him to buy a house on
the hill outside the tiny village of Arriac, he still kept his identity a secret and his PO box number in Cahors. His publishers,
exasperated that even they were not allowed to know who he
really was, were encouraged by his equally frustrated agent to
place an advertisement in *The Times*: FIND ERIC CHRIS-
TIAN. *Mystery author of thrillers hiding in France.*

Expeditions were made to the bank in Cahors, but the manager, as instructed by Elliott, was typically unforthcoming and
unhelpful as only a Frenchman could be to an Englishman if he

so chose. Elliott started writing just as paperback publishing began in the United Kingdom. His books were naturals for the paperback market and when the boom came in the Sixties he had the satisfaction of seeing hordes of British holiday-makers traipsing round south-west France clutching copies of Eric Christian thrillers. His fan mail, arriving weekly at the PO box number, was huge and included, much to Elliott's amusement, several letters, full of glowing praise, addressed to "My dear Mr. Christian" and signed Hugh Heron-Sweeney. He went so far as to reply to them and the correspondence became so animated that Elliott felt obliged to identify himself, begging Sir Hugh not to tell anyone who he really was. He never heard from his father-in-law again despite sending many further letters.

Elliott never got over the fact that he was responsible for the boy's drowning and in one way or another he always tried to pay him homage somewhere in each of his books. Elliott remembered vividly how the boy looked and brought him into each story in some kind of subsidiary role, but always describing him in detail. Several fans picked up on it and wrote asking why he did it, but Elliott always evaded the question. He answered his fan mail, typing his letters and even his name, or rather "Eric Christian," at the bottom in case anyone decided to scrutinize his handwriting for clues.

He had been tempted on his way back from Sir Hugh's funeral to drop in and meet his agent in London. They had, after all, enjoyed a cordial correspondence for nearly thirty years and he was aware that the man must be due to retire quite soon. He wondered who would take over. He resisted the temptation and instead contented himself with a visit to his hardcover publishers where he pretended to be a member of the public asking how to get in touch with Eric Christian. Looking around the walls of the reception area he saw masses of photographs of the more famous authors published by the house. In the most prominent position of all there was a conspicuous gap. He moved closer to read the name on the plaque underneath and was amused to see "Eric Christian." In the reception area of his paperback publishers he was intrigued to see that his latest book appeared to be at the top of a list of bestsellers. He asked the receptionist if this was a common occurrence with Eric Christian's books. The girl looked at him in complete astonishment and replied that Eric Christian's thrillers *always* went straight to Number One. In paperback anyway, she added hastily.

He'd just sent his agent his twenty-ninth thriller. No doubt that too would shoot up this all-important bestseller list. But, as his train drew into Cahors, Elliott knew he had to come to terms with the fact that it was 1977, he'd been writing for nearly thirty years and wanted now to embark on something completely different. He had even gone so far as to broach the subject with his agent when he last wrote to him. A panic-stricken reply had arrived by return, asking if he really thought this was wise. Endless arguments had been put to him as to why it would not work, culminating in an appeal to his conscience: how could he disappoint his audience, the mass of readers who looked forward every year to a new Eric Christian thriller?

But the idea would not go away. Times had changed. He took *Time* and *Newsweek* and he read modern novels. People had apparently "come out of the closet." It was OK to be "gay." You could no longer go to prison for being a homosexual. Surely there was a different kind of readership waiting for him to speak to them, who would understand if he poured forth his pent-up frustration and emotion which he had kept in check all these years and embarked upon a novel by Elliott Fitzgerald rather than Eric Christian. Too bad if they didn't go for it in England; he'd find himself a brand new audience. Maybe in America where as far as he knew he'd never been published.

As he urged the groaning Citroën up the hill past the big house called *La Cachette* he saw Luc Chenier on his *mobilette* in his rear-view mirror. He waved and Luc waved back, grinning. Elliott sighed. He couldn't deny it: this boy with his glossy black hair, his long lean legs, his almost angelic face with the blue-gray eyes fringed with long dark lashes and the cute little turned-up nose like a girl's had awakened in him the stirrings of long ago. He had watched Luc growing from a small boy into this beautiful creature. Yet he knew that even more than Luc's looks, Elliott was seduced by the boy's sweet and gentle nature, always so polite and courteous. Sighing again, Elliott drove the final hundred yards down the lane beyond *La*

Cachette and swung the old Citroën into the field in which his own converted barn, *La Folie*, stood.

He was still thinking about Luc as he let himself into the house. It was too bad the boy had to live with that crazy old woman.

PART 5

LUC
1961–77

CHAPTER 18

Callie woke up suddenly. She was curled up in a fetal position halfway down the bed, almost buried under a mountain of blankets and those coarse linen sheets she had come to associate with France. She found she was clutching a long bolster, pressing the top of it to the aching pain between her breasts.

Except that now she was awake she realized there was no pain. It was the dream again. The same recurring nightmare she had had at least once a month ever since she had come to live in France seventeen years ago in 1961. Not that it could be associated with anything French. In it she relived those few moments of agony when she had been given a stomach pump following the overdose she had taken all those years ago. She could still vividly recall the pain as the tubing was forced down behind her breastplate and the hammering feeling she had experienced there as the pills were suctioned up until she vomited them all safely out of her system. They spread the word about the terrible time the suffragettes had had when they were being force fed with a tube, but they kept quiet about the horror of the reversed procedure. She always awoke when the hammering began; once she had even found herself vomiting as she opened her eyes.

In a second she was up and out of bed. If she lay a moment longer and contemplated the past she would crumble. Her hunger for vindication would never leave her, but she knew she had to keep the pangs in check, that the right time would come and until it did, she should curb her impatience.

She wrapped a large woollen shawl around the crisp cotton man's nightshirt she slept in every night and opened a window, reaching out to unfasten the shutters beyond it. The fog outside enveloped her immediately.

"Encore le brouillard," she muttered to herself and slammed the window shut again.

She padded down the wooden staircase into the main hall of the house and cursed herself for not having put on her slippers. The flagged-stone floor of the main hall felt like ice to the soles of her feet. She hopped from one rug to another till she reached one of the doors leading outside where she stopped to don a pair of large wooden clogs. She was standing in one of the two giant halls on the ground floor of her house. There was no plaster or paint on the walls—the original stone had been left untouched like a medieval castle. A huge oak table, some twelve feet long, stood diagonally across the hall. Tapestries hung on the walls—unique tapestries woven by the local shepherd with the untreated wool of his sheep. The rest of the hall was filled with a confusing mixture of furniture: Renaissance antiques, huge trunks covered with zebra and leopard skins, an elegant little Art Nouveau satinwood card table stood between two contemporary French chestnut chairs; a French provincial wardrobe and glass-fronted chest housed large piles of white crockery and sparkling glassware, and at the far end, the embers from the fire of the night before still glowed in the cavernous stone fireplace.

Absentmindedly Callie picked up a poker from the stone ledge below the ashes and prodded them. A wave of smoke rose up causing her to run, coughing, to open the door. Her clogs clattered across the stones, the sound echoing up to the beams above her. She flung open the door and stood for a few minutes, breathing in the fresh morning air. In the short time since she had opened the shutters in her bedroom, the fog had lifted enough for her to be able to see her view. It amazed her that she could still find it so breathtaking, yet every morning she found herself stopping to gaze in wonder at the extraordinary panorama before her.

She had named the house *La Cachette* in memory of her hiding-place in the brothel in New Orleans. Yet it was far from hidden, perched on the very top of one of the high plateaus above the wild valley of the River Lot in south-west France. It commanded an utterly spectacular view of a complete ring of wooded hills, rolling away as far as the eye could see, broken only by the occasional church tower rising out of a hillside village. But the main attraction of *La Cachette* was that it was virtually inaccessible. The house could only be reached via a dirt track which cunningly escaped from behind the graveyard in the nearby village of Arriac and climbed the hill steeply, running through fields and woods till it reached the house in a clearing on the summit. Now, as she watched the first rays of sunlight begin to filter through the early morning mist, Callie heard the incongruous roar of a motorbike coming up the hill.

Luc! He was up already. He must have been down the track to the nearest farm to collect some milk for their breakfast. Yes, she was right. As the *mobilette* roared out of the woods into view she could see the two big churns strapped behind him.

She should be in the kitchen heating the milk for his chocolate. But no, they were out of milk, he was bringing it so she had the perfect excuse to watch him as he came toward her, lugging the churns.

She was disturbed by his appearance. Ever since they had gone together to see the film *The Godfather* in Cahors the week before, Luc had begun to dress like a Sicilian peasant in a collarless shirt, a V-neck sleeveless waistcoat and a pair of shapeless baggy trousers. He had his hunting rifle slung diagonally across his body and on his head he wore a cap. He deserved to be pleased with the overall effect even if it was helped by the fact that he looked not unlike the actor who had played Michael Corleone. Callie liked to see all the new American movies. Somehow it seemed to be just about the only way she could keep in touch with what was happening over there. She had enjoyed the film, especially the part when Michael Corleone was on the run, in hiding in Sicily. She identified with that part for she too was in hiding. And it had obviously made an impression on Luc but for different reasons since she had never told him who he really was.

Luc Chenier was her grandson.

Although she had never really come right out and told him that they were related, she had implied in a vague way that she was some kind of aunt and for this reason he had called her *"Tantie"* ever since he could speak. He couldn't say *Tante* Callie, Aunt Callie, and the child's abbreviation *Tantie* had stuck. Callie knew he must have wondered who she really was, but he had never asked in all the sixteen years she had raised him.

She could still clearly remember the day she had arrived in the Lot with the tiny baby boy bundled up in a blanket in her arms. She knew they had presented a curious picture to the locals—elegant middle-aged American woman in an ankle-length mink coat arriving in a small sleepy market town in south-west France, cradling a newborn baby in her arms, demanding a house to buy and move into immediately. *Immédiatement!*

She had gone first to Paris, of course, and checked into the Georges V, her last act as Mrs. Perry Jay Duboise. She had stayed only one night and she had not offered any explanation as to why she was traveling with a two-week-old baby. She had counted on the management being far too concerned about keeping Perry Jay's patronage to risk upsetting his wife with inquisitive questions and she'd been right. She'd left Luc, as she'd already named him, in the charge of one of the hotel maids for the evening while she slipped away to meet Anita de la Salle.

Anita had moved to the *six-septième* as well as having a large country house in the forest of Rambouillet, south of Versailles. She had never had any children and Thierry had become more and more of a pompous bore. But while some women might have become bitter and miserable, Anita had never lost her sense of fun. She had continued to entertain her lovers in the afternoon and she had just kissed one of them goodbye when Callie arrived to see her.

"Il était merveilleux mais il était trop vieux," she explained to a bewildered Callie. The young man she had seen whistling out of Anita's apartment couldn't have been more than nineteen.

Anita laughed when she saw Callie's expression. "Oh, I

know what you're thinking. What am I doing at my age running around with *les gosses*? Well, I'll tell you. I like kids. Give me a boy of fifteen, seventeen, eighteen and I can do a lot with him. He's still *sauvage*, wild. By nineteen they want to talk as well, and I'm too old to listen. Talk, talk, talk, all about themselves. So boring, darling. But when they are still young I can talk and they will listen, not that there's much time to talk. Ah, Callie, *chérie,* give me a kiss and tell me I'm still as young as when you last saw me."

It was almost true. Anita was still cuddly. Her skin was still pale, almost translucent with the freckles scattered over the cushiony flesh of her chest and the upper parts of her arms. Her eyes were slitty and cat-like with heavily mascaraed lashes and her teeth were tiny little white pearls behind her scarlet painted lips. Her auburn hair was cut short in a poodle-cut of tight little curls and dark blue sapphire and diamond earrings sparkled in her ears.

"I can't remember when I did last see you, Anita," said Callie quickly, since she did not want to get into a journey down memory lane, "but I'm sure you haven't changed a bit. Pour me a drink and I'll tell you why I'm here."

Anita rang for a bottle of Laurent Perrier and asked, casually, the one thing she had been dying to know ever since Callie had first telephoned.

"How's PJ?" More than a year had elapsed since her encounter with Callie's son. She'd had no word from him, but not a day had gone by when she had not thought of him.

"PJ? *Philippe-Josephe,* you mean? That's right, he came to see you, didn't he? Thank you, Anita, although whatever you said to him was a waste of time."

"Did he *tell* you what I said?" Anita almost said "what I did," but stopped herself in time.

"Nothing. In fact he never even told me he'd seen you. He told his father and Perry Jay mentioned it. You see, Perry Jay got to him before I could see him. He turned my son against me. I've lost Philippe, Anita. This time it looks like he's gone for good. But," she added, strangely triumphant, "now I have Luc."

"Luc?" Anita was baffled. Had she had another child? Surely she was much too old?

"My grandson. Philippe's son."

And Callie began to tell her story to the only person she knew she could trust since leaving New York. She told her all about the model, Honey Winslow, and how she was Luc's mother—but not PJ's wife—and finally Callie told Anita how she still had a hold over her husband.

"But, Anita, I have come to France because I speak French. I want you to point me in the direction of somewhere wild and isolated in France where I'm not likely to run into the cream of high society from my past life. A place where I am not likely to run into anyone who knows Honey Winslow. Preferably a place where they might not even have *heard* of Honey Winslow."

"The Lot," replied Anita immediately. "In the south-west of France. You can go and stay with some old friends of ours while you look for a house. They don't actually live in the Lot, but next door in the Dordogne, but I'm sure they wouldn't mind . . ."

"No! Anita, you must not tell anyone where I'm going. When I leave you tonight I am going to walk into a totally new life. I shall not even let *you* know where I wind up. It will just be me and my boy, my Luc . . ."

"But, Callie . . ." Anita was now seriously confused. Here was someone from New Orleans, turning up out of the blue and turning out to be quite ruthless into the bargain, preparing to disappear again only an hour after she had arrived, leaving her with no gossip, nothing. "But, Callie, you will promise to let me know if I can help you . . ." she finished lamely. She was not sure just *how* she would be able to help, but something told her it was safer to be for Callie rather than against her.

"Oh, I will, believe me, I will. I'll be in touch," Callie told her as she gathered up her things to return to her baby Luc at the hotel. And as she left Anita realized she still didn't know what had happened to PJ.

Callie turned and walked slowly back through the great hall which served as a dining room, through an archway to the long, narrow kitchen which ran along the back of the house. It had been an old bakery when she arrived, with the huge stone ovens still intact. Part of her had wanted to keep them, but deep down she knew that ultimately they would not be practical.

From the moment she started living in her house in the Lot,

Callie knew she was going to have to do everything herself. She was no longer Mrs. Perry Jay Duboise. She was just plain Madame Chenier, a stranger in an area where people did not take kindly to strangers. The people of the Lot were a friendly enough community amongst themselves, but they harbored a deep suspicion of the sophisticated rich from Paris and even farther afield who descended upon their wild and beautiful countryside in search of weekend places or sometimes *à Dieu ne plaise,* a permanent home in the country. This suited Callie well enough. She had sensed their hostility in the little village of Arriac when in 1961 she had arrived at the little *auberge* in search of a room. At the station in nearby Gourdon she had asked a taxi driver to take her to a village, a *small* village, with an inn. He had had a little difficulty understanding her French which, although grammatically correct, had a slight twang to it, but finally he had nodded his head several times and told her: *"Arriac, madame. Je vous emmene à Arriac."*

But when she had walked from the taxi into the bar filled with a thick fog from the smoke of a mass of Gauloises, she had sensed the abrupt end to several conversations as a dozen pairs of eyes turned to look at her.

"Est-ce que vous avez des chambres, monsieur?" she asked the man behind the bar who appeared to be the proprietor.

"Pas de chambres," snapped Vincent Rocaud without even bothering to take the Gauloise out of his mouth. He turned his back to her and started to pour a *Pastis* for someone else.

"Mais . . ." Callie turned beseechingly to the men around her. There was not another woman in the room. They stared back at her until she couldn't stand it any longer and looked away.

The man behind the bar had disappeared and the sounds of a heated discussion could be heard coming from a back room. Suddenly a large woman in a drab black dress with a sleeveless overall half covering it stepped into the bar and reached across to grab Callie by the elbow.

"Mais vous avez un petit!" she exclaimed, looking at the tiny bundle Callie cradled in her arms. *"Regarde, Vincent, elle a un petit bébé. Il est onze heures du soir. On ne peut pas la mettre à la porte si tard. C'est un peu dur."*

Callie listened hard. From what she could understand Madame Rocaud was pointing out to her husband that it was a bit rough to throw out a woman with a tiny baby at eleven o'clock at night. Callie took advantage of the situation.

"Et on n'a pas mangé depuis midi. On a faim, madame." Surely if she told this woman they had not eaten since midday she would give her something to eat and some milk to warm for Luc's bottle.

"On est fermé," Vincent Rocaud told her firmly.

"Eh bah?" returned his wife. Who cares? And before Callie could stop her she swiftly took Luc from her arms and into the back room. *"Venez!"* She beckoned Callie to follow her into the kitchen at the back where she motioned to her to sit down at a little wooden table in a corner.

"Je peux?" asked Callie hesitantly, starting to slip the cumbersome mink off her shoulders.

"Vincent!" screeched the woman till her husband sullenly came and helped Callie out of her coat and took it away into the bar.

Then, once his wife had swiftly and efficiently warmed a bottle of milk for Luc and given him to Callie to feed, she prepared for Callie her first taste of *la cuisine Perigourdine*, the mouth-watering food of the part of south-west France Callie would come to make her home. The meal she served Callie was relatively simple—an *omelette aux truffes*, a small green salad with some *cabecoux*, all washed down with one or two glasses of the heavy red *vin Cahors*. Madame Rocaud prattled away as she cooked—*omelette aux truffes, specialité Perigourdine*, was so simple to make, all you needed was some eggs, *naturellement*, two tablespoons of water, one of goose fat, some salt, some pepper and don't forget the truffles. If madame liked *les truffes*, she had come to the right place. Perigord, the Lot, was where they came from, dug out from under the earth by specially trained dogs, or sometimes by pigs. The salad? Well, everyone knew how to make a salad and the *cabecoux* were just another *specialité de la region*, little round patties of goat's cheese, Madame would find them anywhere round here. *Comme dessert?* Madame just had to try *les merveilles*, the wonders—their name alone made them sound appetizing. Talleyrand, who came from the Perigord, had liked nothing better than these crisp fine biscuit-like concoctions which could emerge in any shape, long or round like sugar-coated Indian poppadums. And afterward a *petit café* with a *digestif*, a glass of *eau de noix* or a delicious *Reine-Claude à la liqueur*, juicy plums soaked for months on end in the intoxicating local *eau de vie*.

Exhausted after such a feast, Callie stayed awake barely long enough to ensure that Luc was properly prepared for the night, before she slipped into a nine-hour sleep.

She awoke next morning, horrified. How was it that Luc had not woken for his feed in the middle of the night? Naturally, when she had had PJ all those years ago, she had had a nurse-maid to watch him through the night, but she had still been around her own son enough to learn a little of what went into caring for a tiny baby. After she had taken charge of Luc, it had come back to her easily enough, even after twenty-odd years, and within days she was changing Luc's diapers, coaxing wind out of him and preparing his bottles with no qualms whatsoever. This last night in the little inn at Arriac had been the first she had slept through without waking since she had begun to look after Luc.

But she need not have worried. Noelle Rocaud had heard him the instant he'd woken and rushed in before Callie stirred. Now, at ten-thirty in the morning, she brought him in and laid him beside Callie in the big old *lit de campagne*, a kind of Napoleonic bed, high off the ground, whose tall wooden ends curled outward in circles.

Noelle had brought her a steaming bowl of hot chocolate and some *brioches* being kept warm inside a red and white checked cloth in a little basket. The woman seemed in no hurry to leave and perched on the end of the bed while Callie ate her breakfast. As she had done the night before, she chattered away and if Callie's silence unnerved her she did not show it.

"Oui, enfin, je viens pas d'ici. I don't come from round here myself. I'm from Brittany, from a little fishing village. I miss the sea. I'd give anything to see the sea again, but Vincent, he hates it. I met Vincent just after the war in Nantes. I fell for him straightaway and when he asked me to come and be his wife here in the Lot I never thought twice about it. I said yes straightaway and we were married by the end of the year. He had a good job helping out behind the bar at the *auberge* and since it was a family business he knew when his father died he would take over the running of it. Ah, but you should have seen it when his papa was alive. Old Papa Rocaud, he was a charac-

ter. He ran a real *auberge* with a proper restaurant. The menu
was *superbe*!" She pressed her fingers to her thumb and kissed
them in the air.

"He knew how to cook, old Papa. It was he who taught me.
The people used to come from miles around to taste his *civet de
marcassin, marcassin*, you know, like little boars, *délicieux*!
And then there was his *truffe en croute. Meilleur du monde!*
Everyone said so. But when he died it all fell apart. Vincent, he
never had the gift. Just wasn't interested if you ask me. And
then . . ."

Callie was only half listening to her. She glanced down at
Luc who was still fast asleep. Why was this woman confiding in
her so much? Was Noelle Rocaud really so desperate for someone to talk to? Were outsiders really so ostracized? If so, then
Callie had certainly come to the right place. As Noelle rattled
on and on, telling her about this and that, Callie was grateful
that she made no effort to get the American woman to talk,
although surely she must be wondering what she was doing
here. As she listened, Callie began to think to herself: maybe it
would be a smart move to trust this woman, tell her a few
things in return—oh, not why she had come to live in such a
remote place as the Lot, but ask her help in the things she was
going to need.

"Madame Rocaud," Callie interrupted at what seemed like a
natural break.

"*Mais oui, madame . . . madame? Excusez-moi, je ne con-
nais pas votre nom.*"

"Chenier." Without the slightest hesitation Callie reverted to
her maiden name.

"*Madame Chenier. Vous desirez quelque chose?*"

"*Simplement un maison.* Somewhere to live. *Immédiatement.*"

And that was when she first heard about *La Cachette.* The
house on the top of the hill was empty. It had been empty for
several months since the death of the old man who owned it.
They said he died of a broken heart, tumbling into the grave
beside his beloved wife only six months after her death. There
was a mass of children and grandchildren who could have
made good use of *La Cachette* as a holiday home, but it was
soon learned that they preferred the more fashionable pursuits

which could be found in St. Tropez. They wanted the house sold as soon as possible.

"Of course, it's quite big," Noelle Rocaud told her. "It's built in the local stone and it has these two towers at each end. There are about five bedrooms upstairs including the two vast upper rooms in the tower which are open to the roof. Downstairs there are two main halls between the two *salons* on the ground floors of the towers. At the back there is an old bakery which I think they used as a kitchen. I don't believe there is a proper modern bathroom in the entire place. But, as I said, it's not exactly a little cottage. It would be perfect if madame has more children. Perhaps madame's husband is bringing them later?"

So the woman was fishing after all. Well, it was only natural and in order to keep her as an ally, Callie knew she had to tell her as much of the truth as she could.

"I shall be living here on my own, Madame Rocaud, with just Luc." She didn't offer any further explanation, nor did she indicate whether or not Luc was her child. "But the house sounds perfect."

And it was. Callie made an offer within hours of seeing it. She hired a lawyer in Gourdon to act for her while the sale was going through and in the meantime she lived at the Rocauds' *auberge*, having all her meals sent up to her on a tray by Noelle. Callie had gone down that first morning to find the same crowd of Vincent Rocaud's *copains* hanging around in the bar. As she entered, one of them was parading up and down in her mink to the raucous sound of catcalls from the others.

"Eh, Jean-Paul, ça te va bien!"

"Hey, good-looking, want to go for a ride? Or are you afraid you will get your fancy coat dirty?"

"Got a rich lover, Jean-Paul? Did he buy it for you? Will he buy one for me?"

Jean-Paul adjusted his beret to a more rakish angle and pulled the mink tightly around his paunch. Ash dropped onto the fur from the Gauloise dangling from his lips. Suddenly he caught sight of Callie standing in the doorway and drew himself to a halt before her. With an exaggerated gesture, he shrugged the mink slowly down his shoulders till it slipped off altogether and fell on the floor at Callie's feet.

"C'est à vous, madame?" he spat at her sarcastically.

Callie stepped around it, ignoring him, making no effort to pick up the coat.

"I wish to rent a room here for a number of days," she told Vincent.

"*Je regrette . . .*" he shrugged.

"And here is half my down payment." Callie bulldozed her way through his words, and threw a huge wad of notes onto the bar. "The other half is on the floor." She pointed over her shoulder at the mink. "I shan't be needing it anymore."

She knew he would not be able to refuse and it would make him hate her at the same time. That was fine. She did not want this crowd to come knocking at her door. Once she'd moved into her house she wanted them to leave her alone and only make themselves available when she needed them to do something for her—for money. So they might as well know that she had some. She was aware that they would gossip about her for a while, but as time went by, it would die down and they would just come to regard her as some eccentric who lived on the top of the hill. If she left them alone they'd keep out of her way.

Except for Noelle. She needed Noelle. And so when the time came for her to move into *La Cachette* she asked Vincent Rocaud's lonely wife if she would like the idea of coming to clean for her, become her *femme de ménage*.

Callie knew that it had changed the woman's life. And, indeed, Callie often wondered what she would have done without her. Noelle showed her the nearby farm where she could get fresh eggs and milk every morning. She took her round the market town of Gourdon and pointed out the best butcher, the best greengrocer, the best *pâtisserie*. She took her to nearby Gramat where she could buy perhaps the best black peppercorns anywhere in the world. She tipped her off about a good source to supply her with the casks of the incredible *vin Cahors*. She helped her supervise the builders who came to put in a bathroom and shower and remodel the old bakery into a modern kitchen. She showed Callie how to plant an herb garden outside her kitchen door and instructed her how to use its yield in her cooking and for making restorative *tisanes*, refreshing herbal teas which, it seemed, could be a remedy for absolutely anything. She helped Callie coax little Luc from his bottles onto solid food and later it was Noelle who introduced Callie to the *principal* who ran the local *Jardin des Enfants* when the time came for him to start kindergarten. She even managed to turn the former Mrs. Perry Jay Duboise into a washerwoman. All the women of Arriac took their washing to a natural spring which gushed out of the hillside just below *La Cachette* into a drinking trough for cattle on one side and a large square stone pool on the other. Here they rinsed their laundry and scrubbed it on the large stone slabs on either side, shooing away the cows who strayed too close. They sang while they worked and Callie sang with them. She knew she was not part of them and they did not accept her despite the fact that she came with Noelle. But she did not care. She had *La Cachette*; she had Luc; she had Noelle. But for how long?

But perhaps the thing she would be most grateful to Noelle for was the way in which the younger woman helped Callie through the menopause. Callie knew it would come sooner or later, but she had hoped to at least get settled in her new house before it struck. But it was not to be. For some reason Callie had always known that she would have a rough time, but she was not prepared for the grueling eighteen months she had to endure. It was her first winter at *La Cachette* and it was a harsh one, the temperature sometimes dropping to four or five degrees below the freezing point. During the really heavy snowstorms Noelle could not get her bicycle up the hill and Callie had to suffer alone. It seemed to her that she was afflicted with virtually all the complaints associated with the so-called "change of life": she had the "hot flashes," she had palpitations, headaches, insomnia, fatigue and constant anxiety and depression. And on top of it all she was supposed to be raising a baby boy in the midst of his own agony: teething. Luc cried night after night for what seemed like six months on end. But each time Callie thought she was on the verge of going completely crazy—far more crazed than she had ever been in the institution—Noelle would gently restore her to an even keel. The woman seemed to have endless patience. Time and time again Callie swore to herself that she would make it up to her, but always put it off. Noelle still prattled on endlessly about how lonely she was, how Vincent had stopped talking to her, how much she missed her family in Brittany, how she felt she might never adjust to life in this isolated part of France, beautiful though it was. But Callie never really listened to her properly.

Until it was too late. Too late to thank Noelle for all she had done. Too late to make it up to her, buy her some nice clothes, send her back home on a trip to her beloved Brittany to see the sea again. They found her one morning around eight o'clock. It seemed she had climbed up one of the telegraph poles and electrocuted herself on the wires.

Callie could not believe it. She had attempted suicide herself once and failed. It never occurred to her that one day she would grow close to someone who would succeed and that that person would be someone she needed. For a short time Callie had felt warmth in her life and in response to it she had begun to change, to feel less destructive and vindictive. In time she might have forgotten all about Honey Winslow. But with Noelle gone she was on her own again with just a child for company, an impressionable little boy who had no idea his mind would slowly but surely be poisoned against his own mother.

CHAPTER 19

Noelle's death unnerved Callie and she reached out blindly to the only other person to whom she could turn for love, completely overlooking the fact that he was a very small child.

For a while she and Luc grew reasonably close. She took to tucking him in at night and sitting with him till he fell asleep. She even offered him the warmth of a maternal embrace every now and then, desperately trying to get him to return it. If he fell and hurt himself she was particularly attentive, but if she cut her finger she would thrust it forcefully under his nose, demanding that he "kiss it better." She could never wait for him to come to her of his own accord.

She wrote a single anguished letter to Anita expressing her love for this child, and in it Anita recognized the same obsession growing in Callie for Luc as she had had for PJ. Anita worried desperately that Callie was placing too much hope on this defenseless little boy, but she could not reply as Callie had carefully not revealed her whereabouts.

But Luc was not his father and as he grew older Callie was forced to accept this. In her more lucid moments she saw that while Luc resembled PJ as a little boy he was in fact an entirely

different type of child altogether—a little French country
urchin—and gradually, without realizing what she was doing,
in her disappointment she began to withdraw her affection.

Luc Chenier never *really* believed her story that his parents
had been killed in a plane crash on their way back to France
from America just after he had been born. Callie had felt it
would be best to stick to the truth about his being born in New
York since there would be no record of his birth anywhere in
France should he ever try to check later on. She explained that
she was a relative of his father's (true) who had been traveling
with them, but had taken a later flight home bringing him with
her, and following his parents' death, she had immediately
taken steps to adopt the tiny baby and take him down to live
with her in her new home in the Lot. This story would tally
with those the locals would tell him later about her arriving in
Arriac in a mink coat cradling him in her arms.

When he asked about his parents she told him that his
mother was an American (true) and his father a Frenchman
(partly true, the *Cheniers* were originally from France even if
the Duboises weren't), and that his father had been working in
New York when he had met Luc's mother which was why Luc
had been born there. But when Luc wanted to know about his
American mother—did she come from New York? did she have
any family he could visit? could he call himself half-American?
—Callie only laughed and patted him on the head, always
evading his questions.

Luc never realized Callie was American. For the first year of
his life he was confined to his *parc*, as the French called the
playpen, dumped on various strategic sites on the stone slabs of
La Cachette where Callie could keep an eye on him as she
supervised the unloading of her favorite pieces of furniture and
paintings which Teddy Lenoir, the only person in America who
knew where she was, had arranged to be shipped from
Coinchenier. During this year and the following one she
learned, with Noelle Rocaud's help, to perfect her French and
pick up a slight local accent at the same time so that by the
time Luc could understand her and learn to speak himself he
assumed she was French.

Callie raised him as a French child 100 per cent, sending him
aged four to the local *Jardin des Enfants* in the next valley till
he was six and then on to the *Cours Préparatoire*, the little

village school with a courtyard in the middle where he stayed till he took his CEF exam when he was twelve to get him into the *Sixième* at the big school in Gourdon.

Callie never mixed with the other parents. At the *Jardin des Enfants* and the *Cours Préparatoire* she deposited and collected him in her little black Deux Chevaux, waiting a little way round the corner so she would not be observed by the other mothers. Once he got to the *Sixième* he was collected at the bottom of the hill every morning by the school bus. Nor did she allow him to invite his classmates home. This was a little unfair to him, she realized, but she particularly did not want to encourage any contact with the outside world. There was always the possibility that word would spread about her, what she looked like, what the inside of her house looked like, and someone would track her down. She knew the *ouvriers* who had carried out the building and electrical work on the house had probably gossiped, but that was a long time ago. Every now and then she had to summon someone to fix something, but they never stayed long and she never engaged them in conversation for a minute longer than was necessary. She went to a doctor in Cahors to avoid local gossip in that department and mercifully she had never had to summon him to the house to see either her or Luc.

Since he could not bring children home to play with, much of his time as a young boy was spent watching television. He began with *Bonne Nuit, les Petits* with the three glove puppets whom he adored: Nicolas, the little boy, Patronel, the little girl and Nounours, the bear who put them to bed. If only Nounours would put him to bed too. Then he graduated to *Zorro* and finally he became hooked on old films, *les comédies* with Bourvil and Louis de Funes, otherwise known as *Fufu*. They made him laugh, but it was small compensation for the fact that he was desperately lonely.

And then one day he found himself watching something rather gruesome. He'd heard about *Le Vieux Fusil*, knew that it had been shot locally and a castle on a hill above a nearby village had been used. The film starred Philippe Noiret and Romy Schneider and told the story of a doctor in Occupied France during the Second World War, who sees his wife and daughter killed by Germans and seeks revenge. But his isolated upbringing had in no way prepared the eight-year-old Luc for the brutal scene where Romy Schneider as the wife is reduced to ashes by a German bazooka before her husband's eyes.

Almost hysterical with fright, Luc backed away from the television, his clogs clattering over the flagged-stone floor till he reached the wooden staircase to the first floor. He knew Callie was upstairs. The wooden floorboards were not carpeted and he could hear her moving about. The roar of the bazooka and the huge jet of flame he had just seen corresponded in his subconscious to a similar sound and image: that of the airplanes he heard passing overhead, and without realizing it, he had mentally pictured those airplanes caught in the flames of the bazooka, burning, exploding, plunging out of the sky.

Instead of Romy Schneider, he had seen his parents being burned to death.

"Tantie!"

He found her in her dressing room and hurled himself into her lap. She did not return his embrace but she did not push him away either.

"Did they burn up like that, *Tantie*, did they?"

"Did *who* burn up? What are you talking about, *ma'fant*?"

Her use of Cajun dialect was the only sign Callie gave that she was concerned by his distress.

"*Ma mère et mon père,* did they burn up? Did they catch fire in the plane?"

"Now, now, now, don't worry yourself about that." She pushed him from her now. "There were no survivors, that's all we know. Don't think about *how* they died, that's taking it too far."

Damn! What had set this off? Had she been a little too creative with the plane crash? Should it have just been simple pneumonia? Well, it was too late now.

"I want to see their pictures."

This was a recurring demand and she had her answer ready. Furthermore, she spoke the truth.

"I don't have any pictures of them. I've told you before, truly I don't. And think how terrible it would be if you knew what they looked like and then had to imagine them being burned to bits."

Luc shuddered and lifted his head to stare at her. To his horror he saw she was actually smiling at him, grinning.

"I just don't believe they were burned, *Tantie*. They *couldn't* have. Please, tell me it was all a story."

"You want a story?" She had turned away from him and was studying herself in the mirror. She looked different, he noticed. Her face was pale, almost white like a ghost and her eyes were like two dark holes with strange black lines drawn all round them. Her mouth was a huge gash of crimson. All over the surface in front of the mirror were scattered little pots and jars. "Don't!" she shrieked at him when he reached out his hand to one, "Don't you dare touch my make-up," and she snatched it away from him. "Now, what did I just say? Were you listening? I asked you if you wanted a story?"

Luc nodded. This was something new. She'd never made any effort to entertain him before. He wondered what was coming.

"And," she continued, drawing him toward her again, "while I'm telling you the story, we can play a little game. Now, once upon a time," she began in time honored tradition, "there was a witch. Stand still, don't wriggle." She was reaching for her pots of paint and the little brushes as she tilted his face toward her. "And the witch lived in this place called Mississippi far far away. They called her the Honey-witch. Are you listening? The *Honey*-witch, remember that. Stand still, *cher,* how many more times do I have to tell you?"

It was hard. She was smearing something cold all over his face and it made him want to squirm. He forced himself to stand immobile before her.

"The Honey-witch fooled everyone," continued Callie, "because on the outside she was the most beautiful little creature you ever did see, just like a princess. She had long fair hair and it was all shiny and glowing and her skin was all creamy and soft just like mine, see, now, feel it . . ." She raised his hand to her cheek, but what Luc touched seemed to him to be dry and flaky like very thin paper. "But *inside*, inside she was mean and evil. But no one knew, especially men, especially little boys. I mean, Luc, you should have seen your papa . . ."

"My *papa*? She knew my papa?"

"Yes, she did. The Honey-witch had a special eye on your papa, and on *his* papa, that's your granpapa. Fact is, she fed them her honey and in return she took away their little boys. She took your papa away from your granpapa and one day she's going to come along and try and take you away too . . ."

"But how can she take me away from my papa when I don't even have a papa? Did she take my papa away from me when he was killed in that airplane crash?"

Callie let out a hideous cackle, shaking her head from side to side so that her long jet earrings swung out violently and darted at Luc like snakes' tongues.

"You're a clever little boy, you know that? Cleverer than I thought. Come here and let me put some *Baton Rouge* on those sweet little lips of yours. See, I kept all the old *Bayou Beauty* products. They're the best. Come on, purse those lips at me, pretend you want to kiss me, stick them out, not too much, just a little pout, *thaa . . . aat's* right, that's just perfect. Yes, that airplane crash was the sort of thing the Honey-witch liked to do. To cause people pain and anguish and heartache. And there's just one thing we have to do to save you."

"What's that, *Tantie*?"

"One day, *cher,* we have got to go back to New Orleans and ask the voodoo man to tell us how to get hold of the Honey-witch's heart."

"Her heart? Does she really have one?"

"Not everyone has a *kind* heart, Luc. The Honey-witch, she has a *bad* heart, an evil heart, and the only way to conquer her is to rip her heart right out of her body, cut it out and leave a big red gaping hole."

Luc shuddered. To think this Honey-witch might one day come after him!

"If I see her, *Tantie*, I mean later on, if she, if we don't get to the voodoo man before she comes after me, what I want to know is . . . how will I know it's her?"

"That's why we're playing this game. Look in the mirror, little Luc, look and see what I've done. Now, aren't you pretty?"

Luc looked in the mirror and immediately turned away. He glanced around him, besides Callie there was no one else in the room. Finally it dawned on him that the other face reflected in the mirror was his and his eyes widened. This only increased the bizarre effect. Like Callie's his little oval face was painted a ghostly white. His eyebrows had been outlined by a kohl pencil in two graceful arcs and below them his eyelids had been coated in smoky gray eyeshadow. His long lashes were caked in mascara and his mouth blazed *Baton Rouge*. But it was the heavy black beauty spot high up on his left cheek to which Callie pointed.

"*That's* her mark. If you see a beautiful fair-haired lady with that mark, you'll know it's the Honey-witch come to get you!"

Luc's nightmares about the Honey-witch woke him at least once a week. He did not know it, but he cried out constantly in his sleep.

Callie never heard him. Her room was at the other end of the house in one of the two huge towers. Sometimes he got up and went along the passage to her door. If it was shut he looked through the keyhole. Now and again she left it ajar and he could stand in the shadows and watch her. He went to her for comfort, but by the time he reached her door he had resigned himself to the fact that she wouldn't respond to his needs. As the months went by he had begun to realize she was getting worse. She never went to bed, it seemed, but stayed up all night long. Often her lights were out and he watched her by moonlight.

She was always naked and never still. Round and round her room she roamed, pacing up and down. He watched her go to the windows, particularly on stormy nights of which there were many, and throw them open letting the rain lash in on her. Sometimes she stood in front of her looking-glass and stared at her gaunt, naked frame. Other nights she would beat her fists against the wall and scream.

One night she wasn't in her room and the smell of cooking drew him downstairs. He found her in the kitchen and the sound of his bare feet moving down the wooden staircase had alerted her to his arrival.

"I'm preparing a feast," she declared. "A feast for your birthday. You did know it was your birthday tomorrow, didn't you?"

As it happened he didn't. She'd never done anything for it before.

"Can I ask my friends from school, *Tantie*? They could bring me presents."

"*Non!* You know you're not allowed to bring anyone here. And as for presents, if you didn't even know it was your birthday how do you think your friends would have found out?

They won't have any presents for you—but I will. I've got a
very special present for you. You'll see."

The following evening she cooked a spectacular dinner—
shrimp gumbo (Queenie's old recipe from *Coinchenier*), *gratin
de quenelles de poisson, tournedos sautes chasseur* with *pommes
de terre gratin Dauphinoise* and a *salade verte* followed by
fromages and a huge *flan du Perigord*. Luc would have much
preferred a simple bowl of *soupe à l'oignon* made with the local
goose fat and a plate of *biftek et pommes frites* followed by
some ice-cream. It was the first time Callie had prepared a
Louisiana dish since she had left America and she was sad to
see that Luc so obviously found it rather unsavory.

She had dressed him up in a frilly white shirt and a pair of
black velvet pantaloons, white stockings and black patent
pumps with grosgrain bows on them. If she did but know it, he
was thanking his lucky stars that he had not been allowed to
bring his friends from school home if this was the way she
would have him greet them. He had never felt such a ninny.

As usual she had lit the twenty-one candles in the circular
iron chandelier which hung from the ceiling above the huge
oak table. Luc sat at one end, presenting a forlorn little figure
and while Callie's place was laid far away at the other she spent
most of the meal hovering between him and the kitchen, ad-
ministering to him constantly, demanding to know if he was
enjoying himself. The only other light in the huge hall came
from the roaring blaze in the huge fireplace, and if Luc's mind
had not been so obsessed with the threat of the Honey-witch,
he would have realized that if anyone looked like a witch it was
Callie in her long jet evening gown dug out of a trunk with her
shadow dancing on the wall behind her, magnified to grotesque
proportions. Two pomanders, balancing on the grate over the
fire, were wafting pungent aromas and making him feel slightly
sick.

Finally she allowed him to open his presents. Excited, he
rushed to look behind the log basket where she said she had
hidden them. But there was only one and it was *tiny*! A small
square box wrapped in silver paper. Trying not to show his
disappointment, Luc undid the wrapping and lifted the lid of
the little box. There, nestling on a bed of cotton wool, lay a
slender silver bracelet with a silver dolphin charm hanging
from it.

"Et voilà!" exclaimed Callie triumphantly, *"ton petit dauphin.* It was your father's and I knew you would want to have it. Of course it's a bit too big for your little wrist right now, but soon you'll be able to wear it all the time . . . Why, Luc, what are you doing? What's the matter?"

Luc had had enough. All this anticipation building up to absolutely nothing. Just some silly little *bracelet*, something little girls wore. What did he want with her stupid *dauphin*? In his rage he flung it in her face and fled outside. A storm was raging round the house, lightning illuminating the panoramic view from the top of the plateau. Refusing to give in to his tears of frustration, Luc tore down the hill into the forest below, too wound up to worry about the fact that he might be disturbing the wild boars who roamed the area and who charged anything which provoked them.

Far removed from the Louisiana banquet at *La Cachette*, Elliott Fitzgerald was preparing a modest supper. He had got into the habit of making himself an omelette every night and taking rather a long time about it. He rather liked pottering about his kitchen at *La Folie* in his slippers, breaking a couple of eggs into a bowl, popping outside to snip some parsley, some chervil and some tarragon which grew wild outside his back door. He generally drank a glass or two or three of wine along the way. He often saved *La Dépêche* to read at this time of day and he had it now spread out on the kitchen table. Then he remembered the chives. He always forgot the chives. It was pitch black out there now. Would he find them? Of course he would. He knew exactly where they grew. If he just snipped away in that direction what did it matter if he brought in a few weeds as well?

The pouring rain encouraged him to be a bit quicker than he might have been and it was while he was running back to the open kitchen door that he saw the little figure streak past him down the hill. It was the boy from *La Cachette.* He'd be soaked to the skin in no time and terrified out of his wits if he ran into a boar.

Elliott dropped the chives and set off in hot pursuit. The boy, hearing sounds behind him, assumed he was being chased and attempted to move even faster, but the thickening undergrowth only served to hamper his progress. Elliott soon caught up with him and had the good sense not to grab the child. Instead he called out to him.

"Arrèt! It's OK. Don't be frightened. I'm here to help. Here, give me your hand and I'll lead you back up the hill."

The boy turned and as he did so the moon came out from behind a cloud and illuminated him. Elliott gasped. It was Little Lord Fauntleroy, all dressed up and nowhere to go.

"Viens-là!" he tried again, speaking softly as if to a recalcitrant dog, and this time the boy moved toward him, tripped and began to cry. Gently Elliott helped him to his feet and together they made their way up the waterlogged hillside, Luc's black patent shoes squelching in the mud.

Luc allowed himself to be led into *La Folie.* It was the first time he had been there despite its close proximity to *La Cachette.* He basked in its warmth, not just from the open fireplace at the end of the kitchen, but from the welcoming simplicity of the room. There was none of the opulence of *La Cachette.* The plain whitewashed walls and the flagged-stone floor were unadorned save for a couple of watercolors, a wooden shelf on which stood a line of bottles of local *eaux de vie* and another housing a row of paperback books with orange spines.

"You seem to be in the wars."

Luc stared at him. Elliott suddenly realized he'd reverted to English.

"It's my birthday," the boy informed him as if that explained everything. *"Mais j'en ai marre . . ."* he finished, his voice almost rising to a scream.

Elliott understood. The boy was fed up. He'd had enough—but of what? *"De quoi?"* he asked Luc.

"Tantie," he spat out the word.

Elliott tried to listen, tried to understand, but it was all too much for him. The boy was rattling it out much too fast—something about a Honey-witch whatever that was and a silver dolphin and a plane crash and a German bazooka shooting flames. None of it made any sense.

But what he saw before him was a scared little boy in tears and his heart went out to him. He reached out and drew Luc into his arms and gently rocked him against his shoulder, patting him on the back until the hysterical sobbing subsided.

Then he said: "I was just making myself an omelette. Would

you like to share it with me?" and Luc Chenier, who had eaten
a three-course feast only an hour before, nodded his head vigor-
ously. He loved omelettes. This was turning out to be a good
birthday after all.

Over the meal Luc chattered non-stop about his school and
what he watched on television, telling Elliott all the things Callie never wanted to hear about. Then suddenly, when there was
a moment's silence, they could hear Callie's voice calling his
name. The storm had died down and Elliott insisted on walking
him back across the field which separated *La Folie* from *La
Cachette.* Luc would not let him come the whole way and Elliott understood. The boy's visit to *La Folie* was to be their
secret. That way he could return.

Callie was waiting for him in front of the house and when she
saw him she reached out her arms to him. After the warmth of
Elliott's embrace it was like being crushed by some kind of
sinister skeleton and he wriggled away from her. She was stung
by his rejection and tried to grab his arm.

"See this?" she dangled the silver bracelet in front of him,
"you're going to wear it if it kills you. It's your *dauphin,* your
identity bracelet, it says you're a Chenier." She forced it over
his hand and onto his wrist, holding it there tightly so that it
cut into his flesh. "It fits you now. I've fixed it so that you can
wear it. I never want to see you without it. *Never!* Understand?"

Luc nodded. Then he ducked down and bit her hand hard.
Screaming, she let him go and he raced into the house. When
she followed him upstairs she found he had locked her out of
his room and she had never even known there was a key in the
door.

Across the field at *La Folie* Elliott sat at his kitchen table and
admitted to himself what Luc's visit had meant to him. He had
reached out to a child, a child who had responded and who
would return for comfort and, possibly, love. A child who
made him remember that he had one of his own, who had
grown up without him.

As Luc grew up he and Callie went their separate ways. As the
years went by she retreated more and more into a world of her
own and this suited Luc fine. Provided he never brought any-

body to the house or disturbed her when she was upstairs in her room, he could do anything he liked, have whatever he wanted.

At the local fairgrounds, the village *fêtes* of the summer, Luc became the star of *les manèges*—the booths, the stalls and most of all the shooting galleries where he won an endless stream of soft toys and ugly cheap crockery which he took home to a bewildered Callie. When he was fourteen he demanded of her that she buy him the obligatory status symbol of all French teenagers: the *mobilette*. At first she refused, terrified that he would kill himself on it, but then he pointed out that if she refused everyone would think she had no money. Everyone rode to school on their *mobilettes* once they had them. Those without still had to ride the school bus. He couldn't face the humiliation. Reluctantly she gave in, knowing it was only a matter of time before the *mobilette* was followed by drinking and sex. Already he sported the inevitable leather jacket and even though he kept the door permanently closed, she would often catch an incriminating whiff of Gauloise black tobacco smoke as he went in and out. But when she challenged him, he always shrugged his shoulders and said in taunting response, "Well, at least your Honey-witch hasn't got me yet, *Tantie*."

Then, when he was fifteen, something completely unexpected hit him between the eyes. Something for which he had not prepared himself at all.

He fell in love.

She was in his class at school, had jet black hair like his own, huge dark brown eyes, a long thin nose and a little wet rosebud mouth. She wore her hair in a long braided ponytail with an endearingly shaggy fringe falling over her eyes. Her name was Marie-Michelle and she had no idea Luc existed.

Her family was rich and she lived in a grand *manoir* by the river about five miles from Gourdon. She was cool and aloof, but she had something no one else in his school had: she had class. Here was someone who would understand the grandiose dinners he had to endure with Callie every evening. Marie-Michelle and her family probably dined in style all the time. But that was about all they had in common. Luc worshipped Johnny Halliday, Eddy Mitchell, the Rolling Stones, while Marie-Michelle liked Mozart, Schumann and Grieg, perhaps a little Schubert from time to time. She was not partial to clinging onto someone's back as they roared around on a *mobilette*.

She preferred to spend her time sitting at the piano, perfecting her Chopin. Or reading the new Françoise Sagan. She spurned the *film noir*, preferring instead the more lyrical films of Eric Rohmer and Claude Lelouche. She had been told she looked like Anouk Aimée in *A Man and a Woman* and each time she saw the film (sixteen in all), she saw herself and surrendered to yet another wonderful orgy of adolescent weeping.

Unfortunately Luc had never seen *A Man and a Woman*. He'd never even heard of it. As for Chopin . . .

He had almost given up hope when one evening she consented to let him buy her a *vin cassis* in Rocky's bar on the way home from school. She did not have a *mobilette*, she had a bicycle which she insisted on riding in convoy with him. This meant he couldn't go very fast or show off his fancy Steve McQueen stunts.

Marie-Michelle sipped her *vin cassis* and looked politely around the bar. "How quaint," she said in a patronizing tone. Then she said something which made Luc's blood turn cold.

"Isn't this the bar run by that man whose wife killed herself on the telegraph wire? Why do you suppose she did it?"

Luc looked down at his feet, his ears turning red. He hoped Rocky hadn't heard her. He had heard about Noelle Rocaud from Callie, but he had no idea that she had killed herself.

"Have another drink," he suggested quickly, without answering her question.

Slowly but surely Luc plied Marie-Michelle with glass after glass of *vin cassis*. He knew the local *crème de cassis* was more alcoholic than most and combined with the wine even one glass was pretty potent, let alone the three or four she had drunk. By eight o'clock she was in no condition to ride her bicycle and for once Luc had no trouble persuading her to cling to him on the back of his *mobilette*. He took her into Gourdon where the annual *fête* was in full flow. Fairy lights were hung throughout the branches of the trees in the main square and a local band was playing while people danced. An accordionist was wandering in and out of the couples, swaying from side to side as he squeezed and serenaded them with typically French country music.

Luc drew Marie-Michelle into his arms and gently rubbed her back as they danced slowly, cheek to cheek. Later, on the way home, he stopped by the river and led her down to the water's edge to lie on the moonlit grass under a willow tree. He did not try to do anything fast, merely laid his face next to hers and let his long, dark eyelashes flutter over her face.

"Oh, how perfect! What are you doing?" she asked.

"Giving you a butterfly kiss," he whispered, "lie back and close your eyes and imagine a mass of *les citrons* flying over you." *Les citrons* were the brilliant yellow butterflies found in the area.

Suddenly she opened her mouth and her tongue darted out to give his lashes a quick lick. Before she could draw it in again, he had covered it with his mouth. They kissed for what seemed to Luc like hours, very slowly, drinking each other in further and further. She seemed to want to go on forever and each time he withdrew, hoping to go on to something else, she sucked him back in again. Except that she did not notice what he was doing to her clothes. She was wearing a thin, cotton print dress which buttoned down the front. Luc undid them all while she continued to kiss him. She was not wearing a bra and as Luc pushed her dress aside he could see why. She did not need one. Her breasts were tiny, her nipples little points on her chest. He had never seen skin so pale and when he felt it he thought he was touching white silk. Until he came to her lace-edged panties which *were* silk. He pushed them down her thighs and brought his hand back up to gently rub her black pubic hair. He began to move his index finger imperceptibly toward the entrance to her vagina. She let him insert it and begin to work on her. Just as she began to moan he slipped his erection out of his jeans and brought the tip in his hand to the edge of her vagina. Slowly he rubbed it against her clitoris until he felt her reach down and take over.

Then she stopped. Suddenly. She sat up and let go of him.

"You are not circumcised?" Marie-Michelle was a Jewish *princesse.*

"Eh bah?" Luc had no idea what she meant, but he figured there might be a chance he could bluff his way back between her legs.

"No, of course, you aren't. How stupid of me. You're not Jewish."

"So?"

"So, I can't take you home to meet my parents."

"Tant pis! We'll stay here instead," and he plunged his hand back into her wetness.

Marie-Michelle erupted into little high-pitched screams when she came. Luc thought he was hurting her and paused for a second, but she pulled him back down to her. At the back of his mind he registered briefly that for someone who was only fifteen she sure knew what she wanted. *Eh bas?* Whatever it was, he had to give it to her.

She was very spoilt. She made him do *every*thing for her. All day long it was fetch and carry. If a pencil rolled off the desk while they were in class she would shoot him a glance, knowing he would run to pick it up.

But more important than anything was her beauty. Every day he had to tell her how gorgeous she was. Preferably several times a day. Never once did she indicate that his shock of jet black hair and his dark luminous eyes made him something of a dreamboat himself. If she noticed the other girls at school drooling over him she never said anything. Just so long as he didn't notice *them.* He must have eyes only for her.

She never asked him anything about himself, which was just as well since he had begun to worry about how he would explain Callie. She always talked about herself and about the things she liked she was quite knowledgeable. Luc could have learned a lot about classical music if he had cared to listen, but he invariably switched off when she got started on one of her intellectual dissertations and concentrated on sucking one of her nipples instead. But it always came back to her beauty.

She wanted to be a model. She made him look through hundreds of old fashion magazines which she brought to their riverside hideaway every day in a plastic bag. She showed him endless pictures of world-famous faces—Jean Shrimpton, Celia Hammond, Veruschka. She pored over them from every angle, their faces, their shoulders, their necks—were they long enough, was hers as long?—their busts, their legs, their feet, their hands. She compared herself with all of them and pretended to find herself wanting. She appealed to Luc. She wanted to hear that she would be more beautiful than any of the models in the photographs. Luc wasn't born yesterday.

"You are already more beautiful," he told her, "so I'd say it was a bit of a foregone conclusion."

"Even more beautiful than her?" Marie-Michelle showed him an old *Vogue* from the Fifties, an American edition. She pointed to a picture of a woman looking coquettishly at the camera, her hair swept up in a chignon. Her head was slightly tilted back and she appeared to be looking down her face, laughing, teasing. She was wearing a tight black turtleneck sweater which accentuated her high pointed breasts. Her waist was nipped in by a wide black patent leather belt. She had obviously just swung around to face the photographer and the movement had caused her wide red felt circular skirt to swirl up in the air revealing perfect legs encased in sheer black silk stockings. She was the most perfect creature Luc had ever seen.

"Who is she?" he breathed.

"Don't you *know*?" Marie-Michelle looked at him scathingly. "She's my idol. I want to be like her more than any other model in the world. 'Course she's not working anymore, not as a model anyway, she's too old. Look at you drooling, Luc! That picture was taken years ago. You don't think she was more beautiful than me, do you?"

"Oh, for heaven's sake, how can you say such ridiculous things?" Luc came to his senses just in time. "That's impossible. Anyway, how can she be in competition with you? She's a blonde and you're a raven-haired beauty. Who is she anyway?"

"Honey Winslow! Surely you've heard of Honey Winslow?"

And at that moment Luc noticed the small black dot high up on the model's left cheek.

"The Honey-witch," he whispered.

It was agony having such a beautiful girlfriend and not being able to take her home and show her off to anyone. OK, he didn't have any parents, but he was bursting with so much pride that he would even have taken her home to Callie if he had been allowed to.

Then an idea hit him. He would take her to meet Monsieur Fitzgerald. Ever since that disastrous birthday night he had returned to visit the Englishman on a regular basis, never staying very long, just twenty minutes or so. Light, easy conversation, but it was a comfort to him to know the old man was there. Luc had never proffered much information about himself, but he had an instinctive feeling that if he ever needed help he could go to Monsieur Fitzgerald. He had become like a *grandpère* to him, had even begun to teach him English over the past eighteen months. It was only fitting that he take his girl to meet him. In fact Monsieur Fitzgerald must be wondering what had become of him. Since he had become involved with Marie-Michelle she had taken up all his time. He had not paid Elliott a call in over four months.

Elliott could not have been more delighted. He felt flattered, no, honored, that Luc should want to introduce his *fiancée* to him. Of course they were not engaged, but clearly she had made an enormous impression on the boy. Elliott fussed for a week as to what he should give them to eat. In the end he decided that if he made too much of a fuss it would embarrass the young couple. He must make it look as natural as possible, as if he had people in to dinner every other night and they were just two more welcome guests. In the end he settled on a simple *quiche lorraine* followed by *pot au feu.*

As it turned out, he spent most of the time cooking, but he enjoyed himself more than he had in years. He took his time making the pastry for the *quiche,* kneading the dough and rolling it out on his wooden kitchen table. He used ham instead of bacon and no cheese. It was one of the first things he had learned when he started teaching himself to cook: a true *quiche lorraine* contains no cheese. He cooked the *pot au feu* in a huge round heavy iron *marmite* which hung from a hook above the open fireplace in his kitchen.

He sang as he cooked and was surprised to find he was singing hymns—"Jerusalem," "Oh God, Our Help in Ages Past," "All Things Bright and Beautiful." Seeing Amy so recently at the old boy's funeral must have left its mark.

He shook himself and went to stir the contents of the *pot au feu* which had been simmering all day above the fire. The aroma of succulent tender boiled beef and a variety of vegetables wafted through the house. For dessert he had made a cold lemon *soufflé* which he had stood on the windowsill to set. He had no refrigerator and until now had never really needed one. Normally he ate everything himself the minute he cooked it.

The meal was a disaster. Not Elliott's cooking which was superb, but Marie-Michelle ruined everything.

First of all she would not touch a morsel of the *quiche.*

"Oh, *won't* you, please, just try a little bit? I have no inten-

tion of poisoning you, I assure you," Elliott told her, exerting
as much charm as he was able.

"What about my diet?" she whined. "Didn't Luc tell you?
I'm going to be a model, I have to watch my figure. At home
we just have a little *consommé* or a salad." When he produced
the *pot au feu* she looked at him as if he were mad. *Pot au feu*, a
simple peasant's dish when she had been asked out to dinner,
her expression said. In the end she helped herself to a small
trickle of the juice—in lieu of her precious *consommé*, thought
Elliott—and a carrot. She declined the lemon *soufflé* altogether.

Worse was yet to come. While he was making coffee in the
kitchen having ushered them into his tiny living room, Elliott
heard her tell Luc in a loud whisper: *"Mais il est pédé, ce mec*,
he's a queer, your friend. Why have you brought me all the way
over here to see an old queen? *Tu me prends pour un folle?* Do
you think I'm nuts?"

Elliott wondered what he was going to do about her. He
cared about Luc and this girl was not right for him. He had
known that the minute they walked in. Furthermore, he knew a
thing or two about Mlle. Marie-Michelle Steiner. He'd seen her
in Gourdon recently on a number of occasions when he'd
driven in to sit and while away the evening sitting in a bar.
She'd probably told Luc she was at home doing her homework,
when all the time she'd been swanning round town on the arm
of someone else. Should he tell Luc? Would the boy listen to
him? Probably not and he was going to find out one day anyway. Whichever way it happened the boy was going to be hurt.

After dinner Marie-Michelle decided to remember her manners.

"What a *charming* house, Monsieur Fitzgerald. So compact.
My parents prefer something larger but really, I think they are
so extravagant. Luc tells me you're English. I'd *never* have
guessed. You have no accent, none whatsoever. So clever of you
to learn our language. What brings you to our country? You're
a writer? Really, how *interesting*."

She prattled on and on. My God, thought Elliott, she's only
just turned sixteen, but already she sounds like an artificial
bourgeois matron. Poor Luc. But poor Luc appeared to be perfectly happy. He sat between them, smiling brightly, turning
from one to another, not really understanding the nuance of the
conversation. He had eaten well. He was enjoying a rare li-

queur, one of Elliott's excellent *Reine-Claude a l'eau de vie*, and all was well with his world. He had not understood what Marie-Michelle had meant by saying that Monsieur Fitzgerald was a *pédé*. He did not really know exactly what a *pédé* was. He drifted off into a dreamy state.

Suddenly his reverie was broken by Marie-Michelle almost shouting.

"I don't know what you mean, monsieur. It sounds as if you have been spying on me. Oh, all right, since you insist, yes, I was with someone. *Mais il est Juif!* Don't you two understand?" She turned to look imploringly at Luc. "I need never have told you if this silly old man hadn't brought it up. Etienne Loewenthal. I met him last year when we were on holiday *sur la côte*. At St. Trop as a matter of fact. He's a nice Jewish boy and my parents approve. And he's rich. Or he will be one day. I mean, look at you, Luc, who are you? You never take me home to where you live. They say you live with an old lady or something. I'm sorry, Luc, but I'm going to be a famous model, I'm going to have a career, I'm going to Paris soon. I want to be seen with the right people. It was fun with you for a while, but you're not going anywhere . . ."

"He's only sixteen," Elliott pointed out gently.

"That's exactly it," Marie-Michelle retorted, *"only* sixteen!" and with that she pulled on her coat and left.

"She never even thanked you," Luc said, shaking his head in utter amazement.

"She's a spoilt brat, Luc, you're well rid of her," Elliott told him, thinking that however much Madame Chenier had neglected her duties in Luc's upbringing, she had at least taught him some manners. He was wild in many ways, but at base he was gentle and polite and now he insisted on helping Elliott with the washing up.

"She called you something, what did she say? *Un pédé?*" Luc began tentatively.

"You don't know what that is?"

"I don't think so. I guessed, maybe, it was . . ."

"It's when a man prefers other men . . . making love, he prefers to make love to men rather than women. It's all right, it doesn't make him any different in any other way. Often he becomes lonely because no one wants to have much to do with him and he can't find real friends. Often he wants to be just friends with men . . . and with women but people think he is abnormal."

"And you are like that, Monsieur Fitzgerald?"

"Yes, Luc. But you are not. You have had sex with Marie-Michelle, have you not?" Luc nodded. "And with others?" Luc nodded again. "There you are then. You enjoy it with girls. And you are quite safe with me. We *'pédés,'* we look out for our own kind. It's hard to find someone. I've been searching for a number of years now. I don't think I will ever find anyone, not buried away down here like I am. I go to the bar in Gourdon every now and then—that's where I saw Marie-Michelle and that young man she talked about. But it is not a bar for our kind and they don't like me to go there too often. The customers get embarrassed. So you see I need my friends, Luc, friends like you."

He did not add that he had no other friends. That would have been too big a burden to place on the boy. He need not have worried. Luc embraced the old man and gently patted him on the shoulder. Then he raised his head and said proudly: "Women! All the same. She was just being stupid. *Idiote!* I'll get her back, you'll see. Thank you for a wonderful meal, monsieur. *Bonsoir."*

But he never saw Marie-Michelle alone again. The next evening he rode into Gourdon on his *mobilette* and hung around the square. He saw her on the arm of a tall young man with a distinctly Parisian air about him. He had to be at least eighteen. For a start he had a car. And he was dressed in white linen slacks and a short-sleeved shirt with a little crocodile on the breast pocket. Over one shoulder he had casually slung his blazer. Luc had never seen anything so smooth. Marie-Michelle caught his eye, then looked away abruptly.

Luc followed them everywhere. He saw them eating in five star restaurants, going to discothèques, going to movies (all the *films noirs* she professed to hate), and finally he watched her lead Etienne to the spot by the river beneath the willow tree. *Their* spot. Etienne might have been a gent in all other areas, but when it came to sex he was as impatient as a tom cat. He unzipped his fly and pushed her back against the trunk of the willow tree without even waiting to lay her down on the ground. He deftly unbuttoned her (he must have had a lot of practice, Luc thought bitterly) and grasped her panties until they ripped.

Luc couldn't watch any more. He leapt on to his *mobilette* and rode back to *La Cachette* at top speed. For once he disobeyed the rules and ran upstairs to Callie's room.

"*Viens, Tantie*, we're going to the movies." He had to seek some distraction. They would go and see that new American film, *The Godfather*, which had opened in Cahors. Callie was so surprised she allowed herself to be strapped onto the back of the *mobilette* and carried off to Cahors.

It was a violent film and at the end of it Luc had clapped. From then on he started to dress like a Sicilian bandit and his dark good looks went a long way to complete the image. And for a while Callie emerged from her own closed-off world and began to wonder how long it would be before he found out who he really was.

A week later they were having breakfast together in the kitchen at *La Cachette*. Summer was over. Autumn had begun. Outside there were still traces of the early morning mist. Suddenly Luc shouted: "*Il arrive, Tantie.*" He leapt up and went to the front door. The *facteur* touched his cap, but did not even bother to get off his bicycle as he flung Callie's *France-Soir* onto the front steps.

Callie heard Luc coming back through the dining hall, munching on an apple. He called out to her and the words froze her blood.

"*C'est qui, Perry Jay Duboise?*" Who is Perry Jay Duboise?

So it had come. He had found out who he was. Relax. Act normally. Decide how to deal with it. Don't pretend there's anything strange.

"Why do you ask, Luc?"

"He's dead, whoever he is. It's all over the front of *France-Soir. Crise cardiaque*, poor bastard." He glanced at Callie and saw the look of shock on her face. "Why, did you know him, *Tantie*?"

Callie let the air out in a rush and hoped he hadn't heard. He didn't know. He had no idea.

"I believe I met him once or twice when I lived in Paris, years ago," she lied. "Let me see." She held out her hand for the paper.

There it was. AMERICAN COSMETICS TYCOON DEAD
OF A HEART ATTACK.

So he was dead. She was a widow. And soon there would be
the reading of the will. Surely now Philippe would realize that
the time had come to be reunited with his mother, to seek out
Callie, and when he did, she would show him his son. He
would contact Teddy Lenoir and Teddy was the only person in
America who knew where she was. All she had to do was wait
for PJ to get in touch with her.

That night Callie's world collapsed around her. They were
watching the news on television and suddenly Perry Jay's face
flashed upon the screen. Callie sat, mesmerized. She could not
believe what she was hearing. At any moment she expected
them to announce her name, but of course it never came. A
reference to Mrs. Perry Jay Duboise was made, *the deceased's
estranged widow still living as a recluse at the family home,*
Coinchenier.

Callie fumed. Just as well they hadn't called her Madame
Chenier. But what about the will? What about PJ?

When Honey Winslow's face appeared on the screen Callie
screamed for a very long time, so long in fact that she missed
what the announcer had said. Luc had crept near to the set and
turned to tell her:

"All his money, *Tantie*—and by the sound of things he had a
lot. All his money and his business . . . hey, he ran the company that makes all those pots and paints you use, *Bayou
Beauty*! He's left 50 per cent of that and his estate to her, to
Honey Winslow."

And suddenly it dawned on him. This was the woman
Marie-Michelle worshiped. And there it was, high up on her
left cheek, her beauty mark.

"Why that's . . . that's . . ."

"That, *cher*," Callie told him in icy tones, "is the Honey-
witch. That's the bitch whose heart we've got to tear right out
of her body. She stole your papa, but she won't get her claws on
you *or* your papa's money. I'm going to wipe her off the face of
the earth."

CHAPTER 20

Honey had long since moved out of her apartment in the Village. For the last few years she had been renting a suite at the Sherry-Netherland Hotel and it was to this suite that the Press were arriving in droves to interview the new heiress to the Bayou Beauty fortune.

In fact, thought Honey, the only person who hadn't shown up was that Goddamned girl who was supposed to be doing a profile on her. She still hadn't reappeared after rushing back to England.

Honey was in seventh heaven. Morning, noon and night she embarked on her own private celebration. She hadn't seen or heard from Perry Jay Duboise since she'd had the baby seventeen years ago and nobody had been more surprised than she to learn that he had left his 50 per cent of Bayou Beauty to her, along with a Park Avenue apartment, a villa in St. Tropez, a house in Gstaad, another in Antigua. She didn't need the money. It was ironic that this legacy should have fallen into her lap when she was wealthier and more successful than she had ever been. *Winslowear* was expanding all the time and diversifying into children's sportswear and other areas. What really appealed to her was the possibilities Bayou Beauty opened up to her. She had all sorts of plans. But there was one slight snag.

She only had 50 per cent. The other half belonged to Callie Chenier. She had been astounded to discover that Perry Jay had power of attorney over the voting of his wife's shares. That power of attorney had passed to her and somehow it made her feel distinctly uneasy, because no one seemed to have any idea where Callie was.

Maybe she was living down at that plantation in Mississippi, but if so then why didn't anyone know that? Honey just couldn't believe it when they told her that no one had answered the telephone down there in years. It seemed the only person who had known where Callie Chenier was was Perry Jay and now he was gone. Of course nobody realized that he hadn't had a clue either. The one person who did know was the wily old Chenier family lawyer, Teddy Lenoir, but Teddy hadn't breathed a word. He had sent Callie a wire breaking the news to her, but he had omitted to mention that Honey had inherited. He'd deal with that if Callie ever showed up.

So where was Callie, Honey asked herself over and over again. There'd been no mention of her in the Press whatsoever. Where had she been all these years? Honey cursed herself for not having kept tabs on the woman, but then she'd been too busy running her own life, finally quitting modelling at the ripe old age of thirty and then for the last five years building up *Winslowear*.

The house telephone startled her.

"We have a Mr. Duboise down here, Miss Winslow. Can we send him up?"

Honey jumped. Had the old man returned from the dead to reclaim what he'd left her?

"Put him on," she snapped nervously.

"Honey, it's me. Can I come up for a drink?"

PJ. After all these years PJ had turned up. Well, it made sense. He was bound to come sniffing around sooner or later. She'd inherited what might have been his . . .

As she waited for him to come up in the elevator, she recalled the last time she had seen him and recoiled slightly. It was a long time ago, but she still remembered it as being good. Clearly he hadn't thought so since he hadn't been back for more.

She eyed him warily as he came through the door, looking rather good in baggy Armani linens. A few lines around the eyes, but as yet no gray in his glossy black hair. Honey had come up a bit in the world since she'd last seen him and she realized he had a lot more natural style than his father had ever had. Perry Jay had been a bit of a sleazeball when you got right down to it, but somehow PJ had always had something classy about him. Maybe it was because of the good breeding on his mama's side.

PJ gave her a quick peck on the cheek, nothing suggestive, just a casual greeting.

"What'll you drink and why are you here?" she asked him.

"Jack Daniels on the rocks and why do you think?"

She fixed his drink and poured herself a kir royale. She had plenty of champagne to get through.

She carried it over to the window and looked down on 5th Avenue, the lights twinkling way into the distance. Then she turned and looked past the Plaza Hotel to a similar view along Central Park South. She was aware of PJ behind her, sitting down, relaxing on the couch when she hadn't even invited him to. He must be planning to stay a while. She heard the two thuds as he kicked his loafers off and they hit the floor.

"Sorry about your daddy, PJ."

"Hell you are, Honey. Don't waste your condolences on me. I wasn't exactly close to my father."

"When did you last see him?"

"About sixteen, seventeen years ago."

Honey swung round. "And Callie?"

"Same thing."

"You mean you haven't seen your family all this time? That's mighty peculiar."

"Well, have you been down to see your mother? No? I thought not. Anyway, I don't see Perry Jay and Callie as my family anymore. They're next of kin, but they're not *family*, never were."

"But your mamma loved you, PJ. You knew that." Honey was shocked to hear him talking like this.

"You may be right, but she had a funny way of showing it."

"You lonely, PJ? Sounds like you are."

"Not especially. I know a lot of people in New York."

"Still fooling around with your little magazine?"

She saw him jump. So no one knew it was him. Still kept it as his little secret.

"That little magazine, as you so sweetly call it, happens to have an extremely healthy circulation. I do pretty well out of it."

"OK, OK, don't worry. I won't tell nobody it's yours. You always were a dark one, PJ. Still making with those weirdo disguises you used as a kid?"

"Some," he said off-handedly. "You're looking good, Honey."

Actually he thought she had lost her looks just a fraction. She had hardened, she had lost that wonderful fresh All-American healthy look she had always had. She had lost her youth and while she still looked young, there was an edge to her beauty now. Her make-up was too perfect, her eyebrows outlined in perfect arcs above brilliant eyeshadow and heavy mascara. The rose glow on her cheeks now came from carefully applied blusher and the shape of her lips had been redefined in a dark wine color by her lip pencil. Her black linen Italian pants were expertly cut and the shoulder pads in her black silk shirt added to the overall look of power dressing. Her jewelery was discreet, a gold chain hanging loose inside her shirt, gold hoops in her ears and a Van Cleef & Arpels watch on her left wrist with the odd diamond in the strap.

"Thanks. Hey, before I forget, there's a model in your last issue I want to get ahold of for *Winslowear*, looks Puerto Rican or something. You got her dressed as a maid, or undressed I should say, serving dinner in the illustrations which accompanied that cookery section you had. Pretty good that was, I recognized some of Queenie's old recipes in there . . . you been back to *Coinchenier* lately?" She sneaked in the last question, hoping to catch him off guard.

"Glad to see you've been reading *Eros*, Honey. She was a hooker on Forty-second Street and I don't think she'd do for *Winslowear* somehow, but more to the point, no, I haven't been near *Coinchenier* in years. I told you, I haven't seen Callie."

"Is she down there?"

"Who knows?"

"She wasn't at the funeral."

"Nor was I," PJ reminded her.

"I think that was terrible. You should have gone to your own father's funeral."

"You're a hypocrite, Honey. Did *you* care about him? Of course you didn't. You just went because he left you his loot."

"PJ, are you sore at me or what?"

"No, not particularly," he replied truthfully.

"It's because of *Bayou Beauty* and your daddy not leaving you a bean, isn't it?"

PJ didn't answer.

"Because if it is, I want to tell you my plans. I want you to join me at *Bayou Beauty*. PJ, what do you say?"

He said absolutely nothing, of course. He knew she'd just said it on the spur of the moment.

"Chrissakes, Philippe, can't we have a conversation? What in hell is the matter with you?"

"You're talking and I'm listening. That constitutes a conversation in most people's book."

"So what do you think about joining me at *Bayou Beauty*?"

"I never joined my father. Why should I want to join you?"

"Because I have plans. I want to start a new line in perfume. For *men*!"

She waited breathlessly for his reaction.

"You have been talking to too many *fegelahs*."

"No, it's a new thing. It's not so much a perfume, more a *fragrance* to make you feel rich, exciting, desirable. . . . I want you to be my partner in setting it up." She was almost whispering now. "It'd be your baby from the start. I'd give you free rein. You could choose the name, the launch campaign, *every*thing. And then we'd go on to something new, create something breathtaking together, rebuild *Bayou Beauty* as a team."

"Oh, stop talking such a load of crap, Honey." PJ was irritated now. "I've got my hands full with *Eros*. What do I want with *Bayou Beauty*? You get free advertising in *Eros* in case you hadn't noticed. Isn't that enough for you? I may not be in the public eye all the time, but I like it like that. Have you any idea what it's been like all this time keeping *Eros* going? Thinking up new ideas, new angles, getting new writers, new photographers? Who else would have put a real live hooker from Forty-second Street in their cookery section and make it work? *Eros* keeps me alive and I'll say this and I'll only say it once, Honey,

I'm grateful to you for giving me my first cover. You talk about creating something new together as a team, well, we did it way back then and that was enough for me. Now, I'll bet all you see me for is a good piece of copy for your publicity guys. *'BAYOU BEAUTY* HEIRESS TEAMS UP WITH SON OF *BAYOU BEAUTY.'* Give me a break."

"But, PJ, sugar . . ." she began and stopped when he turned and hit her with the full force of his explosion.

"You never listened back in Mississippi, so God alone knows why I think you might now, but one day you're going to have to figure out that I want nothing to do with my father's company. *Nothing!* I've never wanted my father's pickings. That's why I've never been near you in all these years. You want to know something? I fell in love with you when we were kids back home. Yes, I did! But all you wanted was my father and what he could do for you. Well, I have to admit it now, Honey, you were one smart little cookie. I don't begrudge you your success and yes, I have been hearing things about you over the years. You were damned beautiful as the *Honey* girl, you were damned smart to start up *Winslowear* and you're still one hell of a looker. But you're *Bayou Beauty* now. You're part of what I hate. I have to confess I was curious at the notion of coming to see you, but I didn't come to talk about my daddy's business. If you want it, you can take it. You deserve it, but you are not going to get me along with it. Although frankly, I do have to confess I don't understand why he did leave it to you. You been seeing him all this time?"

"That's just it, PJ." Honey was relieved he was back on an even keel. "Truth of the matter is, I'm mighty mystified too. Of course I wouldn't breathe a word to anyone else, but I can tell you. There's only one reason he would have left me money and that's the baby and I haven't seen him since then."

PJ was alert. "The baby?"

"Yes, you know I had a baby. You must have read about it in the papers. It was kidnapped . . . and that brings me to something you have to know. Something I never told anyone. It's our secret and it always will be. I should have told you before and I'm sorry, I truly am, but I didn't know whether I should approach you and then, well, it was too late."

She had his attention now.

"It was your baby," she whispered.

"What?"

"Seventeen years ago right after you saw me in my apartment I discovered I was pregnant with your child. I thought about telling you then, oh, believe me I did, but I didn't know whether you would be able to cope with the responsibility. And in the end, well . . . you probably read about what happened. It was so awful, PJ. My baby . . . *our* baby was kidnapped. And murdered. Our precious little boy, dead before I could even bring him to show you . . ."

PJ yawned, then told her: "You're full of shit, you really are. Do you seriously think I can swallow that crap? I know you had a baby. I read the papers like everyone else. And I also know my father bailed you out. Plus you were servicing him at the time on a regular basis so I understand. We're not talking about the death of *our* son here, we're talking about the demise of my bastard half-brother."

"It was yours," Honey shrieked.

"I saw him, sweetheart. I saw him go into your building right after I left you that day, so quit pinning it all on me with your sob stories."

"Can't you see, you dumbo, it could have been *either* of you, but somehow I just know—they say the mother always knows —I know it was your child."

"Yeah, yeah, yeah, so there's an outside chance it could have been mine. But the kid died so where does that leave us now? Wait a second."

"What is it?"

"Luc Chenier."

"Who?"

"Luc Chenier. That's what I came to see you about. Who is he?"

"I don't know."

"Jesus, Honey. Didn't your lawyer read you my father's will? I went over to take a look myself, just to check whether the old bastard had fucked up and left me something after all, but no, he kept his word and cut me right out. Still, that doesn't matter. He left everything to you, Honey, *for your lifetime.*"

"Yes, I know that, PJ. Quit rubbing it in. You can't embarrass me, not now. And I intend to live for quite a long while yet."

"But didn't you notice what happens when you die?"

"I get to leave what's left to whomever I choose, I guess."

"No, you don't."

"What?"

"You don't. It says after you die it's entailed to this Luc Chenier, whoever he is."

"Chenier. Callie's name."

"Yeah, there's loads of Cheniers around, but I don't know of any Luc."

"So who do you think he could be?"

"Think back to what you said earlier . . . about the only reason he would have left you anything being on account of the baby."

"But he died . . ."

"Are you sure? Who actually told you?"

"Perry Jay."

"Did anyone else come and see you when you had the baby?"

"Callie."

"Callie!"

If Luc Chenier was Honey's baby then the entailment of her legacy to him could only mean one thing: Perry Jay had known the child was alive when he made out his will. And there was only one other person who might be able to shed some light on Luc Chenier's identity. They looked at each other and silently asked the same question: Where was Callie?

CHAPTER 21

Callie was packing. Furiously. Throwing things into a couple of battered looking Louis Vuitton suitcases. Luc watched her in total bewilderment.

"But, *Tantie, why* are you going to America? Why are you rushing off so suddenly? I don't understand. You never mentioned anything about going there. How am I going to take care of myself while you're gone? How long are you going for?"

"I don't need to keep you advised of all my plans," snapped Callie, holding up what appeared to be two identical navy silk blouses and looking from one to the other as if she couldn't decide which one to take. "Anyway, you're going to Paris to stay with your *Tante* Anita. You'll be well looked after by her."

"Paris? I've never been to Paris! And who on earth is 'my' *Tante* Anita?"

"She's your . . . well, she's, she's your godmother," Callie finished lamely. "High time you acquired some kind of polish before we let you loose in society. You're going to Paris to be finished by your *Tante* Anita. Can't have a Chenier behaving like a hick."

Luc didn't much like the sound of the word *finished* which had a distinctly terminal ring to it.

"Besides," continued Callie, "you're seventeen years old and you've never been farther than Cahors in your life." She omitted to mention it was entirely her fault since it was she who had kept them in hiding all this time. "You're going to be taught the way of the world, Luc, and who better to teach you than Anita de la Salle."

Anita had other ideas. It was understating it a bit to say that she was rather surprised to hear from Callie after all this time. She had assumed when she didn't hear from her that Callie had gone back to America. But Callie had not forgotten one of Anita's remarks all those years ago: *give me a boy of fifteen, seventeen, eighteen, and I can do a lot with him.* Well, of course, thought Callie, Anita must be getting on a bit now, just like me, but still, who else can I ask?

"Have him to *stay*? With *me*? Thierry will have a fit, Callie, have you taken leave of your senses? I mean, I know I used to have my little bit of fun with *les garçons* but, darling, you know I never let them stay longer than an afternoon and only when Thierry was out of . . . Oh, you don't mean that? Oh, *quelle bêtise!* Silly, silly me! Oh, but of *course*, we'd *love* to have him, darling boy, it's high time he met his Uncle Thierry and his *Tante* Anita. Can we say we're his godparents? *Ses parrains?* It would be *so* much easier, you *do* understand, one has to keep up appearances. But why can't I mention you? How on earth am I going to explain who his parents are, where he comes from? Say they're dead? A plane crash? *Superbe!* Such drama, I *am* going to have fun, but you know I have to say *where* he's been brought up and by whom if I'm going to present him as *un jeune homme bien élevé, comme il faut* and all that. Oh, don't be ridiculous, Callie, everyone knows I haven't got a brother, I can't pass him off as a child of a dead brother. Well, I suppose I *could* do that . . . but which side of the New Orleans branch? Does he sound American? He can't speak *English*? Not at all? Well, I don't suppose it matters that much except . . . Will I *teach* him? Callie, are you insane? I'm not a schoolmarm. Oh, all right, send me his picture. If nothing else it might amuse me to take him about for a few weeks . . . although, heavens above, Callie, it's a bit much after all these years . . ."

Callie sent a recent photograph of Luc looking his most

beautiful and sultry, leaning against a tree. She enclosed a short note which informed Anita that if she didn't hear that he was not welcome in Paris, Luc would be on the *Capitole du Soir* arriving in Paris after dinner on the Thursday two weeks hence. He would bring with him a letter from her which would explain in detail just exactly what she wanted Anita to do with Luc.

Luc lost the letter the day she gave it to him and promptly forgot all about it.

Elliott Fitzgerald saw Luc coming across the fields to *La Folie* and automatically cracked another egg into his mixing bowl. The boy would join him in his omelette. He always did if he turned up at the hour because it meant that he had something on his mind. Elliott was sensitive enough to know that if he was invited to share the older man's evening meal, Luc would have time enough to relax and get whatever it was off his chest.

These visits had become a regular occurrence and Elliott was always amazed that he could still marvel at the boy's beauty. Yet as he watched Luc strolling across the meadow, running his hands nervously through his jet black hair, the late afternoon sun catching the youthful glow of his cheeks, he was aware that yet again his heart was beating a little faster and his hands surrendered to clumsy, jerking movements leaving him unable to continue whisking the eggs. He sat down to regain control of himself. He had made a pact with himself that he would never involve Luc in his emotional feelings for him and the fact that he might even go so far as to consider sexual feelings was out of the question. Yet Elliott was openly affectionate with the boy, encouraging him to feel they shared a bond not unlike that of grandfather and grandson.

"*Gruyère* or *champignons*?" he asked Luc as he came through the door. "What kind of omelette shall we have?"

"Could we not have both?" Luc grinned.

"I don't see why not. Pop outside and bring me some herbs, if you will."

Elliott warmed some *potage* on the stove and quietly laid a place for Luc at the kitchen table.

"So how's things?" he asked as they began to sip their soup, and nearly dropped his spoon as the dam broke and Luc began to pour out his troubles.

"Oh, Monsieur Fitzgerald, everything's gone crazy." Elliott

smiled to himself. He loved the way Luc said Monsieur *Feetz*gerald. "*Tantie*'s going to America and I'm being sent off to Paris and I just don't know why."

"Heavens," said Elliott, "when did all this happen?"

"Day before yesterday. She just announced it."

"Does she come from the South, Madame Chenier?" Elliott suddenly asked him.

"The South?" Luc was puzzled.

"Of America. I've always thought I could hear the slightest twang of a Southern American accent in her voice and I just wondered if this *Bayou Beauty* thing could have anything to do with the general upheaval. It's just an idea . . . I could be wrong."

"You think *Tantie* is American?"

"I know so, Luc. Or at any rate she certainly isn't French. On the odd occasions when we've met she's talked to me in English and that's when I've noticed her accent. It's American with this strange ring to it. Surely you must have known where she was from, Luc? What relation is she to you exactly?"

"I don't know. A friend of my parents, maybe no relation at all."

"And your parents, do you remember them at all? You've never told me about them."

"Don't know anything to tell you. They were killed in an airplane crash and that's it."

"But you must have pictures of them. Do you look like them?"

"*Rien!*" The boy spat out the word. *Nothing.*

Elliott realized he was drawing blanks all over the place. It really was most odd. He marveled that he had never thought to question Luc before. He had sort of always taken it for granted that the boy was French, but of course he wasn't. He was American born and raised in France. It was more than likely that he had family in America he had never met, never even heard about judging by the extraordinary behavior of that crazy old Chenier woman. Yet what could he, Elliott, do about the situation other than provide a welcome for the boy whenever he chose to come across the field for a visit? It wasn't as if Luc had been ill-treated in any tangible way. He was well fed and had a comfortable home. It didn't look as if any violence had ever been used. Yet something wasn't right. One day Elliott would get to the bottom of it.

"So whom are you going to stay with in Paris?"

"My *Tante* Anita."

"So you have family in Paris?"

"Oh, she's not my real aunt. She's my *marraine* so *Tantie* said. She's going to *finish* me whatever that means." He grinned.

"Bless my soul," Elliott laughed. "And where exactly in America is Madame Chenier going?"

"She won't say."

"But she'll leave you an address, somewhere you can contact her?"

Luc shook his head. "She says I mustn't contact her."

"Why ever not?"

Luc shrugged. "I wouldn't want to anyway," he held up his head proudly. "I'm quite capable of taking care of myself." He looked defiant, but Elliott sensed how insecure he was.

"You don't like her very much, do you?" The old man was taking quite a chance with such a bold question, but the more he thought about it the more he felt instinctively that it was important to form as close a bond as possible with the boy before he went off to Paris. Then Luc would know he had *someone* who cared for him.

"It's not that I don't like her so much as I . . ."

"You don't trust her."

"*C'est ça!*" Luc nodded. "I mean, Monsieur, here she is going off to who knows where without any explanation and I've no idea when she'll be back. I've finished school now so it's not as if I have to stay around here, but it's my home. I've never been anywhere else even in France, let alone America. Don't tell anyone, Monsieur Fitzgerald, but I'm a little nervous at the idea of going to Paris . . ."

Elliott took a piece of paper and scribbled something on it.

"Here's my telephone number. If you run into problems in Paris, you give me a ring and I'll see what I can do. Does that make you feel any better?"

When he walked back to *La Cachette* in the moonlight, Luc was feeling decidedly better. In fact for the first time he was actually looking forward to going to Paris. Elliott had spent the rest of the evening telling him of all the delights to be found in the city, painting vivid pictures of Montmartre, the Left Bank, the Louvre, the Champs Elysées. Oh, Luc was in for a real treat.

But when he let himself quietly into the house by the kitchen door he found he was also in for a shock.

Callie had already gone. Disappeared, suddenly, into the night without a word of warning.

In fact Luc was due to leave for Paris the next day, but somehow he had always imagined that Callie would wait to see him off before she herself left. It wasn't a problem; he could take his *mobilette* to the station and leave it there when he caught the train. If anything it was what he had come to expect of Callie, that one day she would abandon him.

Yet now he was able to cope with it for the simple reason that he knew he had someone who really did care about him, someone he could count on: Monsieur Fitzgerald. They might not be related, but he felt far closer to the old man than he did to any genuine next of kin he might have.

Flying high across the Atlantic Callie suddenly began to panic. She was going home to America for the first time in seventeen years and she was totally unprepared for what she might find there.

As she sat in her first-class seat she began to shake and moan and the airline stewardess, mistaking her for a nervous flyer, rushed to offer words of reassurance. She was used to apprehensive passengers, but even she was shocked by the venomous hiss of Callie's words: *"Get away from me, you hear? Leave me alone. I'm on a mission. A mission of revenge. I'm going to destroy her. Understand? DESTROY HER!"*

Not only had Luc lost the letter Callie gave him for Anita, but he managed to miss the *Capitole du Soir* which would get him into Paris late in the evening. It never occurred to him to wait until the next day. He merely hung around the station and caught the next train to Paris which left Cahors at ten-thirty in the evening.

He slept most of the way and awoke as his train drew into the Gare d'Austerlitz around five o'clock the next morning. The station was deserted and there was no one to help him with his luggage. He dragged it behind him until he found a taxi parked in the forecourt with the driver fast asleep behind the wheel.

Luc banged on the window and the man jumped. Luc gestured toward the backseat and tried to open the passenger door. Five minutes later he succeeded in getting the driver to wind down his window. Luc shoved the piece of paper into his hand on which Callie had written Anita's address.

"Ah, non!" snapped the driver, shaking his head, *"dix-septième, non, non, non, ça n'est pour toi. Tu te trompes."* He began to wind up the window again.

Luc was bewildered. What did the man mean when he said Luc had got it wrong?

"C'est tout près de l'Etoile," he offered, remembering what Callie had told him. At that the driver gave him a real look of disgust and let out a stream of abuse. Did the kid think he was mad? Of course he knew it was near the Etoile, he'd been driving taxis for twenty years, but he'd never taken a ruffian like Luc to an address near the Etoile, Luc must have it wrong, dressed like that he'd be lucky to get a bed in a cheap hotel . . .

Luc rummaged through his pockets to see if he could find further evidence of Anita's address and in doing so he pulled out a large wad of notes which Callie had given him. The driver was out of the car in a flash. Suddenly there was no problem at all. If Monsieur wanted to go to the *dix-septième* then that's where he would be taken. Suddenly it was a respectful *vous* instead of the more familiar *tu* the driver had used to begin with. Luc's bags were deposited in the trunk and they were off. The inside of the taxi stank of stale Disque Bleu and the seats were covered with garish plaid. A fluffy pink poodle danced on the end of a string in the back window.

The driver insisted on pointing out to Luc the sights they passed on the way to rue Anatole de la Forge where Anita lived.

"A votre gauche, vous avez le Jardin des Plantes," he intoned as they sped along the Quai St.-Bernard, *"et puis à votre droit vous voyez l'Ile St.-Louis et L'Ile de la Cité—Notre Dame, le Palais de Justice . . ."*

They crossed the Seine over the Pont Neuf, swept past the Louvre and up the rue de Rivoli to the Place de la Concorde. From there it was a straight run down the Champs Elysées, round the Etoile and the Arc de Triomphe and into the Avenue de la Grande-Armée. Rue Anatole de la Forge was the first turning off to the right.

They drew up at a pair of high wrought-iron gates. The cab driver positioned himself in front of the meter so that Luc could not see it and demanded double the amount due. The next thing he knew he was being flung against the window, his head colliding painfully with the glass. Luc thrust some notes into his hand, opened the trunk himself and grabbed his bags.

The iron gates were locked. Perfect! How was he supposed to get in? A curtain moved imperceptibly at a window just inside the gates. He turned back to the cab. The driver was nursing his bruised forehead.

"Mais il faut sonner, idiot!" he spat out of the window, reverting to his former self, pointing to a bell in the wall by the gates. Then he sat back behind the wheel to see what would happen. They would never let this brat in.

Luc rang. The curtain twitched again. Nothing happened. Luc put his finger on the bell and kept it there until he was distracted by a terrible clanging sound. A woman was coming out of a door just inside the gates dragging a huge dustbin behind her. She peered suspiciously at Luc standing outside in the street.

"Oui?"

"Madame de la Salle, s'il vous plaît."

"Elle n'est pas là."

"A cinq heures du matin? Elle est en voyage?"

"Elle n'est pas là."

Luc tried to explain further, but the *concierge* hurried back inside to drag out yet another noisy dustbin. The cab driver had ventured outside to lean against his taxi and watch the proceedings. She clearly didn't like this. She unlocked the gates and pushed the dustbins out into the street, undoubtedly waking up the whole *arrondissement* in the process.

"Allez! Allez!" She rushed at the cab driver, flapping her arms at him, *"il n'y a rien à regarder. Ce n'est pas le cinéma ici!"* The driver remonstrated that it was a free country and if he wanted to stand around and watch he could, whereupon she began to rain insults on him, making an even louder noise than the clanging of her dustbins.

Luc knew a lengthy argument when he heard one. Quietly

picking up his bags he slipped through the iron gates, under an archway and into a little paved courtyard. He found his way to Anita's apartment up two flights of wide stone steps. Faced with an imposing pair of tall white double-doors he stopped dead. It was not yet half past five in the morning. He had never met this woman. He could quite easily go back out into the street again and spend the next few weeks blowing the money Callie had given him on his own kind of Paris education. Despite the fact that he had arrived when the city was still asleep he knew it was going to be his kind of place once everybody woke up, what did he need with some old friend of *Tantie*'s hanging round his neck . . . ?

The sound of the *concierge*'s raucous screeching as she came hobbling up the stairs after him made him change his mind. He pressed down hard on Anita's doorbell.

"ALLEZ! ALLEZ! ALLEZ!" roared the *concierge*, grabbing Luc by the elbow.

Thierry de la Salle flung open his front door.

"Taisez-vous, Madame," he snapped at the *concierge* and turned to Luc, who was grinning with delight at seeing the woman being told to shut up. But Thierry de la Salle gave him a quick once over and then slammed the door in his face. Luc promptly rang the bell again.

The time a plump little woman with dyed red hair ducked underneath Thierry's arm. She was clasping around her a flimsy white *peignoir* which barely concealed her freckled bosoms. Her face was old and wrinkled, but her eyes still sparkled, especially when she saw Luc.

"Qui êtes-vous?" Anita asked, staring in wonder at this beautiful boy with his shock of glossy black hair, long lashes fringing blue eyes. He towered above her, propped up nonchalantly against the door. The things she noticed most about his face were that he had very white skin—pale, almost translucent, and his eyes were like smudged blurs in an out of focus black and white photograph. But if Anita didn't notice the filthy long woollen overcoat, two sizes too big, reaching down almost to Luc's ankles, and the strange baggy pants underneath held up by a pair of suspenders, Thierry did and tried once again to slam the door.

"Je suis Luc Chenier."

And Anita knew it was true. It was just that he was even

more beautiful than his photograph. The only problem was that she had forgotten to reply to Callie's letter to tell her that it was out of the question and of course Callie had taken it that that meant the boy could come. And here he was. Except she didn't have a story ready for Thierry.

Luc came to her rescue. He clicked his heels together and bowed and, apologizing profusely for having woken them up, he addressed Anita as Aunt Anita, and said, of course, he knew it was a bit late for a bed, but could he please spend a night or two with them on his way back to his family in Alsace-Lorraine? He had just flown in from visiting relations in New Orleans and he had run out of cash. Surely Madame de la Salle would like to hear news of New Orleans . . . his grandmother remained in America when she, Madame, had married Monsieur de la Salle . . . and Luc flashed Thierry a brilliant smile.

Thierry shrugged. It was all quite irregular, but he was due in court in less than four hours and he needed his sleep. He was due to have retired years ago, but if he had enough sleep he knew he could keep going a little longer, providing young idiots didn't wake him up in the middle of the night. Anyway, he would be leaving for Geneva later that day. He would be gone for at least two weeks. If Anita wanted to play nursemaid to her friends' irresponsible children she could do it while he was gone.

For the next few days Anita de la Salle kept saying to herself: "If only he'd arrived ten years ago . . ." She was now sixty-five years old and she hadn't indulged in what she called her "little bits of fun" for five years. It was really too late to start that sort of thing all over again . . . but in the meantime what on earth was she supposed to do with the boy? He slept every morning till about eleven o'clock, he spent two hours having breakfast, he showed no interest whatsoever in her suggestions that she take him to the *musées*—after all he had never been to Paris before and he had never even been inside the Louvre. Nor did he want to go to the theater. Worst of all, he had apparently forgotten to bring Callie's letter explaining what Anita was meant to do with him. In any case she doubted Callie even knew.

She knew she could have called Callie and asked her about Luc, explain about the letter being lost, but there was something about the boy's pathetic, shabby appearance and appalling taste in clothes that made Anita reluctant to speak to her former friend. This boy was a hick. There was clearly no point in speaking to Callie; she must have given up on him years ago.

She could tell he was uncomfortable with her and understood that she must appear to him nothing more than an old woman to whom he felt obliged to be polite. At least he had a few manners, that was *some*thing, but she knew it was only as far as she was concerned. She had heard him being abominably rude to the servants, ordering them to bring him his breakfast in bed, demanding that they change his sheets, bring him a clean shirt.

It was when Jacqueline, her housekeeper, came to her clutching a bundle of his clothes, a bewildered expression on her face, saying she didn't know what to do with them, that Anita decided to take matters into her own hands. And in fact it was the mention of clothes which was the first thing to arouse his interest.

"Luc," said Anita, knocking lightly on his door and going into his room, dropping the bundle of clothes on the floor, "I thought we might replace a few of these, they all look like they've seen better days." He was on his feet in a flash, pulling on his filthy overcoat. Anita realized she'd never been outside with him, that she couldn't be seen walking along the street with him in *that* coat, she was ashamed of herself for admitting it, but she simply couldn't.

"No, no," she said gently, "it's not that cold. I'll lend you a pullover of Thierry's. There's about fifty years between you, but you're still the same size."

If Luc was a little disappointed at the places Anita took him to buy clothes, he was smart enough to keep quiet about it. They didn't have to go very far beyond the Champs-Elysées before they came to the kind of de luxe men's *prêt à porter* that Anita had in mind: Givenchy Gentleman in the Avenue George-V, Christian Dior in the rue François-ler, Lanvin in the rue Gambon, Pierre Cardin in the rue du Faubourg-St. Honoré. These were the places where she was known, where she came to buy presents for Thierry or accompanied him on his own shopping sprees. She was greeted warmly everywhere and when she introduced a rather awkward Luc as the grandson of an old friend, it was understood immediately what was required. Be-

sides, the young *monsieur* was a dream, they couldn't wait to
get their hands on him. First *le costume, un costume qui est
eternel,* something that would last forever . . . suggestions
were made, suits were produced, *un costume en laine, finement
quadrille* if *Monsieur* liked checks? Or perhaps something in
prince de Galles? Prince of Wales check? Or *à rayures*? Striped?
Finally at Dior Anita chose for him a classic anthracite gray
double-breasted wool-flannel suit. Luc chose his own shirts,
also at Dior, going for pale yellow, pink and blue—anything to
add a bit of color. Then there were *cravates,* silk ties chosen by
Anita; *vestes,* waistcoats which Luc tried hard to resist, but
which were thrust upon him nonetheless; leather belts, beautiful soft Italian leather shoes, more gray flannel *pantalons,* a
cardigan *en cachemire* and another *en lambswool, un blazer en
gaberdine noir* from Cerruti, *pullovers en laine à col Polo* and
finally, at Luc's insistence, a chunky leather *blouson.*

They took a taxi back to the rue Anatole de la Forge. There
was barely room for the two of them and all the packages. A
strained silence hung between them until finally Luc muttered:
"Listen, Madame de . . . eh, *Tante* Anita, I mean, I suppose I
should thank you . . ."

"De rien," Anita smiled, giving his head an absent-minded
pat, "your grandmother wouldn't want you to be seen running
round Paris in rags. Why, when she was a young woman married to your grandfather she had such style and I remember
your father when he was about your age, he toured Europe and
you never saw such a well-turned-out young . . ." She stopped
abruptly as the memory of PJ's visit surged up.

"Tantie is my *grandmother*? You knew my *father*?" Luc was
clinging onto her hand.

Oh Lord, thought Anita, Callie hasn't told him a thing. How
am I going to get out of this? How am I going to find out what
kind of story she did spin him?

"Don't you remember your father?" she asked hesitantly.

"How could I?" snarled Luc. "He was killed in a plane crash
along with my mother just after I was born. They were flying
home to France from New York. Did you know my mother was
American?"

"Why, yes, of course I did, just like me," replied Anita.

"You're American?"

"Well, in fact, my family were originally French, but they

emigrated to America, to New Orleans and that's where my family met yours."

"Mine? My mother's family came from New Orleans?"

"No, Luc, I'm not sure where your mother's family came from," Anita told him gently, "but your father's family came from Louisiana and Mississippi, from the South. Your *Tantie*'s family, your *grandmother's* family. Callie is your father's mother, surely you must have known that?"

By the way the boy was staring at her, shocked into total silence, Anita realized he had not known that he and Callie were so closely related. What, oh, what, must Callie have been thinking of all these years? Well, she would try to get him to trust her, try to break down the barrier of suspicion he had built around himself. He seemed to be on the point of explosion one minute, frozen into polite silence the next. She had heard him being aggressive with the servants, she had watched him slip with terrifying ease into the role of spoilt young clothes-horse in the shops they had just visited, and now he was a frightened teenager unable to name his own grandmother.

The taxi stopped in the rue Anatole de la Forge and the driver came round to help with the packages. Luc snarled at him so that he retreated and left Luc to help Anita out of the cab and escort her to the iron gates, loaded up with packages.

"*'Nosy folks'll peek through their shutters!'*" remarked Anita drily as the *concierge*'s net curtain fluttered back into place.

"Who?"

"*Oklahoma.* 'The Surrey with the Fringe on Top.' You've seen *Oklahoma,* surely you have?"

"Never heard of it."

Anita was astounded. "It'll be on TV again one of these days, then you can see it. Come to think of it, I think I'll put my feet up and watch a little TV after lunch. Shopping's so exhausting!"

Jacqueline served them a light lunch off a trolley in Anita's own little sitting room. Luc felt and looked uncomfortable and out of place in the ultra-feminine *salon* with its walls hung in fabric patterned with little pink shepherdesses, the same fabric covering a sofa and button-backed chairs. Circular tables were hidden by heavy pink material cascading to the ground while their surfaces displayed a mass of little silver photograph frames and ornaments bathed in pools of light from rosy shaded lamps.

Anita let him eat in silence, noting that he filled his own glass several times, but failed to offer her more wine . . . and she had thought he had at least *some* manners. It seemed they came and went when it suited him.

"That letter Callie gave you—" she began tentatively, "the one you lost, do you know what was in it?"

He shook his head, his mouth full of *fromage blanc*.

"What I really want to know, Luc, is the reason *you* thought you were coming to Paris. Didn't you know who I was? Didn't Callie tell you?"

"SHE NEVER TOLD ME ANYTHING!" he exploded and Anita pushed away her plate and folded her napkin. Here it comes, she thought, here it comes . . .

"She never told me who my mother was or where she came from. She never told me she was my grandmother. She wouldn't come to my school and meet my friends or their parents. She wouldn't let me bring my friends home. She wouldn't help me with my homework, she never wanted to hear about what happened to me at school. Sometimes she didn't speak to me for days and then suddenly I had to dress up and dine with her, downstairs every night, four or five course meals after which I couldn't sleep. And you know, she was *strange. Really* strange! She didn't have any friends, still doesn't. No one ever came to the house. The telephone never rang. I don't know why we had it. She never used it. She'd spend hours in front of the mirror making up her face. Until I stopped her she used to try and make up mine. And then she would dress herself up in these old clothes, fabulous furs, long slinky evening dresses made of gold lamé and that kind of thing, and she'd wander round the house talking to herself, having these weird imaginary conversations. Sometimes I'd answer her and she'd look at me with a blank stare. She hadn't been talking to *me*, she hadn't been aware I was there. Sometimes she wept for days on end, locked herself in her room and sobbed her heart out. She's just a crazy old woman, *Tante* Anita, I feel nothing but pity for her. Now you ask me if I knew why she was sending me to Paris. Well, she told me that story about you being an old friend of hers from New Orleans and I was to say I was your godson. I didn't even know she was American. No one down there knows. She used to get letters from New Orleans now and again—they stood out, they were the only letters she ever received. All I know is she wanted me to learn a bit about life in the city. I don't want to go on acting like a country boy, now do I, *Tante* Anita?" He flashed her one of those irresistible grins reminding her so much of his father.

"But what are you going to *do*, for heaven's sake? I'm an old lady. You won't learn much about *la vie mondaine* from me . . . I like to be tucked up in bed with a good book by nine o'clock at night these days . . ."

He looked so crestfallen that she bit back the rest of her sentence. How could Callie have ignored him so? There was so much to do with him, he was perfect raw material just waiting to be moulded. But how, and for what?

"Never mind, Luc. We'll work something out. Why don't you start by going upstairs and trying on your new clothes, walk about in them a bit, get used to wearing them? Then come downstairs and watch a little television with me. I think there's an old American movie on *Antenne deux* in about an hour. You can use it as your first English lesson with me."

He rose awkwardly and shuffled out. Anita sat for nearly half an hour thinking about him, how he had never had a mother—or a father for that matter. How confused he was, how terrifyingly bright, how sharp and jagged at the edges, but how forlorn and vulnerable at his center. For seventeen years he had been raised as *un gentilhomme* within the lonely confines of his own home and left to find his way outside it amidst a totally different milieu. Anita wondered what kind of stories he had handed out to his schoolfriends as he was growing up, how did he explain Callie's strange behavior? Who else had influenced him besides Callie? For somewhere along the line he had acquired an air of menace about him as if he thought he was being threatened in some way. He was half child, half man— *l'enfant sauvage, l'homme brutal* and potential playboy, all rolled into one. And for the time being, he was hers until she worked out what in the world she was going to make of him.

He *looked* wonderful, always. *Pas de problème* in that department. But he was so ignorant! So unsophisticated. She had had to teach him all about opening doors for her, ordering food and wine to go with it. He had appeared to drink only the heavy red *vin Cahors* and now that she thought about it, Callie had never really been much of a one for wine. Finally, Anita resorted to drawing a little plan for him showing him what to order with what: with shellfish, *hors d'oeuvres,* salads, something light and dry and white like a Muscadet, Chardonnay, Macon Blanc, Chablis from a light year; with *charcuterie* and some firm-fleshed fish a fresh, lively Beaujolais, and on to a medium-bodied red to go with the meat and cheese, a Bordeaux or a Cabernet Sauvignon or a bottle of Saint Emilion, and so on. To her horror, he kept pulling it out and referring to it. She had recommended some good years and sometimes when the *sommelier* had suggested another, he had dragged out his wretched plan again and waved it in the man's face. Well, of course he was only seventeen. She must make allowances. But if only he would grasp the simple task of tipping, understand how it paved the way, *everywhere*, and how to do it discreetly. If he put his hand in his pocket and pulled out what appeared to be the national debt one more time she would die. He would spend minutes sorting through his notes before finally selecting one and waving it at her, asking if it was enough while the recipient hovered uneasily beside him. And if he did manage to remember to slip it quietly into the man's hand, he invariably dropped it *en route* and flung himself to the floor to rescue it.

He's still a baby, thought Anita. He's still living in that fantasy world he was brought up in. He knows he's beautiful and he thinks it will carry him everywhere. How could Callie be so cruel as to send him to me, knowing that it was only a matter of time before he left me and returned to her. I haven't rung her because I am jealous of her, envious that she has had this exotic plant growing in her greenhouse all this time, furious that she has not given it the love and attention it so desperately needs and probably will never recognize it in its real form. This boy is destined to be treated as a plaything, tossed from person to person, choice fruit for the highest bidder. I could stop it, stop what I myself have started. I could talk to him tonight . . . make him understand. I'll do it. I'll start now . . .

"Luc . . ."

"Here's the mail. This one looks like an invitation." He handed her a large square envelope with a card inside it. "How exciting. Can I open it?"

Anita nodded wearily. Really, he was too much sometimes.

"Oh, *la!*" he exclaimed, "listen to this. It sounds like it could be worth going to:

> *Monsieur André Vauniashevsky*
> *serait heureux de recevoir*
> *Monsieur et Madame de la Salle*
> *a l'occasion des dix-huit ans de sa fille Sylvie*
> *le samedi 16 septembre 1977 a partir de 20h 30*
> *au Pavillon de Pré Catalan."*

"Oh yes, the Vauniashevsky girl. I recall she was due to turn eighteen around now. Le Pré Catalan, how wonderful! It's a beautiful place, Luc, right in the middle of the Bois de Boulogne, a little pavilion with French windows leading out onto the Bois. The perfect setting for an eighteenth birthday party. If *only* I could take you. I shall speak to Thierry, see if we can ask if we can bring you. After all, maybe you and Sylvie . . ."

"Who is this André Vauniashevsky?"

"Why, he's the *Redacteur en Chef*, the Editor of *Mode*, the biggest fashion magazine. *Every*one will be there." Anita perked up considerably at the thought of it. Here was something to look forward to!

Luc sauntered into the *Pavillon*, his hand guiding Anita's elbow, very smart in his new *"smoking"* from Dior. The Pré Catalan was an unusual part of the Bois de Boulogne in that it was kept almost as a private garden out of bounds to both dogs and bicycles. The doors to the pavilion were open and the guests, who had already arrived, were wandering in and out to sip their champagne on the immaculate green grass.

Luc stared at the mass of sleek forms passing this way and that in their Saint Laurent, Givenchy, Dorothée Bis, Sonia Rykiel, Chloë and lots of lively Jap. Even Anita fitted in perfectly in a discreet little piece of black chiffon floating from side to side as she walked above tiny peep-toe black and gold high-heeled sandals.

He tried to hold on to Anita, but she was gone. There was nothing left but to move along the line of guests waiting to be greeted by their host. Sylvie Vauniashevsky looked positively virginal in a frothy child-like creation of white organza and primrose lace, but the direct, amused, come-hither look she gave him when he shook her hand left Luc convinced she'd expose her breasts to him right there and then if he asked her to. He was about to ask her for a dance later in the evening when there was a huge commotion behind them.

"WELL, KISS MY ASS! It sure is good to be back in Paris again!"

The photographers went wild, rushing in from the garden, dodging between the guests, all trying to get up close to catch the arrival of the latest guest.

Luc turned and stared as the whispering began around the room.

She paused in the entrance. She stood nearly six feet tall and her skin-tight silver lamé sheath dress, slashed in a straight line across her breasts leaving her nipples perilously close to exposure, gave her the look of a mermaid. Her shoulders were bare, her only adornment a diamond choker around her throat. She turned briefly to hand a silver fox stole to someone and there were gasps around the pavilion as everyone saw the slit in the sheath which went all the way up the back of the skirt to show the little silver lamé panties covering her buttocks.

Luc was mesmerized. He felt as if he were in a dream. It was the Honey-witch herself.

"Excuse me, young man, I want to introduce Honey to my daughter." André Vauniashevsky was trying to bring her through. Luc leapt back a step or two, but didn't move away. She barely glanced at him as she leaned forward to kiss Sylvie on both cheeks. A waiter arrived, bearing a tray of champagne. Without stopping to think, Luc reached out, grabbed a glass and stepped forward to present it to Honey.

She could hardly refuse. The glass was almost underneath her nose. She was about to turn and thank him when she seemed to go into some kind of shock.

She didn't take the glass. Instead she grasped him by the wrist so that much of the champagne in the glass splashed over her. She was staring at his *dauphin*, his identity bracelet with the tiny silver dolphin charm.

Luc asked her to dance. He never knew what gave him the courage. André Vauniashevsky was trying to propel Sylvie toward him. Honey was still grasping his wrist.

To his everlasting surprise she nodded, relaxed her grip and allowed him to take her by the hand and lead her out onto the dance floor. The band, which up to now had been playing background music, quickly switched to a foxtrot.

Luc might have learned an exceptional number of social graces over the past few weeks, but one thing he hadn't been taught to do was dance. He and Honey were the same height. She placed her left hand on his shoulder and held out her right hand for him to hold. They set off around the floor, strolling slowly rather than dancing.

They had no idea they were being applauded. They made a spectacular couple: she with her long wheat-colored hair floating down the center of her spine; he, a raven-haired, pale-skinned almost ethereal *gamin* worshipping her sophistication. He was putty in her hands, they all said, except for poor Sylvie who sulked. *But who was he?* Nobody knew. Not even André Vauniashevsky.

Gradually Luc became aware of the circle of guests watching them, clapping, raising their glasses. Honey was smiling at them, waving every now and then. Luc's hand accidentally brushed the top of the slit in the back of her skirt. He blushed. If only he could think of something to say to her to break this awkward silence between them. Wait a second, she'd said something to him, asked him a question . . .

"Comment?" He looked at her and bent his ear to her lips.

"Can you tell me something? Where did you get that dolphin bracelet?"

"THERE YOU ARE! My God, I've been looking *every*where for you. I really have. Your Uncle Thierry and I want to know everything you've been doing. Oh, I *am* so sorry. I didn't mean to interrupt, I *truly* didn't. Silly, silly me. But do you think I could just sort of borrow him for a minute? Would you mind? Really? How divine you look! Oh, yes, you *do*! Honestleeeee! Trust my nephew! Never satisfied with *les jeunes filles*, you know, always prefers a woman of the world and why not, I say? Of course Thierry doesn't agree with me but then . . . oh, *there's* Thierry, come along, come and say hello . . . *au 'voir, madame . . .*"

Luc simply couldn't believe it. Here was Anita literally dragging him away in mid-sentence. He could not understand what had come over her. What was more she didn't take him anywhere near Thierry. She marched him straight through the crowded room and out the door.

Sitting in the back of the car as Thierry's chauffeur drove them out of the Bois, Anita breathed a sigh of relief. She knew it was terribly unfair to drag him away from the party with no explanation but she knew that she had been the only person in that room, including Luc and Honey, who knew that Luc had been dancing with his mother. She was not sure she approved of the way Callie had brought him up, but if she had opted not to tell him his mother was Honey Winslow, then she must have had her reasons and who was she, Anita, to jump in and cause confusion by telling him now? She had simply had to get him away from the Pré Catalan before he found out.

But, thought Anita as she looked over to his brooding figure slumped in the corner, what on earth was she to do with him now?

CHAPTER 22

"Thierry!"

There was no reply. Thierry de la Salle was still sound asleep
—or pretending to be. It was Saturday morning, Goddamnit,
and he'd been up till the early hours of the morning at the
Vauniashevsky bash. Had himself quite a good time as a matter
of fact. Anita had taken it into her head to leave early having
spent the whole of the week before babbling on about how she
was going to dance the night away. But she had taken that kid
with her which had left Thierry free to have himself a ball, ha
ha. He chortled to himself under the bedclothes. Oh yes, that
little friend of Sylvie's—what was her name? Elodie? Oh, she'd
been a delight and so experienced for one so young. Where did
they learn it these days? Shame he hadn't been ten, or even five
years younger, he'd have shown the naughty little filly a thing
or two, as it was things were already beginning to stir down
below . . . he moved his hand tentatively to the opening at his
pyjama bottoms . . .

"Thierry!" He felt a sharp kick in his backside.

"What *is* it?" He hoped she wouldn't twitter on for hours so
that he couldn't go back to sleep. He had never really regretted

marrying Anita, but he simply could not abide her twittering. She never knew when to stop. At dinner parties he frequently had to slide down in his chair and move his leg to kick her under the table to shut her up. He wondered if she twittered to herself when she was on her own, and she was on her own a lot, poor thing. They should have had children. Of course, Anita had never been able, that was always the problem. It was a tragedy for someone so naturally maternal. In the beginning she had consoled herself with pet dogs, but they had soon been exchanged for affairs with young boys. Scandals had been avoided but only just. Ah well, he'd better hear what she had to tell him.

"Raoul is dying." Anita waved a letter in his face.

"My condolences," muttered Thierry and prepared to disappear under the bedclothes again until his curiosity got the better of him.

"Who is Raoul?"

"Oh, Thierry, *really*, he's my cousin."

"Ah."

"Not just my cousin, my most wonderful, darlingest cousin and he's passing away without me. It's too, too dreadful. I swear I don't know what I'll do if—"

The words "I swear I don't know what I'll do if—" always heralded endless twittering so Thierry interrupted.

"Where is he, eh, Raoul?"

"New Orleans."

"So go and see him."

"Oh, Thierry, may I really? Oh, how divine, to go back to New Orleans after all this time and see everybody. Why, honey, I'd have a ball, wouldn't I just? I could show them all my Paris wardrobe, I may be almost an old lady but, my, will they be jealous!"

"I thought you wanted to see someone who was dying—"

"Why, yes, of *course* I do, but then when poor angel Raoul dies, bless his soul, there'll be a funeral for him and I can see everyone there, don't you see, Thierry? Now, I'm going to call the airline and I must go shopping and I—*oh, my Lord!*"

"Now what?"

"Whatever shall I do about Luc?"

"Can't you send him back to that Chenier woman? He can't stay here forever, Anita . . ."

"But she isn't at home, she's in America and he doesn't know how to get in touch with her."

"Ah, Christ, Anita! You are not letting him stay here with me. If he doesn't go when you do then I am not letting you go at all."

"Well, that's that then," purred Anita, "he's coming with me to New Orleans."

Elliott Fitzgerald was in a hell of a state. He was given to fussing and fretting, but today was a real disaster.

He had come to terms with it long ago: the fact that he had been responsible for the death of a young boy and the guilt was never going to go away. If he didn't have anything else to fret about, he worried that they'd found out, that they were on the point of coming to get him, the game was up. Ironically, now that the one person who *could* give him away, Hugh Heron-Sweeney, was dead, he felt even worse.

It was only in the last six months that he had embarked upon a plan of action which might in some way assuage his guilt and help him expiate his sin. He had, for the first time, written a serious novel, breaking away from his usual crime formula. But it was not strictly a novel. He had written his own life story in novel form, as fiction. It began as what he had discovered by reading reviews in *Time* magazine as a coming-of-age story, but told from the point of view of a young boy discovering his homosexual tendencies. It told of the boy's attempts to understand what was happening when he failed to encounter any similar reactions in his friends, his loneliness, his reluctance to follow his father into his Guards regiment. It described his courtship of a bright blue-eyed girl whose pale gold hair had inspired him to write a poem about her. The second part of the book began with his marriage and dwelled on his constant feelings of inadequacy toward his wife, moving on to depict the horror of war in the eyes of a fragile, sensitive young man and the inevitable "awakening" which awaited him in Paris, resulting in the breaking down of his marriage after the war. But perhaps the most vividly written section of the book was the chapter about an extraordinary drowning accident off Wales' Gower Peninsula—a bizarre story relating how the hero had actually swapped clothes with a young boy and the young boy had subsequently drowned, leading everyone to believe that it was the hero whose body had been washed up several days later.

Elliott had agonized for some time as to how he could end the story. Did he take the character right all the way through his life, in which case he would have to reveal that he now lived in south-west France? Eventually he decided that he would not bring the story right up to date if only for the reason that thirty-odd years in the life of a man living on his own in an isolated country house made for rather boring reading. He decided to end the book with the hero retreating to face a hermetic, possibly suicidal existence for the rest of his life. He didn't specify where.

A rather tragic story but it was, he knew, quite the best thing he had ever written. He also knew that he didn't quite have the guts to send it to his agent in London, especially after the rather hostile response to the feeler he had put out about writing a different type of book from the Eric Christians.

No. He would not send this one to London. The market for this book—for which he still did not have a title—was in America. He had never been to America, but he had an instinctive feeling that they would respond to it despite the fact that it was not set there. He had an almost fatalistic attitude toward his new book. If it ever came to be published then it must be because it was *meant to be. Le destin.* He wanted to chance it all to fate. If Luc Chenier took it to New York and gave it to someone and that person published it then so be it. And if he never heard about it again then he'd accept that that was what was meant to happen. He wasn't even going to keep a copy himself. It would all depend on Luc.

Luc was due to arrive at any second and the sight of him always stirred up a mixed bag of feelings inside Elliott. First of all he was so beautiful! Elliott did not really have any feelings of desire anymore. He suspected a lot of men of his generation were in a similar position. Aware of their preferences, but unable to give way to them actively. Some, Elliott suspected, had probably never indulged at all. But the sight of Luc was enough for anyone to fantasize a little . . . Then there was the fact that Luc was so young which never failed to instill in Elliott a strong feeling of paternity. He often wondered what had become of his daughter Tessa. She must be nearly thirty by now, probably married with children of her own. He had always been tempted to contact Sir Hugh to ask for information, but he had known the old boy would have given him the brush-off without hesitation. That had been the understanding between them. *They think you're dead; leave them alone. They don't belong to you anymore.*

But supposing he had grandchildren? What did Tessa look like now? Would he ever meet her? Appalling to think that he might meet her and not recognize who she was. And vice versa. He wondered if she ever thought about him, wondered who her father was, what he had been like.

In the meantime he had had time to form his plan. He would give Luc the manuscript, ask him to take it to America and deliver it to a publisher in New York. Elliott had no doubt that once an editor with a good eye read it they would waste no time in publishing it. He had not put his name to it. That was giving away too much. But he was laying himself open to chance by allowing the true story, written out in detail, to leave his hands.

There was still time to stop it. To put the manuscript away under lock and key somewhere or even burn it. He had purposely not made a carbon copy.

Then he saw Luc coming across the field to his front door. He stared. The boy had undergone some kind of transformation. Gone were the ramshackle peasant clothes. In their place Luc was fitted out in a pair of beautifully cut gray flannel trousers, black polo sweater and a black gaberdine blazer. Not exactly appropriate dress for the country, but even so Luc presented the picture of a smart, sophisticated young man, a perfect gentleman. As Elliott opened the door to him, Luc smiled in such a winsome fashion that once again Elliott found his hands were shaking and he plunged them into his jacket pockets.

But it was quite clear the boy had changed.

Before they sat down to their supper of a pâté followed by their habitual omelette and salad, Elliott put on some music. As the rather mournful strains of Albinoni's *adagio pour cordes et orgue* poured into the little kitchen, Luc snapped: "Jesus, Elliott, what is this dirge? Do you have to put on something so depressing? We're supposed to be celebrating my departure for America, aren't we? Is this your idea of a celebration?"

Elliott. Luc had called him Elliott instead of the respectful *Monsieur Fitzgerald.* Elliott realized he ought to be pleased at the boy's familiar use of his name, yet somehow he knew it was not a sign of affection. And Luc had never commented on the older man's choice of music before. Indeed, in the past he would never have dreamed of being so ill-mannered.

As the evening wore on, Elliott became rather tired at the sound of Anita's name all the time. She was all Luc talked about, Anita this, Anita does that and . . .

"Do you know who I met? That Honey Winslow woman. She was at this dance we went to in the Bois de Boulogne. Christ, was she beautiful! I danced with her, yes I did! Think she liked me."

Elliott winced at the Americanism. Was this the kind of influence Madame Anita had had on the boy?

"So anyway, Elliott, on the telephone you said you had something for me . . ."

"Ah yes, I wonder if . . . this is . . . would you mind?" and Elliott bent to retrieve something from under the kitchen table. "Here, could you take this to America for me, to New York? Find a literary agent or a publisher and give it to them, ask them to deal with it. It is very, *very* important. It is my life you have there in your hands."

As far as Luc could see all he had in his hands was a large square box.

"What is it?"

"It's a manuscript. Of my latest book. Will you, Luc, please? For me?"

"Can't you give me a name or anything?"

"No, I'm sorry. Just ask someone in New York for the name of a reputable publisher."

"Don't you think it's a bit risky, Monsieur Fitzgerald, just leaving your book with any old publisher? Someone you don't know?"

"I want it to be risky." Elliott smiled to himself at the use of his full name again. "I want this book to be in the hands of fate. If it winds up being published, all well and good. If it doesn't, then that is how it should be. So you'll help me, Luc?"

"I guess," the boy shrugged. "But I'm going to New Orleans, you know, we'll only be in New York but a few days at the beginning passing through."

"Do you have a passport? A visa?" The old man was beginning to fuss over him now.

"That's why I came down—to get my old passport, the one I had when I was a baby. It's an American one, believe it or not. I've been an American all the time. All I have to do is exchange it for a new one at the American Embassy in Paris. Anita's cross because it's holding up her trip. I just came down to get my passport and now here it is so I can be off . . ."

Elliott turned away so the boy would not see his look of immense disappointment. He had thought Luc had come down to say goodbye to him. He realized that if he had not accidentally seen Luc in the distance over at *La Cachette* and called him on the telephone the boy might not even have come to visit him. Yet he wasn't a boy any longer. In six weeks he had become an arrogant young man and he didn't need old fools like Elliott Fitzgerald anymore.

"You'll write?" Elliott asked hesitantly.

"Sure." Easy to say. Luc was almost pawing the ground in his impatience to be gone. "Got a train to catch, Elliott. Gotta be back in Paris tonight. And hey, if my *Tantie* shows up tell her I've gone to America, same as her." And he chuckled with delight at the irony.

Elliott nodded and stood at the window watching him striding across the field away from *La Folie*. He had not even had time to give him a farewell embrace. But a part of the old man was going with him to America in the square cardboard box Luc carried under one arm.

When Luc was out of sight Elliott Fitzgerald sat down suddenly on the steps below his kitchen door. His feet nudged the thyme and rosemary growing wild on either side of him. For a long time he had not allowed himself the indulgence of wallowing in his loneliness. Indeed, for many years he had not even felt the need. Ever since he had met Luc, the boy had been a source of comfort in the old man's life. Unknowingly, of course. Elliott was sure Luc would never know how much he had meant to him.

But now he had gone and Elliott knew he must face up to the emptiness stretching before him. He was solitary by nature, always had been. A loner. And loners were never lonely. What rubbish! They needed love and affection just like everybody else. The only difference was that they were prepared to accept it from just one or two people, people they might see on an infrequent basis and in between they were capable of feeding themselves with enough attention to get by.

But when their props collapsed and the precious few people they depended on deserted them, then they were lonely. Doubly so for they had no wide circle of friends to fall back on.

And now Luc had gone. Elliott realized he was lonelier than he had ever been in his life. He had the feeling that there was no one anywhere in the world who spent a moment of their time thinking about him.

And for this reason, for the first time in years, he wept.

CHAPTER 23

Someone *was* thinking about Elliott Fitzgerald. Ever since she'd arrived back in New York, Tessa found she couldn't stop thinking about her father. Not that she had a specific face to picture in her mind, but the time she had spent at Bellcloud had brought back her obsession to know more about him. Perhaps it was because Amy had talked about him, but somehow Tessa had been able to feel his presence, almost as if he had been there with them.

Another person on her mind was Jack Fern. She'd been back a week now and there had been no word from him. She'd tried to call several times. She had a perfectly good reason to do so— they were supposed to be doing a job together. She'd made contact with Honey and they had a date set up to meet. Now all she had to do was reach Jack and have him come along too. But he had not returned her calls. She knew he wasn't away because at PIA they always told her he'd "just stepped away from his desk."

Of course, there was another reason she wanted to reach him. He'd said those words to her, *"come back to me soon,"*

and she could have sworn he meant them. So why was he
avoiding her? What had happened while she'd been away?

> "Hello, Bill,
> Where ya goin', Bill?
> Downtown, Bill,
> To pay the gas bill,
> How much, Bill?
> A *fifty dollar* bill?"

Jack Fern was up on 125th Street, near the Apollo Theater. He
often spent time in Harlem taking pictures for his own portfo-
lio. Only black and white. Black and white was the thing. Except, of course, when it came to most of the work he was paid
for: in advertising work, color was what the clients wanted.
Black and white didn't mean much to them. Yet slowly but
surely he was managing to build up a collection of his own
work in black and white and soon he would be able to try and
get an exhibition.

For some time now he had been torn into a kind of split
personality. Part of him was proud to have become a success as
a working photographer, in demand by advertising agencies
and magazines, secure in the knowledge that much of his earlier photojournalistic work, his new pictures, had been sold by
PIA, syndicated round the world. Yet, as a serious photographer, he had not yet been totally accepted in the artistic sense.
He knew it was only a matter of time, that he did not yet have
quite enough material from which to produce a book or an
exhibition. And that was why these moments he snatched
alone, away from his commercial work, to take his own pictures, the ones he wanted to take rather than the ones his client
wanted, were enormously precious to him.

> "Hello, Bill,
> Where ya goin', Bill? . . ."

The kids were off again, singing their crazy little song as they
played their own particular brand of hopscotch on the sidewalk. On each *"Bill"* they had to place their feet in a particular
square and on the *"fifty dollar bill"* they were supposed to have
reached the last square and slapped the palm of the kid waiting

to take his turn. It was a kind of relay race. Across the street another team was hopping away across the squares they had chalked out. Both teams were aware that they were being photographed and played to the camera. Jack didn't mind. The expressions he was capturing were those of huge enjoyment and at the same time highly competitive spirit. There was an optimism here not often seen in Harlem. Jack was under no illusion that it wasn't momentary, knew that once the game was over the kids would disperse and mooch about the streets aimlessly once again, but while the fun was there he was determined to get it on film. He shot several rolls. Maybe when he came to edit them he would find only two or three usable pictures, but *one* good picture would mean that it had been a successful afternoon's work.

He was going to be late getting back home. Doodle wanted to go to a movie, had asked that he be back in time to make the six o'clock show. It was a quarter to now. He really ought to leave, but the game wasn't over. He was planning a series of photos, a photo essay showing the kids arriving on the street corner, getting a game together, more kids joining in, the supporters clapping in time on the sidewalks, the game in progress, the winning team, the celebration and the subsequent inevitable anticlimax at the end of it all. If he left now he would only get half the story.

"It's *perfectly* all right," said Doodle, acidly polite when he walked in at seven forty-five. "Don't worry about a thing. I didn't want to see the fucking movie anyway." She could get like that at times, studiously polite, no cross words, just an attitude which could leave a guy rigid with guilt.

"Come *on*, you know I'm sorry. We'll catch the eight-thirty show, have a bite to eat after."

"Look, forget it, will you? If you'd wanted to see the movie you'd've come back in time. It obviously wasn't that important to you. Where were you anyway? I looked in your calendar. You weren't working."

"I *was* working. There were these kids up in Harlem. I think I've got some fantastic stuff, wait till you see it."

"Well, you'd better not waste any time, you'd better get into that darkroom of yours and start developing those rolls before they curl up and disintegrate with old age."

"Oh, Doodle, don't be like that . . ."

"Like what? Like WHAT? Like a normal person who would enjoy going out on the occasional evening, seeing a movie, enjoying a meal? It's quite clear to me you don't want me to be like that. What *do* you want me to spend my time doing while you're shut up in your damned darkroom or out taking pictures? I can't water plants all the time. My work at PIA is over and done with by five-thirty every day. You want I should take up needlepoint and sit here on the sofa waiting for you every evening? Fuck you!"

There was no point in saying anything. Jack tried not to look helpless as she put on her coat and rushed out of the apartment. He began to go around the room, picking up the masses of sheets of paper covered in scribbles. Since she'd moved in, he had become aware that her doodling was more than the eccentric habit everybody had thought it was. He had discovered it was a form of neurosis resulting from the constant stifling of a furious frustration she appeared to have.

Everyone had always thought of Doodle as being nothing more than "a brick," someone who could be relied upon totally. Calm, cheerful and easy-going. Along with his desire to achieve some kind of recognition as a serious photographer, Jack had also begun to yearn for a stable on-going relationship, something he had never had. He had never lacked for women. Everybody figured him for a nice guy, good company, a good raconteur with plenty of stories to tell from his assignments all over the world. Amusing. Attractive. Models loved working with him. He always had plenty of witty repartee to make them smile and relax. At home anywhere, Jack Fern always "fitted in." He was the perfect guest, the permanently eligible bachelor. And always the most elusive.

Underneath Jack Fern was a very private person. He was well aware that he had not opened up to anyone, *really* trusted anyone since he had left home all those years ago. Yet the need to become close to someone had grown and going to bed with Doodle after a relaxed and comfortable dinner had seemed totally natural. She was an old friend, he could let his guard down, talk about some of his fears and his hopes for the future. Good old understanding Doodle. What better person to share his life?

But it wasn't working. Living with her had shown him the real Doodle; someone who was so desperate to please others that she wound up constantly depriving herself. A cheerful, generous person on the surface and, he was sure, by nature, but someone who underneath was growing increasingly resentful. He was genuinely fond of her, wanted to help her, but it was clear their relationship wasn't going anywhere even though they'd only been together for a month.

Maybe that English girl was back in town by now, the one with the terrific legs. Maybe he should have waited a while, but Doodle had been *there*. Tessa. Tessa Fitzgerald, he had her number someplace, they were supposed to be doing that Honey Winslow assignment together. Maybe he should give her a call. Maybe . . .

He couldn't concentrate on the tiny island of onions he was frying in the ridiculously large cast-iron skillet he had bought that afternoon at Bridge and Company. He had to keep looking up and gazing at his loft. *His* loft. Owned by him. Not rented from somebody else in whose identity he could lose himself.

He had rushed out and bought it two and a half months ago rather as one might slip out to buy another carton of milk. He had simply come to the end of rented apartments, of moving from one place to another, of running away from himself. With the loft he had bought something far more important than a place to live in: he had acquired permanence and the necessity to come to terms with who he really was.

It shook him. Even now he had to turn off the flame, push the heavy pan to one side and bury his face in his hands. He felt —he searched for the word—dislodged. Recently he had begun to play a cruel game with himself. He composed copy for a fantasy profile of himself which might appear in a glossy magazine only too aware that it never quite delivered: son *but not heir* of *Bayou Beauty*; brilliant owner and the brains behind the successful *Eros—yet nobody knew it*; accomplished lover, *but unmarried and unloved*.

Unloved. It hurt, but he had only himself to blame. He had withheld himself from the real world and contrived to live in an extension of the fantasy once created for him by his mother. She had highlighted his beauty at an early age and encouraged him to live off it instead of alongside it. OK, so he had not exactly entered the adult world as the beautifully made-up drag queen Callie had created in her bathroom, but he *had* hidden behind disguises and he had made the critical mistake of persuading himself he did it for his own amusement. Yet there had been nothing amusing about it, he was well aware of that now.

And he was guilty of another deception. Making love to many different women did not necessarily mean that he was receiving love himself. For years he had kidded himself that he was surrounded by love, but in truth his life was totally devoid of it. It was as if he had given himself an injection of emotional novocaine years ago which had made him immune to it, immune to feeling generally, and now that injection had begun to wear off. The numbness was thawing and he was beginning to feel pain.

But at least he was feeling something.

The loft was the beginning. He might still be a bachelor in his late thirties, but anyone entering his new home would not recognize it as the conventional bachelor pad. For the first time since leaving *Coinchenier* he had a place of his own to do with what he wanted. He'd had bookshelves built before anything else and the shelves contained as many books by women as by men. He was intrigued by the Women's Movement, not scared by or contemptuous of it like most men he knew. Then he'd supervised personally the installation of a highly practical yet cheerful kitchen in one corner of the loft space. Now, instead of taking women out to dinner every night he cooked himself a delicious meal—soup, pasta (with a variety of his own sauces), salads, filet, entrecôte, cassoulet, choucroute, bollito misto, osso buco—he knew them all as well as numerous Southern dishes from Queenie's cookbook. But his forte was dessert probably because it was his own favorite part of any meal. His zabaglione was the best he'd ever tasted, possibly the best ever. But he had no one to give him a second opinion, no one to share his meal, no one to cook for.

Every Friday night, at great expense, he had armfuls of wild flowers delivered from a florist and then he would spend the best part of an hour arranging them strategically around his loft. He bought several trees and studied them for hours while listening to music, believing that if he watched them long enough he might actually see them grow.

He grew to love his home—so much so that he wanted to show it to someone. As he began to think about it he realized that what he really wanted to do was to talk to someone who would listen. About himself. About his wasted life and what he was going to do to resurrect it. He wanted to tell someone about *Eros* and how proud he was of the way he had conceived it, nurtured it and expanded it. And then he would tell them that that was only a part of him, that he had another side that he was only just discovering right here in this loft. Then, having explained all of this, he would sit back and listen to them.

But who was there in his life who would understand that within the urbane, sophisticated womanizer he presented to the world, there existed a still vulnerable boy who had a lifetime of emotional catching up to do. It would have to be someone with a similar background. Not necessarily in terms of nationality, class or education—but in terms of deprivation of love and affection. He was seeking an emotional next of kin.

It takes one to know one. An old cliché but a true one and in his case it took one to *feel* one. Because now he knew who he was, he recognized himself in another.

PJ knew he wanted more than anything else in the world to open up to Tessa.

The evening started out on a bad note. Tessa had finally succumbed to Larry's eternal query—"You got dinner all sorted out?"—and replied no, she hadn't as a matter of fact and yes, she'd love to go out in search of Chinese on Broadway, when the telephone rang.

It was Jack Fern inviting her to dinner. *That night.* Stunned by the unexpected sound of his voice Tessa heard herself accepting his invitation, agreeing to meet him in an hour at Victor's Café, a Cuban restaurant on 71st, then she turned to face Larry, who was staring at her in disbelief.

"Did we have a date tonight or what? Who the hell was that?" And once again Tessa heard this voice which didn't belong to her explaining that it was work (half-true) and very important and he did understand, didn't he?

"Could I take a raincheck?" she finished lamely.

"Brits don't use that expression," he told her in disgust and mooched off to his room.

Now she and Jack were nearing the end of their meal and Tessa found herself hoping it wouldn't mean the end of the evening. The conversation hadn't stopped from the moment she'd walked into the restaurant and been shown to the table in the glass-encased area overlooking the sidewalk where Jack had been waiting for her with a giant bear hug of an embrace.

He had asked politely about her grandfather's funeral and her stay in England and had tactfully engineered the conversation in a different direction once he'd seen she was not yet ready to talk about that. Neither of them wanted a repeat of their first lunch when they'd found themselves unable to talk about their backgrounds and she was grateful to him for being so perceptive this time round.

He told her about his recent photo session in Harlem and he seemed delighted when she showed an interest in his work and asked to see the pictures. It seemed to unlock something bottled up inside him and he began to talk passionately about his desire to be taken seriously as a photographer, how he would eventually ease out the commercial side of his work to make room for more time on his own pictures and how, already, to this end he had decided to hire himself an assistant to take some of the load off him, do his developing for him, leave him more time for his own pursuits. But in the meantime there was the Honey Winslow job and as far as he was concerned the sooner that was over the better. If Tessa didn't mind he wouldn't come along the next day, he'd rather leave her to it and catch up with them later and spend the afternoon shooting several rolls toward the end of their talks—if she lasted that long, of course. No, he didn't mean Tessa, he meant Honey Winslow and her beauty spot. There'd been another murder down in the Village while she'd been away and yet again the victim was a Honey look-alike.

"So I'd better see you home," he said, taking her arm as they wandered along 8th Avenue looking for a cab.

"But I don't have a beauty spot," protested Tessa.

"I can soon fix that," he told her and taking a felt tip pen from his jacket pocket he drew a black spot lightly on her cheek, holding her face gently with his other hand as he did so. As he finished he dropped a light kiss on her upturned nose and slipped his arm around her shoulders.

In the cab he held her hand and quietly stroked the inside of her palm with his thumb. "You live on West End Avenue and where?" he asked her and she had a momentary pang of disappointment. Why weren't they going to his apartment? Was he proposing to drop her off at hers with just a goodnight kiss?

But clearly nothing was further from his mind as he paid off the cab and followed her into the lobby. "Which floor?" he asked in front of the elevator bank. "Fifteenth," she told him, silently panicking as to what kind of reception they'd get from Larry. But Larry had retired early, probably in a huff. Jack was already wandering down the hall.

"Which room's yours?" he called back to her and she rushed to quieten him, pulling him into her room before he could wake Larry. Once inside she shut the door firmly behind them and he pushed her up against it, nuzzling his face into her neck.

"What I want to do right now," he told her in a surprisingly aggressive tone of voice, "is fuck your brains out and I don't want to see any of that British reserve. OK?"

Tessa giggled into his chest and allowed him to unzip her jeans and pull her sweater over her head. She wanted for him to reach down inside her pants and stroke her, but he had already turned away and was undressing himself in a hurry. She watched in growing excitement as his tall, muscular frame emerged. Obviously he worked out. His body was in peak condition, glowing with health and the last traces of a summer tan. As he turned toward her she silently admired his broad chest with the magnificent burst of blond hair covering it. She removed the last of her underwear and let her eyes wander down his body. To say he was well built was an understatement, but there was something wrong. Instead of a mighty erection his long penis hung limp between his legs. Jack followed her gaze and shrugged.

"He could use a little help." He came toward her and taking her hand he put it on him. Tessa's hand encircled his penis and she began to stroke him, moving up and down from the bottom of his shaft right up to the tip while her other hand caressed his balls.

Nothing happened.

"Come on, baby," Jack whispered huskily, "get me going." She motioned to him to lie down on the bed and stretched out next to him, rubbing herself against him, encasing his penis between her long firm thighs.

Still nothing.

"Go down, baby," he growled, placing a hand on top of her head and pushing her down. Tessa got to her knees and bent over him to lick his tip. There was a quiver of reaction.

"Suck on me, baby." Tessa obeyed. Now things were beginning to happen. She felt him stiffen in her mouth and it excited her. She reached down for a quick dip into herself and found she was already pleasantly moist.

Suddenly he flung her on her back. "What did I tell you I was going to do?" he growled in her ear. "Fuck my brains out," she whispered, wondering if Larry could hear them through the wall.

"Tell me, tell me . . . I'm going to fuck . . . *Aaaah!*" he yelled and collapsed on top of her. He had barely entered her before he came.

He was up in a flash, moving round the room, picking up his clothes.

"You were so good, Tessa. You were terrific, you know that? Weren't we great together? Boy, oh boy. Where's the john?"

He was out of the room before she could stop him. Down the hall she heard another door opening and waited for the inevitable collision in the bathroom.

"Oh hi, how are you?" Jack clearly wasn't in the least embarrassed at being caught half naked in someone else's apartment. "I didn't know there was someone else here. Did we wake you? Sorry about that. Want to go first? No? Well, thanks a lot." Tessa could almost imagine the slap on the back, the leery wink as he slipped past Larry into the bathroom.

Later, after he'd left giving her a quick peck on the cheek and a promise to call soon, Larry appeared in the doorway, a reproachful figure in a frayed toweling bathrobe.

"Well, Tessa," he said before returning once again to his room in a huff, "I guess you finally got dinner all sorted out."

CHAPTER 24

Tessa was getting nowhere with her profile of Honey Winslow. Honey had made a quick trip to Paris and ever since she'd come back she'd been in a kind of trance, totally uncommunicative. Not that she'd been exactly revealing before she left. Tessa was beginning to worry as to what angle she could use to hang the story on. Her usual tack was to take a subject already well known to the public, but instead of presenting the superficial already familiar figure, she would dig deeper until she got through to the person underneath. Then she would profile that person, always sympathetically, and the public would read about someone they had never known existed.

But Honey was proving to be her most elusive subject yet. There were plenty of meaty facts like her success as a model, her building up of *Winslowear*, her outstanding beauty and her inheritance of *Bayou Beauty*, but all of this was boring to Tessa. She was not content just to recap on what people already knew. Nor was she prepared to give up. Yet. Honey must have a vulnerable spot *somewhere*.

But right now she wasn't saying anything. They were sitting

in total silence in her suite at the Sherry. Tessa revved herself up to try again.

"About P. J. Duboise—" she began tentatively, but Honey cut her off at the pass with a question which took her totally by surprise.

"Say, can you write dirty?"

"I beg your pardon?"

"You ever tried writing erotic stuff? There's this magazine, see, called *Eros*. Dirty stuff but good. You might try writing for them. I know the owner."

"I know *Eros*," Tessa told her, "it's good, but it's literary. I'm not sure I'm quite ready for that yet. Do you want me to write an *erotic* profile of you, is that it? In which case you're going to have to tell me a whole lot more about what they call your 'private life'."

"I don't talk about that," said Honey sharply.

"Not to anyone?"

Tessa suddenly got an insight into how lonely Honey's life might be. Did she have any close friends? She decided to ask her straight out.

"No," replied Honey. "I don't talk to a soul, just reporters which is why I'm talking to you. But you know, you're different, you didn't come in here with a whole load of dumb questions about how I am going to run *Bayou Beauty* and am I going to merge it with *Winslowear* and all that shit. No, somehow you act like you want to know about *me*, about the real Honey Winslow."

Christ, thought Tessa, she *must* be lonely. She's projecting like anything. I haven't given her any indication that I'm interested in her as a person. She's just desperate for someone to *be* interested in her and she's picked me as the most likely sucker in town. Well, what the hell. I'll probably get some better copy out of her . . .

"So tell me, Honey, is it lonelier at the top as a tycoon than as a successful model?"

"That's as clear as the day to anyone. First of all I'm a whole lot older now and I need my privacy *and* my sleep. Second of all, now I'm an employer instead of an employee. I'm the one doin' the hirin' and firin' now and folks don't feel they can be themselves with me the way they used to be. And I notice that, don't think I don't. I'm not part of any crowd anymore, I'm out on my own. But I'm successful and I don't question that."

"At the price of having no love in your life?"

"Aw, Christ, what do you want me to say? Listen, Tessa, *Miss* Tessa, I'm an optimist. I've got my success and I believe there's time enough to find love . . . meanwhile I like to have fun. I've just been over to Paris, for some kid's eighteenth birthday bash. One of the biggest parties of the year—out at the Pré Catalan in the Bois de Boulogne. You been there? No? You should. André Vauniashevsky's daughter. You know André? No? Don't you know *any*body? Well, the strangest thing happened.

"Yeah, I'm telling you it was the strangest thing," Honey seemed to trail off as if she were talking to herself. "And yet was it so strange? Maybe it was really him? *So* beautiful, those heavenly eyes with their long dark lashes . . . just think, if he hadn't asked me to dance I would never have seen . . ." Honey was off in a world of her own, a faraway look on her face. She was murmuring to herself, barely aware of Tessa's existence anymore.

"Seen what?" prompted Tessa, her instinct telling her to hold back, to probe gently.

"The Chenier family heirloom!" Honey said as if Tessa had known all along. "It's a silver dolphin bracelet, handed down from generation to generation. Callie gave it to PJ, PJ gave it to me as a love token and when I left the clinic after my baby I noticed it was gone. That's it! She must have taken it, the bitch, right there in the hospital! And when do I see it again? Seventeen years later, in France, on the wrist of this beautiful kid . . . It can't be. It just *couldn't* be . . ."

"So what did you do?" Tessa was treading round the edges of the story, determined not to break into Honey's consciousness.

"Well, suddenly this woman came up and whisked him away and when I looked round for him he'd gone altogether. I asked about the woman and they told me she was some kind of aunt of his or godmother or something. I guess I could have contacted her but what could I have said to her? 'Hello there. Excuse me for asking, but just who was that boy you dragged away from the Pré Catalan that night? Do you happen to know if he was kidnapped seventeen years ago when I was told he was dead?' Oh, forget it! Let's get drunk." Honey's mood had changed, but Tessa was determined to pursue her.

"You think you might have found your own son and you let it go at that? Who else have you told about this?"

"No one. Listen, Tessa, the kid probably found the silver dolphin, maybe he stole it, who knows? They told me my child was killed, who am I to disbelieve them?"

"*Who* told you?"

"Perry Jay Duboise, as a matter of fact."

"And now he's dead so you can't confirm it with him. Maybe someone else knows about this. Don't you even want to try to find out? There must be *something* which made you think this boy was really your son and not just some boy wearing his dolphin bracelet. Did he look like you? Was that it?"

"No," whispered Honey, "but he was the spitting image of his father . . ." She stopped there, and said instead: "So where's Jack Fern, then? I thought he was supposed to be coming to take some pictures of me."

Tessa turned away so Honey would not see if she blushed. She had still not been able to bring herself to think about her night with Jack Fern.

"What do you make of him, Tessa?"

"Oh, he seems very nice. I haven't really had much of a chance to form an opinion."

"No? I've worked with him a couple of times. Good looking fella. A 'take-charge kind of guy' like I told you before. Very sought after. Dependable. Would bore me rigid, but I have to admit he's quite a looker. Still, he's got that girl living with him now, they say, so maybe I'm talking history."

Tessa froze. "What girl?" she breathed.

"Girl who works at PIA. Got a weird name. I've talked to her a couple of times. Seems they went out one night and just hit it off beyond the working relationship boundaries and she moved in. Come to think of it, it's always the ordinary girls guys like that end up with. Wish I could remember her name . . ."

"Doodle?"

"Yeah, that's it. Crazy name, isn't it? Why? You know her?"

"Never met her," said Tessa, "I've just spoken to her on the telephone, like you. Now, about the baby . . ."

But Honey had gone back into her trance.

"I'm sorry, I truly am. I *was* going to tell you, but I thought I ought to speak to Doodle about you first. It was only fair. I never thought things would happen so fast, I knew I liked you but that night when we had dinner at Victor's I realized I also wanted you. Very badly. Don't be angry, please, Tessa."

They were back in the restaurant where they'd had their first lunch.

And Tessa was angry, but not because he hadn't told her about Doodle. But she couldn't bring herself to tell him the real reason. Not yet, anyway.

"So anyway I've spoken to her and she's moving out today. Tell you the truth, I think she was actually pretty relieved. She knew it wasn't going to work out just as much as I did. So we can go to my place tomorrow night after dinner."

And he thinks that'll make everything all right, thought Tessa. Honestly, men were so pathetically simplistic it was almost touching sometimes. They imagined all they had to do was breathe the word *sorry* and the slate was wiped clean. Well, she'd let him get away with it this time, but she'd be watching out for him in the future.

"So how did the interview go?"

"We didn't really get very far . . . Besides, I wanted to think about a new angle I might have on Honey's story—a new slant—something that might make it a sensational news story rather than just another feature."

"How's that?"

"She's got some crazy idea that she might have found the baby she lost," and Tessa went on to tell him about Honey's trip to Paris.

Jack whistled. "Boy, you really might be onto something there, Tessa. Keep me posted. If I could get an exclusive on the pix of the kid if it does turn out to be him I'd really be onto something . . ."

"Hold on," said Tessa, suddenly irritated by his "take-charge" attitude. "Whose story is this? I got there first. You didn't want to come along and take pictures yesterday when you could have been in on the act at the beginning!"

"OK, OK, hold your horses. Listen, I gotta run. I'll get the check . . ."

"No," said Tessa firmly. *"I'll* get the check. I've got an expense account too, you know."

Jack looked momentarily taken aback, but recovered quickly. "Fine, up to you. I'll pick you up tomorrow night. Around eight?"

Tessa nodded and he bent to kiss her earlobe. Then he was gone.

The next evening she dressed carefully in a short, straight tight-fitting black wool skirt and an electric blue jersey top which slipped off her shoulders accidentally-on-purpose if she wanted it too. She swept her hair into a long plait down her back, made sure her make-up gave her face some dramatic color and slipped a pair of tiny diamond studs into her ears. Sheer black stockings encased her legs and her black suede three inch heels accentuated their perfect shape and length.

She was rewarded with a look of drooling admiration in Jack's eyes when she opened the door to him and she couldn't help noticing that he too looked particularly good in an anthracite gray well-cut but casual suit which gave his wide shoulders an exceptionally bear-like quality. She wanted to hug him immediately—and she did.

They ate Italian and Tessa noticed that Jack drank a considerable amount of the excellent Frascati. Again he talked endlessly about his work and his hopes for the future so that when they finally staggered out of the elevator and into his apartment around eleven-thirty she almost felt obliged to ask to see his pictures. His darkroom was back in use and he led her in there.

"This is the stuff I shot the other day up in Harlem," he pointed to a series of black and white prints pegged to a line above them. But as she began to look carefully at them and make what she hoped were suitable comments, she felt his arms encircle her waist from behind and his hands clamp firmly over her breasts.

He led her into the bedroom and told her, quite roughly, to get undressed. He was already almost naked himself. Then he grabbed her to him and held her very close. After a few seconds she realized there was no sign of anything hard pressing between her legs. She slipped her hand down there and encountered his flaccid penis. Any moment now she knew he would want her to kneel before him in a servile fashion and take him in her mouth. And she knew that she wasn't going to.

"Let's get into bed, Jack," she whispered in his ear. And when they were settled she said, "Now, let's just talk."

"What about?"

"About us. What we like about each other."

"What do you like about me, Tessa?"

"I liked you the first moment I saw you. You had a kind of confidence about you which helped me to relax. I trusted you. And I like the way you know what you're doing, where you're going. You're going to be a big success, Jack. I can tell."

It's extraordinary, she told herself silently, I'm the one who's always felt insecure and lacking in confidence in myself. Now here I am boosting the ego of this handsome great hulk instead of the other way round and, funnily enough, I rather like it. It gives me a kind of power. I haven't really talked about myself at all this evening. He's hogged the limelight the whole time and I haven't felt the least bit left out. I don't need to think about myself.

"Plus," she went on, "you've got one of the best bodies I've ever come across. You're beautiful, Jack, quite beautiful," and she bent her head to suck gently on his nipples. Down below she felt a stirring in her hand. He was beginning to harden very, very slowly. She gave one of his nipples a quick, sharp nip and felt his penis give a sudden lurch.

"And most of all," she told him, "I love the fact that you want to *fuck my brains out*."

The magic words! Fully erect he entered her immediately and once again she felt his semen trickle down the inside of her thigh as he came a second later.

He slipped out of her as quickly as he'd entered and she waited for his apology, an explanation which she could brush aside with gentle reassurances, his promise that the next time would be fine. She could hardly believe her ears when he told her: "That was great, baby, sensational. Thanks a lot." And then to her horror he turned over on his side and fell asleep.

Her anger and frustration would not allow her to lie quietly beside him. She slipped out of bed and fumbled her way down the hall in the darkness and into the first open doorway she found. Closing the door behind her she leaned against the wall for a few seconds in the darkness. He was all of the things she'd told him he was and more. Like Honey said, he was a take-charge kind of a guy and that was exactly what she needed

right now. Yet there was clear evidence that in many ways he
needed her more than she needed him and that if they were
going to get anywhere at all in bed, she was always going to
have to "take charge." Could she handle that? Yes, of course
she could.

Feeling better now she flipped on the light and saw where she
was. The kitchen. She remembered the last time she'd been in
this room and with whom.

A man, but a man of such intense power and magnetism that
he had drawn her to him with no need for words, a man who
had given her pure unadulterated sexual satisfaction, but who
at the same time she sensed was in some way still a child in
need.

Where was PJ? Would she ever see him again?

PART 6

TESSA
1977

CHAPTER 25

PJ was driving along a Mississippi highway in a 1950s Plymouth convertible. He'd rented it at the airport in Memphis, Tennessee and now he was on his way to *Coinchenier* to find out what had become of Callie. Since his father's death no one had answered the phone at *Coinchenier* and he had no idea whether he'd find the place shut down or boarded up.

He'd flown to Memphis instead of Biloxi in order to spend a night at the legendary Peabody Hotel. He remembered it from when he'd been taken there as a little boy. Callie had always told him: "Philippe, darling, when you die, heaven's going to be like the lobby of the Peabody Hotel." The best thing about the lobby was the fountain right in the middle. Water cascaded into an octagonal marble pool from a circular basin supported by cherubs, but the thing which had stuck in PJ's mind all these years was the Peabody's band of ducks. Every day the ducks were led from the roof of the hotel down to their fountain to the accompaniment of the *King Cotton March* by John Philip Sousa. They descended the staircase and paraded across the red carpet to splash about in the fountain. To his everlasting delight, PJ found that they were still there.

An hour later he was driving along under the oak trees to pull up outside the front entrance of *Coinchenier*. He got out of the car and paused to look up at the elegant façade with its line of huge white pillars. His hand went out to the long iron bell pull. Should he ring? It wasn't his home anymore. Though if things had not changed the door would be unlocked anyway.

He tried the handle and the old oak door eased open in front of him. He stepped quickly into the hall, uncertain where to go next. Should he call out? He tiptoed over to look into the drawing room on the left. He had always hated this room with its heavy draperies hanging at the windows and the atmosphere now was stifling. The sofas and armchairs were grouped solidly round a fireplace which was never used. The massive porcelain lamps were topped by dull silk shades with long beaded fringes hanging from them. Monstrous paintings adorned the walls, Chenier family portraits with no beauties included. The only dash of color was provided by a deep blue Chinese vase standing high on the grand piano.

PJ looked closer. The vase was filled with giant magnolia blooms and the Steinway was open. Sheet music lay propped up as if recently used. It was the piano part for old Negro spirituals—the only kind of music Callie had liked to play.

Upstairs he found more flowers in Callie's bedroom. Her silk negligee and night-dress were laid out on her bed as if in readiness for her retirement that night. In the bathroom, her make-up was spread out along the counter.

He peeped into what had been his father's dressing room and choked as the dust rose up in his face. Nobody had been in here in quite a while.

Downstairs at the back of the house his father's poolroom was in a similar state of neglect. Yet his mother's study was freshly cleaned and filled with fresh flowers. In the dining room a single place was set at the long mahogany table. Callie's place. And there was something else. Everywhere he went PJ realized he could smell her scent: Guerlain's *L'Heure Bleu.*

He had been wrong. Callie had been here all along, arranging her flowers, making up her face . . . Yet there was something wrong. The house had an emptiness about it. There was evidence of someone living there but it did not feel *lived in.*

PJ felt ravenously hungry. He hadn't stopped since leaving Memphis and there was one area he still had to visit in

Coinchenier: the kitchen quarters. He remembered the way, down the narrow, poorly lit stone-flagged passage round the corner and . . .

He stopped dead in his tracks and cried out in sheer terror.

The chicken was freshly killed. Its outer feathers were intact and its eyes were clear and open, staring at him. It was hanging from a hood in the beam in the middle of the passageway. It had been slit up the belly from the vent toward the breast and the blood flowed freely out of its body, dripping onto the floor.

PJ had walked right into it and his face was covered in its blood.

Then a voice rose out of the darkness beyond: "What you want in my kitchen, boy?"

"QUEENIE!"

"Who dat?"

"Queenie, oh Queenie, it's me."

"Turn on de light by yo' side, boy."

He did so.

"Why, Master Philippe-Josephe, look at *you*! You done walked straight into my *gris-gris*. I put him there each day to protect me from de evil eye, but you done walked straight into him."

"Oh, Queenie, *chère*, do you know how glad I am to see you? Come here, let me give you a big hug."

"No, no, Master PJ, you covered in evil spirits. Go wash you'self at my sink. My, my, my. Thank de Lord yo' mamma ain't arrived yet. She see you look like that, she gone lose her mind."

"When's she due back?" PJ was rinsing the blood off his face. The kitchen was filled with the old familiar smell of his childhood: ground sassafras leaves.

"Any day now I guess," said Queenie.

"She been away long?"

" 'Bout seventeen years."

"What?"

"But she comin' back any day now."

"You've heard from her? Where's she been?"

"Spirits tole me."

"Now, Queenie, come on, cut it out. Where's she been? How d'you know she's coming back?"

"I feel it. I know. Spirits in the air. I got the house all ready for her just how she likes it."

PJ sat down wearily on a kitchen stool. Queenie was getting on, had to be way over seventy by now. He couldn't understand why she was still there.

"These spirits, Queenie, did they tell you *I'd* be coming back? Were you expecting me? Is that why you hung up that sweet surprise in the passage out there?"

"Only works for de women," retorted Queenie. "Female spirits talk to me. Your grandfather, now, he was murdered, yes he *was*! But his spirits, they don't talk to me 'cause he was a *man*."

"Queenie, you know it was Great Uncle Jules who got killed, not my grandfather."

Queenie quickly covered up her mistake, slapped her cheek and moaned. "Stabbed with a knife. In a brothel, oh Lord! On account of the curse, had to be."

"What curse?"

"The curse on your family. On the Cheniers. They cursed. They die bad. Cheniers die from disease and hell and damnation. No Chenier die in his sleep, Lord have mercy."

"Is that how I'm going to die?"

"You ain't a Chenier, Master Philippe-Josephe. You is a Duboise."

"And they're safe from this curse, are they? My daddy passed away recently."

"I killed him," said Queenie proudly.

"No, Queenie, you didn't. He had a heart attack miles away from here in New York."

Queenie shook her head from side to side like a defiant child. She rummaged around in a drawer and pulled out an object, thrusting it in PJ's face.

"There! There's your daddy. That's how I killed him."

It was a doll. An exact replica of his father right down to the black moustache snaking across the upper lip.

"Takes twenty-one days," Queenie told him with authority, getting into her stride. "On the first day I put the doll under your mamma's pillow upstairs and I stuck a pin into it like this," and she pierced the doll's face with a pin. "The next day I stuck another and I went on for twenty-one days like I said. But on the last day I put the pin in the *heart*!"

"I don't believe a word of it." PJ was beginning to feel distinctly uncomfortable. This wasn't the lovable old Queenie of his childhood who used to give him sugar cane to suck on when he visited her in the kitchen. His mind went back to the time when he had dressed up as the new maid. He recalled how disapproving Queenie had been. Maybe he had never been forgiven. Maybe she had a doll somewhere looked just like him . . . Ah, what nonsense. She almost had him believing it himself.

"Going to make *jambalaya* for Mamma when she comes back?"

"Surely am."

"Where's she been, Queenie?"

"Ain't important. Where *you* been anyway? Broke your mamma's heart when you ran off like that. They had to put her in an institution and then she got out and she ain't never been back till now."

"Didn't my daddy try and find her?"

"Your daddy was always in the city. How'd I know what he be doin'?"

"Queenie, are you going to fix me some dinner?"

"Sure will. I'll take the gizzard and the liver from dat chicken out dere and make us some dirty rice like I always done. When was the last time you had dat?"

"Not in a long time."

"You a good boy, Master Philippe-Josephe. But you ain't seen your mamma and you ain't got no nice wife to look after you. Shame, shame, shame. You got a big city job like your daddy?"

PJ shook his head.

"So how you livin' up dere in New York City? Been livin' on your daddy's money and now he gone and left it all to Miz Honey Winslow so what you gone do? Or did you come down here seekin' your mamma to ask her for *her* money? Anyway," continued Queenie, "yo' mamma got 'nother baby to think about now."

"Another baby?" Now what was Queenie on about?

"Baby she took away with her when she left."

"When was this?" PJ demanded.

"Well, I don't know . . . Sixteen, seventeen, maybe twenty years ago. I don't rightly recall."

"She had a *baby* with her. You sure about this, Queenie?"

"Sure I'm sure. Saw him with my own eyes."

"Him? A boy baby?"

"Cute little fellow. I peeked when they was downstairs and there he was. Mighty fine little boy."

"But if it was all those years ago he wouldn't be a baby anymore."

"Well, you're right, he'd be grown by now."

Queenie turned away to prepare her dirty rice. Soon she was sautéing chicken liver, gizzard, green pepper, onion and celery in olive oil in an iron skillet while PJ went in search of some Early Times to quench his thirst before dinner.

They were midway through their meal when the telephone began to ring. PJ leapt up.

"Don't you answer that telephone," Queenie told him firmly. "It's been ringing off the hook since I don't know when, but we ain't gone answer it. It'll bring bad news."

But the telephone wouldn't stop ringing once it had begun. Finally, PJ could stand it no longer, but each time he walked the length of the house to the hall to answer it it stopped, almost as if someone knew he was about to pick it up.

By midnight PJ knew he couldn't spend another minute at *Coinchenier*. Queenie was moaning and singing to herself and lighting candles all round the kitchen to ward off her "evil spirits" for the night and the house was beginning to develop a distinct nightmare quality to it. He wondered how long Queenie would last, all alone with her voodoo. He couldn't turn her out and at the same time he couldn't stay. He'd come down to find his mother and it was clear she hadn't been here in years and there was no evidence that she would be back despite what Queenie might say.

He left a wad of notes on the kitchen table. What had Queenie been living on since his father's death? He blew her a kiss and slipped away, ducking the bloody chicken. As he moved the Plymouth off down the drive he began to wonder about what Queenie had said about that baby. In the stillness of the Southern night he heard the telephone begin to ring again somewhere in the dark house behind him. But he drove on.

Sitting on her bed in her hotel room in New Orleans, Callie wondered why it was that no one answered the telephone anymore at *Coinchenier*.

CHAPTER 26

". . . the extraordinary thing is I can't find Elliott's death certificate. No one can. It just doesn't seem to exist."

Tessa was on the last page of a long letter from Amy, one of the very few she had ever received from her mother. Amy appeared to have taken on a new lease on life. The letter rambled on for pages about her research for the Heron-Sweeney family history and confided that Amy was a little upset that she was not being allowed to write it.

"They're going to find some hack to put together my notes and the material your grandfather has already written. I find it really rather rude that they haven't asked me to do the job after all the work I've done. Writing's in the family, after all. You're a writer, Tessa, it's obvious you get it from me."

First I've heard of it, thought Tessa, although she'd always wondered where her love of writing originated, or, indeed, from whom. Not that she was getting very far these days. She had arrived at Honey's suite at the Sherry-Netherland to find that, according to the maid who let her in, Honey had gone out shopping. Honey, it seemed, could not care less about the article.

Tessa returned to the letter which she kept in her bag. What on earth had induced her mother to go looking for her father's death certificate? It wasn't as if he had been a Heron-Sweeney.

The telephone interrupted her thoughts. Honey's telephone. Well, she'd better take a message.

"Hello?"

"Hello, Honey Winslow there?" A man's voice, soft, alluring.

"Not right now, I'm afraid. Can I give her a message?"

"No, it's OK. Ah'll call back later."

Ah'll call back later. There was a slight Southern intonation in his voice. Tessa knew who it was.

"Is that PJ?"

Silence.

"Hello? Are you there? PJ, it is you, isn't it?"

"Who's that?"

"Tessa Fitzgerald."

"Who?"

What was she supposed to say? *You remember, the woman who stopped for coffee and donuts a month or so ago and wound up getting laid by you in the kitchen* . . . They'd barely said more than a couple of sentences to each other.

"I came to see you when you were in Jack Fern's apartment—" she began tentatively.

"Yeah, yeah, yeah, I know who you are," he interrupted suddenly. "Listen, where's Honey?"

"Out shopping."

"Figures. I've been trying to get hold of her for days. I have something very important to tell her but she won't return my calls."

"Join the club," said Tessa. "Is there anything I can pass on to her?"

"No, I'll catch up with her even if I have to come round there and break into her suite. Listen, how are you? I'd like to see you."

Tessa was caught off guard. She knew that she wanted to see him too, but until that moment she hadn't realized just how much.

"Come on over now," she suggested, "that way you can wait for Honey."

"No, I want to see you on your own. Where do you live?

Near Jack Fern, isn't it? Why don't I come over to your place later on tonight?"

"I could always come to you." A picture of Larry's disgruntled face loomed in front of her eyes.

"No. That won't work. I'll have to come to you. Give me the address. Around nine?"

Tessa waited for another hour, but Honey never showed up. To her immense relief, Larry had left a note saying he'd gone to see his mother in Jersey City and wouldn't be back till the next day. She wondered whether PJ would expect her to feed him. He hadn't said anything about it. She decided to make a salad and put it in the fridge. That way if she was hungry she could get it out and if he said nothing, Larry could eat it tomorrow.

She'd had two baths and a shower by the time PJ finally arrived. The waiting had been interminable. She couldn't decide what to wear and when the doorbell did ring her hair was still wet.

"I'll dry it for you," he said immediately, picking up a strand and sniffing it. "Hmmmm, I love the smell of freshly washed hair."

She went into the kitchen to get him a drink and he followed her, creeping up behind her and putting his hands on her waist. She parted her lips and they stayed locked together, swaying slightly as he kissed her, for several minutes.

"It's good to see you again," he told her as he released her and he sounded like he meant it. "Tell me, why are you seeing Honey?"

"I'm interviewing her."

"You're a journalist?"

"Yes," said Tessa simply, wondering at the fact that they had said so little to each other on their two previous meetings that he didn't even know what her work was. But then now she knew he wasn't Jack Fern she didn't know about him either.

"What about you? What do you do?"

But he ignored the question and went straight on. "Honey's acting insane. Last time I saw her she was in one hell of a state wanting to know where my mother was. Well, I don't know where Callie is either but I just learned what she was up to around seventeen years ago. Go get your hairdryer and I'll tell you about it."

He followed her into the bedroom and began to towel dry her hair, massaging her head as he talked: "I've just been down to my folks' place. They have this big old plantation down in Mississippi. Not a working plantation, just a big house and land. Can you hear me down there?"

Tessa nodded underneath the towel. She was holding her breath, desperate for him to go on. She had no idea why he had chosen to confide in her in this way, but she had no intention of stopping him. Of course, anything he told her might help with her story, might fill in the vital missing links in Honey's background. She told herself that this was why she was seeing him, it had nothing whatsoever to do with the way in which her body was responding to his fingers stroking her head through the towel.

"So anyway, I went down there to see if I could find out what had happened to my mother. My father just died as you must know, and I know it sounds crazy but my mother has literally dropped off the face of the earth—or off the face of America—as far as I can make out. Needless to say, she wasn't down at *Coinchenier* . . ."

"Was anyone there or was the place empty?" Tessa mumbled.

"Queenie was there. Poor old Queenie. She was our cook, big black lady riddled with fantasies. She's convinced my mother's about to come home, but it sounds like she's been expecting her every day since she left."

"Is that what you wanted to tell Honey? About Queenie?"

"No. I wanted to tell her what Queenie told me. Apparently, when my mamma was last there she brought a baby with her."

"And Honey . . ."

"Honey had a baby seventeen years ago. You must have heard about it; she was told it was dead. At least that's what my father told her, but around then Callie goes and shows up at *Coinchenier* with a baby. It all fits and I've been trying to tell her this for days but she won't speak to me. I can't figure it out. Anyway, it's not your problem. Look, your hair's dry. Now I have to comb it out for you."

"You should have done that before you started drying it. It'll be in a terrible tangle by now. PJ, why are you here?" She turned her face to look up into his.

"You know," he whispered. "I wanted to see you again. You

know what we have together. I don't have to tell you. You love
it too."

He was undressing himself now, unzipping his jeans and
stepping out of them.

"Is that all?" she asked.

"No, but it's a start and we're lucky to have found each
other, to be able to enjoy each other. Now, take your clothes off
before I rip them apart . . ."

He made love to her very slowly. She climaxed several times
before he actually entered her and once again—as he had at the
end of their donut session—he told her he loved her as he
exploded inside her. She did not take it seriously, she put it
down to the heat of the moment but she knew that she treasured those words and now, hearing them for the second time,
she treasured the fact that they had come from him. She
brought him the salad and they ate it in bed watching Johnny
Carson.

And they talked.

"There's something I want to tell you about me," he said
suddenly, turning down the sound with the remote control and
gathering her into his arms. Her heart pounded not because she
was in any way frightened by what he might tell her, but in case
he changed his mind and postponed his revelation or never told
her at all. She wanted to know everything there was to know
about him, but she knew she had to let him tell her in his own
time.

He told her about his disguises and to his utmost surprise
and relief she dismissed them as unimportant, watching him
carefully as she did so for fear of offending him. She didn't
want him to feel his confiding in her was unimportant, but she
didn't want him to see she thought his behavior was in any way
bizarre.

"You think you're so special?" she laughed, "you think
you're the only one? Everyone puts on disguises in some way.
What do you think power dressing is all about? Do you think
every woman sitting in her office shoulder-padded up to the
nines feels as confident inside as she looks on the outside? Who
cares if you couldn't let go of the dressing-up box—sounds like
fun to me. Kid's stuff, sure, but you must promise me never,
never to let go of the child inside you. It's important for everybody to keep that part alive in them. Some people aren't even

lucky enough to recognize it in the first place, that's why
they're not much fun to be with. So don't worry about these
wretched disguises, just so long as *I'm* getting the real you."

"You always have had the real me," he told her, realizing it
was true, that even on their first meeting he had felt so relaxed
with her he had been himself (without actually telling he wasn't
Jack Fern)—that was what had made him see, later, that she
was different.

Afterward she slept in his arms, waking once, twice and even
a third time as dawn broke to succumb to his caressing hands
and the inevitable passion which followed. She knew very little
about him, but she had entrusted her body to him without a
second thought and now, she thought, if he would let her, she
would try and give him the rest of her.

"Honey for you today?" said a bored voice and a spray of scent
was squirted at her.

"Please don't do that without asking first," said Tessa in her
best tight-arsed Brit voice.

"Sorry, ma'am. *Would you care for some* Honey *today*?" said
the assistant and promptly sprayed her again. Tessa wiped her
hand across her neck and looked at the huge poster of Honey
Winslow on the counter.

Tessa was in Bloomingdale's, cutting through the store from
Third Avenue to Lexington on her way to another session with
Honey at the Sherry.

"Tell her to be waiting for me this time . . ." Tessa told the
startled assistant, jerking her thumb at the poster.

"No! It *can't* be! Are you Tessa Fitzgerald?" a voice behind
her said. Tessa wheeled round. The woman standing in front of
her was smiling. She was attractive in a rather nondescript sort
of way, brown hair, brown eyes, medium height, fairly conventional clothes.

"It was the English accent and the fact that you're clearly on
your way to see Honey Winslow. Oh, forgive me. I'm Beatrice
Anderson." She held out her hand. Tessa looked blank.

"Doodle. From PIA," said the woman. "We've spoken on
the telephone."

Tessa stiffened. Doodle. Did she know about her and Jack?
Apparently not.

"Look, are you in a hurry to see Honey? Why not come and

have lunch with me. We can go around the corner. You know Kaplan's?"

"Kaplan's?"

"Kaplan's, it's a delicatessen. There's a chain of 'em. Let's go to Kaplan's at the Delmonico, on 59th Street right by Park Avenue."

"Yes, fine," said Tessa, resigned to eating yet another early lunch. Why did Americans always have to eat lunch at twelve-thirty? No one met for lunch before one o'clock in London.

Kaplan's was a noisy place doing a roaring lunchtime trade. There was a line waiting at the entrance for take-out food from the long counter just inside the door.

"Listen, have a corned beef sandwich or a corned beef and pastrami, nothing like it," Doodle told her once they were seated inside.

"Yes, thank you, lovely."

"Hey, Miss!" She grabbed a passing waitress. "Two CB rye —Tessa, you want pickles? Me neither, hold the pickles. That's it, thank you. Now, Tessa, here's the thing. I want to talk to you. In fact I was going to try and reach you. There's a thing or two been on my mind. Forgive me for asking, but do you and Jack have something going?"

"No, honestly. Absolutely nothing. *Please* don't think—"

"OK, OK," Doodle interrupted her, "it's just that I've moved out, did you know that? Yes. We weren't right together, not like that anyway. We've been friends for a long time, working together and stuff and I thought it might work. He's a wonderful man, don't get me wrong, but I'm not strong enough for him. I irritated him, I could tell. I was always waiting for him to come home and entertain me when all the time he wanted for me to be more independent. I'm not like I seem to be at the agency. It's easy to appear full of confidence when you're handling *other* folks' affairs. It's when it comes to handling your own it gets scary, you know what I mean?

"But, see, he, Jack, he talks in his sleep and he used to say your name. I never dared ask him about it. I always felt I was invading his privacy by listening to him. But he did say your name and not only when he was sleeping. He talked about you quite a lot when he was awake too. It's just I think he likes you, Tessa. He's a private kind of guy underneath, it's hard to know what he's really thinking. I mean, none of us know anything

about him, where he was born, where his folks are, stuff like
that. But I guess you're smart enough to have guessed what you
see on the surface isn't how he really is. Yet when he talks
about you he sounds different. He likes you, Tessa, I thought
you'd like to know that and well, like I said, I don't live with
him anymore."

Tessa felt awful. The truth was she had not even thought of
Jack Fern in days. PJ was right. They had something going
between them, she and PJ, which she had never had with Jack.
Poor Jack. Underneath that take-charge exterior he was clearly
an insecure mess.

"Look, Doodle, I mean Beatrice, you might as well know
that I'm not really with him anymore either. Not that I was for
very long."

"Does he know that?"

"No, I mean, I haven't seen him this week and I'm not sure
I . . ."

"You don't want to go on with it?"

"It's just . . . I don't see any point . . ."

"Any particular reason?"

"No, of course not, it's just . . ."

"He comes too fast, right?"

Tessa was completely taken aback. Here was someone she'd
only met half an hour earlier asking her a direct question about
her sex life.

"Well, am I right or not?" Doodle was grinning in such a
disarming way it was hard not to respond.

"Well, since you put it like that, yes."

Doodle clapped her hands. "I knew it! Poor old Jack. Don't
get me wrong. I like the guy, but my guess is that it's the story
of his life. He's so busy thinking of number one all the time. He
may fool you into thinking he's concerned about your well-
being, but don't you believe it for a second. That boy's living in
the Me Generation, me, me, me all the time."

"Did you have the same problem with him?" Tessa couldn't
resist asking.

"Every single night. Thing is I enjoyed the guy's company, I
liked going out with him, movies, dinners, that sort of stuff. I
never had someone like him before, so I kidded myself what
was happening in the bedroom didn't matter. But then he
started coming home later and later and I knew it wasn't going

to work. Nothing to do with you, Tessa, even if he was seeing you at the same time. I just got fed up with sitting home every night. So, I moved out. Let's talk about something else. Tell me how you're getting on with Honey Winslow. She's quite a handful, I hear."

Tessa was surprised how much she enjoyed her lunch. Doodle was as direct in her own way as Honey, but she was considerate with it. She knew how to listen. Tessa realized she was the first person with whom she had been able to let rip and entertain with her stories about Honey and when they'd finished lunch, Tessa made a date to go and look at the library shots of Honey Winslow which Doodle told her were stashed away in their hundreds at PIA.

As they stood up to leave she saw that the paper tablecloth covering their table was almost obliterated by scribbles. Doodle had been hard at work throughout the meal.

Fifteen minutes later she was hurrying through the revolving doors of the Sherry and into the lobby. Honey would probably be fuming by now, she was so late. Just as she was about to turn right to the elevators a figure at the reception desk caught her eye.

PJ! He had his back to her, was deep in conversation with the man on the desk.

She called out, overjoyed to see him. "PJ!"

He didn't turn round.

"PJ," she cried, "it's me, Tessa." The man on the desk tried to draw his attention to Tessa, but he looked swiftly over his shoulder and down again.

"PJ. For God's sake, can't you hear me? It's Tessa."

By now everyone in the lobby had turned to look at her. Except PJ who completely ignored her.

Shaken, Tessa rode up in the elevator to the 14th Floor where a seething Honey was waiting for her. Tessa had been going to tell her all about PJ's visit to *Coinchenier*, but now she couldn't bring herself to even mention his name.

Only last night he had told her he loved her. Now he was acting as if she didn't exist.

CHAPTER 27

Luc Chenier was in a state of shock. He had been ever since his arrival in New York the day before.

He grasped the address given to him by the man on the desk at the Sherry and stumbled out through the revolving doors onto Fifth Avenue, impervious to Tessa's cries behind him.

How was he to know he was the image of his father? Until yesterday he had not even known who his father was and he still had no idea who he looked like.

It had come as a shock when Anita de la Salle had started to tell him who he really was thirty-eight thousand feet above the Atlantic Ocean. He had just finished watching the movie—a movie! in the air!—and was beginning to feel a little drowsy when Anita's words rendered him fully alert in a second.

"Luc, I have to talk to you. Are you listening to me? That woman at the Pré Catalan, the one you were dancing with when I interrupted, she was your mother."

He hadn't been able to bring himself to turn and look at her, had hoped that if he kept absolutely still she'd tell him it was just one of her little jokes, *silly me*!

But she went on, brushing away the stewardess when she

came to offer them more coffee: "I've been thinking about this for weeks. It's really not for me to tell you but if I don't, I don't know who else will and you have a right to know. Callie, your *Tantie* as you call her, well, I already told you she's your grandmother. She brought you over to France when you were just a tiny baby. I don't know why she never told you the truth, but when she finds out what I've done she'll probably never speak to me again. Not that we've been exactly close all these years. We both grew up in New Orleans, you see, and that's why I'm taking you there with me now. We're going to track down Callie and find out what's going on and what she plans to do with you now your grandfather's dead."

"My grandfather?"

"Oh, yes, silly me, you don't even know about him, do you? He was Perry Jay Duboise, Cosmetics King of the South, founder of the *Bayou Beauty* empire, creator of *Honey* perfume . . ."

"Honey," breathed Luc, "the Honey-witch is my mother . . ."

"What's that? He called it after your mother, Honey Winslow, the woman you danced with . . ."

"But who was my father?"

"Perry Jay Duboise was married to Callie and they had a son, Philippe, and he was your father . . ."

"And Honey Winslow was his wife?"

"Well, no, I'm sorry to say she wasn't . . ."

"But why did my grand—" he stumbled over the word, "—mother take me away from my mother?"

"I'm not sure, *mon chéri*. If I knew I'd tell you, believe me. That's why we're going to New Orleans to get some answers."

"And your cousin Raoul?"

"Raoul! Bah! If he hasn't died of drink by now it'll be a miracle but no, he's not the reason I'm going back. I'm returning to New Orleans for your sake, Luc . . ."

"You lied to Uncle Thierry?"

Anita made a moue. "It won't be the first time. And it's in a good cause. You're important to me, Luc darling. I care about you. I've had no children of my own and now for the first time I have a chance to do something for someone else's. You are going to discover so much about yourself in such a short space of time and I want to be with you when you do to help you

come to terms with it all. Callie must have known you couldn't
stay hidden down in the Lot forever, yet somehow I don't trust
her to introduce you to your family properly. It's all going to
come as a tremendous shock to you, Luc . . ."

"So I'm American through and through?"

"Well, yes, I suppose that's something to start with . . . I
don't know your family other than Callie, otherwise I'd tell you
about them. But I do know Teddy Lenoir and I'm going to take
you to him . . ."

"Teddy Lenoir?"

"He's Callie's lawyer—if he's still alive. He'll advise me what
to do with you . . ."

And in the meantime they had a day's stop-over in New
York before taking the train to New Orleans. The awesome
beauty of the Manhattan skyline was lost on Luc. New York
was such a far cry from the dignified splendor of Paris and the
wild countryside of the Lot that he felt he had been catapulted
into a fantasy and what Anita had told him about his background only served to embellish it. He was an American but he
could barely understand a word these people said. He thrust
the piece of paper into the hand of a passer-by and recoiled
when the man rattled off a couple of sentences.

"You foreign?" Luc nodded. "Well, see, you're on Fifth and
you want to get to Sixth. Over there. Next block. Simple." He
pointed and Luc hurried off, murmuring thanks over his shoulder.

He had asked at the desk for the name of a good publisher,
preferably one close by. Now he entered a huge building and
once again flapped his piece of paper in front of the security
man.

"Seventeenth Floor," snapped the man without even bothering to take his cigarette out of his mouth.

Riding up, terrified by the swaying car, Luc clutched Elliott's
manuscript to his chest like a lifebelt. When he arrived at the
17th floor he ran out of the elevator and deposited the box in
front of a startled receptionist without a word, disappearing
before she had barely a chance to register him.

Going down to the street again, he found he could not help
but be convinced that whoever his official next of kin might be,
Elliott Fitzgerald and Anita de la Salle were, in their own way,
his real parents.

Alphonse Lenoir walked quickly to his special place in Central Park and bent down to scrape away at the earth. Before long he uncovered his shrine, the tiny altar at which he worshiped Honey Winslow. On it stood a bottle of *Honey* perfume and, performing the ritual he now carried out every evening, he anointed himself and began to pray. He sensed that Honey was at the start of something momentous in her life and wanted to be sure that his prayers would protect her from the dangers which might lie in wait along her path to success. He was getting closer now, closer to that moment when he would be able to contact her. Meanwhile, each time he saw her he would protect her the only way he knew how.

He buried his shrine and made his way back through the park to Fifth Avenue. From there he took a cab to the apartment in Yorkville which Teddy had bought for him, turned on the television and wondered if they would hang Honey's picture in Times Square again if her new project was a hit. He was tired of having to worship alone.

Honey was in the midst of preparing for the launch of a brand new fragrance. Only this was different. It was *Bayou Beauty*'s first ever fragrance for men and they had finally come up with a name for it.

Money.

She had originally conceived the notion of producing a scent for men soon after she had taken over the running of *Bayou Beauty.* Ever since then she had been developing it and progress had been made in almost record time. Honey knew that it invariably took between six and eighteen months from first consultation to delivery of the final product. First she had had to find her "nose" and brief him on the impression she wanted her particular brand of scent to project and the taste or image of themselves to which its prospective buyers would aspire.

Honey had spoken of a blend of *power* and *success* and *elegance* and *exclusivity* and *old money* and a *good cigar* and *fine wines* and *young men whose dreams can come true* and the "nose" had gone to work in the silence of his laboratory, juggling with as many as two thousand natural scents and three thousand synthetics, daring at times to mix up to two hundred and fifty components in one scent.

And so it had been made in record time, in under six months and even then it was not ready. It had still to go to the factory where it would macerate for up to two months in stainless steel vats filled with alcohol. During her trip to France for Sylvie Vauniashevsky's eighteenth birthday party, Honey had found time to visit the factories of Christian Dior Parfums near Orléans where she had been deeply envious of the forty-odd pure copper vats they had succeeded in preserving.

And then she had had to come up with a name. And it was when she started to say to herself over and over again *Honey* and . . . *Honey* and . . . that she inevitably arrived at *Honey* and *money*! *Honey* for Her and *Money* for Him. She worried for a while that it would seem a little vulgar to some people, but soon dismissed the thought. It's realistic. It's what everybody in America wants. It'll lend itself to a perfect selling slogan: MONEY—EVERY MAN'S AMERICAN DREAM. Might cause a few worries in Export, but let them handle it when the time came . . .

The bottle and the launch itself were going to be all important. Sitting at her desk she surveyed an array of polystyrene models laid out in front of her. Originally everyone had been sold on the idea of having the bottle the oblong shape of the dollar—but eventually that had begun to pall, too obvious.

Honey found herself returning more and more to the delicate, simple packaging of *Honey* with its fresh, country-girl yet sophisticated image. The *Honey* bottle was a little round ball filled with the honey-colored perfume and topped with an exquisite little gold-splattered stopper in the shape of a bee. Honey realized she wanted *Money* to stand beside *Honey*, to complement it, to be linked with it. She wanted to see *Money* in a little gold nugget of a bottle, the stopper for which would not be the fragile little bumble-bee but a strong, powerful golden eagle reminiscent of the double eagle twenty-dollar coin.

Honey knew that this was exactly the sort of thing she ought to be telling Tessa about. For the Englishwoman to be able to reveal Honey's plans for a brand new fragrance would be something of a coup. Yet at the same time Honey knew that this was not the sort of thing Tessa wanted to write about her and she was wary of her, frightened Tessa would force her to bring her past too sharply into focus. Honey felt that for the first time she was doing just fine with her life and she wasn't about to do

anything which might rock the boat. Not even if it meant post-
poning an investigation into the identity of that boy she'd met
in Paris.

OK, so maybe she was behaving like an ostrich, pretending
he didn't exist, but it wasn't as if she was the motherly type and
even if he did turn out to be her son what on earth would she
do with him? No, her best plan right now was to ignore Tessa
Fitzgerald, ignore PJ's telephone messages, get on with the
Money launch and hope that the skeletons rattling around in
her past would quieten down.

So when the telephone rang two minutes later, she ignored
that too and let them take a message downstairs. She was more
than a little miffed when they told her the message was not for
her but for Tessa. Jack Fern wanted her to call him.

Jack Fern. Good-looking, take-charge kinda guy. All-American guy, just what she needed to help her get *Money* off the
ground. She'd have him photograph the entire campaign.
Quickly, she dialed PIA's number and delivered her command
for him to be at her suite at the Sherry in forty-five minutes.

He arrived with his camera and some lighting equipment and
Honey laughed to herself. He obviously thought she wanted her
picture taken. Well, why not? It'd been quite a while since she'd
played model. It would be fun to pretend for a moment or two.

They exchanged greetings, told each other how good they
looked, how wonderful it was to see each other again and
Honey poured him a cup of coffee.

"You want anything special?" he asked. "They told me to
come right over and there was talk of booking a studio so I
thought you must want some shots right away. Lucky I was
free. Things are pretty hectic these days."

Honey took on board his attempt to tell her how successful
he was, ignored it and told him: "It's not as if my hair and
make-up are fixed for a full-scale session . . ."

"So you just want something natural. Well, if you could just
step over to the window so I can see you better. Now, muss
your hair a little, that's it . . ."

Taking charge again, thought Honey. Well, let him. It was
nice to hand over the reins to someone else for a second. The
window was open and the slight breeze lifted her hair away
from her face. For a split second she was back at the height of

her modeling career in the Sixties, harsh studio lights glaring down on her, the wind machine blowing in her face sending her long blonde hair streaming out behind her, a skimpy little dress riding up her thighs, loud music with a pulsating beat making her want to *move*—this way, that way, head back, head forward, sultry pout, roaring laughter, come hither gaze, hands on hips, arms folded, finger resting against cheek, legs wide apart, legs crossed, legs kicked high, legs, legs, legs, going on forever and always the man behind the camera calling to her, making her laugh, flirting with her, seducing her with his lens . . . oh, how she missed it.

Snap out of it! She had work to do. Today's work.

"Sorry, Jack. No pictures, at least not of me." And before she got carried away with more trips down memory lane she plunged straight into outlining her plans for *Money,* ending with: "The first thing we have to do is find a face to launch the campaign, someone who—"

"Someone who will do for *Money* what you did for *Honey,*" Jack finished for her.

"Exactly! You got it! Someone young, I think it should be. They'll be expecting us to aim it at the already successful man, someone a little older, but I want *Money* to be a mass-produced fragrance, appealing right across the board so that a kid who hopes he will be somebody someday will buy it too."

She was close to him now, breathing fast in her excitement.

"I could have gone to an ad agency first, but I want to go to them with the look already in place, telling them exactly what I want to say. Will you help me, Jack? Will you help me find the right look, the right face, and photograph it for me?"

He didn't need to say yes. Her excitement was infectious and he found himself caught up in it. He might have a shot at the big time with this one. If he pulled this off he'd be a Name. He'd be in demand but able to call the shots. He'd be able to do just one or two major commercial jobs a year and spend the rest of the time on his *art*, gathering material for his exhibition . . .

All of a sudden he wanted Honey Winslow. She had *success* written all over her and he wanted some of it to rub off on him. Literally. He reached out and grabbed her arm roughly above the elbow, pulling her to him.

Her eyes gleamed into his, encouraging him.

"Harder!" she breathed.

Jack couldn't believe his ears. "Like this?" He gripped her other arm and shook her, mauling one of her breasts, pushing her down onto the couch.

"Is that the best you can do?" Honey goaded him, laughing in his face.

"What I can do is to fuck your brains out," shouted Jack. If Tessa had been there she could have told Honey exactly how long that would take.

But Tessa wasn't there and Honey hadn't heard anything so exciting in quite some time. She was ready for him, feeling his hands roughly pushing up her skirt, ripping her tights. It seemed Jack was interested in being a take-charge kind of guy in every department and in this particular instance she was happy to let him go right ahead. In fact, if he didn't enter her soon she was going to come on the spot, so randy was she after such a long lull in her sex life.

So whereas Jack left Tessa feeling frustrated and unsatisfied, when he plunged violently into Honey, shouting at her that he was going to fuck her till she fell apart, she climaxed so quickly herself that she never noticed that it was all over for him seconds before. Not that she would have worried if it hadn't been. The fact that she was satisfied was all that mattered.

"That was so wonderful, baby," Jack murmured and Honey purred, taking it as a genuine compliment rather than the token banality it really was.

"All in a day's work," she told him, "of course, now I can expect you to give the *Money* campaign your extra special attention, can't I?"

CHAPTER 28

PJ's disguises were a thing of the past, dead—but not yet buried. There still lingered within him a guilty hankering after the pulp horror-novel world his mother had created at *Coinchenier* and the disguises were part of that world. He knew he had to find one last fantasy role to play, some way in which he could go out in style and then leave it all behind him.

One night it hit him. For some time he had been thinking it was time he did a feature in *Eros* on the notorious night club, Studio 54, about the people who went there and the depraved behavior that went on if you knew where to look for it. He'd been there from time to time, but this evening he had decided to go in disguise. The ultimate disguise, quite outrageous, if he stood well back Steve Rubell would let him through the door without a second thought.

Tonight he was going to be Honey Winslow.

It took him half an hour to get the hair right and the clothes. Then another forty-five minutes for the make-up. He *had* to get that right, do her proud. He looked at himself in the mirror. Almost there. But there was something missing. Wandering back into the bedroom he flicked through an old magazine till he found a photo of her.

Her beauty spot! He'd forgotten her beauty spot.

Whistling once more to himself he picked up a black eyeliner pencil and applied the finishing touch.

Then he let himself out of the apartment and rode the freight elevator down to the street.

Damn! It was raining. He'd never get a cab and his dress would be ruined.

Not for the first time since leaving Jack Fern's apartment in such a hurry he wished he had rented somewhere farther up-town. It was an original idea renting a huge loft down in SoHo but when it came to finding cabs in the rain it was a nightmare.

He tripped his way along the sidewalk in his high heels. He had to pause after only a few steps, stand on one leg like a heron and tip the water out of his shoes and it was then that he heard a voice call softly behind him.

"Honey?"

PJ turned, but could see no one.

"Honey?" called the voice again. "This rain's terrible. What do you say we shelter in the alleyway here? When it stops we can share a cab. What do you say?" The voice was coming out of a dark alley to his left. PJ was intrigued. Did this man really think he was Honey? Had he actually fooled someone already? He should have asked himself what a friend of Honey's would be doing lurking around SoHo streets in the rain, but he was too wound up with excitement that his disguise had worked so well.

He ventured tentatively into the alleyway. The game would be up once he got close enough, but it would be fun to play it as far as he could.

They were almost face to face now, but he still couldn't see the man in the shadows. PJ felt a little uneasy. Was this a mugger? Should he make a run for it? But then again the man whispered: "Honey? Beautiful Honey? Show me your beauty spot."

"Oh, come *on*," said PJ, laughing. "Did I really fool you? Who are you anyway? Did you *really* think I was Honey, was it the beauty spot that fooled you, here, take a look at it!"

He turned his cheek with the beauty spot toward the man.

Too late he tried to duck and felt the point of the blade plunge into his cheek.

PJ's thoughts began to rush through his mind like a tape being wound on fast forward. This man was trying to kill him. There was a murderer in town killing women; his disguise as Honey Winslow had nearly got himself killed. Might still . . . the man was getting ready to slash him again, the glint of the blade hovering above him propelled him into action.

The fact that the knife was high above him could only mean one thing: his attacker was tall. PJ couldn't see him clearly, but he could make out a skinny frame lurching toward him. A clumsy movement. PJ was lithe and wiry. He dodged the blade and dived for the man's legs, bringing him down. He leapt back onto his feet and brought his heel down on the man's wrist until he released the knife. PJ kicked the knife away, registering that it came to rest in a puddle of rain up the alley.

Now, taking full advantage of his stiletto heels, he ground them into his attacker's kidneys until the man groaned in desperation, pleading for mercy.

"What kind of a woman are you? Stop! Please. I won't move, I swear it."

"You think I'm going to buy that? Take me for an idiot? HEY, YOU!" PJ called to a figure passing at the end of the alley. "Call the cops, will ya? I need help here."

"Sure thing," yelled back the passer-by, racing off with a backward glance.

"You're a man," muttered the man on the ground.

"Shut up. Don't move or I'll kick your face in." PJ leaned down. "Look at me, will ya? Look over here so I can see the kind of face I'm gonna kick the shit out of if you move . . . JESUS CHRIST!"

The man turned his head and looked at PJ, his face illuminated for a second by the moonlight.

"Alphonse!"

"If you know me all of a sudden, why are you beating me up?" A whining tone had entered his voice.

"Because you tried to slash me to ribbons. And you know me. It's PJ. PJ Duboise."

"Nnnnnooo . . ." stammered Alphonse, "you're Hhhh-honey. You look like Honey Wiiii . . . nnnslow."

"True," muttered PJ. "Were you trying to kill Honey?"

"Not kill her." Alphonse tried to shake his head. "I was worshiping her! And now you're dressed as Honey. That's mighty peculiar." He began to cry.

"Everything's mighty peculiar, Alphonse," PJ said grimly.

Later, down at the Precinct, PJ wished his father were alive for the first time since the old man had died. For a start he needed someone to help him explain to the cops exactly why he was dressed not only as a woman, but as the prime target of the Beauty Spot murderer. His father would have ranted and raved about his being a no-good pansy, but at least he would have given him some identity. Meanwhile the cops were just taking him for a weirdo.

Alphonse didn't stop talking from the moment they hand-cuffed him. He raved on about Honey being some kind of deity. Only by killing her, he assured the cops gathered around, could he save her soul from the corruption he saw all around him. He had, he informed them confidentially, been able to recognize her by her holy symbol, a small black mark on her cheek, and every time he saw it he knew she had to be "saved." PJ listened in horror, recalling the vacant, faraway look on Alphonse's face when he had first known him, the sudden outburst of violence at Honey in the diner, the boy he had traveled with all over Europe. How could all this have been festering away inside his head? Was it Vietnam that had turned him into a maniac? Looking now at Alphonse calm and happy as he cheerfully justified the string of vicious murders which had been terrifying New York, PJ felt not disgust, but pity.

He tried to call Honey from the police station, but as usual she wouldn't take his call. He had to be content with the knowledge that Homicide would be paying her a visit at the Sherry to explain what had happened. There remained the question of Alphonse's bail. PJ knew there was only one person they could turn to for help, ironically the only person who might also know where Callie was.

With one last glance at Alphonse sitting smiling to himself in his cell, PJ told the police to get in touch with Theodore Lenoir in New Orleans.

Theodore Auguste Panama Lenoir was nearly eighty years old yet he still lived in the same house in the French Quarter of New Orleans in which he had been born. Indeed, he was not much younger than the house itself, a mansion which had been built in the 1820s, entered through a wide carriage drive paved with flagstones leading to a plant-filled courtyard with a three-tiered fountain.

Teddy Lenoir loved that courtyard. Most of the rooms on the ground floor of the house opened onto it and, every morning, he would throw open the French windows and stand for a moment or two listening to the soothing sound of the water cascading down the fountain.

Then, wrapped in his robe, he would lift a delicate little satinwood table out into the courtyard and, providing the weather was not inclement, eat his breakfast there.

His *petit déjeuner* was always the same: strong hot chicory *café au lait* and *beignets,* sprinkled liberally with powdered sugar. He prepared it himself. He knew at his advanced age he ought to have a live-in housekeeper, but the thought of it filled him with gloom. He was still in complete command of all his faculties to a degree which astounded his friends and former associates. Indeed, most of them regarded him as an extremely wily old fox and not someone to be crossed under any circumstances.

He had never married. He had loved one woman, but she had married another and left Teddy to pick up that man's pieces. He'd had to act as the man's legal counsel to get him paroled. He'd done it for Callie, the second worst mistake of his life. The worst had come not long before when she had called upon him to help the cad weasel out of a manslaughter charge. But it was not until he had gone to visit her in the institution where she was incarcerated by her monster of a husband that he had realized to his eternal sorrow that really she was destined for such a place.

He had asked her when she wanted to be released, told her that Perry Jay had no right to keep her there, that she could walk out any day she wanted, he could arrange it. And she had just looked at him and told him he didn't understand: didn't he realize that Perry Jay would come and get her himself and that if he had put her in the institution then she *deserved* to be there? She had been a terrible mother; was Teddy so dumb he couldn't see that? She had committed a crime against her son, she deserved to be where she was.

Callie might consult Teddy Lenoir about legal matters and

take advice from him on certain issues, but he had no idea about her sexual activities and knew nothing of her estrangement from PJ or the reason for it. Nor did he know about her suicide attempt.

All Teddy had seen before him was a woman in a pitiful situation and no reason for it. And a woman who did not want his help in anything which might bring her closer to him, Teddy Lenoir.

Teddy had withdrawn, making a silent vow to himself that if ever she needed his help in the future he would be there to give it.

When, in 1960, she had called him in the middle of the night from *Coinchenier* to tell him that she was moving to France and taking her grandson with her, he had been overjoyed. It meant that he would not see her for quite some time, but it meant also that she was separating from that monster Duboise. No good had come of that marriage. How Callie must have suffered. How he had longed to go to her in France and comfort her. But he had waited, hoping that one day she would summon him of her own accord. And once again he had waited too long. He had not heard from her in years and while he knew he ought to contact her and tell her about the contents of Perry Jay's will, somehow he couldn't bring himself to do it over the telephone. He'd had an exhausting time when that scoundrel Duboise had died. Everyone had wanted to know where Callie was, but he'd insisted she was locked up at *Coinchenier*, grieving, shunning the public eye. He'd eventually played the protective lawyer part to the hilt, and eventually they'd swallowed his story and gone away. But he had to tell her.

He had decided he was going to do it personally. He knew where she was, living in some godforsaken isolated part of south-west France, and very soon now he would take himself off down there and pay her a surprise visit, break the news to her gently.

He bit into a *beignet* and swore under his breath as he heard the telephone begin to ring, shattering his early morning reverie. How could anyone be so ill-mannered as to ring at such an hour? It must be urgent.

Tightening his robe around him, he stepped nimbly across the courtyard, through the French windows and into his library.

But he never answered his telephone.

Callie Chenier stood beside it, a crazed look on her face, her arm raised high above her head, her fist clutching a carving knife.

"If you don't tell me," she hissed, *"right now* where I can find Honey Winslow I'm going to thrust this blade into your heart just like my daddy killed my Uncle Jules. . . ."

CHAPTER 29

For some time now Jack Fern had been at his wits' end. He had a distinct image in his mind of the type of face he wanted for the *Money* campaign and it seemed that there wasn't a single model agency in Manhattan who could provide it. If it meant searching the country coast to coast he wasn't sure he was up to it.

And then, not less than twenty-four hours ago, he had glimpsed a figure going into the Sherry-Netherland Hotel as he came out of the Pierre where he had been having a drink with a rich Texas matron, whom Honey had promised he would photograph wearing her new *Winslowear* track suit.

From that moment on he had staked out the Sherry. One glimpse had told him it just might be worth it. And it was.

"STOP!"

He raced across Fifth Avenue waving his arms, dodging traffic, ignoring the menacing approach of an advancing cop.

He couldn't believe his eyes.

Coming out of the Sherry right in front of him was the boy he'd been stalking for the *Money* campaign.

His brief had been quite straightforward: everyone thinks

having a lot of money is just a dream. Let's take some pictures which show it can become a reality. Which meant he had to find a face for the *Money* campaign which the public could identify with, but which also looked expensive. A youthful face but a successful one. A confident face but not an arrogant one. A good-looking regular job who, because he was wearing it, looked like he had money. And this kid was a natural. There was something innately childlike about him. But he also looked urbane, sophisticated. Yet he did not look remotely threatening. Moreover he looked vulnerable. Successful but vulnerable. *I have everything but I need you too,* his face seemed to be saying, *I have* Money *but I want you to have it too!*

"*Qui êtes-vous?*" Luc, momentarily stunned, reverted to French without thinking.

"You're French? Even better. *Je suis Jack Fern, je suis photographe,* I'm a photographer. *Je veux vous employer pour les images d'un parfum pour les hommes,* you know? I want to take some pictures of you . . ."

"Ah, *non!*" said the boy, reacting violently, backing away as Jack got out his camera and quickly began to take pictures. "*Tante* Anita!" he called out to a small woman with dyed red hair who came tottering out of the Sherry in heels far too high for a woman of her advanced age. In direct contrast to the boy she smiled coquettishly at the camera until he took her firmly by the elbow and marshaled her into the yellow cab which the doorman had flagged down for them. Jack moved in close so that he could hear the destination the woman gave to the driver.

Jack's luck was in. Within seconds he was able to get another cab in which to follow the boy. Jack's driver lost them for a few minutes, but ultimately caught up with them after a mad dash across town at the station.

The boy was quick, ducking in and out of the station crowds far too nimbly for Jack to keep track of him. The older woman appeared to have disappeared until finally Jack caught sight of her trotting beside a porter pushing a mountain of luggage toward one of the gates.

In the end Jack was not able to speak to either of them but he did grab a few further shots of the boy as he raced after the woman onto the platform. And by the time the train had drawn out of the station Jack had managed to ascertain via a small bribe to the ticket collector that the couple were traveling to New Orleans.

Tessa was beginning to wonder if there was any point in continuing to get anything out of Honey Winslow. The last session a couple of days earlier had been a complete wash-out. Admittedly she had been fretting about the way PJ had ignored her downstairs in the lobby. She had even begun to wonder if he had been visiting Honey. Maybe they had had some kind of reunion, rekindled their teenage passion for each other and now he felt guilty about having started something with Tessa. Or was she just being paranoid? Surely if he had wanted to get something going again with Honey, he would have done it years ago. On the other hand, hadn't he said he'd been trying to reach her by telephone for days? Was that just an excuse?

And Honey was so uncommunicative all of a sudden. Tessa felt like calling it a day and going home to London. What was she doing here interviewing a former model? For an item which would probably only wind up as part of a much larger story. It wasn't even as if she could work her usual magic with this exasperating woman. There was clearly a good story lurking behind the scenes, but Honey Winslow was damned if she was going to let Tessa anywhere near it. And forget about the All-American candid, open, sunny personality. The real Honey Winslow was closed for business.

Tessa gave herself a mental slap on the wrist. What was the matter with her? What she had to do was to be much more aggressive with Honey, needle her, wear her down, chisel away until she got to the woman behind all the glossy exterior, the woman who had had a baby seventeen years ago, a baby she thought had died, a baby she believed she'd seen recently at a party in Paris. But, when at their last session Tessa had begun to ask her about it Honey had dismissed the subject altogether, refusing to talk about it. Well, this time she wouldn't get away with it. Tessa was going to take control of the entire session. This time she was going to get what she wanted.

It was in this positive frame of mind that she knocked boldly on the door of Honey's suite and without waiting for an answer, found it open and stepped inside. They had an appointment. Honey should be waiting for her.

But she wasn't. There was no one in the sitting room, the

kitchen or the bathroom. Tessa called out Honey's name but
there was no answer. That left the bedroom. Damn her,
thought Tessa furiously, if she's still lazing around in bed at
eleven o'clock in the morning when she knows she's got an
appointment with me I'll kill her. But as she flung open the
double doors leading to the bedroom telling Honey it was high
time she was up and . . . she stopped in mid-sentence.

Honey was indeed in bed or rather *on* the bed, stark naked,
lying on her back, draped across the peach satin sheets. Her
head was arched back, half hanging over the edge of the bed
and her blonde hair cascaded to the floor. Her long white neck
was partly hidden from view by the tousled head of the man
who was lying on top of her, gnawing at her earlobe.

The man's broad back looked familiar to Tessa and as his
buttocks began to heave up and down she began to close the
doors, but not before she had once again heard Jack Fern's
empty promise: "I'M GOING TO FUCK YOUR BRAINS
OUT."

Tessa sat down on the sofa in the sitting room and began to
laugh. She didn't think they'd seen her and, frankly, by now
she didn't care if they had. She was laughing with relief. Relief
that she need no longer worry about how she was going to
extricate herself from her relationship with Jack Fern—and to
think she had actually been sensitive enough to be concerned
about hurting his feelings! Relief too that while the possibility
of Honey two-timing Jack with PJ could not be ruled out,
somehow having witnessed the scene in the bedroom a few
seconds earlier, she felt confident that she was not.

She went to the front door of the suite, reached outside and
rang the bell. She hovered in the corridor for a few seconds
until the door opened a fraction and Honey's face peered round
it. She was in a robe and didn't bother to hide her disheveled
state as she beckoned Tessa inside.

"I've got a friend here," she said by way of explanation.
"You'll meet him in a second. No, wait, you know him. Jack
Fern. You guys are working together on my story, right? Well,
he's just been getting some pictures in the bedroom, you
know?" She winked at Tessa as she went into the kitchen to
make coffee.

Tessa was enjoying herself. Honey had no way of knowing
she had ever been to bed with Jack. When Jack came out of the

bedroom Honey would be crowing over her little coup, but when Jack saw Tessa it would be a different story for him.

"You were wonderful, baby, just sensational," he said as he opened the bedroom door from the inside.

"Was I?" asked Tessa innocently, sitting demurely on the sofa right in front of him as he entered the sitting room.

"Oh hi, Tess, good to see you." He marched over and gave her a smacking kiss on her left cheek.

"Darling!" cried Tessa, loud enough for Honey to hear in the kitchen, "why haven't you called? It was so *marvelous* the other night, I just can't tell you. I didn't know we had a date with Honey today, but it's just as well you're here, we can talk about what pictures are going to accompany my text. Jack, it's so good to see you." She managed to be clinging to him, pressing up against him when Honey stormed out of the kitchen with a tray of coffee and banged it down in front of them.

"Close working relationship, huh?" she spat before stomping off into the bedroom to get dressed.

Jack slumped down on the sofa. "Tessa, what do I tell you? OK, so I've been with her and it's not the first time. We just sort of hit it off the other day when I came to see her about a job she's hired me for. She's dynamite, Tessa."

"And I'm not?"

"Aw, come on, I didn't say that . . ."

"Oh, Jack, it's all right. I understand, I really do. Let's you and I just keep on working together. To be honest, if you can help me get through to her you'll be doing me a huge favor. I'm having a tough time trying to figure out what she's all about."

"To tell you the truth, Tessa, the same goes for me too. We hit it off in the sack and I suppose that means I've got to first base without a hitch, but beyond that it's a mystery. She's all talk, talk, talk about herself all the time, but it's all about her career."

It's probably why the two of you will get along fine together, thought Tessa. Neither of you is *really* interested in the other, you just mirror each other's huge egos. Well, go right ahead, be my guest.

"The sex is terrific," Jack confided and Tessa squirmed inwardly. She didn't want to know about this and it was a bit of a tacky thing to say to the person who, as far as she knew, had been his last lover. "But I didn't come here this morning to get laid. I came to show her these . . ."

He passed Tessa an envelope. Out of it she took a bunch of black and white prints which slipped out of her hand and fell all over the cushions on the sofa. As she retrieved them, Tessa started. They were pictures of PJ.

And yet? It *wasn't* PJ. This man was far younger, but he had the same penetrating dark eyes, the same straight nose, the same shaped head only somehow this boy's was finer, more fragile-looking. Then she picked up one of the young man's back view and realized that this was the person she'd seen in the lobby of the Sherry downstairs the other day, the man she'd mistaken for PJ. But it hadn't been him. She realized her mistake and her heart gave a lurch.

"Who is this?" she asked Jack.

"No idea, but he's a cinch for the *Money* campaign."

"What campaign?"

"Honey hasn't told you about it? She's launching this new fragrance for men and she's hired me to find the right face and photograph it. Could have taken me months, but I got lucky just two days later with this guy. He's perfect. I saw him right here in this hotel, couldn't believe my eyes."

"Is he still here?"

"That's just it. He left town, gone to New Orleans with some old biddy. I want to go down there and find him, but first I wanted Honey to see his face, confirm she shares my excitement about him. If she thinks he's right I'm going to go after him. But when I arrived this morning we got sidetracked—" He smirked and Tessa quickly changed the subject.

"How old was this boy? He looks quite young from these photographs."

"Oh, 'bout seventeen, eighteen."

Seventeen years old. The image of his father. She picked up one of the photographs and saw it immediately: the silver dolphin identity bracelet hanging off his wrist. She remembered PJ's words: *Honey had a baby exactly seventeen years ago. She was told it was dead. Callie shows up at* Coinchenier *with a baby. It all fits.*

It was PJ's baby. This boy was PJ's son, so like his father that she had thought it was PJ. "Do you have any idea who he is?" she asked Jack tentatively, unaware that Honey had come into the room and was standing right behind her staring down at the pictures.

"Sure. It was easy. I checked downstairs at Reception just now, showed them the pictures and they told me right away. Said the boy was French, arrived with his aunt, a Madame de la Salle."

"What name did he check in under?"

"Luc Chenier," said Jack and stared in amazement at Tessa as Honey, hearing the name, collapsed gracefully at their feet in a dead faint.

Later that same day, as dusk fell, Tessa was still sitting on the sofa in Honey's suite frantically scribbling notes, trying to make sense of all she had learned in the last seven hours.

Honey and Jack were on their way to New Orleans. Honey had fainted not only because of Luc Chenier, but because shortly before Jack's arrival that morning she had had a visit from the police. What Jack had not realized when she had flung herself into his arms on opening the door to him was that she had been seeking comfort, not sex.

Homicide had told her about an attempt on her life and of course she had reassured them that no such attempt had been made. She was quite safe and sound, they could see for themselves. Then they had explained that it had been someone else who had been attacked, someone disguised as her and gradually she had taken in the bizarre story of PJ's encounter with Alphonse Lenoir.

Honey was far more shaken by the news than she let anyone see. It was all very well for people to say she had had a lucky escape, that she was safe. She might be still alive, but in a way she *had* been murdered, many times over. It had been her face he had seen before him each time he had attacked all those other girls. He had wanted her dead and no doubt he still did. The police insisted that she must not blame herself in any way, that Alphonse Lenoir was a sick man, but it was when they told her that they would be contacting his guardian Theodore Lenoir in New Orleans about Alphonse that she knew she must get to Teddy Lenoir before they did. There must be no question of Alphonse being let out on bail. Teddy might be an old man by now, but he was no fool. When it came to Alphonse's defense he'd see to it that his ward had the best. The trial was doubtless way in the future, but until they locked up Alphonse for good Honey knew she would not rest easy.

And then there was Callie Chenier. Where was she? Without realizing what she was saying she had blurted out her fear to Jack and Tessa that that crazy old woman would reappear and claw back everything she, Honey, had fought for. Teddy Lenoir would know where Callie was and suddenly, now that her past seemed to have opened up, Honey made up her mind to go down to New Orleans. And, of course, she might find Luc Chenier down there, too. Honey had stared at the photos, stared at the silver dolphin bracelet, had continued to gaze for a long while at the pictures of the boy she knew now must be her son.

Honey had wanted to go alone to New Orleans, but Jack had insisted on accompanying her. For a fleeting moment Tessa had wondered whether she ought to go with them, but then another plan had begun to form in her mind. Now, closing her notebook, the beginnings of a story once again mapped out in detail (only this time she knew there would be a middle and an ending), she gathered up the few remaining pictures of Luc Chenier which Jack and Honey had left behind. Then she consulted her little black book, dialed a number and told PJ to expect her in twenty minutes. He had given her the number when he left Larry's apartment the last time they had seen each other.

After the ride up in the freight elevator to the ghostly SoHo loft she slipped inside when he opened the door and allowed herself to be taken wordlessly into his arms. She stroked the back of his head tenderly and cupped his cheeks in her hands, looking into his eyes.

He winced and, moving into the light, she saw with horror the scar on his cheek where Alphonse's blade had nicked him.

"I'm OK," he told her. "It's all over."

"No, it isn't," Tessa said and fumbled in her pocket for the photographs.

He would not look at her after he had studied them. After a while he tossed them across the room.

"You know who it is, don't you?" she asked him.

"I have a pretty good idea."

"His name's Luc Chenier. That's your mother's maiden name, isn't it? He arrived in America from France and now he's gone to—"

"I KNOW WHO HE IS!" he shouted at her, anger blazing in his eyes. Tessa thought for one second he would hit her.

"Then say so," she shouted back at him, "tell me who it is. Admit it. What are you hiding?"

"He's my son. I screwed Honey Winslow just once, just one time in my entire life and this is the result. Has to be. He looks just like me. For a second I thought it *was* me. Queenie knew what she was talking about. This must have been the baby my mamma brought back to *Coinchenier*. Well, maybe Honey will talk to me now, not that there's anything left to say. Have you seen her?"

Tessa explained what had happened, that Honey was on her way to New Orleans.

"There's only one person who can tell her what she wants to know and that's my mother and if Honey's got any sense, which she hasn't, she'll stay away from old Callie. I've steered clear of her for nearly twenty years."

"That's very sad, PJ." Tessa led him over to the futon mattress on the floor underneath a vast ten-foot window. They lay down together fully clothed and he held her to him. He began to talk softly.

"I'm glad you came. I've been meaning to call you since the attack, but I'm in one hell of a state and frankly, I wasn't sure how you'd react. I'm pretty screwed up, keep myself to myself. I've never trusted anyone, not 100 per cent at any rate. But you're different. I know that sounds like a cliché but it's the best I can do. I know next to nothing about you, but I sense that you're smart and you don't give out with a lot of bullshit like most women. The way we fucked the first time we met was sensational and I'll never forget it. Most women would have twittered away for hours beforehand, but you knew as soon as I did what would happen and you let it happen, naturally. Now, I want to know a bit about you, just a little, mind, we're going to have plenty of time to find out about each other."

"All I know now," said Tessa quietly, "is that I've never fallen in love before," and felt his arm tighten around her on the word *before*. "I don't know what it is about you either—and perhaps if I could define it it wouldn't be the same between us—but I have the feeling that I want to be with you, close to you, and I have no need of anyone else in the world. It's fact that we don't need to talk. We can just be together. There are times when I feel like a terrible misfit, that nobody else thinks the way I do and I'm an oddball who doesn't fit and somehow I sense that you feel that way sometimes too. I sense that in some way you're alone in the world, more so than I am even. You have a family, your father was a well-known public figure, yet somehow they were not your family. They did not care about you in the right way, in a way which you could feel . . ."

"And your family?" he asked gently and listened while she talked about Amy. When she described her father and the mystery surrounding him and his death, he nodded in understanding.

"No wonder you know about my being alone in the world," he said, gazing at her. "I've built up what I imagined to be an impenetrable defense mechanism with my disguises and my switches from apartment to apartment, nothing permanent, nothing to hurt me. You've crept in under that somehow, not to hurt me, I know, but you know what I'm like without my having to tell you and it must be because you too have a similar family: they're there and they're not there. At the end of the day you can't depend on them."

"And really we shouldn't have to," said Tessa, "we're no longer kids after all."

"We are, you know," said PJ. "Both of us. We're both of us looking for someone to take care of the other. It's not that we can't do it ourselves, we can, only too well. I run a successful magazine, you write, but for both of us that's not enough."

"Why haven't you ever got married?" she asked.

"It never came up. It was something other people did. I suppose I could use the old excuse that my parents' marriage was such a shambles but that wasn't it. You know, Tessa, most of the time I don't feel like a normal person, or what I imagine a normal person feels like. I'm approaching forty, yet I don't own a house, I'm not married, I don't have any kids, I don't look after my mother. I'm a drifter who's drifted into one place and stayed there. Talking of staying here, what about you? Will you stay here?"

"Are you asking me to stay?"

"I can't do that, Tessa. Not yet. But if you do decide to stay I'll be here for you. I won't ask you why you aren't married. I don't want to know anything about your past lovers. I want us to start afresh."

They kissed for a long time and slowly undressed each other. She smoothed a parting in the dark hairs covering his chest and planted kisses there, ending with her lips enclosing his nipple, sucking gently till he half rose and pushed her onto her back. He lay inside her for nearly half an hour and told her over and over again that he loved her and when she told him she felt the same way about him she thought she had never seen anyone look so happy.

Afterward, as they lay together in the darkness, he began to talk with great excitement about his plans for the latest issue of *Eros*.

"What's *Eros*?" Tessa asked and nearly fell off the futon when he sat up abruptly and switched on the bedside lamp.

"This," he said proudly, leaping up and showering her with piles of magazines.

"*EROS! That Eros.* Of course I know *Eros*. Oh, no . . ." The penny dropped. "You said you run a successful magazine. You own *EROS*?"

"There's a lot you don't know about me—a lot I'm going to let you find out. I've got great plans for *Eros*. I don't want it to stagnate. This latest issue, for instance, is going to focus completely on the gay market. A totally gay *Eros*—all the advertising, all the features, even the fiction. And here's the best part, we've found a sensational new mystery writer."

"Why mystery?"

"The manuscript was left at the publishers' reception by a stranger who didn't identify himself and rushed away before they could stop him. When they read the manuscript it turned out to be brilliant. The most original, fresh, honest piece of writing they'd seen in years. They had to get it retyped, because the guy'd sent a really messy typescript, full of holes. It's a gay novel and we're going to use an excerpt from it in *Eros*. I want you to read it. I want to know what you think of it. I want your opinion on *every*thing from now on. Will you read it for me?"

Tessa laughed. She loved his over-the-top enthusiasm.

"Of course I will. But not now. Now we have work to do." And she pulled him back down to the futon. She flipped over a few pages of a back number of *Eros* till she found a photostory. "Let's just read this together and see where it takes us . . ."

"Will you have to go to New Orleans?" she asked him in the

middle of the night and at dawn, when he rose and slipped into his jeans, she had her answer.

"I haven't been able to sleep," he told her. "I have to go down there, speak to Teddy Lenoir. Let me call you from there, tell you where I am and maybe you can come down and join me. I'd like to show you some of the South, but there are a few things I want to sort out first."

"Let me know what happens with Honey down there. I'm going to come down anyway and follow up on the story of her and . . ."

"What? What's the matter?"

"Well, it'll be the story of her baby, her son, *your* son . . ."

He knelt down and kissed her on the forehead. "That was something that happened a long time ago. Maybe it is my son, and Honey's, but we're neither of us equipped to deal with him. If Luc Chenier is my son then when Honey dies all her money goes straight to him so he'll be OK financially. I guess I'll have to make sure someone's looking out for him until then, not to mention the fact that it'd be interesting to find out who's raised him up to now . . . old Teddy Lenoir's going to have a lot of questions to answer. Now, you stay right here and get some sleep. I'll call you later."

But after he'd gone, Tessa remained wide awake. She lay there staring up at the huge expanse of the loft which towered above her from the floor level of the futon. After a while she gave up trying to go back to sleep, got up, made herself a cup of coffee and rooted around for the manuscript PJ had asked her to read.

She took one look at the author's name and her hand began to shake.

Elliott Fitzgerald.

CHAPTER 30

She couldn't leave him lying there in the library.

But she was in her seventies and it wasn't easy for her to sweep an old man's body and deposit it wherever she wanted. Maybe there would be some rope somewhere which she could tie around him and use to drag him along the floor.

She opened a drawer in his desk. It was a silly place to look for rope, but as she started to close it, something caught her eye. Breathing hard, she removed a small pearl-handled revolver and clutched it to her bony chest.

When she checked she found it was loaded—and it gave her the extra strength to pull Teddy Lenoir's inert body out of the library and across the hall. Just as she reached the kitchen, she heard footsteps echoing over the flagstones into the courtyard outside.

Dropping Teddy's body she slipped outside to lie in wait behind the fountain.

"Oh, my, isn't this pretty," cried Honey as she and Jack emerged from the covered carriage drive into the courtyard.

"All these exotic plants and such a darling fountain! It's like a
wedding cake."

"I didn't know you were familiar with wedding cakes," Jack
teased her.

"Oh, stop it, *please.* Jack, I feel bad about rushing in like
this. It's not even ten o'clock in the morning and Mr. Lenoir is
an old man. Maybe he sleeps late."

"I called earlier," Jack said, taking charge again. "There was
no reply, so I thought we'd wait for him. We *have* to see him,
Honey, and the sooner the better."

Honey shrugged. "OK, go on in and take a look around and
I'll just sit here and throw a few coins in the fountain, make a
wish, that sort of thing."

Jack left and she sat there in the morning sun, trailing her
fingers through the water, the gentle sound of the cascade lull-
ing her into a sense of calm.

The tiny bullet raced through her left arm leaving a flesh
wound which began to bleed heavily. The shock caused her to
topple over and fall into the fountain and she was dimly aware
of two strong hands pressing her head down, keeping it under
water . . . she barely had time to struggle or to register the
pain in her arm before she lost consciousness.

Standing in the library, Jack heard the crack of the revolver
and rushed to the French windows. As soon as she saw him
appear, Callie relinquished her grip on Honey's head and
turned to hobble away down the carriage drive. Jack started to
go after her but, as he reached the courtyard, he saw the bloody
water around the fountain and ran to pull Honey out. He sat
her down on the warm flagstones and thumped her hard on the
back to get the water out of her lungs. Gasping, Honey choked
and spluttered to get her voice back, clinging to him as she
croaked, *"Who?"*

"Old crone," Jack said, breathing hard. "Black hair scraped
in a bun. Gaunt, scrawny, crazy eyes . . . Honey, are you all
right?"

"It was Callie . . ." she whispered. "She tried to kill me."

"You're all right now. Just stay here while I go call an ambulance."

"You can't leave me out here all alone. You just can't, Jack."
Honey was plainly terrified.

Jack carried her across the courtyard and into the library,

laying her down on the *chaise longue* while he telephoned for an ambulance. And because she would not let him leave her for a second Teddy Lenoir's body lay undiscovered not ten feet away in the kitchen.

But before the ambulance could arrive, two other unexpected visitors called at Teddy Lenoir's mansion.

Luc *adored* New Orleans.

He loved the streetcars, the narrow streets, the spoken French he heard everywhere, the buildings with their elaborate ironwork, he even liked the perpetual damp atmosphere caused by the warm rain.

Anita had booked them into a small European style hotel in the French Quarter. Luc drank gallons of steaming chicory coffee and munched on croissants feeling more at home there than at any other time since he had left France.

As an introductory treat to the city, Anita took him to dinner at the legendary Antoine's on their first night, run by the same family for more than a hundred years. The menu was entirely French and the waiters clearly appreciated the fact that for this tourist, for once they did not have to translate.

Now, on their second day, they were doing a tour of New Orleans and Anita was going into ecstasies as they passed her old familiar haunts. She pointed out to him not only the house on St. Charles Avenue where she herself had been raised, but the one next door where Callie had lived. Luc was impressed by the size, but somehow he sensed that the house had a melancholy air about it and he had no wish to linger outside it.

In a fit of enthusiasm Anita had hired one of the authentic old horse-drawn carriages to take them about and was rewarded by Luc's obvious amusement at the horse's flower-and-ribbon-trimmed hat. They had been driving for about an hour, and were ambling down a narrow street in the French Quarter, when Anita suddenly cried out to the driver to turn left. Luc watched in surprise as they passed through an archway into a covered carriage drive and emerged in a courtyard.

"This is Teddy Lenoir's house," she explained and, allowing the driver to help her down, she clattered across the flagstones on her high heels.

"AIIIIYEEEE!" Her scream echoed round the courtyard. She had seen the blood swirling around in the water and clutched the rim for support. Luc ran into the house through the open French windows, looking for help. There, on a *chaise longue* before him, was the Honey-witch.

Jack was kneeling beside Honey. "Holy shit!" he said, as he got to his feet. "It's the boy I told you about, Honey."

"He's Luc Chenier," said Honey simply.

"Oui," Luc nodded. *"Vous êtes blessée."* He pointed to Honey's arm. A piece of white linen cloth was wrapped around it, but the blood continued to seep through it.

"She was shot," said Jack shortly.

"Callie shot me," Honey said, looking directly at Luc.

"Tantie?" he whispered, "she's here?"

"She's gone, she got away before I could get hold of her," Jack replied. Luc looked down. He could think of nothing to say.

Honey reached out, wincing as she did so, and took hold of the boy's wrist, fingering the dolphin bracelet.

"You look like your father," she told him simply.

He still didn't answer and pulled his hand away from her sharply. He didn't want her to see him crying.

She persisted. "We've met before, remember?" She tried to coax him toward her. "We danced together in Paris." Still no answer. "Listen, I'm sorry about your grandmother."

"She wanted to kill you!" He broke his silence at last. "Why did she want to kill you? What did you do to her?"

"If I die you will have *Bayou Beauty,*" Honey almost pleaded.

"But she was like a mother to me," he said flatly. "You weren't my mother. You weren't there. You only *danced* with me, once. That's all you've ever done. *Tantie,* she . . ."

"She took you!" Honey raised herself with an effort. "Don't you understand, Luc? I didn't know where you were. I didn't even know you were alive. They told me you were kidnapped and that you died, didn't anyone tell you? Who did you think your real mother was? Didn't you even ask?"

"Tantie told me my mother was killed in a plane crash," Luc said sullenly.

"It wasn't true, Luc. Listen, you're grown up now and you've turned out beautiful. I couldn't have raised you any better. Callie—your *Tantie*—did a fine job." She noticed Luc looking at her with a cynical expression; maybe she'd struck home, maybe he was remembering just how strange Callie was, maybe now was the time to move in on him. "I am your mother. I was the one who gave birth to you. I can't start playing mother to you now, but what say we just try to be friends?"

The sound of the ambulance siren approaching prevented any further conversation. Luc moved to the other side of the room and stood with his back to the window as they carried Honey out of the house.

"Don't worry, Luc," she called from the stretcher. She seemed to have recovered some of her poise. "You gonna be working for me!" She turned to Jack who was walking by her side. "You're damn right, Jack. He's absolutely perfect for the *Money* campaign, and what about the publicity angle? Jack, what in hell are you waiting for? Get over here and take some pictures. I want Luc and me all over the papers coast to coast—"

Jack climbed into the ambulance after her. "Want to come with us?" he called to Luc, who shook his head.

"Well, we're going to the De Paul Hospital on Calhoun Street. Got that? Where can I get in touch with you?"

Luc, still withdrawn and in shock, muttered the name of his hotel and stood in silence, watching as the ambulance began to back away down the drive. It had just disappeared when Anita came flying out of the house.

"Get him back, get him back! We need him!" she shrieked.

"*Tante* Anita, she was here, you know, *Tantie* was here. She tried to kill Honey. *My mother*," he added awkwardly.

"But Teddy, poor darling Teddy. He's dead. Come and see."

She dragged him into the house, across the hall and into the kitchen. There, lying among the powdered sugar from an overturned bag of *beignets* was the body of an elderly gentleman, a knife protruding from his ribs.

Anita began to gabble. "Teddy. That's Teddy, Teddy Lenoir. I knew the family. He came to my débutante ball. He told me I would be the Queen of the Carnival one day. Poor darling Teddy. *Il est mort. Il est partie.*" She crossed herself several times and was about to collapse in tears into Luc's arms, when a husky voice growled:

"*Pas encore.* Don't bury me before my time, Anita. You always were a silly little thing. Quit your twittering and get me to my feet."

Teddy Lenoir was a survivor. Carefully, but without showing a twinge of pain he extracted the knife from his body and in the same movement pulled out a pocket watch on a chain.

"*Très bien!* Hasn't stopped a second. Ten thirty-two. Swiss made. I've worn it for twenty years. Saved my life. Callie meant that knife to go straight through me, so it's lucky she aimed the damned thing straight at my watch instead. Now, Anita, what is all this about? Who is this young man? We must sit down and talk, but first perhaps you'll excuse me for a minute. I fear I should telephone the police. Lord alone knows where Callie's got to by now—"

Brad and Sharleen were on their honeymoon.

Brad had thought it would be fun to spend a few nights at a hotel in the red light district of New Orleans and they had checked into *Le Bordel* that day. Now, after a candlelit dinner and wine which Brad insisted was "genuine French," they were getting ready to turn in for the night.

Sharleen's nipples protruded through her peach satin teddy. She wriggled out of her tiny lace panties and tossed them at Brad who was already sitting up in bed.

"C'mon, baby. Don't keep an old man waiting too long."

Giggling, she pounced on him and they tussled for a while, Sharleen giving out with her tinkling laugh which drove Brad wild.

Then they settled down for some "serious business," as Brad always called their lovemaking.

"Did this place really used to be a brothel?" Sharleen whispered.

"You better believe it and I'm gonna make sure I get my money's worth tonight!" replied her groom of twenty-four hours.

Then: "What's wrong, sugar? How come you got no juicy-juicy for me down there?"

Sharleen shivered. "This is goin' to sound crazy, darlin', but I think we're bein' watched."

Brad sat up. This place might have been a bordello once back in the Twenties, but it was a two-star hotel now and if they had some fancy two-way mirrors installed he was going to get himself up and be down to see the management and . . .

But he couldn't see anything.

"Come on, Sharleen, there's no one here but us," and he began to slither down her body.

Sharleen found herself responding. She moaned and undulated and was about to relinquish herself to Brad's flickering lizard's tongue when she saw an eye.

No, two eyes. Dark eyes. Watching her through a crack in the door of the walk-in closet. She went rigid with fright, clamping Brad's head between her thighs. Pulling the sheet up to her chin she hissed down to him:

"There's someone in the closet."

Although Brad tried hard to reassure her there was no one there at all, he knew he was not going to get what he wanted unless he proved it. Sighing, he got up off the bed and began to search the room.

When he flung open the door of *la cachette*, Callie stood there clutching the delicate little revolver in both hands and fired point blank into his throat.

As she hurtled down the stairs and out into the street she knew there was only one place left for her to go.

Queenie was padding about her kitchen at *Coinchenier* muttering to herself. Miz Callie was coming home that night, she knew it in her bones, she had the *feeling*. She had laid Miz Callie's place for dinner at the long mahogany table and placed a vase of fresh camellias by her wine glass.

Now she was going to make her Cajun gumbo, Miz Callie's favorite. And after her gumbo Miz Callie wouldn't want nothing else.

She chopped up several ounces of okra. This was what gave her gumbo its flavor, thickened it too, made it more like a nourishing stew rather than a soup. She took down her favorite heavy pan and tossed in the okra together with a tomato and an onion. Then she smothered them with oil, added some water and left them to simmer.

Now she had a problem. To make her gumbo she needed a chicken. She needed to brown chicken pieces in the rest of the oil and with that chicken-flavored oil she had to make a roux. Then, finally, she'd boil them all together—the okra, the onion,

the tomato smothered in oil, the chicken pieces, the roux from
the chicken oil and she'd let them simmer for an hour or so,
then right at the end she'd spice it all up with salt, pepper and a
whole lot of cayenne pepper.

Her problem was that she was down to her last chicken. And
that chicken was hanging, freshly killed with a slit up its middle, from the beam at the entrance to her kitchen. It was there
to ward off evil spirits. If she took it down and used it for her
gumbo she'd be vulnerable. Those evil spirits might sweep in
and attack her at any moment and she'd be unprotected.
Should she risk it? Once Miz Callie was back she could leave
Coinchenier and go to market to buy more chickens.

She took down the chicken. Only thing to do. It'd be the best
gumbo she'd ever made.

Callie had taken a plane from New Orleans to Biloxi and from
there she'd taken a taxi to *Coinchenier.* She had the driver drop
her at the gates and made her own way on foot up the magnificent oak-lined drive. The trees seemed to bend inward forming
a leafy tunnel and as she passed each massive trunk, Callie felt
as if they were old friends welcoming her home.

The house ahead of her was in almost total darkness. Light
shone from the windows of only two of the score of rooms, one
on the ground floor, the dining room, and the other on the
second floor. As she drew closer Callie realized it was her old
bedroom.

Queenie welcomed her as if she had only been gone for a
night.

"Why, Miz Callie, dere you is. I bin expectin' you. Come on
in. Dinner's almost ready, but I expect you'll want to go up to
yo' room and wash first. I laid out yo' dress already."

And there, upstairs, laid out across the gray satin cover on
her huge bed, lay one of her old Mainbocher dresses from the
Forties. Large circular glass bowls of magnolia blooms were
placed strategically around the room, crisp white linen crackled
on the bed as she sat down on it. Queenie bustled into the
bathroom and soon the smell of Callie's favorite pine essence
wafted into the bedroom. Queenie returned with her silk robe.

"I be downstairs, Miz Callie, in de kitchen. I made yo' favorite. Be ready when you had yo' bath."

Callie dressed for dinner; she hadn't done so for years. Half an hour later she studied her reflection in the long looking-glass on the door of her *armoire*. The elegantly simple cut of the black Mainbocher dress, tight to the knees and moving out in a gentle swirl to the floor, erased in one second the image of her French existence over the last seventeen years. She was back at *Coinchenier*. Once again she was Mrs. Perry Jay Duboise, queen of a cosmetics empire, renowned in the South. A smile of satisfaction spread slowly across her face. The mirror reflected a hideous leer, but Callie was alone with her fantasies.

Frantic with excitement, she rummaged around in the drawers of her dressing table, but could find no jewelery. Of course, she'd been away, so it must be locked in the safe downstairs. Well, she wouldn't bother tonight. But there, at the back of the drawer, there *was* something. Reaching in, she pulled out one of her old long ivory cigarette holders and a beaded jet evening purse. She had long since ceased to smoke, but the ivory holder felt right as she held it aloft, her arm extended, bent at the elbow.

As she started her slow and rather regal descent of the red-carpeted staircase she failed to notice the dust and decay all around her. If she encountered cobwebs, she brushed them aside and if she saw sheets draped over the furniture in the rooms leading off the landings as she passed she merely closed the doors.

As she stirred the gumbo downstairs, Queenie never thought to ask herself why her mistress had arrived home with no luggage. Life at *Coinchenier* for both women had resumed as they had always known it.

Callie sat down at the head of the dining table and placed her jet purse on her lap, tentatively patting its valuable contents which she had transferred from her regular handbag. Only one candlestick stood on the table in front of her place setting. She could barely make out the other nineteen chairs around the table in the darkness. Somewhere at the end of that long mahogany expanse Perry Jay used to sit. She poured herself some wine and raised her glass to him. Shadows jumped around the room in the candlelight. She toasted them too.

"I'm back," she whispered to herself.

Queenie came in and placed a tray on the sideboard. She padded over, removed the candle from the table and took it back to the sideboard with her, leaving Callie in the darkness.

"We only got de one candle till I go to de market tomorrow, Miz Callie."

She ladled the gumbo into a bowl and picking up the candlestick in one hand she placed the bowl in front of Callie and returned the candlestick to its place on the table. Then she took a few steps back and stood behind Callie in the shadows.

Callie reached out a bony claw for her napkin, shook it out and placed it on her lap covering her evening purse. She took her soup spoon and sipped the gumbo.

And spat it out.

"Queenie, this is *disgusting*!"

Queenie stepped forward, bent over and sniffed. "No, madam, dat mighty fine gumbo. You just ain't had it in a while. You forgotten how good it is."

Callie looked up at her suspiciously. Did Queenie seriously imagine she didn't know how gumbo ought to taste? The old servant was clearly a bit past it.

"Sit down with me, Queenie, tell me how things have been. Come on, sit down, here, in that chair. Master Philippe-Josephe's chair if I remember rightly."

"He was here," said Queenie, lowering herself cautiously onto the chair. No one had *ever* asked her to join folks at dinner before. She didn't relax until she saw Callie begin to sip her gumbo.

"Here? At *Coinchenier*?" Callie's spoon paused in mid-air.

"He was lookin' fo' his mamma, 'course he was." Queenie nodded her head several times to emphasize her point. "I told him about de baby. What you done with de baby, Miz Callie?"

"None of your business, Queenie." Callie suddenly changed tack. "What are you doing sitting here gossiping with me, anyway? Go on, get back into the kitchen."

Queenie went, taking the candle with her. Callie sat sipping her gumbo in the pitch black dining room. She liked the dark. Queenie had not drawn the long wine-colored velvet curtains and through the windows she could see the full moon.

Then suddenly she recalled Queenie's words and she remembered why she had come and what she had to do. The hall was dimly lighted by a lamp on the chest beside the door as Callie made her way down the stone-flagged passage to the back of the house and entered the kitchen area.

Queenie had lied about the candle. The kitchen was filled

with them, tall, small, varying heights flickering all over the room. Queenie was very busy. The feathers plucked from the chicken lay scattered across the wooden chopping block in the center of the kitchen. Queenie was taking them one by one and dipping them into a large round mixing bowl and once she had done so she daubed herself and threw the feathers over her left shoulder. Callie watched. She knew what was happening here and she knew it was bad luck to interrupt Callie's voodoo. There was time enough to carry out what she had to do. She could wait.

Finally Queenie reached for the last feather, dipped it into a bowl, splashed it across her sweating forehead and threw it over her shoulder. Then she picked up the bowl with both hands and began to drink the contents. As she reached the bottom she tilted the bowl and the last few drops ran down her chin and onto her white apron, leaving red stains slashed across her huge bosom. It was chicken blood.

Callie knew it was time. She stepped forward.

"You asked about the baby, Queenie. You shouldn't have done that. You know why? Because it reminded me of the last time I saw you. Do you remember what I told you then? Do you, Queenie?"

Queenie stared at her, not saying a word, running her tongue over her lips, savoring the blood.

"You betrayed me, Queenie," Callie went on in a quiet, controlled voice. "You told Mr. Duboise about my father killing my Uncle Jules. I swore I'd get you for that one day and that's what I've come back to do."

Callie reached into her evening purse and drew out the pearl-handled revolver. She began moving across the kitchen toward Queenie, who backed away and finally found herself trapped against the butcher's block.

"Get up, get yourself up on it," snapped Callie, standing rigidly straight in her Mainbocher dress.

Queenie clambered up onto the bloody surface of the butcher's block and perched there, trembling, her eyes rolling at Callie in terror. Callie took two steps forward and placed the butt of the revolver to Queenie's left temple.

"There's a curse on you, Miz Callie," the old woman moaned in a sing-song voice. "On yo' family. They all gone die bad. And I done put my evil spirits on you too. You gone die real bad, Miz Callie." And she cackled.

"SHUT UP!" said Callie dangerously but Queenie only laughed more, her huge body shaking and squelching in the remains of the chicken's blood until the laughter switched abruptly into one long scream as Callie fired a bullet into her temple.

Queenie's blood poured out of her ear to mingle with that of the fowl and Callie breathed deeply for a few moments until she regained control of herself. Then, as if performing a dignified burial ceremony, she moved about the kitchen, stooping and gathering up the bloodied chicken feathers off the stone floor and placing them reverently all over Queenie's body, draped over the butcher's block.

Finally Callie moved four of the tallest candles to stand them on either side of Queenie's head and at her feet. Queenie was dead on her altar. It was fitting.

Satisfied, Callie wandered back through the house and out of the front door to look at the grounds in the moonlight.

As she was crossing the stable yard, toward her favorite stall, an acute pain gripped her. Clutching her stomach, she bent almost double and collapsed on the ground. She felt dizzy, her vision was blurred, she could no longer see the stables ahead of her. Her mouth was extremely dry and she could barely swallow, let alone speak. She thrashed about, but could not cry for help even if there had been anyone there to hear her. In less than an hour her muscles had weakened to such an extent, she could do nothing but lie motionless on the floor of the yard. Out of the corner of her eye she could see a rat approaching from the stables. As it drew closer her pupils became dilated and fixed upon it. Its mouth was open and its teeth seemed poised to sink into her flesh. She tried to breathe and found she could not. Respiratory and cardiac paralysis had already set in.

Queenie had put enough belladonna in the gumbo to poison every single Chenier she had ever known. As Callie died, she thought she saw her beloved PJ before her for an instant. She tried to speak to him, to tell him that she had had love in her heart for him, that whatever else happened in her life she had loved her son and that it was only when that love had been forbidden to her, she had started to die within herself.

PJ was too late to save her. When he had arrived in New

Orleans and heard from Teddy Lenoir what had happened, he had caught the next plane to Biloxi. A quick enquiry had brought forward the cab driver who had taken Callie to *Coinchenier* and he rushed her son there after her.

It was much too late. PJ knelt beside her as she lay in the very spot where he had last seen her. He held her head in his lap as her life ebbed away from her and whispered: "Remember what you always told me, mamma. When you die heaven's going to be like the lobby of the Peabody Hotel."

And then he wept.

CHAPTER 31

Tessa knew she was being stupid but she just couldn't help it. She was utterly miserable. She was angry. She wanted to bang on the table and scream like a frustrated five-year-old.

But she wasn't a child. She was a mature, successful woman in her early thirties. She was in the prime of her life. Her writing career was on the brink of breaking out into something really big. She had almost come to terms with her relationship with her mother. She had just about everything she had always wanted.

Just about. There was one thing which still eluded her and that was PJ. She had his love, of that she was sure. But she didn't have *him.*

She had lost him to another woman, a woman she had never met, but whom she hated with a passion she had only ever imagined reserved for love. And to top it all the woman was dead.

Callie Chenier.

PJ was in the process of mourning the mother he abandoned for eighteen years, for whom he had held nothing but contempt. A woman who had been undisputably evil, destructive and insane. And Tessa was jealous. He had shut her out, retreated into himself with his pain, his guilt, his remorse at having become estranged from his precious mamma. Tessa could not get near him.

Only a few days earlier they had begun what she knew was to be her first serious relationship. It was extraordinary that they should have found each other at all, coming as they did from such different families, not to mention different parts of the world. She felt they were destined to meet, to save each other, to make each other happy. But the relationship was still at an extremely fragile stage. If they did not work at it, talk to each other, grow closer every day, it was in danger of disintegrating.

She had never felt so frustrated. She loved him. His mother had died horribly and she should be offering him sympathy. But he wouldn't let her and she didn't want to. She wanted to shake him and tell him that he was wasting his time, that he was well rid of the old woman, that he should take a look around and notice her, Tessa, ready to give him real love, real affection.

Strangely enough, Honey's jubilation didn't help. Tessa had noticed in the past that when someone was splitting up with a partner it was all right for that person to heap bile and vitriol on the errant spouse, but the minute she started to say something like, "I always knew he wasn't good enough for you," they didn't want a word said against him. It was the same with Honey Winslow's crowing over Callie's death. Her presence at the funeral had been prominent, her smile of victory splattered all over the *Times-Picayune* (she was more than a trifle miffed that *The New York Times* failed to illustrate their story). But when she encountered Honey, Tessa couldn't help thinking of PJ's torment and as the sessions at the Sherry continued, more productive than they had been in quite a while, she found it hard to retain a detached, professional approach to her subject. She was writing Honey's story, Honey's success, but for how long?

If Tessa was angry at PJ for mourning the mother he had abandoned, she was horrified by his total lack of interest in his new-found son. She had asked Honey point blank what *she* intended to do about Luc and had received an answer totally in keeping with the Honey Winslow philosophy of life: "I'm going to make him a star!"

It was, quite simply, in her terms, the best Honey could do for her son. And at least she was doing something.

Honey and Jack went to work and within weeks Luc *was* a star.

Money took off from the word go. All over America people were captivated by the rows and rows of striking golden eagle-topped bottles. It was ridiculous, of course, but there was the feeling that they were getting *Money* for money. It was irresistible. And so was Luc's hypnotic face. He was everywhere: billboards, TV commercials, magazine ads, posters, all reproduced his image twenty to thirty times along a wall.

Honey pointed out to Tessa that it was rare enough for female models to become celebrities in their own right: Barbara Goalen, Fiona Campbell-Walter, Bettina, Suzy Parker, Paulene Stone, Jean Shrimpton, Celia Hammond, Twiggy, Lauren Hutton, Marie Helvin, Jerry Hall were not all household names. How many male models were even known by name outside the world of fashion, advertising and magazines?

Yet Luc had become a personality. He was interviewed, profiled, sought after for talk shows, openings, parties . . . just like Honey had once been. *Had been.*

Honey assured Tessa she would never be a has-been, but she confided she was becoming more and more aware that she was prepared to take something of a backseat for the first time in her life. Luc's success was phenomenal and she was enjoying it vicariously. She felt he was merely following in her footsteps, taking over where she had left off. It ran in the family. She made sure he mentioned her in his interviews, credit where credit was due and all that. The dual publicity for the two of them had gone a long way to getting the *Money* launch to first base. The sentimental angle of Honey Winslow's reconciliation with her son had been picked up by all the magazines and the fact that that son was so extraordinarily beautiful was the icing on the cake.

Yet while Honey was basking in her new success with Jack Fern promoted to an exalted position within Bayou Beauty's marketing division (Tessa decided to refrain from asking what happened to his lifelong ambition to be taken seriously as an art photographer), nobody seemed to remember that Luc Chenier was still only a boy of seventeen who had just undergone a particularly traumatic experience. He had found the parents he had believed to be dead, but they were obviously nothing more than his next of kin in name only.

Tessa was concerned about him. She didn't know him, had only glimpsed him once in the lobby of the Sherry-Netherland when she had mistaken him for his father. Yet whenever she saw his haunting face in the *Money* ads, she was devastated by the look of utter vulnerability in his dark eyes. It was this look which made him so appealing. Right across America people chose to see his beautifully cut clothes, his startling good looks and failed to notice what lay behind them. It was the old story of the glamorous exterior and the hidden terror within; if someone looks successful then they are successful and that's all that matters. Never mind the subtle signals in the eyes which cry out, "Help me, I'm not what I appear."

Tessa sought out Luc on the pretext that she wanted to interview him about his reunion with Honey. She could not have been more surprised when she finally met him. Luc Chenier *was* sensitive and vulnerable, that was quite plain to see, but it soon became clear that the events of the last few months had been something of a watershed in his life and that he was relieved to have come through them.

"All my life," he told Tessa, who reflected that his seventeen years must have seemed an eternity, "I have pretended to myself that I loved my *Tantie* and now she is dead I can say out loud that this was not true. I was afraid of her but she looked after me and I had to trust her. I had no one else except . . ."

"But now you have found your mother," Tessa interrupted him.

"In a way."

"What do you mean by that?"

"Honey Winslow gave birth to me, but she is not my mother any more than Callie was. Even now she is only my mother for the photographs when she puts her arm around me and we say *'Cheese'* together."

Tessa wondered what Honey would have to say about the way this interview was going. It had to be the first time Luc had begun to talk about how he really felt. All his other meetings with the Press could be divided into two areas: his interviews with Honey where she did most of the talking and his interviews about his success as the *Money* star. For the first time he was on his own and able to speak for himself and Tessa

realized that her story was going to work after all. She had just
been interviewing the wrong person. Through Luc Chenier she
might possibly get a completely different perspective on Honey
Winslow. In fact, forget Honey Winslow, she was no longer
interested in her as the central character. Suddenly Tessa knew
that her story was going to be about the whole family: Callie
Chenier, Perry Jay Duboise, Honey Winslow, Luc Chenier and,
if she could bear it, PJ. She would hang the story around Luc,
not Honey. She would use her old magic to weave out of this
boy a picture of Luc Chenier the public had never had presented to them.

"But my real mother is Anita," said Luc, "Anita de la Salle.
She *cares* for me." And he went on to explain to Tessa who
Anita was, how it was she who had brought him to America in
the first place. And she had shown him his real roots. He was
not going to go back to France. He would stay here in America,
but he would not go to Hollywood. He did not want to be that
kind of star. He was Luc Chenier, of the St. Charles Avenue
Cheniers—and Tessa smiled at the pride in his voice as he told
her this—and that's where he belonged. He would go down to
New Orleans and stay with Anita de la Salle for a while and
from there he would explore the area to look for a house. Anita
was going to stay down there too and while she denied it, he
knew it was so that she could look after him.

Little by little he stepped tentatively backward into his past,
painting for Tessa a picture of terrifying loneliness in an isolated region of south-west France. Silently she resolved to seek
out and interview Anita de la Salle and make sure she received
her due credit in this heartbreaking story.

Finally she knew there was one more question she had to put
to him: "What about your father?"

"Monsieur Duboise?" *Monsieur* Duboise? Such a formal way
to talk about your own father.

"Yes. PJ." She couldn't bring herself to tell him that she
lived with PJ. That his, Luc's, name had barely been mentioned
by PJ since Callie's death. "Your father."

"Again, in a way," Luc smiled at her.

Tessa smiled back. "I give up," she said, "don't tell me you
have an Anita de la Salle father figure."

"Exactement!" Luc clapped his hands. He often did that
when he was excited or pleased and it was a gesture which had

immediately endeared him to television audiences. *"Meester Feetzgerald,"* he said proudly.

"And who might he be?" Tessa was smiling encouragingly at him, but her smile froze as he spoke.

"His name is Elliott Fitzgerald. He's *un Anglais* and he's lived next to *Tantie* for years, ever since I can remember. He was my father, he talked to me, he cooked for me, he advised me. I love him and one day I will go back and see him."

"But what is he doing down there in France?"

"He writes. He gave me a book he had written to bring to America."

"And what did you do with it?"

"I gave it to a publishing house."

"When?"

"When I first came here, when we were in New York the first week before I went down to New Orleans."

That was it, thought Tessa, the *Eros* piece she had read which PJ was so excited about for his gay issue, it had to have come from this book.

She looked down at her notes, suddenly unable to speak. If this man was who she thought he was, at last she knew his secret, the secret her grandfather had kept from her all those years.

Tessa took refuge in her writing. Each night when she got into bed beside PJ and he turned over and presented his back to her she crept out again and silently made her way across the vast studio to the work table she had set up behind a tall screen. She did not type. She didn't want to wake him although she felt sure he never slept.

Night after night she scribbled down her story of Luc Chenier and his parents and grandparents. Where Candy McCarthy would fit this into her feature on models now and then, Tessa had no idea, but she knew that this was the story she had to tell and not a straightforward banal piece on the success of Honey Winslow.

He seemed to know the night she finished it. About half an hour after she had written the final sentence a hand touched her shoulder and a soft voice murmured: "I've given *Coinchenier* to my son, you know."

PJ slipped to the floor beside her and put his head in her lap.

"Why don't you stroke my hair like you usually do?" he asked her, a small boy assessing whether or not he was to be punished. "I'm sorry, Tessa. I've been a monster but I've been suffering. I've been in hell."

"Why wouldn't you talk to me about it? That's all I wanted. I knew how you must be feeling, but why did you shut me out? I would have listened." Tessa longed to gather him up in her arms, but she knew that if she were honest with herself she did not want to let him off that easily. If they were to continue some kind of life together he had to learn to trust her, to open up.

"I didn't know how to tell you, I didn't know where to begin," he explained. "You thought I was grieving because my mother had died and in a way I was, but in another way I was trying to come to terms with the fact that I was *pleased* Callie was dead. And then at the same time I felt responsible for her death, that she had died because of me and what I had done to her. She genuinely loved me, Tessa, and if I had been able to return that love, who knows, maybe she wouldn't have become the sad, crazed old woman she was. But I rejected her. I couldn't handle her love for me. It smothered me. Do you know what she used to do when I was a boy? She made my face up and dressed me up as a girl. She was weird. I'm telling you, Tessa, I had a weirdo for a mother and all my life I've been wondering whether that made me a weirdo too, whether my children would be crazy, whether it was *in the blood* . . ."

"But you've only got to look at Luc . . ."

"I can't deal with Luc either, not right now. She raised him, my mother raised him, Christ only knows what kind of voodoo she taught him."

"He's fine, PJ. Honest to God, I've met him and he's an incredibly bright young man. You ought to be proud of him."

"I will. In time. But first I have to be proud of myself. I've told Teddy Lenoir to make *Coinchenier* over to Luc. Callie left it to me, but Teddy told me the boy wants to live in the South, that he doesn't want to go back to France. It makes sense he should have *Coinchenier*. He *is* a Chenier, far more than I'll ever be. It's his home, it's right he should have it. He's mighty young to take on such a big property, but Teddy tells me Anita de la Salle is going to stay down South and keep an eye on him.

Tell you the truth, I think she wants to keep half an eye on Teddy too . . ."

Tessa laughed and this time she reached out to touch him. Their lovemaking was cautious, tentative at first, as if each was not sure how far the other would let them go. It made it all the more exciting and by the time he was ready to enter her they were both intense and urgent. It was over quickly and neither resented the fact. There would be plenty of time later for a more languid reunion. Now PJ lay on top of her, breathing softly and after a while she heard him whisper quietly: "I really do love you."

She gave him her story to read and he was amazed. From it he learned of Callie's life for the past seventeen years, of Luc's anguished childhood. His own role was small and for that he was grateful. He knew she had to tell the story of his family in the way she had and he told her he only wished he could do something similar for her.

One day she would tell him that he would be doing just that by publishing Elliott Fitzgerald's piece in *Eros,* but not yet. And in that moment, she understood why he hadn't talked to her about Callie before. She was not ready to tell him about her father. She would, one day, because she loved and trusted him. But for the time being she had to keep it to herself, wait until she knew more.

She mailed her Chenier piece to Candy McCarthy and it was published in England in the same week that PJ ran Elliott's story in *Eros* in New York. Both stories caused a sensation and although Tessa doubted if her mother had registered the fact that an extract from a novel had been published by someone called Elliott Fitzgerald, the book itself was bound to appear sooner or later in an English edition.

Tessa knew it was only a matter of time before she would force herself to face Elliott Fitzgerald . . . but the more she thought about it the more she realized she could not bring herself to do it alone. She needed someone to help her through it. She needed PJ. The time had come to tell him about her father and to ask for his support in facing up to the truth . . .

They had been growing closer all the time, talking late into the night, making love, discovering each other, but one issue lay unspoken between them: that Tessa was an alien, that she did not have a work permit, that she could not stay on indefinitely. If he were to offer her a job on *Eros* that might not solve the problem, even if he were able to overcome the Green Card stumbling block. A simpler solution would be if they were simply to get married. But neither of them was about to be the first to raise the question. And sooner or later Tessa would have to leave, unless . . .

She let herself into the loft and called out to him. It was seven and he was usually back from *Eros* by now. But a particular kind of silence greeted her, the kind which tells you that things are not as they were. She snapped on the overhead spotlights and saw immediately the empty cupboards and drawers. She checked the bathroom and found his robe was no longer hanging on the back of the door and there was no sign of his shaver, his toothbrush, his shampoo . . .

PJ had gone.

Tessa did not go out for forty-eight hours. She ate one slice of bread and a can of soup and threw it up a few seconds later. The rest of the time she just sat and stared into space, putting off for as long as she could the moment when she would have to deal with what had happened.

When the telephone rang the sound reverberated round the huge room until finally she grasped the receiver off the hook and, holding it tightly with both hands, lifted it to her ear, willing it to be PJ.

It wasn't. It was Candida McCarthy telling her that they wanted her to go to south-west France as soon as possible to do a profile on an extraordinary new writer everyone would soon be talking about. His name was Elliott Fitzgerald.

CHAPTER 32

Elliott Fitzgerald was pottering about. If he was totally honest with himself he had to admit it was his favorite occupation. And an entirely useless one since he never really achieved anything.

He had pottered religiously for the last hour. He had gone outside to pick some lavender and then had sat down in his old wicker chair to enjoy the late afternoon sun, so by the time he came in again he had forgotten all about the lavender.

He put on a Mozart record and sat down again, by the fire this time, waving his hand in the air and nodding his head in time to the music. The record came to an end and on his way to turn it over he was distracted by his two-day-old shopping list lying on the kitchen table. He might be expecting a dinner guest; he wasn't sure. At the very least he would have a lunch guest the next day. What to prepare? Ordinarily he would give them an omelette and be done with it. A little local *foie gras* first perhaps, a perfectly stupendous *salade frisée* swimming in *l'huile de noisettes* and some little *cabecoux* to round off the meal.

But would that be enough? The guest was not exactly a local

paysan. Should he make a *casserole du lapin*? Or buy some fresh trout in Gourdon on the way to the station? Yes, trout. Excellent idea. Why hadn't he thought of it before?

Now, he decided, he really ought to sweep the floor. Where was the broom? Had he left it in the barn again? He went outside where he found the lavender waiting for him and forgetting all about the broom, he brought it indoors and arranged it in a plain white jug which he set square in the middle of the big oak chest by the front door. The scent of the lavender wafted through the room, blending with the wood smoke still rising from the dying embers in the fire.

He turned the record over and found himself performing a little dance, bumping into his desk as he did so, so he sat down abruptly in front of his battered old Remington.

His book was to be published. His *new* book. The one Luc had taken to America for him. He missed Luc, but they must have got his address from the boy, those publishers in New York. He had a letter from a man called Walter Finkel who seemed to want him to go to America for publication and tour. *Tour?* What did it mean? He wasn't going, of course, and he'd written to tell them so, as diplomatically as he could. It seemed as if he'd overdone it, offered to accommodate them in any other way and now they'd gone and called his bluff. They were sending someone to interview him. A complete stranger coming all the way over from New York who would be arriving to interview him about his book. He hoped they didn't realize his book was autobiographical.

The lavender wasn't quite enough. He'd have to pick the last few rose buds still blooming in November. He hunted around for his secateurs and after he'd snipped away he stooped even further and plucked some mint, rubbing it between finger and thumb. Taking the roses indoors, he crushed the stems, filled a tall glass vase with tepid water, added a little sugar and dropped in the buds. With luck they'd bloom by the next day.

Elliott drew into the station twenty minutes later (forgetting all about the trout), and rummaged around in the glove compartment for Walter Finkel's latest letter. He'd never actually read it all the way through but somewhere, surely, he must give the name of the journalist who was coming all this way. Elliott had received a postcard giving details of the train time, but he had been unable to read the scrawled signature at the end. Well, all he could do was wait until everyone had been collected and see who was left.

In any event, only two passengers got out at Gourdon. The first, a man, was immediately claimed by two excitable children and their mother.

The second was a tall woman with glorious russet-colored hair, who struggled along the platform with a heavy suitcase. As she came toward him he could see her face was gray with exhaustion. He rushed to her aid.

"*Permettez-moi.*" He lifted his hat with one hand and attempted to take her case with the other. She looked at him enquiringly.

"*Je suis Elliott Fitzgerald . . .*" he began.

"*Et je suis Tessa Fitzgerald,*" she told him and burst into tears.

Tessa opened her eyes and panicked. For several seconds she had no idea where she was. Above her were wooden beams. She was lying in a sturdy wooden bed high above the ground. She could smell lavender and looking to her right she saw a jug filled with it. On her left stood a stem vase balancing precariously on a rickety cane table with two perfect rose blooms just emerging from their buds. Across the room she could see an old washstand complete with jug and bowl and beside it, laid out in a row, a shaving kit—brush, cream in a round wooden tub, a razor and a small pile of neatly folded white towels.

Tessa sat up tentatively and stared in bewilderment at a line of men's shoes on the floor. Brogues and elegant lace-ups, black, brown, old-fashioned with pointed toes, beautifully hand made, bespoke a man with long thin feet.

The walls were basic stone; the floorboards were unpolished. A couple of threadbare Persian rugs were strewn diagonally here and there. A heavy old *armoire* stood wedged into a corner under the beams. Tessa vaguely registered the name of the author on the book spines before she climbed out of the high bed and staggered across to the window to open the shutters. And there she remembered. Opening the window she looked out on a remarkable view, wooded hills stretching as far as she could see and there below her a flock of goats, forty-five at least, swarming around the meadow nibbling at the grass, their bells tinkling as they dipped their heads.

Turning back, her eyes rested on a chest of drawers and the silver-framed photograph which held pride of place on top of it, a black and white picture of a woman with a baby in her arms.

Although it was taken many years ago, the prominent nose and the large mournful eyes belonged unmistakably to Amy Heron-Sweeney.

Tessa heard footsteps on the stairs and rushed back to bed realizing for the first time that she was wearing a man's nightshirt.

The stairs rose straight into the room. There was no door on which to knock and Tessa watched as a gnarled hand with long fingers appeared and made a fist. Knuckles rapped on the beam. "Come in," she whispered, but he had heard her. He entered bearing a tray which he set down on the rickety table beside the roses and Tessa tensed, fearing it might collapse with the weight.

"Here," he said, "see if you can get this down." He handed her a bowl of steaming hot chocolate. "You've been fearfully ill, you know. You more or less collapsed at the station, and I'm afraid I took the liberty of bringing you here and putting you straight to bed. Did you have a terrible journey?"

Tessa nodded. For the moment it was all she could bring herself to do. She had had a terrible journey. First the transatlantic flight from New York to Paris, then—sheer lunacy—instead of spending the night she had left straightaway, continuing her journey by train. She had been pestered on the train by a particularly egotistical Frenchman, who simply could not believe that she didn't want anything to do with him. And she missed PJ more than ever and had still had no word since he had left the SoHo loft two weeks before. Had she done the right thing in leaving New York? If he returned would he think she had abandoned him? But he had abandoned *her,* he didn't want her anymore. Their relationship had moved too fast for him. She had frightened him off. What *was* she to believe?

Meanwhile she had to deal with the fact that this fine-boned old man was her father. She was just wondering whether he realized who she was when he spoke gently: "Tell me, how is your mother?"

How could he appear so casual? Unconsciously Tessa replied in kind.

"Well, I think, but you know I haven't seen her in quite a

while. I live in New York and she'd never go there in a million years."

He chuckled. "Amy in New York. Great heavens! What a marvelous notion. No, you're right, she wouldn't go near the place. Nor would I as a matter of fact. Well, I hope she's all right." He coughed and plunged on, "I haven't seen her myself for years as you well know since you've read my book."

Tessa stared back at him. "Are you saying that whole story is true . . . that you . . . ?"

"More or less. I am homosexual, or at least I was. I realized it during the war before you were born. Yet I loved Amy; I wanted to be married and I was delighted when you were born, but at the same time I knew the other wouldn't go away. When your grandfather found out—that whole bit in Wales is all true, you know—he banished me, killed me off literally. I was weak, I know. I should have stood up to him, that boy's drowning was an accident. I could have taken you and Amy away with me, but you know Amy loved Bellcloud. She would have been miserable anywhere else. I doubt I would have been able to make her happy. I hoped that if she thought I were dead she would remarry one day."

"She did."

"Good Lord, who to?"

"Uncle Johnny. Johnny Simpson."

"Johnny Simpson, bless my soul. Are they still together?"

"No, he ran off with Fluffy."

"Fluffy?"

"His secretary. She had fluffy blonde hair. Mummy always called her that."

"Poor Amy. Did she mind terribly?"

"Not a bit as far as I could make out. I'm not entirely convinced she's cut out for marriage."

"You could be right," said Elliott. "I'm not sure I was either. Well, clearly not in the conventional sense. You were most likely well rid of me . . ."

"Oh, *don't* say that. But how did you know, about me, I mean, who I was?"

"When you're in a fit state we'll stand side by side in front of the looking-glass and you'll see quite clearly that you couldn't be anyone else but my daughter. But I'm going to insist you stay tucked up in bed for the time being. Now, what about a little breakfast? I've a freshly baked *baguette* downstairs. I have my own bread oven like a lot of the houses round here. And my chickens have come up trumps. Three eggs this morning. Nothing quite like a freshly boiled egg . . ." He was already halfway down the stairs. She opened her mouth to call out to him —and stopped. What should she call him? Mr. Fitzgerald? Elliott? How ridiculous. The man was her father.

"Daddy . . ." Although she'd never used that word before, it came easily. His head surfaced, and he smiled shyly.

"Stay as long as you like, my dear Tessa."

It had all been so simple, so natural. She had never trusted someone so instinctively, so completely. He fussed over her, bringing her tempting snacks on trays, cups of *bouillon*, rearranging flowers, plumping up her pillows and gossiping. He turned out to be a wicked mimic to boot. After thirty years he could still imitate Sir Hugh's pompous voice—*"My dear Fitzgerald, the Heron-Sweeneys don't"*—and Tessa laughed, with guilt at first, but ultimately she had to admit to herself that she hadn't really liked her grandfather.

It seemed as if they chatted for days on end. Elliott pestered her for details of New York life. Looking around the house she saw he was clearly a magazine addict and all she really had to do was to bring to life with colorful anecdotes the people whose pictures he saw in the society pages. She told him about Luc's success and assured him the boy would be back to visit him one day. She had brought with her her piece on the Duboises and the Cheniers and he devoured every word of the story of Callie's bizarre death.

"Whoever would have thought that I had Madame *Bayou Beauty* herself living right next door to me all these years! Crazy old woman!" Eventually, after they had talked about everyone else in their strange, muddled lives, Elliott asked his daughter, rather diffidently, to tell him about herself.

Tessa neatly turned the question. She wasn't sure she was ready to talk about herself yet.

"Well, my job is to write profiles, but I'm not sure I can do one on you now. Your book is going to be a huge success. It's beautifully written and it's different. It will capture the public's imagination whether it's true or not, but I don't think you should do any publicity. You should remain a mystery . . .

but I do have to turn in a story, so I've thought of another angle I can use."

"What would that be?" Elliott was intrigued.

"Eric Christian."

"How did you know I'm Eric Christian?"

She pointed to his Remington typewriter.

"Forgive me, but I saw the books upstairs and then there's your typewriter—"

"What about it? It's old, I know, but it's in good nick," the old man protested.

"Of course it is, Daddy, except for the *O*s, look, there, on the page. They don't work. I still have the letters Eric Christian wrote to Grandpa—same thing, same typeface, no *O*s. I just put two and two together. Have you any idea how popular your Eric Christian books were in England, still are? But no one knows anything about him. I could tell them your story, where you live, unmask you . . . if you're up to it, that is."

"Write what you like, my dear. I trust you. But on no account give away my exact whereabouts. I simply couldn't bear it if people come traipsing down here to bother me."

"Don't worry, the only person who's going to come a-traipsing is me," said Tessa.

The next morning when she came downstairs, Elliott was making fig jam in a big round copper vat.

"One of the greatest pleasures of my life is my fig tree. Such a yield this year. Look here now, I've peeled the figs and in they go with lemon, cinnamon, cloves and *sucre de vanille*."

"*Sucre de vanille?*"

"Yes, I'm not sure they make it in England. *Vanilla sugar* would be the literal translation, but all you do is take a few sticks of vanilla and bury them in a jar of sugar for a month *et voilà, sucre de vanille*. By the way, you've got a letter, over there—"

PJ! Tessa thought immediately, he's found out where I am. But it was from Amy to whom she'd written a carefully worded letter soon after her arrival in the Lot, gently breaking the news that she'd found her father.

"My God!" she exclaimed.

"My God, what?"

"She's coming. She's coming down here to see you."

"Who is?" Elliott looked terrified.

"My mother."

He sighed. "Is she really? You wrote and told her, I suppose.
Well, why not? Of course, she saw me at the old boy's funeral,
you know. When does she arrive?"

"Tomorrow."

"Ah, well, I'd better go and prepare the guest room. It's a
shambles. I'm sleeping in there at the moment."

"Where will you sleep when she . . ."

"When Amy arrives?" Elliott allowed himself a wry smile.
"Well, even though we're man and wife I think I'll sleep down
here on the couch. I often do when I'm writing so I can rise in
the morning and go straight to work. Do you love your mother,
by the way?"

The question caught her off guard.

"No, not really," she admitted, "but I'm enormously fond of
her. She's a mess, I warn you. Go easy with her."

"She always was and I always did," he told her quietly and
she knew it was true. "It was that damned father of hers who
ruined her. Why do those closest to us have the power to destroy us so?"

"Do they?" she asked, looking at him hard, "always?"

"Well, let's hope not always," he conceded. "Now, lunch,
saucisses grilled on the fire. What you do, Tessa, is you put
some fresh thyme on the fire and it flavors the smoke and, in
turn, the sausages . . ." and he was off outside to pick some
thyme.

Amy, true to form, marched along the platform in a particularly unflattering pair of corduroy trousers. She had to walk
across the tracks to reach them and began waving furiously as
soon as she saw them, drawing attention to herself. Tessa
cringed with embarrassment, but Elliott was unmoved.

Amy behaved as if she'd only been parted from her husband
for a day or two rather than more than thirty years.

"There you are, Elliott. Didn't keep you waiting, did I? Why
on earth did you have to go and bury yourself down here?
Perfectly ludicrous!"

Elliott kissed her on both cheeks, French style, and Tessa
could see that secretly her mother was pleased. Amy's constant
barking comments all the way back to *La Folie* were, Tessa

understood now, merely a cover for her embarrassed pleasure. Why, oh why couldn't she just relax and show Elliott how delighted she was to see him again?

It took time but in the end the reunion was a huge success. Tessa found it enormously touching, watching the elderly couple drawing closer and closer, rediscovering the friendship they had obviously once shared—not romance, not passion, but simple companionship. Would Amy stay? Of course she would never really be happy anywhere but Bellcloud. But she would come down and visit him as one would visit a friend.

"And what about *me*?" a small voice inside Tessa asked as she sat with her parents in Elliott's garden. What about PJ? He would never have a family reunion such as this one now. He needed her, didn't he realize that? He needed her to start a new family. She had called New York from a bar in Gourdon and learned that he *had* returned for a few days only to disappear again and no one knew where he was. Luc was at *Coinchenier* and hadn't seen him. And Honey said he hadn't been near *Bayou Beauty*.

Elliott was aware of his daughter's sadness. He hadn't said anything, but he recognized it for what it was. She was missing someone just as he was still missing Luc.

Yet, there as he looked, sauntering across the field toward him from *La Cachette* . . . it couldn't be, was he dreaming . . .?

Elliott stood up to get a better view. But Tessa was already on her feet, rushing across the fields, arms open wide. She knew who it was. She couldn't reach him fast enough. As she flung herself into his arms, PJ whispered: ". . . but you knew I'd turn up here sooner or later, didn't you? Callie left me *La Cachette*. After all, I *am* her next of kin."

ABOUT THE AUTHOR

CARLY MCINTYRE was born in London in 1946. She traveled widely in her childhood while her father was in the British army, living for several years in Egypt, the Sudan and Paris. She was educated at the S.H.A.P.E School, Paris and St. Mary's, Calne, Wiltshire. She has worked in a variety of areas including the film industry and as a photographer's assistant and now divides her time between New York, London and France. *Next of Kin* is her first novel.